A

Darkness Realized

By

Jessie Grigsby

First Published in the USA in 2016 by the author

First edition

Cover Design by Adrijus

http://www.rockingbookcovers.com/

ISBN:978-0-692-74056-9

Acknowledgements

This book is dedicated to my grandmother, Annette, and to Amy Grigsby. Grandma, thanks for paying me 25 cents to read a book and write a report about it on an index card when I was younger. Amy, thanks for giving me a paperback copy of *Cujo* when I was 8 years old and starting me on my love for the King. I love you both and am eternally grateful.

This book is also dedicated to the men and women of the armed forces. I very proudly served 6 years in the Army with 27-months deployed to Iraq. I have personally known fellow brothers and sisters in arms who have committed suicide, died overseas, come home and become addicted to drugs or alcohol, been diagnosed with many forms of deployment-borne diseases, gone through messy divorces, and suffered severely from PTSD. We lose 22 veterans a day to suicide. The number for veteran suicides from OIF and OEF has recently surpassed the number of American soldiers killed there. One veteran suicide is too many!

I created a website that is veteran owned and operated. I am using a portion of each book sale to start and fund a non-profit organization for veterans. Let's all rally together and help our veterans. You can view the site here: http://warrioraddiction.com/

—Jessie

Table of Contents

Chapter One: Touchdown

Of the sixty troops from the 25th Infantry Division currently crammed uncomfortably into the jump seats of the C-17 cargo plane, Specialist David Jones was one of the most experienced ones, even at twenty years old, having previously completed two deployments, including a year in Afghanistan. For many of the others, this was their first tour of duty.

The C-17 was one of four cruising in the standard flying v formation, all headed for Iraq. The planes droned on in an incessant harmonizing baritone, a sort of mechanical barbershop quartet, oblivious to the thoughts and feelings of those who sat stoically inside.

Those that had been previously deployed there knew that Iraq was a kind of hell on earth and those who hadn't would soon find out. The mood of the group was akin to a football team returning from an away game after a brutal loss, all their fire and enthusiasm deserting them in this moment of truth and harsh reality. Despite the inner turmoil of emotions they were experiencing, they remained silent, only staring straight ahead at the belly of the bird, trying not to catch the eyes of their companions.

Though each plane, and indeed each soldier, was overloaded with the necessary equipment, DJ always found a place for his iPod. He considered it a lifeline, a touch of normal life within chaos, a link to sanity. Currently, it was cranking out The Red by Chevelle into the tiny buds inserted firmly into his ears, but he was completely oblivious to its random choice of track.

Instead, he was lost in memories from his past.

The last time he'd been in this specific type of plane had been during his Airborne training, when he'd willingly, but with a touch of trepidation, jumped out of it. Thankfully, this particular excursion didn't require such a drastic method of deplaning; but he couldn't help recall the moment; and his father's reaction when he'd informed him he was attending Airborne.

"Why would anyone want to jump out of a perfectly good airplane?"

It was the type of question that only a loving parent could have conjured, and the fact that he'd heard the mild concern in his father's voice, even though he was a military man himself, had led DJ to examine his own decision and admit his own mild fears. In the end, he'd seen the training through and survived the experience, even come to enjoy it, but he hoped he would never have to execute it for real in a hostile situation.

When the overloaded, monster bird had struggled its way off the runway and into the air in Kuwait, DJ had immediately fallen asleep, exhaustion overtaking him. He managed to remain that way for a blissful hour or two, but now he was wide-awake, facing the remainder of the twenty-two-hour flight with nothing to occupy him except his thoughts and his iPod. He shifted in his seat, stretching out the long legs of his 5'10" frame and closing his brown eyes.

Instantly, an image of his wife, Clara, filled his mind's eye, and a small smile flickered fleetingly across his lips before the pain of being separated again cut through him like a knife. DJ had been an army brat, moving wherever his father had needed to be, finally settling long enough to attend high school in Copperas Cove, Texas. It was there that he'd first seen Clara, and from that first encounter, he'd been smitten. Thanks to his perseverance, they'd become high school sweethearts, loving each other in the cliché manner that only two kids from small towns in the ass end of nowhere could accomplish. She had been the love of his life then and still was to this day. He couldn't believe it might be months before he had the means to tell her how much she meant to him again. With a sense of despair, he recalled their parting, her sad smile as he'd kissed her and stroked her cheek.

"Just make sure you come home to me," she'd said softly.

"I can't make promises I can't keep, but you know I'll do my damndest."

"Do you have to go?"

"You know I do, but I'll think of you every minute of every day."

DJ ran a hand through his dirty blond hair as if to wipe the painful memory from his head.

Feeling rather than hearing the shift in the drone of the quad engines, DJ opened his eyes to see the others fidgeting around him, checking the positions of their gear, and stretching their limbs as best they could in their cramped allocated space. With a sigh, he reached down to his iPod and shut off the music.

"What's happening?"

The man next to him glanced over.

"Typical Army maneuvers, taking the long way round everything. They've just announced we're making our first pit stop."

"Where?"

"Alaska."

"Holy crap, we circumnavigating the entire globe?"

"Musta figured it was the only safe place to land these days."

DJ snorted, amused by the comment, and not surprised that their final destination had been the only information revealed to them regarding their trip. They were strictly on a need to know level.

He felt the plane touch down and waited patiently for the order to move, gathering his kit and filing out in an organized manner with the rest of the troops, heading for the normal civilian sections of Anchorage International Airport, most in search of bathrooms, conversation, and chow, and not necessarily in that order. DJ allowed himself to be carried along with the crowd for a while, splitting from them when something caught his attention.

Standing in awe, he was face to face with a foe that made him shiver; something that horrified him more than the first time a rocket had ripped through the tent next to his during his first tour.

The largest Kodiak grizzly bear ever recorded loomed over him, standing tall on its hind legs, its gigantic claws hanging from humungous paws, its mouth open to reveal fearsome teeth. Okay, so the bear was in a glass case and stuffed in many ways resembling something from an old b-rated horror movie, but in spite of that, it was very real, and some guy had stared into those eyes, reaching within himself to overcome possibly debilitating fear, and killed it before it killed him.

Fascinated by the display, he dug out his camera and snapped off a shot, knowing that he and Clara would marvel over it on his return. He wandered off, keen to see what other treasures he could find among the displays of wildlife, vintage airplanes, and local art. Before he knew it, his plane was refueled and ready to go.

As he settled back into his allocated seat, he mentally loaded a third bullet into an imaginary handgun. To him, these tours were akin to playing Russian roulette, and this was his third spin of the barrel. Every time that clicking sound slowed to a stop, and he pulled the trigger to create that hollow, empty thud, he had to add another hollow point .45 round to another empty tube, decreasing his odds of making it through another turn. There wasn't any real point to this little mind game he played, apart from the fact that not only was it a good representation of the truth, but it also kept things exciting. The day he could no longer make things exciting was the day he would lose his edge, and that could be the day he'd die.

He knew that if he allowed himself to become complacent or jaded, it wouldn't be long before the enemy caught up with him and he'd find himself in a home video being broadcast on Al Jazeera. He'd wake up on his knees in front of four hooded men with dull knives; his arms tied behind his back. One of them would grab his head and pull it back, and the last thing he would know would be the pain of them sawing and hacking at his throat followed by the quick jerking motion as he literally drowned in his own blood.

He understood that for the majority of them, this grim threat that hung over their heads wasn't a soldier's worst fear. Their worst fear was that the video would end up somewhere, accessible to their loved ones. They were the ones that would have to relive the moment over and over, unable to erase it from their memories.

After another pit stop somewhere in Germany, DJ fell asleep again with his ear buds firmly pushed in place, waking up to the familiar feeling of the flying mammoth making the combat maneuver known as the corkscrew, a technique the pilot began at a very high altitude, making a series of sharp, right-hand banking turns during a rapid descent. He knew that this must be the final approach to the base, using the technique to touch down as quickly as possible without being shot down in the process.

The trick landing hit him with a g-force that reminded him briefly of his ride on The Mamba, at Worlds of Fun amusement park in Kansas City. The roller coaster had a two-hundred-foot initial drop at speed, but the G's there were nothing compared to this little ride. As Incubus' Make Yourself played almost inside his head, he glanced over at the young soldier in the seat opposite.

Private Craig Hardwell was a first timer, at just eighteen years old and on his first deployment. DJ knew the kid and liked him, but he could see he wasn't faring well during his first corkscrew. His café latte skin tone had a greenish tinge, and he was staring blankly into his upturned helmet, making the face of a drunkard about to experience his lunch all over again. DJ was certain he was going to fill the thing.

"Hey man, take it easy, it'll be over soon," he yelled, hoping the newbie would hear him over the roar of the engines.

Whether he filled it or not, he would be required to put his helmet on before exiting the plane. DJ wanted to save him the discomfort and humiliation if he could. He continued to yell encouragement, keeping Craig focused on him. The kid managed to hold it down, and DJ breathed a sigh of relief as the tires screeched on the ground; the heavily laden plane using everything it had to come to a halt.

As soon as the cargo door opened, the occupants were hit by a blast of heat and sand that was nearly unbearable. DJ winced, likening the experience to heating an oven to three hundred and fifty degrees Fahrenheit then sticking your face inside, throwing some grit in it for good measure.

Loaded down with every possession they had to their name in a duffel bag, their weapons, and their battle gear, the company marched down the ramp and away from the plane until they were at a safe distance to cross through the jet wash, which was blowing hotter and harder than the Iraqi wind. They quickly got into formation in a large, empty sand lot next to three massive metal buildings.

DJ recognized the Commander that approached, at least by sight. His name was Martinez, a proud, third-generation Army man. That's what came of being an army brat; you often crossed paths with people who would pop up again later in life. He risked a glance at the other three hundred and fifty-nine soldiers, all staring at the Commander, waiting for direction and encouragement. Word had it that Martinez had only just graduated the Officer Academy, and this was his first deployment in his current post. DJ was reserving judgment for now.

Martinez cleared his throat and jumped into his speech without trepidation. "Welcome to Camp Speicher. This is the last time we will ever form up as a company. We're close to enemy territory, and we don't want to give the Haji's a chance to take us all out with a single rocket. Behind the formation, you'll see three hangers, and they're what we'll be calling home from now on.

There are a few basic campground rules. Don't go behind the hangers for any reason. There's an active landmine field that hasn't been cleared yet. The Marines and our infantry have literally just captured this base, which is an eighty-four square mile former Iraqi airbase. There are buildings with suspected chemical weapons and bunkers that haven't been cleared out. Do not, I repeat, do not go wandering off and always carry your chemical suits with you at all times. Also, watch out for the wildlife, as everything here is poisonous and wants to kill you.

There are no decent latrines, no showers, and no chow hall yet. Clearing the base and scavenging for materials to construct the necessary buildings will be part of your duties here. I hope you all followed the packing list and brought baby wipes, as those baths are the best you'll get until we sort things out. As for food, MRE's will be handed out at designated meal times, which will be staggered depending on your duties."

Internally, DJ groaned. The ready to eat meals were light to carry and convenient, so were great when away from camp on recon, but you didn't want to live on them full time if you could help it. Basically, they tasted like shit. He sincerely hoped Martinez would be pushing hard to get that chow hall up and running. He turned his attention back to his Commander's words.

"The airfield is all dirt and sand, so all aircraft maintenance will be conducted in the hangar next to it. Working outside isn't recommended, this sand clogs up parts in a heartbeat. Our motor pool will also be staged here when the rest of the equipment arrives.

"After this formation, I want you all to swing past Hangar #1 and pick up a cot. Take the cot and your gear into either of the other two hangars and set them up with just enough space remaining to stow your gear underneath. It's going to be tight, and space is at a premium, use it wisely.

"The arms room, supply, and the head shed will also be in hangar #1 where you pick up your cot. The good news about this place is that it's solid, and has a fence right around the whole perimeter, as well as the two guard towers. We'll have twelve-hour guard duty rotations starting tonight on the base perimeter.

"I know this is a tough time for everyone, and that being away from our families is hell. I've got a wife and a two-year-old son back home myself, so I know what you're going through. My open-door policy is effective immediately, and the Chaplain is also available if you need to talk. Keep your heads down and on a swivel. Dismissed!"

"A real home away from home," a sarcastic voice muttered in the crowd as the troop about turned and marched towards the hangar, lining up to collect their cots.

DJ wasn't sure if he agreed with the sentiment, or if the constant busy work in the arid heat would be preferable to hours and hours of staring into that dry, dusty landscape, trying to catch a glimpse of a threat in the baking sun. He had a feeling he might just prefer digging latrines.

Chapter Two: Wake Up Call

DJ tossed and turned, trying to find a comfortable position on the thin, flimsy mattress. He glanced at his watch, the soft luminosity of the hands and dial informing him it was 0230 hours.

In the pitch black and plummeting temperatures of night, he could hear the soft, muffled sound of someone crying. With so many men sardined together in the vast hangar, there was no way to tell who it was or where exactly it was coming from. *Probably a first timer, missing his Mom and Pop,* DJ thought. The ones who already had families of their own weren't usually criers, but you could never rule it out. He had to admit it was a helluva deployment to pull as a first outing, but that was just military life and the luck of the draw, as you didn't get to pick and choose. Rolling himself up in his rough, grey, military issue blanket, DJ finally found a comfortable position and drifted off to sleep.

Two hours later, he was jolted awake by the ever familiar concussion of a rocket violently ripping through the night and impacting somewhere inside the base. He knew it was close, because as well as hearing the sounds, he felt the concussion knock the wind out of him like a punch in the gut.

All around him, in the deep darkness, he could hear the sounds of complete chaos, three hundred and sixty soldiers scattering like rats from a sinking ship, trying to take cover, some cursing, some silent, one screaming. The sound was cut off abruptly, and DJ could imagine a meaty hand being clamped over the mouth from behind as the panicked soldier was silenced and yanked off his cot.

Together as one, they hunkered down alongside their cots in a futile attempt to seek some sort of cover. In silence, their sleep deprived and already dehydrated brains worked out the severity of the situation, horrifying enough for even the most battle-hardened of them. The camp did not yet hold any safe haven. No cleared concrete bunkers, no reinforced buildings, no long-range equipment to mount a counter attack and ward off their enemy. Crammed together into two hangars this way, they were sitting ducks. There weren't even a few Humvees on site to hide beneath. All they had were three, or maybe less now, decrepit, old Iraqi hangar buildings. They smelt of old oil, as if it were a junkyard garage from the 1950's. The stench of sand, urine, and now fear hung in the air.

They all ducked lower as they heard a second rocket screaming through the night sky, flinching as it made a loud popping sound overhead. Crouched inside the windowless darkness, they missed witnessing the beautiful orange light streaking across the deep navy colored sky, rivaling even the likes of the Hale-Bopp comet. In the heart of the dessert, there was no light wash to detract from the vast expanse of the galaxy that twinkled and glittered above, putting on its magical show that was rarely seen by city-dwellers. It was doubtful that any of them would have appreciated the view right now.

Still lying on his cot in Hangar #1, Twenty-two-year-old Specialist Joey Stevenson was probably the oldest in the troop and the exception to the reactions of the others. Having already spent a year in Iraq, he'd refused to join in with the frantic confusion after the first strike. His 5'9", 210-pound athletic and muscular frame was still stretched out in a relaxed position.

"Those cowardly fuckers are taking pot shots at us," he said, still groggy from sleep. "But that last one was a dud."

A small, trembling voice somewhere in the hangar responded. "How can you tell?"

"Because you never hear the one that kills you," Joey replied, a voice of confidence aimed at the inexperienced, drawing from knowledge gained over his previous tour. "Besides, there was no concussion at the end. Most of the shit they shoot at us is old, unused Russian artillery. They bury it in huge caches in the sand, then dig it up to fire at us. More than half of them will be duds."

"Yeah? What about the other half?"

"Well, they're the ones you've got to worry about," he replied, his grin evident in his tone.

"This just gets better and better."

DJ smiled, recognizing the sarcastic tone from earlier in the day. He had a feeling there were going to be some good guys in this company, making things bearable. As it goes, it is your duty as a soldier, to protect and die for the man next to you; it makes it so much easier when you actually give a shit.

"So what do we do now?"

"Nothing much we can do," Joey said, shrugging even though no one could see. "Most of the equipment isn't here yet, and we can't engage with hand weapons and rifles at this distance. I don't hear any screaming, so I don't think the other occupied hangars were hit. Nobody to help, and nobody to attack."

"I'll take a look outside and check," DJ said, rising to his feet.

He snagged his duffel from beneath the cot, fumbling around blind inside for his flashlight. Finding it, he clicked it on, causing pale faces to turn away from him, some protesting.

"Shit, that hurts."

"Could have used a little warning there man."

"Sorry; didn't mean to blind you all."

"Do you think you should have a lighton? Aren't we supposed to stick to blackout or something?"

"This isn't the Blitz, kid. There aren't any other buildings for miles around, and I think they already know we're here. Besides, they can't see into the hangar any more than we can see out. I'll turn it off as soon as I get to the door, I just didn't want to be falling over all your sorry asses on the way."

Nobody answered. DJ could imagine some teen, huddled in the dark, biting his lip and feeling embarrassed. Instantly, he felt sorry, forgetting that the younger crowd might not be used to the sometimes-harsh banter.

"It was good thinking, though, and under other circumstances, you'd have been spot on," he added, attempting to soften the impact of his earlier statement. "Any form of light, from a cigarette to the sun glinting off your weapon can reveal your position, and if we were going for stealth, I'd gladly let you string me up for using a flashlight."

A few chuckles rippled through the hangar, and DJ felt pleased he'd managed to lighten the mood and relieve some of the tension. He hoped the kid felt better about his question. After slipping on his field jacket, he walked down towards the door end of the hangar, his footfalls heavy in his desert boots. DJ had known better than to remove them tonight. He'd removed only his field jacket, a bulletproof vest, and Kevlar helmet before lying down to sleep.

He never underestimated an enemy. The arrival of the four planes wouldn't have gone unnoticed, and all it would take was a pair of high-powered binoculars to know that the camp was now full of troops and not much else. Strikes when they'd only just arrived and were still floundering to find their feet had been inevitable, although he hadn't expected it quite this soon.

"I'll come with you."

DJ turned to his left, catching a pair of long legs, also booted, swinging off the cot to the ground before the soldier rose to his feet, and appeared in the flashlight beam. He moved with an assurance that spoke of experience, and with a stealthy grace that only hinted at his 2nd generation Cherokee blood. His light grey and tan camouflage field jacket were open over his light tan t-shirt, but DJ caught the eagle insignia attached to it, identifying the man as an equally ranked Specialist.

"Joey Stevenson," the man said, sauntering over to DJ.

"David Jones, DJ to my friends. Pleasure to meet you."

"Better circumstances would be nice, but we take what we can get," Joey agreed. "Let's see how much of a mess we have to clear up."

The two made their way to the small door cut out of the left-hand side aircraft access. DJ clicked on his flashlight and then pulled the door open. They stepped outside and closed the door behind them.

Of the eight hangars, the decision makers had chosen the most intact three to use as temporary bases. One of the other eight - only two away from hangar #3 - had been almost completely demolished. Its roof and most of the four walls were gone, only one small section still standing, another part hanging from it, swaying gently with an arthritic wheeze. The rest of it was just a blackened pile, wisps of dirty, dark smoke curling up towards the heavens.

"Shit," DJ breathed. "That would have been some carnage."

"Yep, if that had been one of ours, we'd be digging graves instead of latrines come first light, and any closer might have caused the whole lot to collapse on us. We're lucky the ground's so damn impacted. If it had embedded deep, the shockwaves still might have brought the roof down on our heads."

"Frankly, I'm surprised any of these tin cans are still standing. They're in pretty bad shape. Think they'll be anymore tonight?"

"Been quiet for a while, so maybe they're out of action or ammo. Shit gets clogged up with sand pretty quick. It's a constant battle to keep equipment free and firing here."

"You've been here before?"

"Yeah, spent twelve months in this hellhole; and to think I signed up to get away from a deserted nowhere."

"Where was that?" DJ asked, already liking Joey.

"Some hick little place called Oskaloosa, Kansas, but don't judge me."

DJ chuckled. "I won't. Besides, I'm in no position. After hauling our asses from state to state, Copperas Cove in Texas is where I call home. I don't suppose it's much better."

"Army brat?"

"Yep, born and raised to this life."

"Glad to hear it, but I don't think is the best place for idle chatter, do you?"

Both men turned towards the voice, snapping to attention and saluting as they saw Commander Martinez standing beside them.

"No Sir," they responded.

"At ease. What are you clowns doing out here, and why the hell aren't you wearing your full gear?"

"Checking for damage and casualties,to see if there was assistance required, Sir," DJ responded.

"Unless necessary, we weren't going more than few steps away from the hangar, Sir. We put the speed of investigation above the need for full gear," Joey added.

Commander Martinez nodded and sighed, looking at the destroyed hangar. "Well, not much we can do tonight, and you've only got…" he glanced at his wrist, "…an hour before its time to rise and shine. I suggest you get back inside and get a little more sleep if you can, and don't ever let me catch you outside the hangar out of full battle uniform again."

"Yes, Sir."

The Commander walked away, leaving the two soldiers to look sheepishly at one another.

"That could have gone a lot worse," Joey said as they slipped back into the hangar.

There was no time for DJ to respond as their battle buddies inundated them with questions.

"Well, how bad is it?"

"Anything we can do?"

"Anyone hurt?"

DJ held up a hand to silence them, clicking on his flashlight with the other. "Just one of the empties, everything's fine. Try and get some sleep."

He noted that each soldier was dressed in full battle rattle, all standing either beside or at the end of their cot, ready and willing to leap into action should they be required to do so. He and Joey glanced at each other, silently acknowledging their appreciation. Already, they were working together as a unit, making decisions without orders, coming together as a team, willing to risk their lives under rocket fire to go and assist where they could. They nodded to each other before returning to their cots, both knowing that sleep would elude them for the rest of the night.

***

Tired but eager to be released from the confinement of their metal cage, DJ and Joey shared Joey's cot as they sat and wolfed down their MRE breakfast; their compartment trays balanced on their laps. It was a little after 0600 hours, and both wanted to get to work. The sooner work began, the sooner the base would be a safer place.

"So what do you think of the Commander?" DJ asked between mouthfuls.

"He's young, but not dumb," Joey replied, taking a swig of his bottled water and grimacing.

He glanced at the label, shaking his head at the Arabic writing. "Bitter," he said, rummaging through the selection of thick, taupe brown packets spread out on the cot beside him until he located a slender sachet.

He ripped open the package, gripping the open bottle between his knees. He shook some of the powder in and tossed the rest, the water already turning a bright, synthetic raspberry red. He grabbed the bottle and covered the opening with his thumb, shaking it hard. He took another swig.

"Better. Yeah, Commander Martinez. I heard he'd newly graduated, but I liked his intro yesterday. I think he's going to be okay. What about you?"

"I think the same. With a good team, good command, and a lot of hard work, there's a small chance we could survive this," DJ replied, mopping up his marinara sauce with the last of his tortilla.

"That's if we survive the MREs," Joey replied. "Nothing like beef stew for breakfast. Oh boy, you ate the jalapeno cashews? You'd better take my moist wipe as well as your tissue; you're gonna need it."

"I need every last one of my twelve hundred, nutritional, packaged and processed calories thank you very much, and you can keep your moist wipe, I've got a cast iron stomach."

"Cast iron or not, that's going to sting on the way out," Joey grinned. "Check it out, looks like some of the guys are struggling."

DJ glanced around, seeing the new soldiers on first deployment struggling with the packages in the awkward space, or carefully reading the instructions on the flameless heater or the other packages that would magically turn into edible food and acceptable drinks if given the right treatment. Others had negotiated their way through the process, but were struggling to force the food down.

Noticing one soldier sitting on his bunk, knees raised, staring morosely at his unopened MRE pack; he called out to him.

"Hey, kid."

As soon as the teen raised his head, DJ recognized him as Craig Hardwell, the private who'd nearly filled his helmet during the corkscrew.

"Who me?"

"Yeah you, why aren't you eating?"

The private shrugged his shoulder. "The trip, last night…"

20

"Come on over here and take a pew. Bring your breakfast with you."

Craig did as he was asked, perching himself sideways on the opposite side of Joey's cot.

"Not feeling so hot, huh?" DJ asked.

"I'm okay; I just don't feel like eating."

"We understand, kid," Joey said. "And you're going to see a lot worse in your career that will really make you sick to your stomach, but you have to carry on. You grab rest when you can, and you eat when you can because you can never be sure when you'll next get the chance."

While Joey had been talking, DJ had been opening Craig's pack, shifting through the various packet and sachets until he found something useful. He opened the packet and held it out to Craig.

"Here, dry crackers, just take a little bite."

Craig looked at it dubiously, but he took it and pulled a cracker out. Tentatively, he took a nibble.

"Good, now another."

Craig tried another, finding it went down easier than the first, then nodding, he crammed the rest of the cracker into his mouth, suddenly ravenous.

"That's better," DJ laughed, already shoving the entrée into the heater and stuffing it back in the box to warm.

He'd known that the cracker would settle Craig's stomach and that his appetite would return. "Must admit, I still feel a bit peckish myself."

He stood up and addressed the hangar. "Any who doesn't want their pound cake can throw it my way," he called.

Two pound cakes came flying through the air. One he caught, the other bounced off his head. "Hey, watch it," he laughed. "Who's got the lousy throw?"

The door of the hangar was open, allowing the emerging daylight to brighten the vast interior. Suddenly, the light disappeared, blocked by a silhouette in the doorway, the sun a fiery ball low in the sky behind him. Recognizing that only a sergeant would stand there with that authoritative stance and not speak, they scrambled to their feet, trays and packets flung aside and hands frantically wiped as they tried to make themselves respectable and presentable.

Without entering, the sergeant flung a roll of trash bags down the center aisle between the cots. "Get this mess cleaned up and get outside. You've got five minutes tops."

"Yes Sergeant," they chanted as the shadow figure disappeared.

Joey got to his feet and snagged the roll, opening and peeling off two sacks, handing one to DJ. He threw the sack to the guy on the next bunk.

"Anyone who's done grab one and pass it along. Anyone who hasn't finished, eat what you can and stash the rest for later, you're going to need it. You heard the sergeant, move it!"

Chapter Three: Friendships Forged

After compacting down the trash bags as best they could and stacking them in a corner until further instruction, the men had donned their full battle rattle and filed outside. The outfit consisted of desert boots, camouflage trousers, a light tan t-shirt, camouflage field jacket, bullet-proof vest to which a chemical mask was attached, ballistic sunglasses, a Kevlar helmet, their weapon, and a camelback hydration system.

The uniform was designed the best that it could be with both safety and maneuverability in mind. Some soldiers who had never been anywhere, but military training camps or bases in the homeland grumbled about having to wear the full kit at all times on the base, a complaint that seemed justified when they stepped out into the open. Although the sun was barely up, already the arid heat was stifling, catching and drying the back of their throats. They could tell that soon the heat would be blistering, and they longed to remove the helmets and strip down to only trousers and t-shirts.

The more experienced of them knew that even though they were inside a base that was now under U.S. command, they were still on enemy soil. At any second, on any given day, that soil could become a combat zone. Those were the ones that welcomed the kit, despite the added bulk, the weight, and the dehydration it would cause as they sweated under the fiery ball of the desert sun. They dreaded the day that the newbies would learn their lesson the hard way.

The troops had already been split into four platoons, with hangar #1 containing 1st and 2nd platoon. They formed their groups and separated, standing a distance apart from one another, avoiding formation as they'd been instructed. The men from hangar #2 were doing the same.

Eight squadron leaders were already waiting impatiently outside Hangar #1 for the occupants to organize themselves, allowing them some leeway in this unfamiliar setting, a luxury that would not be afforded to them in future. They made fast work of allocating squad numbers to the men, splitting each platoon into four groups. Whichever group they landed in now would form their squadron for the entire deployment, and the squadron leader they were assigned to would be their first link in the chain of command.

"Right, Second Squad, Top put out the marching orders for today, assemble on me."

DJ walked towards his designated squad leader, recognizing the voice as the one who'd ordered them out of the hangar earlier. It had the rich tone and slight drawl of the Southern states, and the man that belonged to the voice was a tall Caucasian with brown hair and hazel eyes, and carrying around two hundred and ten pounds of solid muscle. While the squad leader was waiting for everyone to join him and settle, DJ glanced around, pleased to see that both Joey and Craig were in the same group. Once everyone had found a spot, the sergeant continued.

"Top wants half of my guys out on a little recon mission. You're going to scavenge all the other Haji hangars for anything we can use or build with, paying special attention to anything that might help us get latrines up and running. They're our priority, so the other half will join first squadron, who are going to start digging and prepping them."

Joey jumped in quickly before anyone else had the presence of mind to speak up. "Hey sergeant, I got my group, and I want recon duty."

He quickly snagged DJ and Craig, pulling them closer to him, then randomly tapped five other guys nearby. He looked at the sergeant, confident and assured, holding his gaze. "We've got this Sergeant."

Sergeant Will Heard examined the group, noting the two Specialist insignias among them. He looked back to Joey, who hadn't dropped his gaze. He admired his confidence and balls, but idly wondered if this guy was going to be a problem in the future, thinking maybe he was a little *too* confident. Making a split second decision, he figured that today would answer his question one way or another. Either he would lead his chosen team to do a great job, or he would use the recon as an excuse to goof around and lead the others astray. It was best to know what he was dealing with here.

"Fine, you got it, move out."

The group of eight split from the rest; falling into a steady march as they circumnavigated the other squads of men receiving their marching orders.

"So, who's going to tell me where we start?" Joey asked cheerfully as they walked. "Not you DJ, I know you'll give me the smart answer."

"We should start at the closest building," a heavyset man with dark brown hair and eyes responded.

"Okay, what's your reason?"

"Shit man, 'cos it's the least distance to walk!"

DJ and Joey allowed the group of privates to have their laugh, already judging with an expert eye that the young man had probably struggled to make weight and might be the least fit of the group. Still, Joey's question was a serious one, and once they'd settled down, he resumed the opportunity for a lesson.

"It's a fair answer, but your reasoning might be a bit simplistic. Yeah, it makes sense to start close, that way, if we find anything useful; we can get it over to the digging crews quickly. Also, it does make sense to keep the walking distance shorter initially, as we might have Humvees in a few days and be able to use one for the further outlying buildings. Anything else?"

"If this was an Iraqi hold up, they might have caches stashed or buried inside the hangars. Any explosive material should be moved further away from the occupied hangars ASAP, in case of future air or rocket attacks."

26

DJ smiled at Craig's answer. He'd always liked the kid, and now he was proving his smarts too. He only needed to toughen up that stomach, and he'd go far in his chosen career.

"Ding... ding... ding... you've won yourself a prize," Joey joked.

"Yeah? What do I win?" Craig said, playing along.

"You get to go in first!"

The group roared with laughter, their spirits high, a moment of camaraderie and joy that would be held onto through the nightmares that were to follow.

"How about we play a little game of getting to know you while we walk. I'll start. Specialist Joey Stevenson, Oskaloosa, Kansas, second deployment, all Iraq," he chanted in time with their footfalls. "Next."

"Specialist David Jones, Copperas Cove, Texas, third deployment. Afghanistan, Afghanistan, and now Iraq. Next."

"Private Billy Knowles," a tall teenager with blond hair and blue eyes said. "Wheeling, West Virginia, first deployment. Next."

"Private Craig Hardwell, L.A., California, first deployment and in case you hadn't noticed, second generation African American and Caucasian mix."

The group cracked up along with Craig.

"Well heck, if I'd known we were disclosing our ancestry, I'd have made it a guessing game," Joey said. "But we're approaching our first destination, so we'll have to get to know the rest of you a little later."

"Proceed with caution from here on in guys," DJ added. "We don't know how hard they fought for this place yet. For all we know, the enemy might have rigged it before lying down and handing it over. Never assume anything is safe. Besides, it's next to the one destroyed in the blast last night; the structure might be unstable."

"Great; and I have to go in first. I'm only eighteen, too young to die."

Craig had meant it as a joke, but the sobering reality hit the group hard. All good humor was forgotten, and the team was strictly business on their final approach. The hangar that stood in front of them was a giant, imposing and terrifying, yet possibly the key to making the camp a better place to be.

"Stand back. DJ, with me," Joey said, approaching the personnel door.

DJ unshouldered his rifle, an instinctive reaction to the opening of any previously unopened door and entering any unexplored building. Logic told him that it would have been checked and checked again by the team that had captured the base, but who was to say someone hadn't hidden themselves well on the huge acreage, perhaps deep in the bunkers. Then moved with stealth at night throughout the place, awaiting their chance to escape or wreak havoc upon them. In war, you could never assume that somewhere was safe. He stood close by Joey's shoulder as the Specialist eased the door open, the deep, creaking groans echoing through the cavernous space.

Nothing but sand and dust stirred inside. Joey clicked on his flashlight and stepped in, making room for DJ to join him. They scanned the area, looking and listening for the tiniest sign of movement or life, in any form.

Without nearly two hundred regimented cots and living, breathing men inside, the hangar showed its true colors. Designed to contain five or six fighter planes with room to maneuver them and work on them, the dimensions were massive. Joey's flashlight barely penetrated the intense blackness inside; the light almost swallowed up by the unknown. They could make out large shapes that cast eerie shadows as Joey flicked the light around, trying to get a better sense of the building and its contents.

"Will you just look at all this shit," he breathed as his light landed on a pile of crates to their left.

They too were huge, although they appeared smaller in the vast space. They were stacked four or five high, ending way above head height.

"We're going to have to work fast to go through this lot," DJ agreed. "And that's just the stuff we can see. Lord knows what's back there."

"What, or maybe who," Joey said, backing up DJ's earlier thoughts. "I say we try and get the big doors open so we can get a better idea of what we're dealing with."

DJ shouldered his weapon and clicked on his own flashlight, joining Joey in his examination of the massive steel and tin doors on the flight line side of the hangar. They were the roller kind, suspended from metal tracks on top and with wheels on the bottom. Seeing no locking mechanism, he tried to slide the right-hand door open.

The door didn't budge. He tried again, putting his back into it, but still the door refused to do any more than rock slightly. Working his way along the door, he soon found out why. About three quarters along, crates and other piles of equipment had been jam-packed hard against it.

"These rollers are out of action until we clear a ton of stuff," DJ called as he made his way back. "How's it going on your side?"

"It's all jammed up with grit and sand, but otherwise clear. Maybe if the two of us put our backs into it, we'll get it moving."

Holding their flashlights in their mouths, they both applied two hands to the door.

"On three. One, two, three!"

The huge door held fast, then began to move, squealing, then screaming in protest as it picked up speed along the uneven, dirt filled tracks, any soothing balm of oil in the mechanism long since dissipated. The two men let go as it slammed and locked at the end of the tracks, both of them already sweating after this simple exertion.

They switched off their flashlights, blinking in the brightness of the sun, coughing with the sand and dust cloud they'd stirred up. A low whistle came from outside.

"Look at this place; you could work on a Boeing 747 in here!"

The privates moved inside, sticking close and remaining alert while they examined their surroundings.

"I reckon it must be about two hundred and fifty foot long, what did they expect to be keeping in here?"

"Don't know what they expected, but they ended up with a handful of old Russian fighters and helicopters," Joey replied.

"That's probably why they didn't care about blocking the doors," DJ said, looking up at the peaked roof that was about fifty foot high at the point. "They ended up just for storage. Maybe we should try and pack everything into one and leave the others clear, in case, we can make them secure and utilize them."

"That would be the long term goal once we've hunted down anything useful. It'll take days to search through them all if they're all like this."

Now that daylight illuminated the hangar, they could determine what had been causing the eerie shadows. As well as the massive stacks of crates that seemed to be everywhere they looked, toolboxes and random tools were scattered around, as well as wheel separators, floor jacks, chains, and fuel tanks. It looked like an aircraft graveyard, the skeletal bones of crafts abandoned to turn to dust.

"This place reminds me of a documentary I saw about the Mary Celeste," Billy said. "It's like one minute they were working, then the next minute, they were just gone, disappeared, their tools falling where they were standing."

Craig shuddered. "Way to creep me out, man!"

"Nothing creepy about it," a tall, lanky private commented. "We know exactly what happened to them, the U.S. military. Where do we start, I can't wait to see what perks we can scavenge."

Joey looked at the teenager with mild amusement. "I don't think we've had the pleasure yet. Introduce yourself, soldier."

"Private Jacob Johnson, but I prefer Jake."

"And where do you hail from, *Jake?*"

"Dallas, Texas, and before you ask, this is my first deployment."

"I never would have guessed. Since you're so keen, we'll start at the front and work towards clearing that other door. Go ahead and climb on up there and see what's in that top crate."

Jake looked up at the precariously balanced pile of crates. "Up there?"

"All the way to the top."

"Aw shit, why did I open my big mouth?"

"We were wondering the same thing," DJ chuckled. "But consider it a lesson learned. Besides, you must be what, at least six ft."

"6 ft. 2" actually."

"There you go then, the rest of us would have further to climb."

"Very funny."

"Come on; you'll get first pick of anything you find that we can't use for the base."

Jake unshouldered his rifle and passed it to Craig to hold.

"Nothing ventured, nothing gained. Here goes," he said with a grin, digging in his pocket to pull out a pair of black leather, reinforced gloves.

After slipping them on, he shook out his arms and shoulders while jumping from foot to foot, like an athlete limbering up before an event. He scrutinized the stack one last time then began to climb, agile and fast, reaching the top in seconds.

"I'm impressed," DJ said, raising an eyebrow at Joey.

"Not bad at all," Joey muttered in return. "But we won't give him a swollen head just yet. Hey, monkey boy! What do you see in there? Can you lift it to pass it down?"

"Aircraft parts; fuel gauges probably, foreign writing."

Jake lifted the corner of the top crate, testing the weight, his feet balancing on the crate corner sticking out below. "Too heavy to lift down, maybe if I toss a few down first?"

"Long as you're sure they're not explosive devices, we'll catch them," Billy joked.

"Split into two teams," Joey ordered. "I'll go up the next stack and do the same. Anyone who hasn't introduced yourself, do so when you catch something unless someone else is talking at the time."

"Incoming!"

The first gauge was tossed down to Billy, who caught it and began the trash pile on the floor. Joey climbed the next pile of crates with less speed, but more grace and finesse than Jake had, peering into the top crate.

The stockier soldier was the first to introduce himself. "Private Jimmy Wayne, Richmond Virginia, first deployment," he called as he caught the gauge and added it to the pile on the oil-stained concrete floor.

"I got tires in these," Joey called down after a quick glance to see who had spoken. "I'll leave it up to you whether you want to catch them on the bounce or not."

He hauled the first tire out of the crate, easing it down as far as he could before letting it go. Both DJ and a slim man with brown hair and eyes and a deep olive complexion made a grab for it. They caught it together, DJ nodding at him to speak as he took the tire from him and added it to the trash.

"Private George Ates, Detroit, Michigan, first time deployed."

Another voice followed almost immediately. "Private Justin Gibson, Harrisburgh, Pennsylvania, first time out."

"I think I can lower this top crate down now. Get ready guys."

With the introductions complete, the group worked on in amicable silence, concentrating on making headway in their daunting task. By the time the sun was directly overhead, they'd brought down and emptied at least seventeen stacks of crates, clearing the area in front of the other main door. They'd restacked the contents neatly in the corner, leaving the door free. Their chests were heaving and beads of sweat formed and dripped from their foreheads, but they were all pleased with their accomplishment.

"This is good, strong wood," DJ said, closely examining one of the crates. "And the slats are pretty large. I think they'd be suitable to build with, even if it's temporary."

"I haven't seen anything better yet," Joey agreed. "I think we should take some of these back and see what they reckon. No use walking for miles around each hangar if these will suffice."

"Maybe there would be some manageable bits of metal from the hangar hit by the blast. We should check it out on the way."

DJ looked at the private that had spoken up. "Jacob Johnson, wasn't it? That's not a bad idea JJ."

The teen looked pleased, proud to have been assigned a nickname from a Specialist. It was a sign that he was considered a valuable member of the group, that he was accepted.

"Do we all think we'll manage to carry two of these between a team of two, one on either side with the crates on top of one another?"

Justin snorted. "Two is for pussies; I bet I could carry three on my own."

"This isn't a competition," DJ said. "It's about getting the job done efficiently and safely and still having the energy to carry on for as long as it takes. You're not acclimatized to the heat yet, and I bet that back in Pennsylvania you barely see ninety, let alone one-thirty with zero humidity and a sand storm blasting in your face. I admire your eagerness, but we need to learn to pace ourselves out here when we can. We'll try the two between two to start with. No point killing ourselves if they don't like them. Collect your gear and choose your battle. Give it a try and if you think it's too much, take one. I'd rather take less than have to haul anyone's ass back to base because he collapsed on the way. Jimmy, you're with me."

Joey approved of DJ's call, understanding that he wanted to keep an eye on the stocky private, worried about his fitness levels in the heat. DJ would set a nice, steady pace for him, and take more of the weight if it looked like he was struggling. He motioned for George to

35

join him. He'd been pretty quiet so far, and Joey wanted to make sure he felt like part of the team.

"So you're a city boy?" he asked as they walked, carrying the crates between them.

"Yes, born and raised in Detroit."

"This place must be a shock to the system then."

"Not so much, except Detroit's a whole lot flatter. It has it's built up inner city, but it sprawls out too, just like this place."

"Yeah, I can see that. You got a wife waiting back home for you?"

George shook his head. "No, I'm only eighteen. Even if I had found that special someone, I'd probably have been too stupid and immature to know it before my training."

"Made some mistakes?"

"A few, but I'm over them now. I feel I'm on the right path."

"I'm glad to hear it. You know, if you ever need to talk or ask any questions, you can come to me at any time."

"I appreciate that. What about you, have you got someone waiting and worrying back home."

"Yes, my wife, Carrie. We just celebrated our two year anniversary before my departure date."

A moment of silence followed, Joey thinking about his life back home, George thinking about what it would be like to leave someone behind for this.

"So what do you like to do in your free time, any hobbies we can try to accommodate once we get this place fully functional?" Joey asked, pulling himself back to the present.

"I used to box in high school; I was hoping to take that up again."

"I'm sure we might persuade Sergeant into a few friendly matches one day. For me, it was football and lifting weights. Anything else?"

"Just music, listening and playing."

"What do you play?"

"Guitar, since as far back as I can remember."

"Me too, I started playing when I was eleven years old. Who were your inspirations?"

"Metal is the only music man! Always has been, always will be. If I weren't carrying these crates, I'd show you my tribute to my hero."

Joey laughed, pleased to hear the passion and enthusiasm in George's exclamation. He'd hit on something that really opened him up, which was exactly what he'd been hoping for.

"You going to tell me who it is, or do I have to guess?"

"You'd never guess so I'll just tell you. It's Dimebag Darrell."

Joey had hoped it was a name that he'd instantly recognize. A blank look and a shrug would damage the forming bond between them before it had even had a chance. If George admired them so much he'd had an image permanently inked on his skin, it was important. He scanned through his mental catalog of musicians, coming up trumps when he recalled the story of the guitarist being shot and killed on stage by a crazed fan, and with that, the band's music flooded his memory, making him smile.

"Pantera, good choice."

"You know it," the kid grinned.

Finding common ground other than their current circumstances, the pair continued to chat animatedly about one of their favorite subjects, passing the time before they hit base. Judging by the sound of chatter and laughter behind them, the others were doing the same.

Chapter Four: Darkness Approaches

DJ glanced anxiously at his watch. "It's going to be dark soon; we'd better head back ASAP. Let's get these doors shut and gather our gear."

The day had gone well. The wooden crates and intact, if blackened, sheets of metal they had retrieved had been well received by the rest of the squadron. After a short break for lunch sitting on upturned crates, they'd gone back to work, searching the rest of the hangar and making sure it was clear of anything dangerous, living or otherwise. They'd split into two teams, one team emptying out crates and stacking the ancient Russian parts, the other team carrying the crates to base. After a while, they'd swapped over. With this technique, they'd worked their way through the first hangar, were almost clear of the second, and had given the third a brief inspection, pleased to find it practically empty already. Although keen to carry on, they were still relieved when DJ called a halt and told them to prepare to move out.

"Hold up, I can't take the chance of those latrines not being ready when we get back, I need to go squat outside," Justin declared, heading for the door.

"Stop right there! What about your battle buddy?"

"Come on Joey, can't a guy have some privacy to take a dump?"

"Not until there's a closed door to take it behind, and maybe not even then. You know better than that."

"I'll go with you," Jimmy said, gathering his camelback and rifle.

"I hope you've got a clothes peg in that kit JDub; you're going to need it."

"Don't go too far boys, remember the land mines, and hurry it up for God's sake," DJ said with another glance at his watch.

"And don't forget to bury it afterward," Joey yelled at the two backs disappearing out the small personnel door.

Justin's answer was to shut the only remaining open door behind him, plunging the men inside into total darkness.

"Wise ass," Joey said as they all clicked on flashlights and found themselves makeshift seats. "We all did good work today. If we get to stick with this task, we'll get this one finished early tomorrow. Maybe the rest won't be so bad."

"Once we've been through them all, would it be better to shift all the junk to the farthest away hangar so that when equipment arrives we can use the closest ones for maintenance and storage, or would it be better to have everything spread out over the base?"

"That's a good question, Billy, but it probably won't be our call to make. Top or above will decide that when the time comes. It might be that we won't get any of the good stuff for a while yet, not until we've got things secure here. They hate risking their hawks."

As they discussed the merits and disadvantages of various tactics, only DJ was aware of the passing time. He stood up and began to pace, glancing at his watch for what felt like the hundredth time.

"It's been twenty minutes; we could have been back by now. What the hell are they doing out there?"

"I can check on them if you want," George offered, rising to his feet. "JJ, battle?"

"No, I'll come with you, just in case they've got some situation they can't handle out there," DJ said. "Besides, if he's goofing around, I want to be the one that kicks him in the butt."

They opened the door, finding it already twilight outside.

"Dammit," DJ said. "We're going to be in deep shit for being this irresponsible."

They made their way around one side of the hangar, seeing no sign of their missing teammates. Increasingly aware of the fading light, they retraced their steps and headed in the opposite direction. As soon as they turned the corner, they spotted their two squad members pressed up against the side of the hangar, trying to inch their way along. DJ was instantly on high alert, scanning the area for a threat. Seeing none, he began to march towards them.

"Stop," Justin hissed, his voice carrying in the still night air.

"What's wrong," DJ half-whispered back, unsure if he were to be concerned or irritated.

"Snakes," Justin said. "They're everywhere. We've been pinned here for ages. Every time we move, they get interested in us."

Cupping his hand over his flashlight and keeping it pointed low on the ground DJ clicked it on. The light at Justin and JDub's feet revealed two snakes meandering slowly around, their skin a silvery color in the beam of light, a dark grey Aztec pattern clearly displayed.

DJ couldn't help but laugh as he turned off his flashlight.

"It's only two, and they're rat snakes. JDub, didn't you say you were from Virginia? You must have had corn snakes there, right?"

"Well, sure."

"Similar markings, similar species. Totally harmless, so move it."

Justin bolted towards them, lifting his feet high as he ran, causing DJ and George to hoot with laughter. He was still checking the ground, wide-eyed and fearful when he reached them. JDub approached more calmly, walking away from the snakes unchallenged, a sheepish expression on his face.

"Sorry, I just didn't know what I was dealing with out here. Justin here freaked out, so I assumed he knew something I didn't."

"I did not freak out! I was justbeing cautious that's all."

"That why you ran back here like a little girl?"

"I did not."

"Don't worry, your secret's safe with us," DJ said, clapping a hand on his shoulder and winking at the other guys. "We won't say a word."

"Yeah, right. I bet a good laugh at my expense will be the first thing you do."

"We won't be laughing at you; we'll be laughing with you, as soon as you come out of your embarrasment and see the funny side."

"Might be awhile," Justin said with a grin.

They turned to walk back to the hangar door, but a familiar whistle froze them in their tracks. Instinct screamed at them to run in the opposite direction, but they needed to fight it. Ahead was possible death, behind was certain death if they just ran blindly into the landmines.

Get them safe, we can make it before it hits, DJ thought; judging quickly that the attack was coming from a similar position as the night before.

"On me," he yelled, praying that all of them would follow the order as he broke into a full sprint up the side and along the front of the hangar, the whistling growing louder in his ears.

Reaching the door, he yanked it open, shoving each man inside, first George, then Justin. *Shit, where was JDub?*

"Incoming, take cover," he shouted, slamming the door shut and racing back round the side of the hangar. JDub was still where he'd last seen him, only now he was crouched down, his arms wrapped around his head.

DJ ran, and then skidded to a halt beside him, hunkering down.

"I've got you buddy, we're going to be fine," he had time to say before the rocket hit, the blast trembling the ground beneath their feet and knocking the wind from them. There was no sound of screeching metal, no sound of collapse. The rocket had hit empty ground. This time.

"We move, now," DJ yelled, grabbing JDub and practically hauling the two hundred and ten-pound man to his feet. "Come on soldier, before they fire again."

DJ didn't let go, dragging JDub along, his feet stumbling over each other on the way. Finally, JDub's body kicked into autopilot, and they picked up pace. Their path was illuminated by the bright orange tail of light streaking across the sky, and they could hear the second frantic whistle growing ever closer.

They practically flung themselves into the hangar door, both of them tumbling onto the ground, DJ stretching out a leg to kick it shut, JDub scrambling on his knees to find any cover he could. DJ still had his foot on the door when the rocket hit.

Indirect, but somewhere out front, he thought as he felt the pressure push the door in against his foot, his leg trembling as he tried to prevent it from bursting inwards under the force.

Suddenly, Joey and Craig were at his side pushing two heavy-looking crates. DJ twisted and rolled out of the way as they slid them in front of the small door, jamming them hard up against it.

"Center, now," Joey yelled.

While they had been filling crates and moving them upfront, the others had created a three crate high square in the center of the hangar, leaving a small opening. They piled in, pulling the crates into place behind them to seal the gap.

They huddled there as two more rockets fell, the hangar reverberating to a deafening level, but standing true during the messy and inaccurate attempt at an attack.

"They're having too much luck tonight with that old Russian junk for my liking," Craig said, finding his voice through the fear.

"Four for four, next one's bound to be a dud," Joey said.

Remarkably, he was right. They heard the impotent popping far and high above them. The next was also a dud, and the night went quiet.

"That was too damn close for comfort," Joey breathed.

"Yeah, just as well I'd taken a dump, or I might have crapped my pants."

"It was you and that dump that had us stuck out here in the first place."

"Hey man, blame the snakes, not me."

"Snakes?"

"We didn't get a chance to tell you. Justin was held at fang-point by two fierce, terrifying rat snakes out there," DJ informed Joey.

"Rat snakes, huh? I think we'd better see if we can get top to get his hands on some educational material about the wildlife here."

"Justin *is* the wildlife out here."

"Hey, watch it! I have feelings too, you know," Justin laughed.

"Let's get the hell out of here, just in case they decide to start again."

The group prepared themselves mentally and physically for the journey back to their hangar, pushing their way out of their makeshift bunker and shifting the crates from the doorway.

Joey paused before opening it. "We move fast but we travel with stealth, No lights, no noise, and we'll keep to whatever shadows we can find. I'll take point, and DJ will bring up the rear. Stay between us, no matter what, and if we give you an order, you don't hesitate to follow it. Everyone got it?"

He made out the nods of agreement by flashlight before he turned it off and tucked it away, easing the door open. He peered out, the acrid scent of the explosives filling his nostrils. He didn't really want to lead the men out there, but they couldn't stay here all night. The enemy position seemed to favor the most outlying areas of the base. They would not only be safer back at the main camp, but they also needed to report info to the Sergeant. Joey wasn't looking forward to that, but knew he had bigger problems to worry about right now. It would only be an issue if they actually made it back alive. Hearing and seeing no movement, he gave the team the hand signal to follow and moved out.

In single file, they moved fluidly across the barren expanse, feeling naked and exposed until they reached the shadows created by the moonlight from the next hangar. Joey halted them with a closed fist held up above his shoulder, taking a moment to scan the area again, checking for movement, but also looking to see if he could identify any damage done by the rockets. A full status report on the hits might go some way to redeeming themselves with Sergeant Heard. There was enough light for Joey to determine that none of the buildings had taken direct fire, unlike the night before. He'd already seen the crater left behind by the second strike some ways in front of the hangar they'd vacated, and the lack of a visual of any others told him that the rockets had fallen well short of their intended targets. That information was only mildly reassuring. There was nothing to say that the enemy hadn't altered their position and were preparing to resume fire right this minute. With that in mind, he gave the silent forward command and headed out, trusting his men to follow, trusting DJ to watch their backs while he scanned ahead for threats.

They had further to go this time before they reached cover, the next hangar being nothing but a pile of twisted metal. The night gave the base a different feel. Devoid of the movement and chatter of over three hundred men, it felt fraught with dangers unknown. The hangars cast ominous shadows, dark places where anything could lie in wait. The dirty, dusty brown of the ground could easily conceal creatures far more harmful than the rat snakes encountered earlier. Even the mountains surrounding the base felt sinister, only discernable by their impenetrable blackness against the midnight blue skyline. On a cloudy night, their existence would be completely concealed to the naked eye.

Onwards they moved, making it to the first hangar they'd cleared that day. Joey paused again, taking note of the ground damage off to his right. Once again, it was well short of any important targets, but it concerned him more as it was closer to the occupied part of the base. With that haven now clearly in his sights, he had to fight the natural urge to make a dash for it, forgetting stealth, and running full pelt to perceived safety. It was an instinct that few soldiers could be trained out of, only trained to push aside and ignore. He moved forward at the same pace as before, as quickly as he dared while maintaining composure and giving himself time to spot danger ahead.

When they reached hangar #1 without incident, they all let out breaths they hadn't even been aware of holding, some knees beginning to tremble now that the immediate danger had passed. Their relief was short-lived when they spotted Sergeant Heard waiting for them outside the door.

"Where the hell have you been? Status report, now!"

Despite his tone, the men could read the concern on his face. Joey stepped forward. "All present and accounted for. We were pinned down by enemy fire and holed up in the hangar we'd been working in. Ground damage only, but of the four that hit, I only got a visual on two areas, one in front of Hangar #7, and one in front and to the right of hangar #4. Presumably, the other strikes were too far out for me to see in the available light."

Relief flickered across Sergeant Heard's face, but he couldn't let the matter drop that easily. "You broke protocol by even being out there in the twilight, never mind after dark when the enemy started firing at us. It was stupid and irresponsible."

Justin stepped forward. "It was my fault, I had …"

"We don't play the blame game here. You were out as a team, you work as a team, and you make decisions as a team. Pointing fingers when you all get blown to pieces doesn't help. You had two senior members of staff with you who should have provided a better example and more responsible leadership. If I were going to place blame, I'd be looking in their direction. As it is, they showed some initiative and got you all back in one piece under difficult circumstances. We'll let it go for now, but if I ever find you breaking curfew again, there will be serious consequences."

"We don't intend to, trust me," Joey said, the thought of those young lives in his hands still too fresh in his memory to give in to utter relief just yet.

"Good, now get some rest. Tomorrow, I need you to ensure that the closest and most stable three hangars are completely cleared and fit for use."

The group didn't say a word as Sergeant Heard left, they filed in the door in silence, ignoring the sea of faces that all turned their way as they entered. It wasn't surprising that they found the cots rearranged. Their sleeping arrangements hadn't been officially allocated and were probably temporary. It made sense that as squadrons had been assigned and men had worked together all day, friendships had formed, and the hangar had been altered to reflect those alliances. DJ noted the eight empty cots now placed nearer the door, arranged around Joey's original sleeping place, and about forty bunks down from where he'd been the night before. He found he liked the idea; the team was a good one.

As they all moved to the empty bunks and began removing their battle rattle without complaint, the room seemed to heave a sigh of relief and chatter started up, creating a white noise around the exhausted men. Gladly, they fell into bed, although sleep was a long time coming for all of them, those orange trails of fire and light burned across the retina of those who'd dared to look at them.

DJ was the one it hit hardest, and he tossed and turned, trying to calm or ignore his racing thoughts, but sleep eluded him, and before he knew it, men were stirring around him, preparing for the start of a new day.

Chapter Five: A Welcomed Sight

"Listen up everyone; I've got good news for you."

Sergeant Heard stood outside with his squadron gathered around him, pleased to have something positive to relay to them today. "A lot of equipment is going to be convoyed in from Kuwait, arriving in stages throughout the day. We should be receiving at least some Humvees and the portable maintenance shops and tools. Your LMTV troop trucks should also be coming in with the shipment today, as well as the rest of your personal bags."

The squad gave a massive cheer, thrilled to be receiving the rest of their personal items that couldn't be carried with their standard kit when they traveled.

"Yes!" George said, fist pumping the air. "I'll get my guitar. Did you bring yours Joey? We could jam."

"I'm more excited about a change of clothes right now, but yeah, it'll be there, and I'll look forward to seeing what you can do."

The Sergeant interrupted their conversation. "You eight already have your marching orders, so get to it. We haven't had confirmation of exact times of arrival yet, so get to work ASAP and make sure those hangars are ready before the convoys start to appear."

"You got it!"

The men departed, setting off at an enthused steady jog, anxious to get to work and ensure they were ready for the deliveries.

"So will our stuff have taken the same secret and diverse route to get here as we did?" Justin asked as they crossed the base.

"No," Joey said. "It would have been driven by our own guys from 25th ID out of Hawaii to wherever the cargo ship was loading up. Once our guys received word that the ship was fully loaded with all the equipment, the men would have been flown to Kuwait to await its arrival. From there, it'll get loaded back onto trucks and driven out by them to our current base."

"Cool, so more of our unit will be showing up?"

"Yep."

"That's great, but I don't know where they're going to sleep. I barely fit on my cot as it is so I'm not sharing!"

"It'll be a bad day for the US military, the day we have to think about sharing cots."

"I'd rather sleep on the floor."

"Really? Even with all those nests of snakes slithering all around you?"

Justin shivered as the men laughed. "Yeah, maybe not then. I'll just have to look for a short, skinny guy that doesn't take up too much room to share with."

"Fun time over guys, we're here, so it's time to get to work. All three hangars we inspected yesterday seemed sound and watertight, so I reckon all three will be good to use. We'd better get everything we stacked up in them out of there and ensure they're ready to receive. I did think we'd have more time to work on that, but we can't complain that equipment is arriving much earlier than expected. However, it gives us a very tight deadline, so put your backs into it, boys."

Enthused by the arrival of equipment and the sheer joy of having made it through another night, they made quick work of clearing everything out of three strong, secure hangars, freeing the loading doors and opening them fully to air them out. They were sweeping them out with a couple of old brooms they'd found when they saw the first of the huge trucks and flatbeds arrive.

"The first convoy made it safe and sound," DJ said with a grin.

Even though there was no chance of the men from their unit seeing or hearing them, they applauded and whooped anyway, eager to express their appreciation. The drive would have been a dangerous one, with every chance of the enemy intercepting the convoy in an attempt to prevent the base receiving the means of fighting back against their strikes, or planning their own strikes against them.

Knowing they still had work to do, they turned to moving all the items they'd carried outside to a further outlying, less intact hangar.

They'd each made two trips and were about to make a third when they heard approaching engines.

They all turned, wiping the sweat from their brows and shielding their eyes from the sun to watch as two large LMTV trucks kicked up violent dust trails on their way out to them. They waited until the trucks had come to a halt and men in battle rattle spilled from them.

"Good to see you guys, good job on making it."

"Thanks, it was hairy in places, but we didn't lose any trucks on the way this time."

Hearty greetings and introductions were made all round, then the driver of the first truck looked around, assessing the situation.

"This place is bigger than I expected. Are you the Armament dogs?" he asked, using slang for the official title of the Avionics, Electronics, and Armament Systems Repairers in charge of the Kiowa Warrior Helicopters.

In layman's terms, it meant that anything that had an avionic component, a spark to it, or a weapons system, it was their job to maintain it or repair it.

"That's us," Joey said, standing a little taller.

Each soldier had a role to play, and whatever area they were trained in, they were usually good at it, and therefore proud of their accomplishments.

The driver nodded. "We've got everything you packed in Hawaii to set up a line maintenance shop back here. The flatbed will be over any minute with the forklift. Is this the hangar that's been chosen?"

"Actually, we were going to leave this first one for the Motor Pool, since it's closest, and use the next two for Avionics and Back Shop, etc. respectively. All three are sturdy and sound."

"Okay, I'll move the truck along to the next, and we'll start getting her unloaded with what we can while we wait for the forklift. Maybe in between runs, we can help you out by loading this junk and shifting it out of your way."

"That'd be great. We're using that hangar way out there, and it's a long trek to dump it in this heat."

"I can imagine. The truck was reading one thirty-seven just now. Jump in if you can find a space and we'll give you a lift along."

The team spent the rest of the day setting up the equipment as the trucks brought it over and the forklifts lifted it out, including the portable, collapsible and fold out working shop that came complete with electrical outlet sockets. In addition to those were workbenches, cabinets, stools, extensive toolkits and air conditioners. Sergeant Heard had joined them; helping out and making sure everything was placed to his satisfaction.

Everyone pitched in, setting up equipment in both designated hangars, other teams joining them to complete the work quickly. The last items to arrive were the 10 kW, 20 kW, and 30 kW generators, and the spares were parked in rows by the motor pool, arranged by type, out front, and opposite the flight line.

One of the trailer mounted wheeled 10 kW generators with the built in diesel tank was assigned to the team, and Sergeant Heard oversaw its installation, ensuring the power cable reached from it to the shop.

By the time the job was done, the sun was a low, orange ball, just starting to dip behind the mountains. They quickly counted and checked over the equipment before submitting their report to Sergeant Heard, who would pass it up the chain later.

With so many hands appearing to help, the team was impressed with the progress they'd all made in two days. DJ took a moment to take it all in, feeling that the place was actually starting to look like an army base. As well as their own area, the base now had a sheet metal shop where welding work could be done, and a line maintenance shop for line crew work, where heavy mechanics, engine work, transmission work, and repairs to rotor blades could be carried out. Also, there was what DJ referred to as the Window Washers' area, better known as the Crew Chiefs' shop. This was where the day-to-day upkeep of the aircraft would take place, including communicating with the pilots and readying the aircraft for flight. This job, of course, included washing the windows, a source of great amusement to the other teams.

All day, Kiowa Warrior helicopters had been landing in teams of two at the airfield. DJ had kept count, and totaled twenty-two before the steady stream had tailed off. Apart from the ones still in use, Humvees and LMTV trucks had also been making their way out to the hangars, all taking their proper place in rows in the Motor Pool. The organization felt good, reassuring somehow, and DJ knew that everyone would sleep better that night just knowing that everything was there at their disposal should they need it.

"All right men, I'm calling it for the day. Park up that last LMTV and I'll radio back for the ones that are still out to transport us back. I'm not risking what happened last night. I want everyone under cover before dark."

DJ winced, taking the comment personally. He couldn't shake the feeling of letting his team down last night, and blaming himself for the danger they'd been in. Joey, noticed his reaction and sidled up to him.

"You okay?"

"Yeah, I'm okay, just dwelling a little on last night."

"You shouldn't. We'd have been back before dark if we'd left when you called it."

DJ lowered his voice. "I get that part, but I still feel it might have been my fault that the first two hit so close to us."

"What are you talking about, how could it have been your fault?"

"When Justin was freaking out about the snakes, I turned on my flashlight outside to see if I could identify the threat. I know we're teasing him, but if you aren't used to snakes of any sort, I understand why he reacted the way he did. There are plenty of different kinds of a snake with deadly venom out here. Of course, I cupped it and kept it pointed directly at the ground, but I can't help thinking that the light was spotted. They fired almost immediately afterward."

Joey gripped DJ's arm tightly. "Listen to me; they'd have fired those damn rockets whether they'd seen the light or not. They were waiting for nightfall; that's all. You saw how wild all four hits were. It was just pure dumb luck that they got even remotely close to us with the first two. Even if they *had* seen us, they can't aim for shit. You had to assess the situation. You did the right thing, and it worked out for the best. We all got back. What would you prefer? That Justin or JDub got bitten by a deadly snake in the dark?"

"Of course not, that's exactly what I was trying to avoid, but I didn't bank on bringing enemy rockets down on our heads."

"You didn't, so quit thinking it right now, you hear?"

DJ sighed. "I'll try."

"Hey!" Sergeant Heard yelled. "What are you two girls gossiping about over there? Get in the truck before we leave you behind to sleep under the stars tonight."

"You good?" Joey asked DJ, his eyes piercing.

"Yeah, I'm good."

"Great, now let's go and see what's been going on back at camp. With a bit of luck, they'll have some decent latrines up and running, and I won't have to look at your bare ass while I battle you to take a dump."

DJ couldn't help but laugh at Joey, thinking the guy had a knack for knowing the right thing to say at just the right time. They climbed into the vehicle, DJ's spirits lifted and now able to look forward to receiving his personal items.

"Maybe they'll even have the showers up and running, and I can have a proper wash before putting on clean clothes," he said as he settled into place in the rear with his teammates.

"Dream on DJ; we're in a different country, not on a different planet."

"I suppose it is too much to hope for. Man, after all, the blood, sweat, and tears today, that hangar is going to stink tonight!"

"It won't affect you; you won't be able to smell anything except your own ripe pits."

"Better than the stench from your butt when you've eaten the chili and macaroni for dinner."

"It's my favorite!"

"Well, it sure ain't mine, not when you've had it anyway."

Joey smiled at the various voices joining in the good-natured banter. The teenagers on their first tour were beginning to find their feet out here. They weren't relaxing, as you could never really relax in this situation, but they were making progress into learning what it really was to be a soldier in the US Army. Add that to the progress they'd made with the base, and the fact that they'd made it to day two with no casualties, Joey thought things were going better than could be expected. Even the Sergeant's next words couldn't dampen his spirits any.

"I hope you're all still as cheerful in the morning because you've got a change of pace for the next week. Report to me at 0400 hours."

Chapter Six: Checkpoint oo

Groggily, in the early hours of the morning, the guys fought with the freezing temperatures of the desert night, reluctant to leave the pitiful warmth provided by their army issue blankets. After only a handful of hours of sleep, they struggled out of bed and began the difficult morning routine of shaving without mirrors and brushing their teeth without the assistance of a basin or running water. Their hygiene routine consisted of nothing more than being able to scrub themselves all over with moist wipes and bottled water, the soothing lotion turning icy cold as it dried on their skin. It was inadequate at best, but was the best they could do.

After the pathetic excuse for a wash, they had to turn to their clothing, checking it thoroughly for any creepy crawlies that may have made it their home for the night. With venomous snakes, spiders and scorpions in the area, diving quickly into their gear wasn't an option. Once partially dressed, they had to address their combat boots. Some were still sleeping with them on, but those that had removed them had to turn them upside down and pound them thoroughly against the sides of the cots, checking for nasty creatures that might lie in wait inside. Once clear, they had to turn to ensuring that they looked clean and presentable. No matter where the soldiers were, or what they had to endure, their uniforms always had to pass inspection, being intact and as neat and clean as possible under any circumstances.

The eight gathered and talked quietly amongst themselves as they ate breakfast, trying not to disturb others who had different shifts at different times. They'd been joined by another member of their squadron, Pvt. Steve McComas. He'd been on latrine duty the first couple of days, but had been ordered to join them in their new task. He was an old friend of DJ's, so he was welcomed into the already tight-knit group without question or hesitation. He'd been vouched for by one of them, and that was good enough for the rest of them.

After eating, they removed the quarter full bottles of water they'd stuffed in with their MRE heater, making it just warm enough to dissolve mostly the small packet of instant coffee granules supplied with their meal. Using a cutoff water bottle as a mug, they savored the coffee while cleaning their M16-A2 rifles.

Their weapon was the one part of their kit they would never overlook. Every day, they had to remove the magazines and clear the sand and grit out of the weapon. Failure to do so in this environment would lead to the weapon jamming, refusing to fire just when they needed it the most.

"This stuff gets everywhere," George said with dismay as he examined his weapon.

"Tell me about it," Craig agreed, polishing the outside of his rifle. "I'm going to have a sandpit here to play in by the end of the first week."

"Just wait until you experience your first real sand storm," DJ chuckled. "Then you'll know about it getting everywhere. You'll be finding it inside your shorts by the time it's over."

"Ugh, be like trying to make out on a beach, without the fun part."

"Justin, you're from Pennsylvania, when did you ever make out on a beach," Jimmy scoffed. "And who would be dumb enough to be the other half of that."

"I've made out on beaches plenty," Justin protested.

"Are you sure it wasn't in your sister's Little Tyke Turtle with one of her dolls?"

The men chortled, trying to keep the noise down, but Justin's next words sobered them.

"I didn't have a sister. In fact, I didn't really have much of a home life, spent most of my childhood in a boys' home."

"Aw man, I'm sorry. You know I was just messing with you, right? I didn't mean anything by it."

"I know, Jimmy, its fine," Justin shrugged. "Just one of those things I guess."

"You want to tell us about it?"

"No big deal. My Mom had an addictive personality. It started with booze, then moved on. My Dad quit on her, and me, once she moved on to harder stuff. She couldn't take care of herself, let alone a family, so I was taken into care."

"Did you stay in touch with either of them?"

"Not really. My Mom was a lost cause, my Dad I barely remember. I was only about two when he left, and Mom told me he'd gone to Poland to look up relatives. He was of Polish descent, but whether that story was true or not, I never found out. I never heard from him again."

"Man, that's rough, I'm sorry."

"Like I said, no big deal," Justin said, slamming the magazine back into his rifle. "I'm set, everyone else ready?"

"Did everyone take their Anti Malaria tablets?" Joey asked.

"Those things are like horse pills," George protested. "I can barely choke the things down."

"Yeah, can't we skip them?" JJ asked.

"You're kidding! You've seen the size of the mosquitoes here. I don't care where you've come from; you can't tell me you've encountered monstrosities like those before," DJ said. "Get those pills down you and quit whining, they could save your life. Besides, they're not half as bad as the anthrax vaccinations, isn't that so, Joey?"

"Heck yeah. We began a course of them before my first tour in Iraq. It hurt like hell, had to go right into the triceps muscle. It felt like someone had punched you there, and felt like it was on fire. Three shots in, they were pulled as unsafe; apparently some marines had died after having an allergic reaction. Then before my second tour, I found out they'd been reinstated. The kicker was that we had to start over, as we hadn't received enough to make a difference the first time."

"I hate needles," JDub said with a shiver before throwing the huge pill into his mouth and downing half a bottle of water to wash it down.

"And what about that smallpox crap?" DJ exclaimed. "Stabbed in the arm fifteen times with a miniature pitchfork to inject you with a half-dead version of cowpox, the closest thing to smallpox that wouldn't kill us outright. I swear I had an open wound for a month or more!"

"Yeah, and nobody was allowed to touch it because they'd contract cowpox."

"Come on guys, knock it off, you're going to make me lose my breakfast," JDub said.

"Okay, time to go anyway. You know how it is, if you're not ten minutes early then you're already late."

The group stood, checking each other over, ensuring their uniforms were straight. Billy grinned sheepishly at DJ as he ripped off his Velcro insignia from his chest and turned it the right way round before reattaching it.

"Sorry, was still half asleep."

"That's why we always check our battle buddies. Everyone straight?"

The team nodded and followed DJ out the door, assembling outside to await their marching orders from Sergeant Heard. Once again, he was already waiting.

"Okay men, we've been tasked with manning the Entry Control Point for the next week. You guys are on days, the other half of my squad are on nights. Shifts are twelve hours, and yours is 0500 hours to 1700 hours. Understood?"

"Yes, Sergeant," they said.

"Okay, we'll head over to the Motor Pool and check out an LMTV. I'll give further instructions once we arrive at our destination. On me."

Proceeding on foot to the Motor Pool, the guys refrained from their usual banter, unsure if their Sergeant would appreciate their wise-ass humor. Feeling comfortable around him would come, but for now, he was too new to them, making them feel they should be on their best behavior around him. Besides, the night had been a quiet one with no enemy strikes. It made them all nervous, wondering if they were being watched from the hills by unseen eyes belonging to men that plotted and planned from their distant cover.

In spite of their concerns, they made it to the Motor Pool without incident, where they went through the procedure to sign out the troop truck. Sergeant Heard immediately took the passenger seat, leaving the spot open for a driver. The younger, first-time soldiers all scrambled into the back, nervous of performing even the simplest of tasks with their Sergeant right next to them. It was something they'd have done a million times before, but out here, things were different. Back home on base, or in training, mucking up didn't usually mean life or death. Here, it could.

DJ and Joey glanced at each other, wondering if the other had a preference. Joey indicated his head towards the rear, silently telling DJ to go, he would drive. As DJ climbed into the back, Joey climbed into the driver's seat. With his left hand, he held the rocker lever for the glow plugs, waiting until the little blue indicator reported that the truck was ready to start before pushing the large red start button.

This thing is both underserviced and over used, he thought as the old diesel engine barely managed to sputter to life. Joey had been working with his father on engines since he was old enough to pick up a wrench, and he knew this old girl needed some serious TLC to keep her running much longer. Pulling out of the Motor Pool, the engine idled roughly as he waited for someone to leap down from the back and close the doors behind them. Two hard knocks from the back indicated they were ready for him to move on.

Everyone was silent during the twenty-minute drive, those in the back keeping a wary eye on their surroundings, ever alert for movement in the gloom. As they neared the main access gate to the base, two giant metal guard shacks loomed into view, standing like sentries either side of the gate. The boys took them in for the first time, not having had the time to pay much attention since their arrival.

The towers were positioned directly across from one another at either side of the paved access road. Both were two stories high, with an enclosed room at the top with glass windows all round, giving a 360-degree viewpoint. As Joey pulled the truck to a halt and shut off the engine, the men leaped down from the back, arranging themselves to hear their orders.

"Welcome to Checkpoint 00, your home away from home for the next twelve hours," Sergeant Heard announced. "I'll give you the grand tour. As you can see, there are concrete barriers placed down the road from the gate for about a hundred yards. Can anyone tell me the importance of the pattern they're placed in?"

"To create a slalom that slows down any approaching vehicles and gives us time to assess it and the occupants," Craig responded.

"Good, anything else?"

"To provide cover for the men outside the gates on the checkpoint."

"Excellent. There are also two further barriers closer to base at the end of the slalom. These act as the final barrier before the actual gate and its where all ID's should be checked."

The men studied the barriers, seeing the large metal rings buried in each, the thick metal cable stretched between them. The idea was that the cable would remain in place until any vehicle had been cleared for entry, then at that point, would be unhooked by the man on guard and dropped to the ground, allowing the vehicle to drive safely over it and approach the actual gate.

"Now here, we have the guard shacks. Both are already equipped with two radios so you can call back to base without ever leaving your post. You'll be keeping a report of all movement you see and report immediately if anyone approaches the base. I don't have to tell you not to engage without prior permission."

Sergeant Heard glared at them all, waiting until he received confirmation of the instruction. When he was satisfied, he continued.

"Also in the shacks are two tripods mounted SAW's, set up facing the road. We hope you don't have to use them on your first day, but they're there if you do, once you've been given the green light of course."

The first time deployed soldiers glanced at each other, sharing a thought. All of them had used the fully automatic squadron weapons before, but never against a living, breathing target. They could all put their hands on their hearts and swear they'd pull the trigger to protect their men on either side of the gate, but none of them knew how they would actually feel in those fleeting moments before, during, or after the deed.

Sergeant Heard caught the glances but made no comment. How the newbies would react in their first combat situation was a constant worry. Would they panic and forget all their training, becoming a danger to their own men? Would they freeze up and be unable to perform their duty as soldiers, or would they perform that duty then crumble under the weight of their conscience afterward? Even when someone threatened the life of your closest friends, it still wasn't easy to stop that life in its tracks. The best-case scenario was that they would stay calm, utilize everything they'd learned and eliminate the threat, being proud of their actions instead of guilt-ridden. It was a lot to ask of these boys that were barely men. Pushing his concern aside, Sergeant Heard continued with his tour.

"Over here we have two tents that have been allocated for breaks and meals. One of them contains another radio, and I'll be manning that today. At the base of the left-hand tower, you can see a large, square-shaped fenced area. This gentleman is the pit. In another couple of hours, this pit will be crammed full of Iraqis all looking for some work on the base. We've put the word out that we're paying five bucks a day for various odd jobs like filling sandbags, clearing up trash, and help with building work. We've also asked for interpreters that can speak English as well as Arabic. They've been offered the princely sum of seven bucks per day, so hopefully some will turn up."

"Isn't that a bit risky, allowing them on base?"

"Yes, Pvt. Knowles, it is, but we don't have a lot of choices if we're going to get this place up and running. We don't have enough men, and we're spread too thin. We'll put as much security in place as we can with the checkpoints, and we'll allocate them in small groups of ten per soldier. That soldier will be responsible for them for the entire day, and will be guarding them at all times. The pit has its own small guard point there, also equipped with a SAW."

The men looked doubtfully at the aforementioned guard pit, which was nothing more than sandbags stacked three high. Sergeant Heard barreled on with his speech, not giving them time to comment or protest.

"Hopefully, it'll move things along as well as put a positive spin on our presence here with the ordinary people. Ever since the Persian Gulf War, there's no welfare, no social services, no subsidized education, and quite often, the food they survive on is rations from the Red Cross. The work we can give them could help them out a lot."

"Or give them the funds to buy black market weapons," Justin muttered.

"There's that too," Sergeant Heard agreed, catching the comment. "But it's a chance we have to take. We don't know how many will turn up, but prepare for it to get a little hectic. Okay, so now you've got the lay of the land, I'll assign your posts for the day."

The Sergeant consulted a clipboard that he'd been carrying around under his arm. "Pvt. Billy Knowles and Pvt. George Ates, guard tower one, that one on the left. Pvt. James Wayne and Pvt. Jacob Johnson, guard tower two. Move out."

The others watched Billy and Craig head in one direction while JJ and JDub headed in the other, all disappearing inside the towers.

"Pvt. Craig Hardwell and Pvt. Justin Gibson, you guys are the pit security, supporting your guys in there. Keep them safe. Move out."

The two left as ordered, Craig giving DJ a worried backward glance as he left. DJ sent him a reassuring smile in return before turning back to the Sergeant.

"Pvt. Steven McComas, you're outside on ID and vehicle check, so that leaves you two in the pit," he said, pointing to DJ and Joey.

"Figures," DJ muttered, although knowing that the decision made sense.

As the most experienced, having them amongst the natives was the wisest choice, knowing they could possibly spot a potential threat faster than the others might.

"This sucks more than latrine duty," DJ murmured as they walked together to their position.

"I saved you from that two days in a row, I can't save you from every shitty job out here," Joey grinned.

"Yeah, thanks for that. I guess every job out here is a shitty job, so we can't complain."

"We can complain amongst ourselves if it makes us feel better, but other than that, it won't do us any good."

The two men stood inside the pit, watching the access road anxiously.

"When do you think they'll start turning up?"

"A little after daybreak I guess, they have prayers between dawn and sunrise."

"How many do you think will come?"

"Probably not many to start with," DJ said. "And those that do will probably be plants – sent to gather Intel about the base to take back to the bad guys."

"So they'll try to limit the number to ensure their guys get picked?"

"I don't know for sure, but it's what I would do."

Joey nodded, liking DJ's strategy of placing himself in the shoes of the enemy. It was something he'd been taught by his Cherokee relatives when learning to hunt; to always look at things from the perspective of the prey as well as your own. "Yeah, guess I would do that, too."

As it turned out, they were wrong.

By the time the sun was fully up in the sky, the pit had become a teeming mass of vocal Haji's, all shouting and screaming at the translators that had been weeded out by Steve and passed through to the soldiers waiting to pick up their charges for the day.

"There must be at least three to four hundred of them," the dismayed DJ yelled to Joey as they tried to control the rabble inside the fenced area.

Joey nodded back, not even being heard over the voices as he screamed at them to calm down and be patient. The people were akin to obsessed fans at a concert – crowding to the front, pressing against the fence, the mass threatening to crush those in front with the sheer weight and volume of those behind.

From the safety of the security sandbags, Craig shook his head. "This is madness! I can't even see DJ and Joey, never mind spot any threat to them."

"I know man. I wish they'd hurry up and pick so they can send the rest packing. Groups of ten will be easier to watch over."

"Maybe, but it'll be groups spread right across the base. I think I like them better all contained down here."

"I see where you're coming from, but I just want the craziness to end. Thank God, they're starting to pick."

As the soldiers spoke to the translators, and in turn, the translators relayed words back and forth between the Iraqis and the soldiers, the selection process began. When one was pointed out, it was up to DJ or Joey to push and barrel their way through the crowd toward the person selected, giving them a final check for weapons, cell phones, cameras, or impromptu explosive devices before leading them to the gate and passing them through to their guard. The theory sounded simple, but it was a nightmare to execute.

When the whole process was complete, and the pit had been cleared of the remaining angry people unchosen for the day's work, DJ felt drained. He'd lost track of passing time, but felt as if he'd completed his twelve-hour shift already.

"You two, over here."

On shaky legs, DJ made his way over to the tent where the Sergeant waited, Joey walking quietly by his side.

"That was rough, I know, but you'll get used to it. Take a short break."

"Yes Sergeant," DJ said, the relief evident in his voice.

Grabbing bottles of water that had remained semi-cool in the shade of the tent for the moment, the two sat down at a flimsy, folding table, glad to be out of the dry air and dust.

"I'm not sure I'll ever get used to that," DJ said.

"You okay?"

"I'm fine; it just took me by surprise, that's all. It was a bit overwhelming."

"Did it remind you of anything, take you back someplace?"

DJ looked closely at Joey, seeing the concern on his face, but also something more, a steely glint behind the worry in his eyes, a question much darker than the one he'd vocalized.

"If you're asking if I had a flashback, then the answer is no. Sure, things are the same here as in Afghanistan. Sometimes, you don't know who the damn enemy is, whom we're supposed to be fighting.

You can be talking to some young kid one day; then he's standing on a street corner aiming a rifle at you the next. There's no clear parameters, no specific combat zone, no army clearly marked by a uniform. We're supposed to defeat the enemy and protect the civilians, but how the hell can you do that when you can't tell which is which? How can you do your job if, by the time you find out the answer, it's too damn late! The pit just emphasized that. Any one of them could be going back to the terrorists with detailed information of our base and equipment, any one of them could have had a bomb strapped to their ribcage, not caring how many of their own people they took out as long as they got a couple of us. Then again, they might just be farmers with poor crops and six kids to feed. It was madness, and sure, it shook me a little, but I'm not reliving any traumatic experiences from previous deployments, I didn't have a panic attack, and I'm not going to fall apart on you and the team."

"Okay, okay," Joey laughed. "Calm down, I just wanted to make sure you were good, that's all. I never thought for a minute you were falling apart on us. You did a good job in there; we did what we had to do. I agree with you, and the lines are even more blurred than you said. Half the people in their so-called army are there because their wife, son, or daughter is tied up in some rat infested, derelict building, with the terrorists threatening to slit their throats if they don't raise arms against us. What does that make them, enemy, or victim? Believe me; I know where you're coming from."

"I'm glad you do because people back home sometimes don't understand. I've tried to explain it to Clara, but although she hears the words, she can't come to grips with how it feels."

"Clara, that your wife?"

A smile lit up DJ's face. "Yeah. I can't believe how lucky I am to have her. How many guys actually get to marry their high school sweetheart?"

"Not many," Joey agreed. "Those relationships usually die a death."

"Not ours, not ever. I fell in love with her the first day I saw her, and that just keeps getting stronger. Knowing she's waiting for me is the one thing that makes me so damn determined to make it home each time."

"Sounds like she's something special."

"She's more than special, but I don't even have the words to say how much she means to me. She's my everything."

"I'm happy for you, and I get it. I've got a wife waiting back home too, just makes it all the harder to leave doesn't it?"

DJ's face lost its excited animation of earlier. "Clara hates it when I go, always asks me if I have to, and if I can't just stay. Breaks my heart every time, but being in the army is in my blood, it's all I know. I just wish I could let her see what it's really like in places like this. She always says that I'm different when I first come back, and she doesn't like it."

"Places like this can't help but change you," Joey agreed. "At first, when you've been in a place where every man, woman, or child could be your killer, you walk down the street with a different perspective, you can't help it. The trick is to let it fade away once you're home. As long as you can do that, you're fine."

"There are some things you can never switch off, though, right? You ever find yourself in a restaurant, and the first thing you do is check every entrance and exit, make sure you know the fastest route out?"

Joey chuckled. "Sure, some things are drummed into us so hard in training that they become more than second nature. That's just one of them. Heck, I'll probably still be checking for escape routes when I'm a hundred years old and on my deathbed."

"I wish I could get Clara to accept that; she gets upset when she catches me doing it. I know it's out of concern, that she just wants me relaxed and feeling safe and secure when I'm back home, but just because I check doesn't mean I anticipate a threat, it's just a habit. I wanted to document this trip more, took my camera so I could take pictures. I figured maybe if she had visuals to go along with my stories, she'd have a deeper understanding. Not that she isn't supportive, of course, but you know how it is, if you haven't been through it, you can never really know."

"How's that going, the pictures I mean?"

"Not too good. I haven't had a chance since the airport in Alaska," DJ laughed. "It has to be secondary to everything else, it's only important to me."

"Maybe we can get the other guys involved and help. You should carry your camera with you, and if one of us has an assignment that would make it possible, you can hand it over."

"That'd be great, thanks," DJ grinned.

"Anytime," Joey replied, tilting his bottle of water at DJ.

"Break over, gentleman. Go and relieve the privates in guard tower one. I've had confirmation of a small convoy coming in within the next few hours. I'll be able to firm up ETA later, but I want your eyes on it. Do your best to determine if it's been compromised in any way on approach."

"Yes sergeant," they responded, rising to their feet.

After the short break inside the tent, the heat hit them in an oppressive, arid blast as they stepped back outside. Their eighty-five pounds of gear weighed heavily on them as they made their way across to the tower. A momentary relief of cooler air greeted them inside, but it soon faded as they made their way to the glass room up top, the windows serving only to magnify and trap the vicious heat of the blazing sun.

"You didn't ask us to identify ourselves," DJ said to Billy and George as they finished the climb.

"Didn't need to, saw you coming," George replied, removing the binoculars from his eyes and turning towards them. "What's up?"

"I think you're getting a break. Our orders were to relieve you, but I think we're taking over from here on. Has anything been going on?"

George shook his head. "Apart from the cattle market this morning, it's been quiet. Even with these, though," he said, indicating the high-powered visual aid. "The outlying mountains are tough. I've been going cross-eyed trying to get a handle on what I'm seeing. The good thing is that it's too far away for a strike, and if they moved closer, I'd be able to spot them, so I think I've got it covered."

"Good job. Go and uncross those eyes, we've got it from here."

While they'd been talking, Joey and DJ had been taking in every small detail about their new surroundings, noting and memorizing everything they needed to know. The glass room at the top of the tower was a contradiction. The extra height gave a sense of security, as did the panoramic view, yet at the same time, it was akin to being in a goldfish bowl, open, exposed, the occupants in clear sight, and the height making it an easy visual target from both land and air.

Joey walked over to Billy, tapping him on the shoulder. "You can let go now; I've got it."

Billy was kneeling on one knee behind the fully automatic machine gun; the foot-long tripod fully extended and propped up on sandbags to give him the extra height he needed. The knuckles of his hand were white as he gripped the handle, his trigger finger in place at the ready. He was trance-like, his eyes flicking around then darting back to look through the sights, constantly searching for a threat to his base. He ignored Joey.

"Come on Billy, you're on guard duty, not sniper duty, and it's a long shift. You can't keep up that level of intensity for twelve hours, not unless you've been trained for it."

Billy glanced at Joey, but quickly turned his head back to the windows, as if unable to stop watching for even a second.

"Billy, snap out of it!" Joey said with a click of his fingers beside Billy's ear.

"Huh? What?"

Billy seemed to come back to life, his intent concentration broken. He eased his finger off the trigger and removed his hand from the grip, wincing as he stretched out the fingers, the muscles and tendons in his hand, wrist, and forearm throbbing. He'd had no idea he was so tense, no idea of how tight a grip he'd had on the gun.

"Welcome back to earth my friend. What was that about?" Joey asked as Billy rose to his feet.

"What was what about? I'm just stiff from manning the gun; that's all."

"You were away in a world, man, one where you were under attack from every direction."

Billy opened his mouth to protest then closed it again. This was no place for bullshit, bravado, or tall tales. This was a place for truth, a place for openness and honesty, and if he couldn't share that with his battle buddies, he couldn't share with anyone.

"You're right. When they all started arriving this morning, I panicked a little, got behind that spray and pray and couldn't leave it. They were like a swarm of angry yellow jackets and the responsibility hit me hard, like I was the only thing standing between them and my guys."

DJ stepped towards him and placed a hand on his shoulder. "We get it, we were discussing something similar earlier too, but you've got to remember you're never alone out here. We're all here with you, and we all share the responsibility. You've got Steve out there, the other guys in tower two, the guys in pit security, and your battle by your side."

"I didn't do too good a job there," George said. "I should have realized something was going on with him, but I've been too busy watching out there."

"Nothing went wrong," Joey said. "So no harm, but I hope it's been a learning curve. No matter what, you keep an eye on your battle. He's the guy that's going to rush into a burning building to get you, or run through a hail of bullets to drag your ass to cover. We're all here to protect the guy standing next to us and pray to God that he'll do the same for you. I want it like a mantra in your head at all times, check your battle."

"You got it," George said. "I won't be the one that lets anyone down ever again."

Joey knew he meant it, and that from this moment on, he'd be one of the best to have with you in combat. The lesson had penetrated deeply, the message hitting hard.

"Take a break if Sergeant lets you. It'll never be this bad again now we know what to expect," DJ said, sending them on their way with a few pats on the back.

"What do you think?" he asked Joey once they were alone.

"He'll be fine. You said yourself the chaos was a little overwhelming, but we'll be prepared for it in the future, all of us."

"I agree. We've got a good squad here. With just a little bit of guidance, they're going to make fine soldiers."

He wandered over to the window and snatched a look over the base with the binoculars. "Looks like they've put everyone to work, lots of activity out there." Returning to front, he scanned the distant road and mountains. "All quiet, not so much as a goat roaming about. Now we just watch and wait."

Waiting was hell.

DJ wasn't a great words man. He had a feeling that Joey would be better able to describe the feeling, but the most he could do was liken it to that sense of nervous expectation and agitation, that sitting at home waiting for that important call to come through, anxiously awaiting a possible delivery, waiting for guests to arrive. Only back home, the conclusion of the wait wasn't likely to be a battered old car rigged with homemade explosive devices, or three men jumping out and opening fire on you. You also had the option of finding a distraction, whereas here, you could never lose concentration, never take a step back from being on mid-level alert at all times.

The only break in the monotony was the radio check, carried out on the stroke of the hour, every hour. Four hours into their shift in the tower, it crackled to life once again, the disembodied voice a comforting and welcome relief.

"Checkpoint 00 Guard Shack One, this is Saber One Nine radio check."

Joey reached for the radio to respond. "Saber One-Nine, this is Checkpoint 00 Guard Shack One, I have you, Lima Charlie, how about me?"

"Checkpoint 00 Guard Shack One, this is Saber One Nine. I have you Lima Charlie, radio check complete. I have some additional information for you. We have an ETA of one hour on the convoy, confirm please?"

"Saber One Nine, Checkpoint 00 Guard Shack One confirms that. ETA in approximately one hour."

"Checkpoint 00 Guard Shack One, thank you for your confirmation. Saber One Nine out."

Thirty minutes later, DJ had a visual on the approaching convoy. "I see them, four vehicles, three Humvees, and an LMTV."

Joey joined him at the front window. "How's it all looking?"

DJ shook his head. "I don't know, the last Humvee isn't as tight as it should be; it's lagging a little."

Joey checked the situation for himself, agreeing with DJ's assessment. "Should I make a special report?"

"Hold on … yep, it's all good, he's tightened it up. I think he took that sharp decline a little cautiously and was just catching up."

The convoy continued to approach, and DJ foresaw no problems. It took the slalom slow and easy, allowing them an excellent visual. Everything looked in order. Still, Joey manned the SAW while DJ remained on high alert, both relaxing only once the fourth and last vehicle check appeared to be cleared by Steve down below. They watched as Steve ran to the barriers and unhooked the cable, dropping it to the ground. The main gates were opened from the inside, Steve jogging to the opposite side to wave them, through. The trucks rolled onwards.

Neither DJ nor Joey could later explain exactly how it happened, but somehow, as the fourth vehicle passed over the thick, twisted metal cable, it was caught by the wheel and flipped up into the wheel well, where it tangled firmly around the axle. DJ banged on the glass, yelling frantically. Joey rushed to the radio. The driver of the heavy vehicle, oblivious to the problem behind him, continued moving forward, intent on his job of getting through the gates as quickly as possible so they could be closed behind him.

Unable to leave their post or do anything more to get the attention of the men below, DJ and Joey could only look on in horror as the cable snapped taut, events seeming to move in slow motion as the two-thousand pound concrete barrier began to topple. Helplessly, they watched the events unfold. Steve realized too late, managed to poise his body to run, but got no further as the massive weight fell upon him, crushing one of his legs. Time reverted to normal for the watchers, then seemed to go into fast forward. Steve was arm crawling away from the barrier, not realizing that he was leaving his severed leg behind, still trapped beneath. Blood was spewing from the remaining stump, leaving a bright, sticky trail. Shouts, yells, the gates opening, then Steve surrounded by men. A truck blazoned across the base, kicking up a gigantic dust cloud in its wake. The field medics were there, Steve's screams joining the other voices as he was loaded onto a stretcher and realized what had happened.

DJ stood, staring at the pool of blood oozing out from beneath the colossal concrete stone, the base now eerily silent, the only sound the resonating whomp of the helicopter rotors overhead, hoping to save a man's life.

"I'm sorry," Joey said.

"He was my friend," was all DJ could say in return, both palms still pressed against the glass window.

Chapter Seven: Collateral Damage

After six days of twelve-hour shifts on Checkpoint 00, the guys were exhausted. They'd ended each day, hot, dirty, dehydrated, and grouchy. The relief they'd felt that this was the last day of the countless hours of watching and waiting had been palpable as they'd gone through their awkward and uncomfortable morning routine. Even the nightmarish pit had gained a small sense of appeal – the craziness and chaos passing the time better than the long, silent hours at the mercy of the sun and dust.

They were all still slightly shaken by what they'd witnessed on that first day, but they'd received word that Pvt. Steven McComas would live although his missing limb had meant instant discharge from the army. His career had been severed along with his leg, but he was recovering from his injury in a German hospital, soon to be transferred home to adapt to a new and very different life. The outcome had been better than it could have been, and they were aware of it.

As the LMTV headed out to the dreaded Entry Control Point, the guys in the back dozed, some grabbing the opportunity for the snatched moments of sleep, others simply unable to fight the deeply ingrained fatigue, no matter how hard they tried. The rocket and mortar attacks from the enemy were now a daily and nightly occurrence, making undisturbed rest almost impossible at any time.

Far sooner than they would have liked, they were jolted from their light napping by the squeal of brakes as the truck pulled to a halt at their destination. They rubbed at eyes and faces, waking themselves up as they leaped down from the truck, longing for a cool breeze or a sudden, refreshing downpour; all knowing their hopes were in vain.

"I'd kill for a shower," George muttered as they waited for Sergeant Heard and Joey to join them from the front of the truck.

"I'd kill for you to have a shower too, you stink," JDub said. "You smell worse than my kin when we'd been on a week-long hunting trip."

"You like to go hunting?" JJ asked, not having heard this snippet of information before.

"Sure. I grew up in Virginia, what else do you expect? Spent my youth fishing, hunting, drinking beer, and driving big trucks."

"Just a good ol' boy then."

"Like you can talk JJ. Aren't you just a cowboy from Texas?"

Their conversation was interrupted by Sergeant Heard, issuing their posts for the day, but they were able to continue as they found themselves together on pit guard duty.

"I'm from Texas, but I'm no cowboy. I'm from Dallas, so I'm a city boy through and through."

"So what did you do for fun before you signed up?"

"Created hell and lived by my wits," JJ replied with a grin.

"If you're such a hell raiser, what made you sign up for a life of regimented routines and taking orders?"

"I'd been living rough on the streets," JJ said, comfortable enough to share the very worst of his life with this man that he now considered a close friend. "I was surviving day to day on my wits alone. I learned some skills and figured I could put them to use for Uncle Sam's boys as well as myself, and get paid at the same time."

JDub snorted. "Don't put too much hope on those wages; it's a pittance."

"At least I've got a bed of sorts to sleep in, and clothes on my back. Those things shouldn't be taken for granted."

"True, true. So, what are these mad skills you think you can bring to the United States Army?"

"Just you wait and see," JJ said with a wink. "Heads up, here they come."

The two men settled down behind their SAWS; theireyestrained on DJ and Joey in the pit as the approaching locals began to appear on the access road.

Inside the pit, DJ and Joey prepared themselves for the usual onslaught of loud, frantic men, all competing for the day's work to earn a measly five bucks. Each morning had been worse than the first as word had spread around the surrounding area. The pit was filled earlier than ever, and hordes of people were being turned away before they even reached the barriers, the pit already crammed beyond capacity. The soldiers that were required to pick their ten-man crew for the day were trying to be fair, resisting the temptation to go only with familiar faces. The fact that they'd spent time on the base before without incident made them the obvious choice, but they wanted to ensure that everybody had the chance to earn some extra money for their families. Each morning, new voices were added to the chorus, all screaming their worthiness and their need out to the befuddled soldiers, the interpreters unable to keep up with the constant demand on their abilities.

The interpreters they were using were regulars, all Iraqi National Guard, speaking both English and Arabic, as well as often understanding a wide range of the many dialects that varied the language considerably. Since they'd been here on a daily basis since this had begun, their faces and names were beginning to be familiar to those who'd been on checkpoint duty all week, as well as the soldiers who guarded the groups once they were on base. Often, they arrived early, chatting with DJ and Joey in the pit before moving through to take their positions on the other side of the fence with the soldiers.

This morning, amid the usual and expected confusion, every soldier at Checkpoint 00 tensed as they spotted a group of latecomers running along the access road, a stretcher carried between them. Pushing their way through the shouting masses, DJ and Joey made their way to the outside edge of the pit, trying to get a better view. The stretcher might hold a wounded person, or it might hold a concealed explosive device or cache of weapons. Until they got closer, there was no way to tell.

The checkpoint guard outside the gate was shouting for them to slow down, his weapon unshouldered and pointed at the approaching group. As they continued to run, DJ and Joey joined their weapons with his, aimed at the fast approaching cluster and ready to fire if the order was given. Inside the guard towers, the watching squad members were on their radios, reporting everything that they could see as it was happening below them.

"There are women in the group, I don't think this is an attack," DJ said to Joey.

"Do not be fooled; no one is above using women and children."

DJ and Joey turned towards the heavily accented voice that had spoken beside them, recognizing the face of Aban, one of their regular interpreters.

"What do you make of it?"

"Let me go out and talk to them," Aban said, waiting for both of them to give their nod of agreement before exiting the pit.

Aban jogged over to the guard, speaking to him quietly. The guard glanced at Joey and DJ, who both gave him a signal that they'd approved Aban's request. The guard let him go, and Aban proceeded to walk forward, his palms raised in a soothing gesture.

Noting that the selection process had halted, the people in the pit had looked around in anger and confusion, their shouts and yells dying in their throats as they'd seen what was happening outside. Their instant silence didn't register with DJ and Joey at first, their focus entirely on events on the other side of the fence and gate. It was only much later, in the dead of night and alone on his cot, that DJ realized what it meant.

DJ and Joey heard Aban call out, watched as the group slowed down their approach, one man stepping forward with clasped hands to plead with him. Aban closed the gap between them, examining what lay on the stretcher. With a nod, he turned and jogged back to the gate guard, waving a hand over his shoulder for the people to follow. The gate guard halted them; checking ID's before nodding and waving them through. Aban ran ahead to talk to DJ and Joey.

"It is a family from the village of one of the interpreters. The terrorists heard he was working with the soldiers here and attacked his village as a warning to others. They drove through his village, randomly shooting at everything and everyone. Many people died, and this family's daughter has been shot in the head. They have done their best, but they are begging for medical assistance."

As protocol demanded, DJ and Joey had to examine the stretcher, the carriers, and the injured girl before allowing them to pass through.

"Jesus Christ, she can't be more than seven years old," DJ exclaimed when he finally glanced towards the ashen-faced, near lifeless girl on the stretcher.

She was a harrowing sight. The wounds were very fresh, the entry wound bad, but the exit wound where the bullet had passed straight through her skull was even worse. Her entire head had been shaved, and at the exit point, the gaping wound had been crudely stapled shut in a vain attempt to stop the bleeding, which from a head wound, was always profuse. The process must have been agonizing.

It pained them to do it, but they had no choice but to roll her over to examine every inch of her, ensuring there were no explosives concealed on her tiny body, or weapons lying beneath her. A faint mewl escaped from her lips as they did so, shattering a piece of each of their hearts.

Cleared of threats, DJ and Joey escorted the family to the other side of the pit, the people parting like a wave to let them through to the opposite gate. Once there, they waved the three men carrying the stretcher through but prevented the others in the group from following. Thanks to the radio reports, an LMTV was already on standby, troops waiting to escort the girl to their makeshift medical facility on base.

"Sorry, you have to wait for her here," DJ told the remaining members of the family, Aban translating his words.

Some gripped the fence, watching as the stretcher was loaded into the back of the truck, while one woman collapsed to her knees on the ground, sobbing, her tears forming dark splotches in the dusty earth. Joey knelt to offer her a fleeting second of comfort, while DJ watched as only one man was allowed to accompany the girl, the rest being turned back towards the pit.

"Tell them they've got to wait until we've got the pit cleared," Sergeant Heard called to Aban. "Then we'll see where we stand with things."

Aban relayed the words while DJ and Joey went back to work, trying to push their thoughts of the girl from their minds and focus on their duty. There was nothing they could do for her, or the family until they were given further instructions. As hard as it was, they had to forget about it for now. Making a mistake on pit duty could cost a lot more than one life. They were both relieved to see that Aban remained with the family of the girl, forgoing his pay for the day to assist them any way he could.

As the pit cleared, DJ and Joey breathed a sigh of relief, glad that it was over. Two soldiers arrived to escort the girl's family to the second break tent, where they were being allowed to wait for news in the shade.

"Take your break guys, give yourselves an extra five minutes, then relieve guard tower one as normal," Sergeant Heard instructed the Specialists as they locked the pit gates. "Aban, you can stick around here, we'll need you to talk to them when we know more. I'll make sure you get paid the usual rate."

The Sergeant disappeared inside the second tent, returning to his job of manning the radio and to assist with keeping an eye on the family. DJ and Joey both turned to Aban.

"Come and grab a bottle of water with us before you join the family," Joey said. "We'd like to thank you for your help."

"I did what any good person would do," Aban said as he followed them inside the first break tent. "They were scared and desperate, and fear is only intensified when it is accompanied by a foreign language and you cannot comprehend what is happening."

"They've nothing to fear from us, not if they come with no intention to do us harm," Joey said.

"Perhaps," Aban said. "But any association with you is punishable by death as far as some are concerned, and for that reason alone, you are the enemy. It took courage to come to you for assistance, that and having no other option. They may yet have consequences to pay."

"Surely nobody can blame a family for looking for medical help for their little girl. After all, they were the ones who shot her in the first place!" DJ said. "What did they expect them to do?"

"Yes, they shot her, and they didn't care that they had, as long as their message was heard and understood. They expected them to do nothing except learning the lesson not to collaborate with the Americans. They have no problem maiming or murdering their ownpeople; nothing is taboo as long as it furthers their cause."

Aban rose from his chair and raised his shirt, showing several bullet wounds almost hidden by extensive burn scarring. "I speak from experience, having been tortured myself for my association with the American army."

DJ's eyes went wide. "You got all that just for helping us? Why do you keep doing it?"

"Because it is my duty. Alone, I am just one man, helpless to prevent the atrocities, the abductions, the senseless killing, and the torture. At least here, I am a tiny part of something bigger, something that offers us the only hope we have, although many don't see it that way. I'll leave you now, and offer the family what comfort I can."

DJ and Joey were left alone to contemplate the depth of everything Aban had said, and everything he hadn't.

"What kind of enemy are we up against here," DJ asked in despair. "When they'll happily wipe out a whole village just to stop one man from associating with us?"

"I don't know, man, but it makes it almost impossible for any of them– whether good or bad– to welcome our presence here. Soon, they'll all hate us and think we're doing more harm than good."

"I've seen some god-awful things in my time, and lots of casualties of war, but shit, that little girl."

DJ shook his head, struggling to find the words. "She's completely innocent, had done nothing to deserve that. She was probably out playing or walking home from running an errand. Holy crap, she's about the same age as my little sister, Candice. She turned ten this year. I can't imagine her out on the street, not a care in the world, then some bastard pointing a gun at her," DJ's voice choked, and he dropped his head.

Joey gripped DJ's wrist. "I know; I get it. I've got a little sister too, Alicia, she's eight."

"When I think about what must have gone through her head, that split second of confusion, panic, then absolute terror. God, I can't even begin to imagine what that family is going through right now," DJ said, wiping furiously at his eyes, ashamed of his level of emotion.

"We can, and that's why we're taking it so hard, but it's also letting us know that we're still decent human beings. The pain, the heartache, the sorrow, the grief, it's terrible, but I'd rather that than

94

having war numb me to it all. Battle-hardened is one thing, but the day I can look at that and not be affected by it is the day I walk away. Don't ever let me get that callous, promise me."

DJ raised his head, his red-rimmed eyes staring straight into Joey's. "I promise. No matter what, we will always care; we will always do our best. No matter how much they hate us or don't understand our purpose here, we fight the enemy, and protect the civilians."

"I'll drink to that," Joey said, raising his water bottle. "Fight the enemy, protect the civilians."

They bumped their water bottles together before taking a long, deep drink, both wishing they could do so much more. DJ knew that he'd be on edge all day, waiting for word on the nameless girl, knowing that her skinny frame and ugly wounds were burned into his memory forever. Still, they had a job to do, and it was time to get on with it.

They relieved Billy and George from the tower, taking up their positions as they'd done the day before, and the day before that. DJ looked down on the access road, imagining the earlier scene from this vantage point, seeing again the family running towards the base, the stretcher between them. Anything or anyone approaching the base at speed was a worrying, if not frightening, sight, particularly when they refused to slow down when asked. He'd been surprised that Billy and George hadn't mentioned it when they'd crossed over, but they hadn't seen the wounds close up, hadn't seen how young the girl had been, or learned how her injuries had been sustained. All they would have heard over the radio was confirmation of an injured civilian seeking medical assistance. He was glad they hadn't asked more questions. He didn't want to talk about it again.

The hours passed in a companionable silence, but both men allowed thoughts of the awful week to wander into their minds, even while staying alert to their surroundings. It had started out badly for them, and they should have known it wouldn't have ended peacefully. DJ glanced at his watch, calculating how many hours to go before checkpoint duty was over, trying to ascertain the chances of any more disasters in the remaining hours. They were close to being relieved from the tower before Joey spoke.

"You know how they've got the Haji's clearing out those old bunkers?"

"The creepy looking ones with the pyramid shaped stonework above ground?"

"Yeah, those. Well, there's a bit of a commotion going on over at one of them."

"What's happening?" DJ asked, joining Joey at the window that looked over the rear of the base and raising his binoculars.

"No idea, but one guy is waving his arms around like a lunatic, and it looks like he's yelling at the soldier in charge."

"Yeah, and he's not taking it too well," DJ replied, watching as the soldier used his rifle to indicate the man should enter the bunker.

Despite the weapon raised towards him, the local refused to budge or stop his apparent tirade. They looked on as two men pushed past him, heading for the bunker entrance, surprised when the local grabbed them and pulled them back, screaming in their faces.

"I think we'd better radio in," Joey said.

"Someone's beaten us to it I think," DJ said. There's an LMTV heading out in their direction."

"Don't do it, man," Joey said, as the agitated or angry local pushed past the armed soldier and fled across the base, heading in the direction of the gates.

"Shit, do you think he'll shoot him down?"

"I don't know; it depends on what it was all about. I hope not,though; it'd be a political nightmare and create an absolute shit storm."

The man continued to run unhindered while the guard hesitated over his course of action. They could see his indecision, could tell by the trembling of his rifle in his hands, the beads of sweat on his forehead, the worried expression on his face. He was responsible for this man, was his guard. Any negative action on base carried out by the runner would be his fault; the blame laid firmly at his feet. Only by knowing the full details of the runner's problem could a decision be made about his next intention, or the best way to deal with it in order to protect everyone on base.

"Hold it together, there sunshine, back up's close," Joey muttered, urging the man to hold his fire, even though he knew he couldn't be heard. It was more of a request to any unseen force that might be listening than to the soldier himself.

The tension broke as the LMTV reached the man, four men spilling from the rear before it had come to a complete halt. Weapons drawn, they surrounded the runner, who dropped to his knees, hands clasped behind his head. Lifted to his feet, he was escorted onto the truck, which screeched into a rapid turn and sped off in the direction it had come. They saw the young soldier let his rifle hang loose, his head bowed, chest heaving. That time when he would first be required to pull that trigger and end a person's life had passed, for now at least.

"Must be taking him to the head shed for an interrogation," Joey said, referring to the local who had run from the soldier.

"What do you think it was all about?" DJ asked.

"No clue. Maybe he used to work with the Iraqi's here, knew the place was full of unstable explosives or something, but that's just a wild guess."

"Guess we'll find out later. At least this one isn't our problem."

Soon after that, DJ and Joey were relieved from the tower, not seeing the runner being escorted off base and told never to return. Nor did they ever find out the cause of the commotion. The only factual information to be passed down from the top was that the man had refused to carry out the task requested of him by refusing to enter the bunker, therefore negating his right to be on base. His reasons were never disclosed, leaving those that had witnessed the episode to speculate amongst themselves. The only other fact that they were able to determine was that the groups of civilians were given different tasks for the rest of the day, all instructed to abandon the bunkers for the time being. With no further reports, everyone soon lost interest and forgot about the drama, having far more important issues on their minds.

With the closing of his eyes that night, DJ could only see the scene of the stretchered girl, each moment stuttering forward like a series of stills, or a video with a two-second freeze frame. Closer and closer the family came, Aban, holding up his hands, the woman dropping to her knees, her mouth wide in a silent wail of anguish, and the girl, so pale, so still, so small and fragile, those big, ugly staples dominating her delicate features. The tighter he closed his eyes, the more intense the visions became. In the end, he opened them, staring into the pitch dark of the night, listening to the pops and booms of mortars and rockets around him.

It was then that he remembered, then that it dawned on him why the crowd had fallen so silent on sight of the approaching people with the stretcher.

They knew, he thought. *They all knew that it could have been a ruse to infiltrate the pit with explosives and that it might have been meant for us, but just as easily could have been meant for them, just for being where they were. They know what it is they're up against, and what risks they take just to come here. They understand far more than we ever could.*

Chapter Eight: First Blood

With their stint on guard duty mercifully over and the base now up and running as it should be, the men were finally charged with what they considered their real job. Not that every job assigned to them wasn't a worthwhile task, because it was, and they accepted that they had to be wherever they were needed the most, but working with the birds was what they'd trained for, what they'd prepared for, and what they felt they did best.

With the helicopters now out on regular missions and providing air support to the ground troops, they needed constant attention throughout the day, and the Armament Dogs were more than happy to give it to them. The birds in question were Bell OH-58-D helicopters or Kiowa Warriors. They lived up to their name in appearance, sturdy and mean-looking, with a shark-shaped nose, deep body, and a large Mast Mounted Sight above the main rotors, an imposing all seeing eye. This MMS allowed the helicopter to fly and fight in any conditions at the maximum range of its weapons systems, its high-resolution camera effective at target detection even at long range in low light. It also boasted infrared thermal imaging, laser rangefinder, and a bore sight, giving the pilot and copilot as much support as possible at their disposal to peak from behind buildings and mountains, spot targets in the dark even when obscured from actual vision, and a precision aim with their weaponry.

The MMS wasn't the only thing that rendered them ideal combat equipment. Protruding from the sides along the bottom of the body in line with the skids were arms. These arms were, in fact, Universal Weapons Pylons, each able to hold various deadly configurations of impressive weapons. They could hold two 109-pound laser guided Hellfires, or anti-tank missiles on either side, a pod that held seven Hydra 70 rockets or a 50-caliber machine gun with a side mounted ammo tray that could hold up to 500 rounds. Apart from having to ensure that if the machine gun was required, it needed to be mounted on the left where the ammo tray was situated, the weapons could be configured in any way and any combination the Commander chose, depending on what he felt would be most effective in completing the assigned mission. The whole UWP system was designed to be quick and easy to use, ensuring the helicopter could be fully armed and ready to fight in less than ten minutes.

As well as destroy, the helicopter also had systems in place to protect, its turbine, transmission, and rotor system all designed with extra kick and sturdiness to provide speed, lift, maneuverability, and reliability in sticky situations. It was also equipped with an infrared seeker jammer, radar and laser warning receivers, and infrared suppression, the countermeasure suite intended to increase the survivability rate during direct combat. They were also equipped with dual cyclic and collective controls, ensuring that if the pilot, seated on the left, was unable to continue flying for any reason, the copilot – responsible for manning the MMS and the weapons during normal operation – could take over in the hopes of getting them both to safety. They were more than just equipment to the men; they were a lifeline and one that the Armament Dogs were proud to work on, making sure they stayed that way.

As well as the shop for weapons and avionics repairs, part of their job was manning the Forward Arming Refueling Point or FARP for short. The FARP was simply two giant, metal shipping containers placed close together with the open door sides facing one another, essentially mirroring the other's position. It was located on the flight line, as far from the aircraft hangars as possible. The giant fuel container required to keep the aircraft flying was an almost irresistible target, and every man on base knew that if the enemy ever got their aim together enough to hit it, the resulting explosion would be devastating. Its outlying position was a necessity in order to prevent a strike from taking out every hangar and every bird they had that wasn't in the air at the time.

The Armament Dogs had one container, kitted out with spare cots to be used as chairs, bottled water, and a stash of MRE's so that they never had to leave their post. Their job was to arm the helicopters before the initial flight and to keep a steady stream of weapons coming whenever required during their shift, as well as making any basic repairs to the weapon or avionics systems that could be done in situ.

The other container was occupied by the fuelers, also part of the 3/5 Platoon, who were responsible for fueling the birds, trucks, Humvees, and the various generators around the base, ensuring everything was kept running twenty-four seven. Both containers were surrounded by a row of sandbags, the buildings used for protection during strikes.

The group of eight was sitting inside their container, sheltering from the heat. JDub was absentmindedly brushing stubborn sand from the earlier sandstorm off the shoulders and arms of his uniform, watching it fall at his feet.

"Hope you're gonna clean that up," JJ joked half-heartedly.

None of the men cracked a smile. The night before, six soldiers who'd been out in an LMTV carrying out a perimeter check had been caught in the blast of a rocket strike, their vehicle flipped and thrown as if it weighed next to nothing. The four in the back hadn't stood a chance; all were dead on the scene. The driver and passenger had been seriously injured, both loaded for medevac. The driver hadn't made it, dying in the helicopter en route. It was the first deaths caused directly by the frequent but often ineffective enemy strikes, and it had angered and sobered the entire base. The current mood of the team reflected both their loss, and the harsh realities of something that they could never get used to, but had learned to accept as a constant background to their lives.

"What does it matter? Nothing's ever clean around here. I'm sick of this shit everywhere and in everything," JDub responded, kicking angrily at the small pile of dirty sand on the floor. "When the hell are we gonna get some showers around here? I want to wash the stink of this place off me."

"Relax, JDub," Joey replied, flipping cards as he played solitaire on the cot, his face calm. "The showers aren't the issue. You're angry about last night, and we all are; but the choppers are out there today doing what they need to do, and we're here, playing our part in that. That's the way to honor our guys, not by yelling at the management for lack of basic amenities."

"I know, and I know you're right. I just feel so helpless sometimes; it makes me mad, and I wanna punch something or somebody."

"Hear that, George," Joey grinned. "JDub feels like going a few rounds with you."

George grinned. "Nothing personal man, but anytime. Just say the word and I'm there."

"It's such a waste," Craig said, turning the subject back to the young men who'd lost their lives. "A perimeter check for God's sake! Inside our own base, minding our own business."

"No such thing," DJ said. "I keep telling you, US base or not, this is their land, and every inch of it is a combat zone. Everything we do is their business, same as everything they do is ours while we're here."

"I wonder why they signed up if they were proud to die checking that the rest of us were safe," Billy mused.

"I would be," DJ confirmed. "Dying to save a fellow soldier, even if it was just by checking that there weren't any Hajis on the other side of the fence with a rocket launcher, would be the greatest honor, and I guess they signed up for the same reasons as most of us. What about you, why did you sign up?"

"The country mindset I guess. To prove to my Daddy that he'd raised a boy he could be proud of, and wasn't a total waste of space, and love of my country of course."

"Good enough reasons," Joey added, never taking his eyes from his game. "The Daddy thing was part of mine too, and to get away from the small-town mentality."

Some of the others murmured their agreement, knowing exactly what he meant and how he felt. Joey threw down the pack of cards. "Heads up, we're on."

The others strained to listen, finally hearing the approaching sound of rotors in the distance that Joey had picked up.

"Shit, you must have ears like a bat," Craig commented as they all reached for their rubber earplugs, inserting them quickly.

The helicopters should always come in teams of two, and they should coordinate their landing back at base with other pilots, but in combat situations, that planning could go to hell just as easily as everything else could. The Armament team had to be ready for any eventuality, so all prepared until they knew what they were dealing with. Once the earplugs were in place, they all pulled on their FARP helmets. They'd gotten over their initial mirth as the cheesy pieces of tan plastic that created a shell-like protection for the top and back of the head, with the cloth sides framing the face down to the chinstrap, and the bulky aviation headset attached. They might look ridiculous at first, but they were as necessary as the sand and dust goggles that they added once their helmets were secure. Not only did they provide impact protection, but also the headset gave them double hearing protection, and a means of talking to the pilots if verbal communication was required. Kitted up, they went outside to wait.

They stood around the sandbags, close to the entrance of the building, watching as the two helicopters came into land side by side, the pilots displaying expert control of the powerful machines as their rotors spun within inches of each other. The noise was deafening, reducing only slightly as the pilots powered down to idle and signaled to the fuel guys with a thumbs up that it was safe to approach the aircraft. Two teams ran out, rolling their fuel pumps and hoses towards the helicopters, one man from each team running ahead to hook the grounding cables in place. These were thin, metal braided cables coated with yellow plastic and attached to a nine-foot rod buried into the ground at one end, and clipped to the helicopter at the other. They were an essential part of the process as the helicopters generated a vast amount of static electricity while the rotors turned at high speed during flight. The sand that was flung around within them during landing and while on the pad only intensified the problem, building the static fast and creating stray voltage around the bird. Any sparks that might fly when the hoses were attached could be more than enough to start a fire. The cables effectively earthed the helicopter, removing the excess charge safely and lowering the risk.

Once the aircraft were grounded, the fuelers attached the fuel hoses with a quick connector to the fitting on the right-hand side of their respective birds. Flipping down the pump handle, the hose guys signaled to a team member with a circular motion with their hand, letting them know they were clear to start the pump.

The armament team watched the pilot as closely as the pump guys, waiting for the slicing motion of his hand to stop the pump once his gauges indicated his bird was fully fueled. Once that happened, they'd be up next.

"George, Craig, Billy, JJ, you guys take this one," DJ instructed.

He knew the guys had trained for this, but he wanted to see how they handled it under pressure, this being the first time they'd done it for real without himself and Joey leading the teams. In training, there wouldn't be a ground troop pinned by enemy fire, dying somewhere while they waited desperately for air support to clear their exit route, this time, there might be, and that knowledge could make a world of difference to how people performed. The fast and efficient turnaround of the birds always had to be treated as a life or death situation, unless instructed otherwise. He nodded with satisfaction as the four men looked at each other and shifted position slightly, non-verbally deciding on their teams and their roles. It was a good start.

With the teams chosen, JDub moved back inside the building, electing himself as the one that would remain to protect their personal weapons, allowing DJ and Joey to move as far from the building as they wanted to observe – or to intervene should the guys need assistance. Justin followed, throwing his helmet and goggles onto a cot and sighing.

"Don't stress, it'll be your turn next," JDub said, easily reading Justin's blatant body language as he removed his own gear.

"This is Phys. Ed. all over again, getting chosen last. It's depressing."

"Weren't you good at sports?"

"Oh sure, I was good, but nobody else saw it. They saw me as skinny and weak."

"As opposed to what?" JDub asked with a grin.

"Wiry, fast, and agile," Justin said. "Not to mention cunning."

"Uh huh, so all to do with the build and nothing to do with the fact that you were always in trouble; got it."

Justin laughed, unable to resist being cheered up by JDub. "I wasn't always in trouble; I had a few good days."

"I bet they were just a few, too if I even believe they existed at all."

Outside, the chosen four braced themselves as the signal came from the pilot, ready to jog out as soon as the fuel guys had removed their equipment from the pad. They never rearmed and refueled at the same time; the fire risk was too great.

DJ and Joey kept eyes on the four of them. They reached the landing pad, one of them on each team moving forward. Then, up the left-hand side of the bird, bent over to avoid the rotors, faces blasted by the sandstorm kicked up around them, the downdraft substantial even in idle. Leaning over, careful to avoid being in the line of fire of the weapons, George and JJ each slid a metal pin with a 'Remove Before Flight' banner attached inside a small hole on the outside of the UWP rack. It was a simple mechanical safety, but one that offered some assurance that the weapons wouldn't fire accidently.

With that in place, they both stepped over the back of the weapons system on the left side and with their chests hugging the aircraft skin, ducked underneath the tail boom section at the farthest point from the tail rotor, keeping their backs to it. They moved down the right-hand side of the bird, keeping their chests against it until reaching a safe point to step out and over the weapons, pinning the side with the safety mechanism.

"They're doing well so far," Joey commented, talking loudly to be heard by DJ standing right next to him.

"Yeah, almost moving in unison, and always remembering to assume they're loaded."

It was a lesson that would have been drummed into them during training, just because a bird had come back to base, you couldn't assume they were completely out of ammo. They might have only used one type of weapon, the other arms still being fully operational. Accidental fire was always a possibility. Until they received the information from the pilot, the status of the UWP was an unknown.

Now that the weapons were safe, George and JJ looked to the pilot for further instructions. Through a series of hand signals, such as a number and a point towards a particular weapon, the pilot lets them know what they needed. Using the same hand signals, George and JJ relayed the information back to Craig and Billy. Over to the front of the pad on the right, there was a massive wooden pallet stocked with the rockets and Hellfire missiles, all packaged in their own individual metal containers with latches on the sides. It was the FARP team's job to ensure the pallet remained stocked up throughout their shift. Both Craig and Billy ran to the pallet, joined by George and JJ, and together, they picked up rockets.

"Still moving fast," Joey said, glancing at his watch. "I think our record might be in danger."

"Let's see if they remember to fold 'em and tap 'em," DJ yelled in response. "Penalties for mistakes."

All four men out on the pad displayed a healthy respect for what they were carrying, handling them securely, but gently. They all remembered to fold down the three metal fins that would release and guide the rocket straight after launch; pushing them down and flat to enable it to slide into the pod as they walked them.And they all remembered to touch the rear of the rocket against another metal surface, either on the UWP or the helicopter itself, discharging any stray voltage and grounding it to remove the possibility of it launching out of their hands.

"Damn, no penalties," DJ exclaimed even as he breathed a sigh of relief and inwardly beamed with pride.

Having taken these guys under their wings, DJ felt that any mistakes they made would reflect more on himself and Joey rather than these young, inexperienced teenagers. Seeing them blossom into good soldiers was his greatest desire, and they were all getting there already.

"Wait and see how they do with the 50 cals, they might still make a mistake."

"They might, but I think they've got it. You and I need to team up for the next one, show them just how quickly this can go, or else we're going to be redundant around here."

"Could be," Joey agreed, taking another glance at his watch and raising his eyebrow as the teams made their way back over to the pods and under the boom to the left-hand side, where the 50-caliber ammo for the machine guns were kept on a separate pallet.

Each set of five hundred rounds came preassembled in a linked chain contained in a metal container with a handle on top for ease of transportation. The pilots had already electronically retracted the bolt of the feed door of the ammo can to the open position as the teams removed the ammo from the container and used the quick release handle to open up the door. They confidently and quickly slid the ammo down the chute and into the gun, allowing gravity to do its job, then folded the remaining links in a zigzag pattern, stacking it neatly into the ammo can. George and JJ both pointed to the front of their respective aircraft, giving the pilot the signal to close the barrel, catching the metal link holding the rounds together that fell during arming and firing. Once assured that the ammo was feeding correctly through the gun, they closed the gun and ammo can doors.

With the helicopter now fueled and fully loaded, they were on the final stage of their task. One member of each team pulled the safety pin from the left-hand side and repeated their slide and ducking motions to move under the boom to the right and remove the safety pin from the weapons. Once the pins were clear, they removed the grounding cables.

With the pins and cable in hand, the teams made their way to the copilots, showing them the items, confirming the process was complete. The copilots gave them the thumbs up, showing their understanding and agreeing that they had checked the items they held. The armament team then dragged the ground cable back off the pad and retreated far enough back to avoid the propeller wash and remained there, watching as the birds took off, heading back to their mission. Once gone, the four jogged back over, removing their extra gear on the way. DJ and Joey did the same. Seeing Joey glance again at his watch, George couldn't help but grin.

"So how did we do?" he asked.

"Pretty good," was all Joey was willing to say. He didn't want them getting cocky and slipping up next time. "How was it out there on your own?"

"It's pretty intense, but it was good," George answered as they all made their way back inside.

"You know what I can't get used to?"

"What's that, Billy?"

"This whole not greeting the pilots and copilots thing. I mean, they're Chief Warrant Officers, above even Sergeants in rank, and every instinct screams at me to stop and salute and call them sir. I know it's dumb because you couldn't hear an elephant farting right in your ear over the birds, and I know there's no time to stand on ceremony as the fast turnaround is the priority, but ..."

"Speed, accuracy, and safety," Joey interrupted.

"Huh?"

"They all have equal priority, not just speed."

"Oh, yeah, of course, goes without saying that it's got to be done right and done safely too, what I meant is accuracy and safety need to be carried out with speed. Anyway, this whole ignoring them then just communicating with hand signals, it just seems so disrespectful somehow."

"You mean you find it hard keeping your mouth shut for that length of time," JJ said, giving him a punch in the arm.

"He can open it and talk as much as he wants out there," Craig added. "His gripe is that no one is listening, and all he gets for his trouble is a mouthful of sand."

"You can say that again!"

"He can open it and talk.... Hey, that hurt!" Craig said, laughing as a hand slapped the back of his head.

"Okay, enough, guys, we don't need any head trauma around here today," Joey said. "Billy, you do have a point, but the pilots and copilots just want to get in and out as soon as possible. As long as you treat them with that level of respect when they're not flying, it's all good. Besides, they're all pretty decent guys. Don't forget they've usually worked their way up the ranks, the same as you will. They'd have been grunts like you too, then Specialists, then probably Sergeants before making CWO, they remember what it was like to be in your boots, and seem to make a habit of not forgetting that."

Justin looked at Joey aghast. "You did not just call us grunts?"

"I did," Joey said, with a wink towards DJ. "And what are you going to do about it?"

The tension-relieving banter during their down time was interrupted by the sound of rotors cutting through the air. The men scrambled for their extra gear.

"Right then, DJ," Joey exclaimed before they put their helmets in place. "Let's show these newbies how it should be done. Justin, JDub, you're up for team two."

As DJ and Joey made their way to the closest helicopter once the fuelers were clear, they both grinned and gave the pilot and copilot a wave. They recognized them both, had served with CW-2 Brandon Kessigner and CW-1 Mike Taylor on previous deployments, getting to know the men quite well. Joey took the lead, proceeding to make the aircraft safe as the copilot jumped down, patting DJ on the back before heading over to the side of the container to take a leak. The pilot, Brandon, tapped his microphone, indicating he wanted to talk. As Joey moved around the other side of the helicopter, DJ plugged his headphones into the audio jack on the UWP, allowing him to hear and be heard by Brandon.

"Hey there, DJ, good to see you. Back in Armament for another tour I see?"

"You know I can't keep away from you guys," DJ said with a grin.

"Pilot envy," Brandon joked.

"Not a chance, I'm happy down here, thanks."

Seeing Joey ready to go, DJ indicated he would need to wrap up the conversation.

"Sure, I'll let you get on, but there isn't any urgency, we're on a scout mission today, using the cameras to search for stashed rocket launchers in the mountains, and taking them out. Hope it'll be a nice little surprise for the Hajis tonight when they come sniffing around. We've been told to work on the assumption that they're hiding them further from base and moving them in every night, else they might have been spotted already."

"Sounds good. Any issues to report?"

The copilot gave DJ another slap on the back as he returned before jumping back into his seat.

"Nothing, she's good. All we need are seven more rockets to blow that Russian crap to pieces. Tell Joey I said Hi."

"You got it."

"Hey DJ, any chance we could have a couple of fresh bottles of water before we head out. The instruments are telling me nothing else is coming in right now, so we've got a few minutes to spare."

"Sure thing, Mike. We'll get them for you once we finish loading up. Take care out there both of you."

"Catch you next time," Brandon said as DJ disconnected the jack and turned to Joey, reverting to the hand signals to convey what the guys needed.

They moved together to the pallet, making fast work of loading the required rockets. Once complete, DJ relayed the fact that the pilots wanted water using hand signals. Joey nodded and made his way back over to their container, while DJ completed the process of removing the pins. He was waiting by the grounding cable as Joey returned, handing the pilots the bottles. The other team was also ready, standing by the cable, ready to follow DJ's lead. DJ went over with pins and cable in hand, and they received the thumbs up and a final wave from both Brandon and Mike before they moved out and back, allowing the helicopters to be clear for takeoff.

They were watching them leave, still well within eyesight when the two birds flying side by side began careering wildly in the air. DJ gripped Joey's arm as they heard a muffled boom through their double ear protection, and smoke billowed from a tail rotor, the damaged helicopter starting to spin wildly. Before their brain could make sense of what was happening, both birds were on their way down. DJ ripped off his FARP helmet a second after Joey, hearing him screaming back to the container for them to get on the radio, knowing that the guard towers would have beaten them to it, but unable to think of anything else to do.

The horrendous sounds of screaming metal hit their now-exposed ears, and they could hear and feel the hollow thump of redundant rotor blades against the ground, gamely trying to carry out their now defunct duty. It echoed in the pits of their stomachs before the rotors finally gave in and came to a halt, and the screaming engines died a death.

Already there were Humvees flying towards the gates, medical teams heading to the scene, and another pair of helicopters approaching from the distance.

"Please let them be assigned to medevac," Joey said, understanding that requiring medical attention would be a best-case scenario for the occupants of the two birds.

It was, but it wasn't long before several other pairs of Kiowa Warriors appeared, one pair looking for fuel and ammo, meaning they had to remove their attention from what was happening in the distance. Knowing that they wouldn't receive news of the four men in the helicopters, or an explanation as to what happened, until after their shift, DJ and Joey went back to work, unable to push the scene from the minds, but having to work through their concern nevertheless.

As DJ worked, self-doubt began to creep in. Had he made a mistake somewhere in the process that had caused an accident? Had the other team erred, the one he was supposed to be keeping an eye on? He cursed himself for taking those few precious moments to chat, which may have caused enough of a distraction to create a disaster. It wasn't until the remains of the helicopters were unceremoniously stuffed into a shipping container by a massive bulldozer and put into the Armament Dogs' hangar for the crash investigators that he found out what had actually happened.

Both birds had taken heavy and unexpected AK-47 fire from multiple groups of insurgents on the ground, probably in retaliation to their mission to seek and destroy their rocket launchers. A hit by an RPG, or rocket-propelled grenade, had been responsible for the plume of black smoke they'd seen and had taken out the tail rotor, causing the bird to career wildly out of control. It hadn't been anyone on base's fault, but DJ couldn't bring himself to feel any relief. He only felt sadness at the news that CW-2 Brandon Kessigner and CW-1 Mike Taylor, were both dead; and the men from the second helicopter, CW-3 William Brown and CW-2 Alexander Munoz, were badly hurt; with a broken back and heavy gunshot wounds through the arms and legs making up only part of their injuries. Both had been medevac flown to Germany, and it was unlikely that they would learn of their long-term prognosis. Dealing with the two fallen birds before them being inspected would likely fall on the two Specialists in the group, himself and Joey. The thought kept them both awake that night.

Chapter Nine: Memorial

Assigned to the shop hangar for the day, the crew was attempting pointedly to ignore the huge shipping container or Conex, placed there. It's dull, bluish grey, ridged metal exterior, and steel bar locking mechanism appeared bland and innocent, a common sight around the world, the contents normally innocuous. In this instance, even thinking about that container made them shudder, its presence providing a constant, grim reminder of yesterday's horrific events. The moment DJ and Joey had dreaded – the one that had kept them awake allnight – arrived as Sergeant Heard pulled them aside only an hour into their shift.

"I need you two to open that up and clear out the Comsec before the crash investigators arrive. I know it won't be pretty, but it needs to be done," he said, giving the Conex the nod, his face grim, voice low. "I need you to take out the cyclic sticks too. Might as well start straight away, get it over with."

Neither of the two men spoke, simply walked over to the container, and stood at the doors, staring blankly at the mechanism.

"Hey there," George said, coming up behind them. "Do you want a hand with this, or want me to do it for you?"

Suddenly, the entire team was around them, comforting hands on their shoulders, soft words being spoken.

"We can take over."

"Heard you both knew them, let us take care of this."

"Might be best if you don't go in there."

Joey glanced at DJ, then turned to face his battles. "Thanks, guys, we appreciate the offer, but I guess this is something we have to do. I wouldn't wish it upon any of you anyway."

"It's too much, man," Justin said with a shake of his head. "Let me go; I'll handle it."

DJ finally turned; a ghost of a smile on his pale face. "Yeah, thanks, and it's tempting, but a direct order is a direct order. You guys get back to what you were doing. Joey and I have got this, haven't we?"

Joey's heart constricted as DJ turned towards him, his pleading expression desperate for reassurance. "Yeah," he replied, returning the wan smile. "We've got this. We'll be fine."

The six teammates glanced at each other uneasily but nodded, backing off and returning to their duties, all of them making the occasional clandestine glance from the corner of their eyes toward the men they considered their mentors, the ones they respected and looked up to, foreheads creased in concern.

"I can't believe we were speaking to them just moments before... moments before..."

DJ choked up, unable to finish the sentence.

"I know, buddy, I know. Let's get this thing open, get this done with."

Having been handed the key from Sergeant Heard, Joey unlocked the regular padlock and removed it, slipping it into his pocket before pulling the handles out. He pushed on the handles, expecting to hear the sound of the top and bottom locks disengaging with the action. Nothing. He pushed again, and still the small metal feet above and below each door refused to budge.

Taking a step back, he examined the container. Its age was given away by the amount of rust on the metal, and its constant usage was depicted by its slightly deformed shape, having been bashed around by cranes on loading docks once too often.

"Damn thing's all bent out of shape," Joey said. "No wonder it won't pop like it's supposed to."

DJ looked at the container, knowing that the metal tabs attached to one door went underneath the other for locking, meaning that the doors had to open in the correct order, and the only way to achieve that was to do what Joey was trying to do. He sighed, realizing that any sense of ceremony and dignity would have to be roughly cast aside to carry out their task. Once again, their battle buddies surrounded them, all of them pushing, shoving, and trying to manipulate the warped metal to a point where the doors would find their proper position and respond. Suddenly, they gave, and the calling out of instructions and grunts and groans died down as the doors were swung open with a grating creak. As soon as the doors were open, the smell hit the team, causing them to stagger back, some of them coughing, some of them holding their hands over their mouths and noses, their stomach muscles lurching and throats jerking with the gag reflex.

As well as the pungent, acrid odor of recent fire and hot metal, stale smoke and engine oil, the underlying scent of burning hair and the sickly, almost sweet smell of roasting flesh taunted them, tickling at their nostrils, reminding them of the lives that been stolen by licking flames and scorching heat.

JDub ran outside. The remains of his last MRE were rapidly leaving his stomach as thoughts of large family barbecues after hunting trips crept unbidden into his mind. The thoughts of flesh sizzling, popping, and charring causing him to fall to his knees as he tried to blot them out, praying that no one would ever guess the macabre and disrespectful comparison his senses had made without his permission or compliance. Craig and Billy joined him, offering comfort, but also preferring the desert air to the stench emanating from the Conex.

DJ and Joey recovered from the initial shock, gathering handsaws and placing their minds firmly on their mission ahead. The remains of both helicopters took up most of the space inside the container, and one by one, they entered, having to crawl around the twisted metal to locate an entry point. The smell was worse inside, intensified by the proximity to the actual events, almost overwhelming them.

"We got this," Joey said again, as much to summon his own determination as DJ's.

The cockpit of the first helicopter was covered with dark, dried bloodstains, and they could both imagine it as it had been, awash with bright crimson from the multiple gunshot wounds the occupants had suffered, as well as the injuries sustained during the crash landing, both too injured to control the aircraft. They moved past it quickly, unable to face it quite yet. Instead, they headed to the rear of the bird to locate the secure communication radio equipment the Sergeant had asked them to retrieve. The Comsec was a part of the helicopters' equipment that the Armament Dogs were responsible for, required to fill them every morning with the secure anti-jam fill before the initial flight. This was a necessity during deployment, ensuring that the secure communication frequency and hop set numbers could be changed daily. That way, if a bird crashed outside the wire, the codes were only functional for twenty-four hours, useless to the enemy after the elapsed time.

In this first bird, despite the outer damage, the interior was fairly intact, and the Comsec was still located where it should be. DJ and Joey got busy with the handsaws, cutting the device from its location, nestled safely in the rear cocoon of one of the supposedly safest combat helicopters available to the US military.

"Fat lot of good it did them," DJ muttered, his anger rising like a shield against his raw emotions.

"I hear you," Joey replied, following his train of thought. "All the training and hi-tech equipment in the world don't help when you're caught off guard by these bastards."

DJ paused in his work. "Do you think it was my fault, because we were chatting, and they were relaxed and in a good mood, not engaged with their mission right away?"

"This isn't the first time I've heard you trying to lay the blame on yourself for something, and I'm telling you, you've got to quit it, right now. They were trained pilots, damn fine ones at that. They'd have seen them, only too late. The Hajis were already in position, locked and loaded, ready to fire as soon as they went over the wire. They didn't even have a chance to fire back, or you could have bet your bottom dollar they'd have taken them out with them, lit them up and gone down in that proverbial blaze of fucking glory. There was nothing, and I mean *nothing*, that would have distracted these men while flying. It just happened too damned fast for them to react. That's all there is to it."

DJ had never heard Joey's voice so cold and hard. He knew it was anger and sadness at the heart of it, and it wasn't really directed towards him, but still, it surprised him. Joey was always so calm, so laid back and in control. It dawned on him that the deaths of the two men they'd considered friends was hitting him harder than he was willing to show or admit. It was time to stop torturing himself with self-doubt and leaning on his battle, time for him to take charge and offer the strong set of shoulders to carry his friend through this and back to safer ground.

"You're right, and I'm sure there are plenty of pilots out there who want to do it on their behalf. We'll get this shit over with so we can concentrate on the birds that can still fly, and make sure they have the opportunity and support to do so."

DJ attacked the metal around the Comsec with vigor, pouring his rage and impotence into the task, making short work of the rest of the job of removing it. Once done, he slithered his way to the cyclic, hacking at it viciously, ignoring the tears that stung his eyes as he worked. Joey watched, allowing DJ to vent his frustrations in peace, not surprised when DJ launched the now free control stick out the door of the helicopter, where it clanged against the side of the hangar, the sound causing him to wince.

"Everything okay in there? Are you guys all right?"

"We're fine, JJ, go about your business," Joey called, knowing DJ needed to work this out with some semblance of privacy.

He wished he could do the same, but burning hot rage wouldn't come, only an icy cold steeliness that didn't seem to have any outlet or release mechanism. Deep inside, he ached for these men, but his pain had been encased in a frozen layer and locked away, inaccessible to him. *The grief will come when this is over,* he told himself, following DJ to the second helicopter, the one in which his friends had died.

This time, the Comsec was a little harder to find, the helicopter much more warped than the previous one, and blackened by the fire and soot. The damaged tail rotor meant the bird had gone down harder and faster, spinning wildly during descent. If the pilots had still been

125

alive, it would have been a terrifying and fatal roller coaster of a ride. They worked as quickly as they could in the cramped space available to them, removing the items they'd been sent to retrieve. Inside this cockpit, the same dark splashes and stains provided gruesome decoration, but the smell of burning hair and flesh was much more concentrated. Joey wished he had the ability just to hold his breath, to not breathe until he left this scene of devastation, but he knew his lungs and brain wouldn't let him, the survival instinct, and burning pain too much to fight for longer than a few brief moments. Instead, he allowed the core of ice to expand, numbing him to everything around him except his job, successfully blinkering himself to the horrible reminders of the remains of his friends.

Finally, they made their way back to the door of the Conex, carrying the required items, the ghastly mission complete. Placing the items outside, they turned to close the doors, finding them as reluctant to close as they had been to open.

"Close, damn you, just fucking close!"

Joey could only watch as DJ lost it, screaming and kicking wildly at the stubborn doors, causing them to slam and spring open in a never-ending cycle, first one, then the other, as they both received marks and the occasional dent from the bad side of his boot. His anger draining, DJ ran from the hangar, leaving the doors creaking as they swung behind him.

George made to follow DJ out.

"Don't," Joey said "Just let him be. Break the battle buddy rules this once; he won't have gone far, and he'll be back in a moment, full of apologies."

"He's got nothing to apologize for," Craig said. "There isn't a single one of us that doesn't understand. Come on guys, help me with these damn doors."

The team rallied round, eventually succeeding in getting the doors to close and lock into place. Joey slipped the padlock back on and tucked the key away to give back to the Sergeant when they handed over the cyclic sticks and Comsec. Breathing a sigh of relief, he turned and leaned his back heavily against the Conex, exhausted by emotion and mental strain.

Billy was ripping open an MRE, using the heater to warm some water before shaking in the coffee granules. Craig led Joey to a cot, forcing him to sit. Still waiting for better supplies to arrive, Billy handed Joey the lukewarm black coffee in a cutoff water bottle with an apologetic shrug. Joey took it with an appreciative nod.

"Thanks."

"Was it bad?" Justin asked.

"Yeah, it was really bad, so bad; I'd rather not talk about it right now."

"I'm sorry. You should have come right out; some of us could have taken over. You didn't need to put yourselves through that."

"No, sometimes you have to, to do your best for the fallen ones, you know? In their honor."

"I think I get it," Justin said. "But I guess it's something I'd have to experience to understand really. I've never been close enough to anyone to care much if they lived or died before, but things are different now, so don't any of you go dying on me in a hurry."

"We'll try not to," George said in all seriousness, all smartass comments and banter firmly clamped down as a mark of respect.

Joey drained the rest of the strong, black coffee, its tepid warmth nowhere near enough to counteract his inner chill. Before he began to shiver, he rose to his feet, gathering the items from the hangar floor.

"I'm going to go and see if I can deliver these to Sergeant Heard and return the key, so he has it for when the crash inspectors show up."

"You need a battle?"

"Thanks, but I'll collect DJ on the way. If I can't find him, I'll come back for one of you."

As Joey suspected, DJ was right outside, hunkered down against the side of the hangar. Hearing Joey's approaching footsteps, boots crunching in the sand, he looked up.

"I made such an idiot of myself, in front of you and the guys."

Joey hunkered down alongside DJ. "Nope, you didn't. Everyone gets it. You didn't do anything that any normal person wouldn't do, and what we faced was pretty awful."

"It was, all that blood, they were shot to pieces. No wonder they couldn't return fire and control their birds. They might have even been dead before they hit the ground."

"We can hope so, for their sakes."

They shared a moment of silence, heads bowed, until Joey broke their inner reverie. "Ready to get these to the Sergeant?"

"Yeah, final stage then mission accomplished," DJ replied, rising to his feet.

Making inquiries as they went, they were directed to the hangar where the Sergeant had last been seen. Walking along in the desert heat, Joey felt a wave of sadness wash over him as the ice he'd utilized to get through the trauma melted away, leaving behind sorrow and regret. He was relieved when they finally found the Sergeant and handed over the parts.

"Good job," he told them. "I know it couldn't have been easy. Commander Martinez has decided to hold a memorial service this afternoon for them since they were so well known and liked as well as high-ranking Officers. I think paying our respects will help us all move on and give us some closure. I'll see you there. Back to your posts."

***

For the second time that day, the Armament Dogs spent a few precious moments tending to their appearance. They cleaned up as best they could, adjusted their uniforms, removed their boots to brush the dust and sand from them, and re-polished their rifles. Only a few words were spoken as they scrubbed at their faces and hands, trying to ensure any ingrained dirt or oil had been removed from their sweaty skin. They combed hair and ran dry razors across their chins, then checked each other over when they were done, each one wanting to look as presentable as possible for the somber service that was about to occur. They stepped out of the hangar single file and immediately fell into a loose formation as they made their way to the designated point.

The entire company had turned out for the memorial service, formed up inside the hangar next to the one occupied by the Armament Dogs, gathered at the front beside the large doors, facing inwards. In front of the gathered company at the rear of the hangar, funeral monuments had been set up. Two rifles stood, barrels pointing downwards, Kevlar helmets placed on the butt of the rifles, and the men's dog tags hanging from the weapons. The barrel of the gun rested between a pair of their boots, sitting side by side.

The entire display was desperately sad, meant to honor, but more of a stark reminder of the items essential to a soldier that were no longer needed. Of everything there, it was the boots that ripped at Joey's emotions as his gaze ran down the memorials. Those empty boots, never again to stride across the base, a smile on the owner's face as he greeted people along the way, never again to run to his bird, ready to answer the harsh call of duty, never again to expertly operate the highly sensitive pedals of his ultimate war machine.

The men stood to attention; their bodies ramrod straight, eyes forward. Joey's never left the monuments, even when Commander Martinez stepped in front of the group to address them.

"At ease."

The soldiers shifted slightly, moving their left foot to find a more comfortable standing position, careful to ensure their right foot remained static. Some clasped their hands behind their back; others simply relaxed their shoulders and allowed them to hang loosely by their sides. As the slight shuffling sounds died down, the Commander began his speech.

"Men, we are gathered here to honor the memory of two very fine Officers who lost their lives in the line of duty yesterday. These men were true patriots, dedicating their lives to the safety and freedom of the United States of America. Two men who…"

Joey allowed the words to wash over him, his mind wandering. He tried to recall conversations about family, but the memories refused to be caught, flittering away like the fireflies of his childhood. It was with a sense of panic that he found his head playing tricks on him, blocking him from retrieving the information he required. He wanted to say a prayer for the folks back home, the people that had known and loved the man, not just the soldier, but he couldn't remember if there were wives, kids, sisters, or brothers. He knew that he knew; knew that they'd shared the information during many conversations, but right at this moment, not a single fact would come. He assumed it was some coping mechanism, albeit a cruel and unnecessary one, and that the information would come once the pain had faded a little, washed away by the daily routines and constant danger. People always said that time healed, but Joey knew from experience that it didn't. The hole left by losswas never filled. It was a constant. Once it existed, it couldn't be undone, it only hurt less to acknowledge its presence, and even that was just a coping mechanism, the human body, and mind unable to keep up the intensity of raw, unchecked grief for too long.

In the end, all he could do was to pray for everyone, everyone who had known these men for their different roles in life, be it son, grandson, brother, cousin, father, or soldier, all of them separate, yet inextricably intertwined to make up the men they had been. By the time he'd finished, Commander Martinez was wrapping up his speech by giving what little information he had on the condition of the other two pilots, who, so far, were still survivors of the attack.

For the first time, Joey broke his steady stare at the memorials, watching the Commander as he turned right and marched to them, kneeling in front of them. From his off-left and front position, he saw the Commander close his eyes, and his lips move, his words inaudible to the company. With a sudden rise and abrupt about-face, the Commander marched out of the hangar, leaving the soldiers confused, having not been dismissed. Some stayed exactly as they were while others glanced around, looking to see if anyone else had more of a clue as to how they should proceed.

One soldier took the lead, walking up to the memorial, snapping to attention and saluting the fallen Officers one last time before about facing and leaving the hangar. Relieved to have a direction to follow, the soldiers began to line up and one by one, they took their turn at moving forward to pay their final respects. Some left stony-faced, others left sniffing with watery eyes, and some left crying openly. The ritual was carried out in complete silence, not even a murmur of comfort being uttered.

As Joey took his turn, he'd expected to cry, had *wanted* to cry, but as the moment came and went, he found that he physically

132

couldn't. The river of sadness that swirled and boiled within was dammed up tight, the walls refusing to break and allow the flood to come. In a moment of panic, before he turned around, he wondered how his dry eyes and stoic expression would look to the others in the room. Would he be considered heartless and unfeeling, an insensitive, cold fish not worthy of their regard or respect? He wondered if he should try to fake it to avoid their misconception, but in the end, he decided against it. Those that took the time to know him would understand and those that judged him without knowing him weren't worth worrying about. He walked from the hangar with his head high, proud to have known CW-2 Brandon Kessigner and CW-1 Mike Taylor, both serving with them and being able to call them friends, and glad of the chance to say goodbye.

Back in the hangar used as barracks, the group of eight gathered together, seeking companionship from their battles after the highly emotional day. They crowded onto two cots, four a piece and facing each other, their knees occasionally touching due to the lack of space between the regimented designating sleeping areas. Normally, they might have tried to avoid the contact, or made some crass comments and jokes when it occurred. Today, they all appreciated the tiny human interaction, the warmth of a live body close to them. It went unmentioned, and no one was in a hurry to jerk away as they might normally do.

"He gave a nice speech, the Commander I mean," Billy said, breaking the silence.

"Yeah, it was good, uplifting," JDub agreed. "I think I needed to hear something like that. Did it help you guys?"

DJ and Joey both knew that the question was directed mostly at them, being the two that had known the pilots the longest. Joey was reluctant to answer, knowing he'd tuned out for most of it, preferring to pay his respects in his own way. He was relieved when DJ spoke.

"It was so sad, and damn, those memorials hit me hard every time, but yet, it helped and gave me a chance to say a proper goodbye. And also gave me some closure on it. At least now, I have the last memory that's easier to handle. Better than watching the birds go down, or crawling around amongst their blood in the wreckage."

A hand reached out and squeezed DJ's shoulder. He accepted the touch, having no need to identify where it came from.

"You guys did well today, handling that. I'm sorry you had to go through it, and I'm sorry you lost friends," George said.

"I didn't handle it at all," DJ replied. "I totally lost it, and I'm sorry you had to see that. It was unprofessional and set a bad example."

Normally, a comment like that would open up the speaker to a volley of teasing and jibes, but not today. Instead, quiet protests ensued.

"Nobody blames you or thinks badly of you for it."

"You only lost it afterward."

"Yeah, you performed your duty, you weren't unprofessional."

"We get it; we'd have been the same, or worse."

"It was just a form of release, nothing to be ashamed of."

134

DJ looked gratefully around the earnest faces, glad he hadn't lost their respect or friendship during his meltdown. "Thanks, I appreciate that."

It was Justin's next comment that wiped the solemn expressions from those faces, replacing them with ones of surprise.

"If it were any of you guys, I'd have done more than kick a door a few times; I think I'd have scaled the fence and personally hunted them down, not stopping until I'd killed every last one of them, either with my rifle or my bare hands."

The words were spoken with such conviction and venom; they startled the entire group, stunning them into silence. It was JJ who finally gave a nervous chuckle and broke the uneasy tension.

"We appreciate the sentiment, but I think the military takes a dim view of personal vendettas."

"They'd have had to shoot me to stop me," Justin said with bravado. "Nobody messes with my battles and gets away with it."

DJ and Joey caught each other's eye, sharing a moment of silent communication. Justin's declarations were mildly amusing and slightly alarming, but it was also good to know that they'd already created the tight group they needed to help get through a deployment, and to work like a well-oiled machine throughout any marching order top decided to bestow upon them. For many, the army became a substitute family, and for a boy raised without the closeness of loving parents, the newly discovered sense of brotherhood and camaraderie could be all-encompassing. They acknowledged that while the unbreakable bond was a good thing, they would keep an eye on Justin, just in case it overwhelmed him to his detriment at any time.

"I propose a toast," JJ declared. "To finish off the funeral properly."

"Yeah, that sounds good," DJ said. "I've got some fresh bottles of water here."

"I can do better than that, hang on."

JJ scurried to his own cot, reaching for his duffel stashed beneath. He returned triumphantly, sporting a can.

"Sorry, it's just the one, but it's better than nothing."

DJ took the offered can. "Sanabel Lager, Eastern Breweries, Baghdad," he read aloud. "Where the heck did you get this?"

"Didn't I tell you I had a talent," JJ laughed, winking at JDub. "Once I find my feet, there'll be plenty more where this came from. I was saving this for an occasion, and this seems like a perfect moment. Go on, crack it open."

DJ popped the pull ring off the can and took a tentative sniff at the contents, grimacing slightly. "I'll be damned," he said. "Never set foot off base, and produces a can of beer brewed in an Islamic country. I'm amazed."

He raised the can high in the air. "To Brandon and Mike, may you never be forgotten, and fly forever, watching over your loved ones from heaven above."

He took a gulp of the brew, then passed the can along. Each man raised the can and toasted the pilots in their own way, saying whatever they felt was meaningful before taking a swig of the lager. As the last man toasted and drank, the conversation turned to the beverage.

"Not too bad, for a country that isn't supposed to drink."

"Smells like cardboard and grass, but it didn't taste too bad."

"Too sweet for my liking, but any port in a storm."

"It's kind of fruity, no taste of hops at all. I wonder what they use to make it."

"Who cares?"

The lagergone and their exuberant moment over, thoughts of their reasons for the toast returned, bringing with it the return of the somber and reflective mood.

"I'm going to hit the hay, guys," Joey said. "It's been a long day, and who knows what tomorrow will bring."

The others agreed, and the small wake broke up, retiring to their own cots with their thoughts. As soon as Joey closed his eyes, everything came flooding back to him. Faces, names, shared photographs of smiling wives and young children, tales of family trips and cute things the kids had done and said. In the darkness of night, Joey was able to recall it all and say that prayer he'd so desperately needed to say at the memorial service, mentioning each family member by name, wishing them the strength to handle their loss and grief, and find a way to carry on through life while mourning death. When he was done, in the scant privacy of his cot with his face pressed hard against his rolled up blanket, he was finally able to cry.

Chapter Ten: Breaking Point

With missions in full swing, the Armament Dogs were kept busy either in the shop or on FARP duty, the coming and going of the Kiowa Warriors now a constant sight and sound. As the rocket attacks continued and men lost their lives in a variety of manners, the base developed an all-around feeling of resigned determination. A situation of constant danger could never become boring, but the men had little to break the terrible monotony of hardship, pain, and death, that seemed to surround them constantly.

It took six months for the Quartermaster unit to show up with amenities to make life a little more comfortable. With nothing to provide any entertainment except each other's company, the arrival brought with it a stir of excitement on base. Enthusiastic chatter could be heard as the CHU's, or Containerized Housing Units were maneuvered into position. They were set up in pads, which consisted of around fifteen to twenty units to a pad.

These housing units were basically aluminum trailers similar to shipping containers. They weren't much, but they would be a sheer luxury to the soldiers. Before they could be used, they had to be made a little more resilient to the devastating rocket attacks. It was with a sense of impatience that the men watched the Iraqi laborers fill the vast amounts of sandbags that were required to be stacked three deep and about halfway up every wall before the units were deemed safe for habitation. As well as the sandbags, the entire pad had to be surrounded by a giant concrete T barrier, or retaining wall, at each side and behind to offer more protection. Finally, top gave the word that the units were ready, and the Armament Dogs and the rest of their squad were instructed to move their things before their shift began the next day.

"Man, I can't wait to move into CHUville tomorrow," JJ declared. "How do you think they'll be configured?"

"It can vary," Joey informed in. "One tour I did, they were split into two rooms with a tiny toilet and basin in between, but I think that might be asking for too much here."

"Can you imagine a proper toilet with just four sharing, though? Heaven!"

"Dream on, Billy, dream on."

"Yeah," Justin agreed. "I was told that there are separate latrine and shower trailers at the end of each pad."

"Where did you hear that?" DJ asked, constantly amazed at the Intel Justin always seemed to get his hands on. How he found the time to make the kind of friends he needed to find out the level of information he did was beyond even the experienced DJ.

"The usual sources," Justin said with a cheeky grin. "You just have to know the right people to ask."

"We all know the right people to ask; it's their reluctance ever to give a straight answer to a straight question that keeps us in the dark," Craig grumbled.

"You obviously don't have my charm and boyish innocence," Justin replied, fluttering his eyelashes at Craig.

Justin kept his words light but on the inside, he glowed with pride. Being able to be the one to impart important information to the group meant a lot to him. As inexperienced as he was, it was amazing what he'd found to attempt to impress the others, particular DJ, and Joey. He'd discovered he had a knack for getting people talking, and he fully intended to use it to his best advantage. It was the one thing he felt gave him value and a way of competing with JJ's knack of getting his hands on illicit goods.

"No point in speculating about it too much. If you'd all just shut up and go to sleep, you'd be finding out before you know it," George said.

The few grumbled replies soon settled down, and the guys did their best to sleep, all urging morning along. It came, as always, with rising heat, a constant shock to the system after the plunging temperatures of night. The Armament Dogs hurried through their tricky routine of preparing themselves for the day in their tiny allocated space, all the while rejoicing in the fact that it would be the last time they had to do it. Once done, they gathered their meager belongings and packed their duffels, assembling outside with their squadron to wait for Sergeant Heard to escort them to their new living quarters. For the first time, the Sergeant wasn't already waiting for them.

"Typical hurry up and wait bullshit," Justin muttered.

"Relax, it's the dawn of a brand new day," Joey said. "A change of scenery, on the inside at least, new beginnings, that kind of thing."

"Yeah, this should really be a morale boost for everyone," DJ added. "Lord knows we could all use it."

They only had to wait a few moments before Sergeant Heard appeared; an apologetic smile on his face. "Just needed to confirm some last minute details. Fall in, gentlemen, and allow me to show you your new home."

He seemed almost as pleased and excited for his men as they were for themselves, leading them to their pad at a clipped pace. First, he showed them the latrine trailer. The trailer had four built in shower stalls at one end, with four basins and wall mounted mirrors across from them. At the other end, there were four bathroom stalls. It even had a frosted window at one end that allowed natural light to flood in, and the mirrors gave the place the illusion of space.

"Oh my God, sheer bliss!" JJ cried as the Sergeant allowed them to see inside to inspect it. "I haven't seen my face in so long; I've forgotten what it looks like."

"Believe me; you're not missing anything," George said. "But it will be good to shave without guesswork. I swear I use most of my t.p. sheets to blot the nicks every day."

"Look at how white it is, how *clean* everything is," Craig said.

"Make sure you keep it that way," Sergeant Heard instructed, thrilled that his men were pleased with the setup. "The showers and sinks are already operational. Outside, there are two large capacity storage tanks which are full, hooked up, and ready to go, one to supply, and the other to catch the used water."

"Can I jump in right now?" JDub asked.

"I wouldn't if I were you. We're relying on the sun to heat the water, so I'd suggest that you time your showers accordingly with your shifts to take advantage of that fact."

"Cold or not, I don't care. I just want to be beneath running water!"

"Fair enough, but wait until you see what other tasks await you before you decide that's how you want to spend your time before your shift in the shop."

"That doesn't sound good," Craig said. "Don't tell me we have to fill in the old latrines or something."

Sergeant Heard chuckled. "You'll see. Fall in."

The squad did as they were asked, gathering beside their Sergeant.

"Over there, you can see there's a line of Porta Johns, in case the four stalls are already in use, and down here, are your new quarters," he said as he led them to two trailers on the pad. "The trailers are split by dividing walls into three rooms, two to a room, organize yourselves however you want, and then fill in the paperwork to let me know which room, and in which trailer you're in. Make sure you hand it in before you leave for your duties."

"In case we get blown to smithereens, and you can't find our tags?" Justin asked.

"Pretty much," Sergeant Heard agreed. "And so I know where to find you when I need you."

"Fair enough. Can we go now?"

"One more thing. Inside each room, you'll find your furniture, which is flat pack and still boxed. I'd suggest that you all make a start on getting it made up in the time you have before your shift. Be sensible and start with your bed, just in case you don't feel inclined to do any more at the end of your twelve hours."

"Yes Sergeant," the men chanted, all in high spirits as they each decided who was to share with whom.

DJ and Joey decided to pair up, with Craig and JJ taking the room next to them. JDub and George occupied the third room in their trailer, with Billy & Justin taking the first room in the next CHU along.

"Do you think it's wise to have Justin so far from our supervision?" DJ asked Joey as they entered their new room together.

Joey chuckled. "Least he'll be someone else's problem if he gets up to any mischief. Besides, how much trouble can he cause, being only one trailer away?"

"Never underestimate Justin's abilities to create situations," DJ replied, looking at the labels on the boxes to find the ones that displayed an image of a bed frame.

He looked at the box and looked around the long, narrow room. "I don't think we'll both be able to work at the same time, not enough space."

"Then we do each one together, get it done in half the time anyway," Joey replied.

They set to work and soon had the bed frames built. They knew from previous deployments that the standard layout of the room chosen by the men was to place a bed at either side, which left just enough room down the middle to place the two wall lockers, end to end facing towards their beds on either side; effectively creating a partition wall between them that allowed each man some privacy. Joey looked at the bed frames and looked at DJ.

"These are designed to be either free standing, or bunks if you want, see these extra fittings to join them together?"

"Oh yeah," DJ said. "I've never paid much attention before. What do you think? Should we bunk up and have the extra space?"

"I think that's a great idea," Joey replied with a grin.

They fitted the beds together as bunks then unwrapped the plastic from the thin mattresses that went along with them. Putting them in place and making them up with the sheet, blanket, and pillow that had been provided, they stood back to admire their handiwork.

"That looks a lot more comfortable than a piece of rough, stretched canvas," DJ said.

"Not bad," Joey agreed, more admiring the space on the other side of the room. "So what are you, a top, or a bottom?"

"I'm not sure I want to answer that, but if we're talking bunks, I'd rather have the bottom," DJ said with a guffaw.

"You got it," Joey replied, slinging his duffel up onto the top bunk. "I reckon we can still get the desk and the two wall units down this one side, leaving that other side completely clear."

"For what exactly?"

"Our guitars for one, and didn't you say you'd brought your laptop and speakers?"

"Bose speaker," DJ agreed. "And I've got some amazing playlists."

"Then we load this side up with the folding camping chairs for the guys, and this room is party central!"

"Great idea! Once the PX is up and running, we can get a mini fridge right here…"

"And a microwave over here," Joey finished. "And as long as the PX carries adaptor plugs for these sockets, your laptop can be our permanent sound system."

"Everything we need to have some decent down time finally."

The guys high fived each other, pleased with their plan.

"Let's get the rest of this cheap shit built before it's time to go. That way, we can head on over to the Conex and pick up our personal stuff after our shift."

Being engineers, assembling the flat packed furniture was a breeze. They then proceeded to unpack their duffels and store the contents in the newly built wall lockers.

"We might actually be able to turn out half-decent now," DJ said with satisfaction as he folded and placed his final item.

"Sure, and if they get the Wi-Fi up and running, you can use your laptop to call home. I don't mind giving you privacy for that. I can hang out with some of the others."

A shadow crossed DJ's handsome features. "You know what, Clara and I did that on my first tour, but we both talked about it when I got home, and we agreed that it was just too damn hard. Being able to hear each other's voice or see each other on video, but being so far away and not able to touch, well, it just tore us apart. Clara said that the days I left for deployment were hell, wondering if it would be the last time she would ever see me and that every phone call or video call made her go through that same hell, dragging it out throughout my whole tour."

"I can see her point, but isn't that rough on you?"

DJ shook his head. "I miss her like crazy, and there isn't a day goes by that I don't long to talk to her, but in another way, it's a relief."

"How come?"

"I don't know if I can explain this right, but you get into a way of thinking here. The guys around you become your family, the stress, the danger, it all becomes a part of your daily routine. You never forget the folks back home or your own bed, but you push it aside, let it fade to the back of your mind as much as possible. Sometimes I think that being reminded of all that, seeing Clara sitting on our couch back home, or at our kitchen table, it's too much of a reminder, and that reminder makes you hate where you are, reminds you of what you're

146

missing and might never see again. Sometimes, it can just affect me too much, and that type of emotion makes me weak. Am I making any sense?"

"I understand," Joey said. "I've seen some guys crumble after a call home and take a while for them to get back into the mindset. I didn't think you'd be one of them, though, not after three tours."

"No matter how many tours I do, I can never get used to being away from her. I just love her so damned much."

"Fair enough, and it's none of my business really, just curious. I get it, though. So you go with no contact at all?"

"Well, I write to her. Signing off a letter is easier than hanging up the phone. I've written countless letters already, even though the mail flights aren't up and running yet either. I'll probably never send them all, but writing makes me feel as if I'm talking to her direct, without the painful parting at the end. She says she doesn't mind those so much because they're something she can hold onto forever. I know she'll write to me as soon as she can."

"That's good. Shouldn't be too long now buddy, now that the base is starting to get properly equipped."

"I know! I can't wait. Maybe she'll include some pictures that I can show off to you and the guys."

"We'll look forward to it. Well, I think we've done all we can here. We've still got fifteen minutes before we need to head out, will we go and see if any of those numb nuts need a hand?" Joey asked, already in the doorway.

"I heard that!" Craig called from the next room.

"Good, you were meant to."

The trailer erupted in hearty guffaws, setting the men up for a good day. Mostly it was filled with talk amongst the work of DJ and Joey's idea to turn their room into their hangout, a plan that went down well with all the guys. They were excited for the end of their shift when they could head to the storage container and reclaim their personal items now that they had somewhere to store it.

"Oh baby, I've missed you so much," George said as he removed his guitar from the case in the Conex, inspecting it for damage. "Perfect as ever," he declared, giving it a pat.

All the men were equally enthusiastic to retrieve their items, and loaded up like pack horses; they made their way back to their rooms to fill them with their belongings, personalizing the space and making them feel more comfortable.

"Can you believe we've actually got air con?" Billy enthused as he wandered into DJ and Joey's room. "No more sweating like pigs if we're trying to sleep during the day, or freezing our asses off at night."

"Use it wisely," Joey replied. "You've only just become acclimatized to the temperatures here, so don't push it too far either side of that, or you won't be able to handle being away from it again."

"Good point, thanks. Hey, this place looks great!"

"Glad you approve; we're pretty pleased with it ourselves. We've got more plans once the PX is up and running," Joey said, referring to the Post Exchange, which was basically an on base shop that would stock random food, drinks, movies, and sanitary items such a soap, shampoo and deodorant, as well as the small appliances that most men would purchase to kit out their CHU's.

"I heard that's going to happen in the next couple of days," JJ said, entering the room with Justin and Billy. "AAFES are supposedly arriving tomorrow with the goodies to stock it, and it should be open the next day. I also heard that they're going to allow some Iraqis to set up a bazaar. I can't wait for that."

Billy curled up his nose. "What are they going to stock that we'd want? Even their bottled water is bitter as all get out. I can't see any of the local stuff being up to much."

"The beer wasn't bad," JJ replied. "Besides, it isn't so much what they do stock; it's what they don't stock but will be able to get for you with a little persuasion."

"Don't say anything else," Joey said. "I don't think I want to know. I'm heading for a shower."

"Now there's another great idea!" Craig agreed.

The showers were simple with only an on and off switch. After a day of heating in the sun, the water in the tanks was scalding and the pressure supplied by the pump was enough to strip several layers of skin from their backs; but after six months of whore baths, none of them thought that they were any less than amazing. Feeling clean for the first time in a long time was a luxury they knew they would never take for granted.

Even better were the laundry tents that were set up the next day, containing massive industrial sized washers and dryers that finally allowed the men to ensure they had a steady flow of clean uniforms to wear after their showers. Life on base had never been so good, nor had any of the first timers been so appreciative of the simple things they took for granted back home. The only downside was that with the constant sand storms and the continual coming and going, they were finding it hard to keep the dust and dirt out of their trailers. DJ and Joey devised the plan of surrounding most of the exterior of the pad with piles of small river rocks they'd gathered, which created a buffer against the worst of it. The plan worked well, its only flaw presenting itself in the early morning or late evening when the freakishly huge camel spiders were on the move, their size and weight being such that they could clearly hear the clicking sound they made as they scurried across the rocks, reaching top speeds of approximately ten miles per hour. Although non-venomous, they grew up to twelve inches in length and possessed large jaws that could deliver nasty, painful bites that could easily become infected in the less than hygienic conditions they'd been living in until recently. All the men had encountered them at some point, and even the sound of them was enough to make them shudder with revulsion. However, it was a small price to pay for the cleanliness of the trailers.

The guys adjusted to their new environment and continued to customize their rooms, buying the fridges and microwaves they'd promised themselves, and some buying small, cheap Iraqi TV's to use with the various game consoles they'd brought in the hopes of having some free time to enjoy them. DJ and Joey's room became their regular hangout as they'd planned, and their time off was filled with video game tournaments, jam sessions, card games, and general goofing around, with all of them contributing to keeping the fridge stocked with drinks and snacks. The shared work and play only served to increase the bond between them as they each learned more about the others, although they all knew that the relationships formed would be almost impossible to explain to anyone who hadn't lived through a deployment. With things pretty much as good as they could get, the news that the cargo planes had arrived carrying Air Force mail seemed like the icing on the proverbial cake. The squad gathered around Sergeant Heard, waiting in anticipation to see whose names might be called out, to step forward and receive something from home. For some, it was a letter that they tucked into their pockets and retreated to their rooms to read in private. Others, such as JDub and Billy, received large boxes, which they just knew would be filled with their favorite goodies from home, but for some, like JJ and Justin, there was nothing. They hadn't even gathered with the rest of the group, knowing they had no one back home that would even notice their absence, let alone care enough to write them or send them a care package.

"Guys, can we all gather in your room to open this up?" Billy asked DJ and Joey. "I'm sure I'll have some things I'll want to share out, and I'd like JJ and Justin to be part of the experience, without making them feel like I've singled them out 'cos I feel sorry for them."

"Me too!" JDub added. "You guys have probably guessed I've got a sweet tooth. I bet my mama's sent some home baking and a ton of candy."

"That's real nice of you two guys. Of course, you can, right DJ?"

151

"Sure," DJ replied, although he'd hoped for some peace to read the letter from Clara that he was clutching to his chest. "Go get them and we'll see you all there in a few."

JJ and Justin looked uncomfortable as they gathered in the party room feeling set apart from the others for the first time during the deployment. Sensing their awkwardness, the others rallied to ensure the whole thing became a group experience.

"Mine first," JDub declared.

He placed his large box on the floor, splitting open the packaging tape with his knife, but holding the flaps in place. "Okay, everyone gather round and close your eyes. I'll whip it open, and everybody dive in, like a lucky dip!"

"This isn't fair," JJ protested. "I've got nothing to share."

"Neither have most of us; we only got letters, and maybe, if we're lucky, some pictures," Joey replied.

JDub looked at JJ, his face deadly serious, his eyes, and tone pleading. "You've got to, man. You don't understand. I have a good idea of what will be in here, and if you guys don't help, not only will I make myself sick, but I won't fit into my uniform by the end of the week, and my ass will look huge in camouflage."

The men stared at JDub for a second before he could hold his serious expression no longer, breaking out into an infectious laughing fit, which had them all guffawing. Any tension felt over the mail delivery was gone, and they all dived into JDub's box, exclaiming with delight over the treats they pulled out.

152

"I feel like a kid at Halloween," Billy mumbled, his mouth full as he wolfed down one of his favorite candy bars.

"OMG, Dr. Pepper," JJ cried out. "May I have one?"

"Sure, help yourself, but don't you want to chill it first?"

"Nah," he replied, popping the can. "It's fine as it is. You know I'll make this up to you, right?"

"Yeah, with those special talents of yours, I know. Now, I bet you never got this at Halloween," JDub said, pulling out a large, circular, sealed plastic tub.

Reverently, he opened the lid. The contents inside were double wrapped, first in greaseproof paper and then tightly in saran wrap. He undid both carefully, revealing a triple layered cake that had almost survived the long journey. The frosting was mashed all over the paper, the pecans and walnuts that once decorated the top no longer in a display that resembled enhancement. Icing letters were broken or partially crushed, making them unreadable.

"Aww, that's a shame," Billy said. "I bet it looked really pretty."

JDub ran his finger over the greaseproof paper, loading it with a huge blob of the light caramel colored frosting. He popped his finger into his mouth and closed his eyes in bliss.

"Still tastes delicious," he finally declared. "But it won't stay even close to fresh for long now that's it open. Grab some paper plates and we'll dish it up. Might as well eat it while we can."

As the men dished up the cake, using a spoon to scrape some of the toppings back onto their pieces, JDub read out his letter from his family, unashamedly laughing and crying at various points, the others laughing along with him, and patting his shoulder or giving him an encouraging light punch on the arm during the more emotional parts. Once he'd finished, the others followed, taking turns at reading out their letters from home, sharing anything that had been sent, and proudly showing off pictures that had been included. Soon, only DJ's letter remained unopened.

He looked at the expectant faces turned towards him. He hesitated, unsure about sharing this special moment after waiting so long for it to arrive. His and Clara's love was sacred, and it almost felt like a betrayal to share her private words with the group. He reminded himself that he'd taken quite a few photographs of the moment, of the men sharing their prizes, their emotions while reading their letters. *Once she sees those, she'll understand why I had to do it;* he told himself, the thought of not telling her about it never even crossing his mind. Feeling more confident, he tore open the letter, anxious to read the words of love that had traveled so many miles to get to him.

"Dearest David," he began, then paused to clear his throat before continuing. "Dearest David, I hope this letter finds you in good health and that things are going as well as could be expected over there."

He hesitated once more; confused over the formal and almost cold beginning. He caught the glances of the others, knowing they shared his feelings regarding the words he'd read so far. Desperate to reach the part where she talked of how much she missed him, he carried on.

"I realize this is far from good timing, and it's the last thing you need to hear during a deployment, but I felt it only fair that I tell you right away. I'm so sorry, David, but I'm sure you'll agree that our marriage hasn't been all it should be for some time now. It isn't anyone's fault, I think we just married too young, and we've both changed as we've grown. What the fuck? What is this?"

DJ looked around the stunned group, his face a mask of sheer panic. Seeing the pity and embarrassment staring back at him, he slumped, letting the letter fall from his hands. "She's leaving me isn't she?" he whimpered.

"I'm afraid it sounds like it; I'm sorry man."

"We don't know for sure; maybe she just wants to set up counseling or something for when you get home?"

"Don't give up hope; you can win her back."

"This might be just a reaction to you being away again, maybe everything will be fine once your home."

DJ sat crossed legged on his bunk. As the flood of responses came from the guys, he put his arms up over his head, trying to block them out, rocking himself gently back and forth. "No, no, no, no, no, no... this can'thappen," he half-whispered, half-moaned.

Joey moved to sit beside him. "We can't be sure what's happening yet, not until you read the rest of it."

DJ looked up into Joey's soft eyes, his own red-rimmed from the sting of unshed tears. "I can't," he said, his voice cracking and breaking.

"I could read it to you if you want I mean."

DJ's nod was almost imperceptible, but Joey caught it. He picked the letter up from where it had fallen, finding the place where DJ had left off.

"With every tour, you come home different, not the same man I fell in love with. I don't blame you for that; you're just not strong enough to not let it change you, and can't leave it behind when you need to. Before you left, things just weren't the same between us, and at times, I feel as if you'd actually rather be there anyway. All the photographs, all the wanting to tell me about every detail, it's not natural, David, and to be honest, I was relieved when you received word of your next deployment.

Believe me; it hurts me just as much as I know it will hurt you when I tell you that I found I didn't miss you when you left."

Joey hesitated as a piercing keening came from DJ, his head still covered, as if he could ease his pain by muffling the words. George moved to DJ's opposite side and wrapped a strong arm around his shoulders, hugging him tight to still the rocking that was growing increasingly frantic. Steeling himself against the pain, he knew he was inflicting upon his friend, Joey continued, knowing he had to reach the end.

"Trust me when I say I would rather have waited until you were home to tell you in person, but there's been a development that has forced me into having to tell you straight away because I couldn't live with myself otherwise. I've been seeing someone, David, a soldier like yourself, only one that can leave the war behind when he needs to. His name's Sgt. Greg Saddler and he's a good man, David; he makes me happy. I think you'd even like him if you got to know him. He's asked me to move in with him, so I needed to let you know I'd be gone when you come home. I'll leave my house keys with your mother once I've gathered my things.

Once again, I'm sorry to have to tell you this way, but I think we both know it's for the best. Please stay safe out there. Clara."

Joey dropped his head and released a deep, resigned sigh as he came to the end, his heart breaking for his friend. He folded the letter and placed it carefully back in the envelope, placing it on the bed beside DJ, unable to find the words of comfort he wanted to express, aware that nothing he could say could help ease the pain.

When DJ finally looked up, Joey felt the icy grip of genuine fear, for there was no sign of the man he'd grown to love. DJ's eyes were cold, dead, devoid of emotion, empty of the warm and caring personality they all knew.

"I'll fucking kill them," he said, his voice low, menacing. "I'll fucking kill them both."

At that moment, every single one of them believed him.

Chapter Eleven: Celebration

Joey had spoken privately to Sergeant Heard, gaining his agreement that DJ would be more of a liability trying to carry out his shift that day. He'd ordered him to make sure that DJ stayed behind in his room.

"Pick someone to babysit him too, I don't want anyone doing anything stupid on my watch," he'd added. "Oh, and make sure he gets it together and is back to work tomorrow at the latest. I sympathize, but we've got a job to do out here, and I won't have it said that any of my men didn't pull their weight."

"Yes, Sergeant," Joey said, understanding his position and agreeing with him.

If DJ couldn't snap out of it on his own, Joey fully intended to kick his ass until he saw some signs of the soldier he knew. After giving it some thought, he decided that George would be best equipped to stay behind and keep an eye on the broken Specialist. The others would chatter, offering what they believed to be useful opinions and advice, or attempt to cajole DJ around before he was ready. George, on the other hand, had the same ability as Joey to hold his tongue, keep his thoughts to himself, and let someone be. He would sit quietly in the room, maybe strumming his guitar, maybe reading, follow DJ if he happened to move, but wouldn't speak unless spoken to first. He would be a shadow – a specter that would only intervene if absolutely necessary.

George accepted the news of his new assignment for the day in his usual unflappable and quiet manner, taking up his position on one of the folding chairs before Joey left, only glancing once in the direction of the bunk where DJ lay facing the wall, curled into the fetal position. He nodded to the hesitating Joey, letting him know he had it covered.

As Joey suspected, the talk that morning while they worked was dominated by various ways to cheer DJ up, although their resources and options were severely limited – with only their guitars, music, and a few video games at their disposal.

"I know there's at least one ball around, how about a soccer match?" Billy asked.

"I've never heard him talk about soccer," Craig replied. "Besides, maybe the last thing he wants to do is be around a bunch of other guys."

"Something with just us then," JDub mused, trying to think of something different from the usual way they spent their downtime. "If George were here he'd suggest boxing. I can see it being a good way for DJ to release some of that anger."

159

"Yeah, but George's got the advantage. He'd just kick all our butts and make us feel like losers. DJ needs something to boost him, not make him feel like less of a man," Justin said, receiving murmurs of agreement from the others.

"I've heard him express an interest in learning to play guitar, maybe Craig or Joey could start teaching him, give him something else to focus on?"

"Not a bad suggestion, Billy, and I can see it working down the line a little. Don't know if it'll be much good right now, though," Joey said.

"There's only one thing for it," JJ declared. "We need to throw him a party. A loud, obnoxious, get-absolutely-shit-faced-and-talk-bullshit-for-hours party. Let him rant, rave, cry, fight, dance, whatever he needs to do, then forget it all by morning."

"Best suggestion yet."

"Sounds good to me."

"I'd go for that."

"What do you think, Joey?"

Joey smiled. "It sounds good, guys, but I can foresee some problems. Firstly, where are we going to get the booze and secondly, how do you plan to get away with that in CHUville? We'd be shut down within fifteen minutes."

"I've been thinking about that," JJ answered, "and I've already got a plan. Why don't we check out those bunkers?"

"You mean the bunkers that have been fenced off with 'Do Not Enter' signs plastered all around them?" Billy asked.

"Yep, those bunkers. In fact, I figured we could actually check out the one that the Haji almost got himself killed for refusing to enter; see if we can find out what his problem was. It could add some serious excitement to the night."

Joey snorted. "He was probably just claustrophobic or something, but I'm not completely opposed to the idea of using the bunkers. Way out there; we could make as much noise as we like. It would mean crossing the base after dark. Not only would we get our asses handed to us on a plate if we were caught, but we'd be exposed to the rocket fire. Do we think it's worth it?"

The men looked around, catching each other's gaze then answering Joey in unison. "Hell, yeah!"

"Anyway," JJ added, "we've got the incoming warning system in place now so we can take cover if we hear it."

"Yeah right! They're only designed to warn the TOC, we can barely hear those crappy little speakers half way across base, never mind right out at the bunkers. Besides, they only report about half the air strikes anyway."

"You chickening out, Craig?" Justin asked.

"No way! I was just saying."

"All right then, we've got a starting point," Joey said. "We need to do some recon of the bunkers and make sure they're accessible, and we need to try and organize some decent booze."

"I can take care of both," JJ said. "I'll need a few days to arrange the booze, and I can't promise it'll be decent, but I can do the recon tonight. Fancy a short excursion, JDub?"

161

"Sure, I'll come with you, but where are you planning on getting this booze from?"

"I've got a Black Water contact that'll be more than willing to help us out; don't worry about it."

"Okay, so the only problem left is how we get DJ to agree to it," Billy said. "I don't know about you guys, but I don't mind saying that he scared the crap out of me back there. Who's going to be the one to tell him we think he's gonna snap and freak out on us, so we have a party to try and prevent it?"

"How about we don't put it quite like that?" Joey replied. "How about we say we're looking to relieve some of the boredom and stress by cutting loose a little, and that the party is to celebrate staying alive out here for six months?"

"If it doesn't work and he won't join us, can we still go ahead?"

"Sure, JJ, but I'll do my best to make sure he doesn't skip out on us."

"Thanks, Joey, you're the best."

"Don't ever forget it."

With the tentative plans made, the guys could talk of little else and JJ could hardly wait for nightfall to carry out the recon mission. He and JDub snuck out well after curfew, relying on only the moonlight to light their way across the base. They'd both ensured their trousers were tucked in hard and their desert boots tied as tightly as possible before leaving, knowing that standing on scorpions, spiders, or snakes in the dark was a strong possibility. Their boots offered them some protection, and at least the creatures couldn't scuttle or slither inside their trouser legs. They daren't use a flashlight until they were at least past the shop hangars, and maybe not even then if there were patrols out doing safety checks. Sergeant Heard seemed a decent sort, but even he would have limits, and finding his guys sneaking around base after the curfew for all those that weren't on shift would definitely be pushing him a step too far.

The hangars and FARP station were busy that night, the helicopters still coming and going from important missions. Unable to sneak around the back due to the landmines, JJ and JDub walked purposely among those that were working, hoping that everyone assumed they had a right to be there. They went unchallenged, but once they were past the thriving activity, they needed to pause to allow their eyes to become accustomed to the dark once more.

"Ready to do some fence climbing?" JJ asked as they began to move forward towards the outskirts of the base where the bunkers were located.

JDub groaned. "What height are we talking about?"

"I don't know, maybe eight feet," JJ replied with a nonchalant shrug. "Nothing we didn't cover in training."

"As long as I don't rip anything; my sewing skills suck."

After an answering chuckle from JJ, they walked on in silence until they'd reached their destination. They found the gates to be higher than expected, but unlocked, swinging noiselessly open as they gave them a push.

"Well, isn't that handy," JDub said.

163

"Yeah, they probably trust us to follow the rules and think the fence and signs are all they need."

"Guess they didn't bank on you and Justin. You two together are a match made in heaven as far as trouble is concerned."

With a shared grin, they entered the off-limits area.

"Can't we just check out this first one?"

"No, I want to use the one that caused the trouble. I want to see what had the Haji so terrified. It was the third one along, right?"

"Yep."

They carried on walking until they were standing outside the much talked about bunker. It looked the same as the rest. The part showing above ground was an interrupted pyramid; the four flat sides rising sharply before being cut off to a flat top instead of continuing up to a peak. Mounted on top was a box-type structure with a window-shaped hole to provide a lookout point. Moving around the structure, they found the entrance located on the far side from the dirt track road that ran past the odd buildings.

The entrance looked like a doorframe that had been laid down on the sloping outer wall, except it was made of thick concrete and was extremely narrow. Dry, brown weeds and grass were beginning to grow through cracks in the structure and nothing stirred this far from the sights and sounds of the busy base camp. The whole area had a derelict, abandoned look and feel that conjured up nightmare scenarios that they both had to fight to push aside.

"Shit, this place gives me the creeps," JDub said with a shiver.

"All part of the fun."

164

JJ clicked on his flashlight and shone it down the entrance; so dark that the light barely penetrated. "I can't see shit. I'm going in."

"I'll stay here and keep a look out."

"Oh no you don't. You're coming with me."

JJ moved forward, giving JDub no time to protest.

"Damn, they must have all been skinny fuckers," JDub complained as he inched his way down the narrow corridor behind JJ.

The corridor was shorter than the engulfed light had made it appear, and at the end, they were faced with a hinged metal door.

"If we've come all this way and it's locked I'm–"

JDub's words cut off as JJ turned the handle and the door swung open, the creak of dried out, disused hinges echoing loudly in the space beyond.

"Sounds like it's pretty big in there."

"Well, what are you waiting for, get your flashlight in there, and let's see what we're dealing with."

"All right, all right, keep your hair on."

JJ took two steps inside, JDub close on his heels. He swung his flashlight around, lighting up the corners of a good space with only some old Russian ammo crates and other assorted garbage lying around. Both breathed a little easier as they looked around the place.

"Looks perfect. We can use the ammo crates for seats and the laptop. The floor doesn't look too bad either, though."

"Great. Can we get out of here now?"

"What's the matter, JDub, you scared?"

"Not scared, no, more... uncomfortable. It's just too damn quiet out here, makes it a little eerie."

"I know what you mean. We're kind of used to the noise of the siren, the rockets, the chatter, the birds and trucks at all hours; this sudden silence almost makes you feel like you've gone deaf, doesn't it?"

"Time to go?"

"Yeah, we've seen all we need to see."

The two men exited the bunker, closing the door firmly behind them, careful to leave everything exactly as it was when they found it, so they didn't draw any attention to their activity. They made their way back the same way as they had come, stealthy until they couldn't hide; walking as if they belonged through the occupied areas. Reaching the CHU unit, they were surprised to find Joey standing outside with an unlit cigarette in his hand.

"Since when did you smoke?"

"I don't," Joey replied with a shrug. "It's just a cover, so no one asks why I'm out here."

"Why are you out here?" JDub asked, giving Joey a cheeky grin.

"Waiting to make sure you idiots got back here without getting yourselves into a world of trouble and, if I'm honest, taking a break from DJ."

"He's still bad?"

"Worse. He's not even crying anymore, just staring, completely silent, and those eyes." Joey shook his head in dismay. "I've only ever seen a look like that once before when we got two boys back after a team of five were captured and held for interrogation for three weeks.

They had that same, empty, dead look as if their souls had been ripped right out of them and there was nothing left but a shell."

"Quit it, Joey! He was scaring the hell out of me as it was and you've just made it twenty times worse."

"Just don't let him know it. Don't treat him any differently than you did before. So, what did you find?"

"A perfect place for a party!" JJ enthused; keen to change the subject. "Plenty of space and a solid metal door, ideal for soundproofing. Once we shut that behind us, no one would ever know we were in there, even if they came sniffing around outside. We didn't even have to scale the fence; the gatewasn't locked."

"That's useful. Since we don't have any climbing to do, we can safely take the laptop and our guitars. So we're pretty much good to go?"

"Yep, just as soon as my contact comes through with the goodies – and that shouldn't be more than a day or two."

"Good. Let me handle DJ. We should all get back to our rooms now and not push our luck."

They all retired for the night; theirexcitement is only marred by their battle's misery.

Next morning it was business as usual. DJ joined them for their shift without requiring any prompting, but the team was subdued, almost afraid to crack jokes and trade the usual insults for fear of appearing disrespectful to his situation. They all watched him closely but other than appearing robotic and lackluster; he was as efficient and careful as ever while carrying out his duties. Nobody raised the issue of the party, waiting for Joey to take the lead as he'd requested. It was late afternoon before he broached the subject.

Hey, DJ, the guys and I have been thinking."

DJ gave a quick glance in Joey's direction but didn't respond.

Joey carried on talking, ignoring the silence and working as he spoke, his eyes averted from his friend. "Since we've managed to survive six months of this tour, we reckoned we should mark the occasion with a party. Figured we could sneak out to those old bunkers and have a blast; take the guitars and your laptop with us. JJ's taking care of refreshments."

The others waited nervously, trying to pretend they weren't listening as DJ still made no comment. Joey tried again.

"So, you up for it?"

The answer was singular. "Sure."

The tension was broken with the acquiescence. Even though it had been delivered as a reluctant grunt, at least it was given. Softly spoken conversations started up around the shop, the guys still careful not to appear overly exuberant or too happy for fear of triggering DJ's anger or despair.

***

The night of the party was clear, the sky filled with the celestial luminescence of twinkling stars and a perfect crescent moon. The Armament Dogs loaded up and headed out, curtailing their excitement to maintain stealth until they passed the hangars and well on the way to their destination. Reaching the gate to the bunker area and finding it still unlocked, JJ let out a muted whoop.

"Shut it," Craig hissed. "There could be eyes and ears in those mountains right over there. If you get me blown up before this party, I swear I'll haunt you for the rest of your life."

"I'm sure I'd enjoy the company," JJ wisecracked. "Follow me, gentlemen."

He led them through the fenced-off area, ignoring the muttered comments from the others.

"Why do I feel like someone's watching me from every one of those windows?"

"I can't even think what these freaky buildings look like, but I can't help feeling that they're some kind of incubator, just waiting to hatch something awful."

"Watch sci-fi much as a kid?"

"Get lost."

"I'm hoping to, right down at the bottom of a bottle."

"And then the bodies of a hundred dead Hajis will crawl out of the ground and—"

"Shut the fuck up; I mean it!"

Reaching the third bunker, JJ stopped and turned back to the group. "If you children have finished spooking each other with scary stories, this is the one."

JJ eased himself down the narrow, concrete corridor and opened the metal door before stepping inside and turning to light the way for the others with his flashlight. Once they were all inside, and the doors closed firmly behind them, they all clicked on flashlights and inspected their venue for the night.

"Not as great for soundproofing as you thought," Joey remarked. "You didn't take into account the sniper lookout up there."

"Not a problem. This level was probably just for storage, so all we need to do is go down to the level below and we've got it made."

In perfect agreement, the men made their way to the concrete stairs cut into the floor and proceeded downwards, with Joey taking the lead. Once down, they inspected their surroundings. Above, the remnants left behind by previous occupants had been fairly innocuous, but here, they were more ominous, with crates bearing poison warning signs and metal containers that looked as if they would contain chemical weapons.

"Holy crap! I wonder if there's anything still inside them."

"Justin, believe me when I say it would be best not to find out," George said, giving them a wide berth.

"I bet this is what the Haji knew about and didn't want to get anywhere close to. It must be some pretty serious stuff," JJ said, wandering over beside Justin to inspect the containers.

"Will you two get away from that!" Craig said, exasperated with his battles. "Those containers could be so old, the contents have leaked out onto the ground there.Anyway, I thought we were here to have a good time. When's this party supposed to be happening?"

"If some of you go back up and bring down enough of those ammo crates for us to sit on and one for the laptop, it can start right now."

Craig, Billy, JDub, and George complied, each carrying two down and Billy running back up for another. The guys placed the crates in a circle, unloaded all their gear, and took a seat. When DJ made no move to unpack his rucksack, Joey reached towards it.

"May I?"

DJ nodded. Joey proceeded to pull out and set up the laptop and Bluetooth Bose speaker pleased to see that DJ had at least thought to charge it fully before taking it out tonight. He scrolled through the extensive playlists, avoiding anything that sounded even vaguely romantic or slushy. Picking one that sounded promising, he was relieved to find it contained a selection of rock and metal tracks that should keep everyone happy. It was just what they needed to get this party going. He clicked play and adjusted the volume to a suitable level to allow them to talk for the moment.

While he'd been occupied, JDub and Justin had unpacked the selection of chips they'd brought, along with the cheap, overly sweet version of Fanta that the bazaar sold. It was the only soda they currently stocked so it would have to do. The others had also brought snacks, but it was the contents of JJ's duffel that they were most interested in, urging him to display his spoils. First, he produced two aluminum cans similar to soda cans, the label black with Russian writing.

"Russian vodka," he informed them proudly. "You could probably fuel the birds with this stuff. I could only get two, but I think it'll pack a mean punch and besides, that's not all I got."

He then produced two bottles and held them up for inspection. The bottles had a gold label with silhouettes of four men. Justin held out his hand, and JJ passed one to him for closer inspection.

"Four Brothers Whiskey, I've never heard of it."

"Cheap, local Haji crap, but if the beer was anything to go by it'll be drinkable and should do the job. DJ, you want to be the guinea pig?"

DJ took the offered bottle, twisted off the cap, and took a long draw from the bottle. He coughed after swallowing – the raw, cheaply made booze leaving his throat with a slight burn. Everyone looked on, awaiting his verdict.

"Pretty rough, but it'll do."

It was the closest to normal DJ had been for three days, and they allowed themselves to laugh, relaxing as the bottle was passed around and each took a swig. As they drank by the light of their flashlights, Billy looked around the concrete room.

"You know what; something doesn't make sense to me."

"There's a surprise," Craig said, rolling his eyes.

"What's on your mind, Billy," Joey asked.

"Well, if the top level was maybe for storage and to have a man or two up in the watchtower part, and down here would have been their main hideout and protection, how come this room is smaller than the one above?"

"It's actually a good question," JDub said. "You would have thought someone who went to the trouble of creating bunkers of this size and solid construction would ensure that the safest part would be the most substantial part."

George's interest was piqued. He picked up his flashlight and, starting from the door, worked his way around the walls, examining each section carefully.

"What exactly are you looking for?"

"I don't know. Something somebody didn't want anyone to find maybe."

"Ooh, you mean like hidden doors and secret tunnels," Justin said then laughed hysterically. "We're in a bunker on a military base, not a medieval castle."

"Don't kid yourself. I can't think of anyone who has more secrets than the damn military, and that's in any country," George replied, continuing his search. "And here we are, only it's not so secret, more of an optical illusion, especially in the dark."

"What have you found, George," Joey asked, wandering over to take a look.

"This wall here. It's built as solidly as the outer walls, but look, it stops about two and a half feet short, so there's a gap. Because the outer wall isn't far behind and the same, you really don't notice it that much. Especially in dim lighting; and you would have to assume they wouldn't have it too brightly lit unless they used to have something that covered the stairwell to ensure the light didn't creep up and glow out the lookouts."

"See, I told you there was something odd," Billy declared, vindicated by George's discovery. "You can scoff, Justin, but I bet they used that as a secret storage area. The gap's so narrow all they would need to do is stack one pile of crates in front of it, and it's completely hidden from view."

"Question is what would they have been hiding?"

"Why don't we go and take a look," Justin said with a grin. "Maybe whatever it was is still there."

He grabbed his flashlight from the ground and hurried over, pushing past the other two men, keen to be the first to explore the new area. He slid through the gap and disappeared from view, coming back a second later, his eyes bright with excitement.

"Nothing actually back there... except another set of concrete stairs! There's a whole other level beneath us, guys, and I vote that we go exploring."

"Oh shit, give me another hit on that bottle first, I've got a feeling I'm going to need it," JDub muttered.

The bottle had done another full round before the guys all gathered their flashlights.

"What about all our stuff, do you think it's safe to leave it?"

"Yeah, it'll be fine," Joey said. "However, I would suggest that we all put back on any kit we've taken off and brought along our rifles, just in case."

"Seriously?" Justin asked, glancing at DJ for confirmation. "You think somebody could still be down there?"

DJ nodded, backing up the other Specialist's advice.

"I'm not saying it's likely," Joey added, "but you have to expect the unexpected. There could be someone or something that could cause us harm down there and even if there isn't, being prepared for it can't hurt. If anyone had been scrambling to hide down here, we'd have heard them as soon as we came in the door. Down on a third sub-level is a whole different ball game."

"Maybe it would be better if we just left it alone then," Craig said.

"Nope. We've got to check it out now that we know it exists. We can't be up here getting shit-faced if there are a group of Hajis with weapons down there just waiting for their chance to ambush us."

"Isn't that just great. It's supposed to be a party, not a mission."

"Yeah, well, it will be, just as soon as we declare it clear."

The team kitted up and shouldered their weapons with no more arguments, some hoping to get this over with quickly, others excited by the added adventure. They left the music playing, figuring if there were anyone to hear, they would have heard it already. Turning it off would only raise suspicion while leaving it playing might help mask their approach.

Justin moved to take the lead, but Joey stopped him with an arm across his chest and moved ahead of him, his protective instincts kicking in. As one, they moved in single file, adopting their method of moving silently through enemy territory, communicating with hand signals only, moving only when the man on point indicated it was safe to do so. Joey slid through the gap and quickly took in his surroundings before turning off his flashlight and moving towards the embedded stairway. He took the steps slowly, one at a time, pausing between each to listen for any telltale sounds in the darkness below. Now that the flashlights were off, the stairwell and beyond were pitch black, not even a sliver of natural light to penetrate it this far below ground.

As Joey stepped from the final step, he felt and heard the ground beneath his feet change from concrete to rough, gritty sand. He grimaced at the noise he'd made and waited, poised, one foot on either surface. Nothing stirred. Reassured, he moved on, trying to keep his footfalls as light as possible. Once he figured he'd moved forward enough for everyone to be clear of the stairs, he did a quick head count by touch, assuring himself in the dark that everyone was still with him. Unable to tell who was who without further inspection, he tugged on a couple of rifle straps, informing two men that he wanted them to unshoulder their weapons and have them at the ready. The rest, he fumbled for the hands that he knew would still be holding their flashlights, giving them a tap.

"On two," he whispered, having to count in a hushed tone, as even hand signals would be useless when he couldn't see his own in front of his face. They had automatically formed in a back-to-back circle, the most protective stance they could take. On Joey's cue, they turned on their flashlights, the bright LED's suddenly illuminating the space. They fought the assault on their eyes, blinking rapidly and ignoring the pain to focus on what they might be facing.

"Holy shit," Justin breathed. "Look at this place."

There were no crazed insurgents waiting to ambush them, no caches of top-secret weapons or booby traps that they could see at the moment, but still, the place was startling.

Rather than being manmade, it would seem as if this level was natural, or at least blasted out of the very bedrock of the earth. The walls were rough, natural stone, the ground the same sand as outside, except uncompressed by hundreds of feet, vehicles, and aircraft.

"It's a cave," Craig said.

"Only it doesn't have an entrance that I can see, other than the one we came down," Joey replied as the men moved slowly round in their circle, careful not to cover new ground just yet.

"Maybe it got filled in by an explosion or something."

"Maybe. Or maybe it was filled in deliberately so no one would find this place."

Joey used the butt of his rifle to check the area infront of him, stepping only where he'd been able to check. Rummaging in the sand, he gathered several good-sized rocks. "Field glasses on and back up the way you came, men. Make sure you follow your previous footsteps."

They all did as he asked, except DJ, who copied Joey's earlier actions and soon had his own handful of rocks.

"I said back up."

"No, you back up. I've got this."

"DJ, don't do this."

"All right, we do it together. You take that side; I'll take this one."

Joey knew DJ wasn't going to back down so he gave in with a nod, knowing that an argument would only undermine each other's authority in front of the young and impressionable soldiers standing behind them. He looked around, seeing them gathered at the base of the stairs.

"Get back up," he snapped.

"No way. We're in this together, so if there's any IED's planted down here, we all face it. We're not leaving you."

Joey made his decision, figuring they could stand here all night arguing, or he could get this over with and find out for sure. He tossed a rock. It thudded gently and harmlessly into the sand, the walls and floor seeming to deaden and quickly absorb the sound. He threw another, then another, as DJ did the same on the other side of the room. Their hands empty, they both examined the area they had covered.

"Looks like we got it pretty good, I think we're clear."

"Great," Justin said, removing his goggles and stepping forward. "I want to see what that weird obelisk thing is over at the back."

They had all seen the stubby rock pillar that stood by the back wall but hadn't given it much thought due to more pressing issues. It stood about fourfeet tall, its four sides wide at the bottom and narrowing to a peaked top. It looked like natural stone, but was worn smooth, either by hand or perhaps by the constant blasting of sandstorms if it had ever been above ground at some stage.

"Guys, it's got all sorts of symbols on it."

Their interest piqued, they gathered around the small monument with Justin, examining the carvings.

"It looks like ancient inscriptions," Craig said. "It's actually pretty damn creepy."

"You two know a little Arabic," JDub said to the Specialists. "Does anything look familiar; can you read any of it?"

"This doesn't look like any Arabic I've ever seen," Joey said. "In fact, it doesn't look like any *language* I've ever seen before."

"Me neither, but this could be really old. Look how worn the stone is."

"The walls are covered in it too," JJ announced, running his fingers along the etchings, the stone feeling warm to the touch. "Even I have to admit this feels a bit spooky. Do you think this was some ancient temple or something?"

"It could be. Maybe a sacred area, or even a tomb for an important figure," Joey agreed. "Maybe that's why the Haji didn't want to come down, afraid of disturbing it or desecrating it."

"Fucking A," JDub said. "Joey, why do you always have to say just the right thing to make me want to shit my pants?"

"That's just the Haji whiskey," George said, gaining a nervous laugh from all of them. "But even I have to admit there's an odd atmosphere down here. The hairs on the back of my neck are standing up, and believe me I've been in some pretty bad neighborhoods in Detroit and never felt like this before. It's like you know the danger's there, you just can't see it."

"There doesn't seem to be anything to see, nobody down here, no booby traps rigged as far as we can tell. I think maybe it just has that forbidden feel, the one you used to get when your folks told you not to go somewhere, and you did it anyway," Billy said. "Do you think they maybe only found it themselves when they built the bunkers?"

"Might have, or maybe they built the bunkers to hide it," Craig replied.

"Either way," Justin said, "I think we should move the party down here. It's creepily awesome, and I think the weird acoustics will be great for a jam session. What do you say, DJ?"

"Sure, whatever. We'll go get the gear down."

Joey wasn't too sure about the decision but let it slide since the others seemed to be in agreement. DJ was still way too quiet for his liking, and he just wanted everyone to hit the bottles hard and relax as soon as possible. While the others went to fetch the gear, he carried out a final check over on the place to assure himself that no hidden dangers lurked within the mysterious underground cavity. Satisfied that he'd missed nothing, he helped the others to arrange the crates in a semi-circle in front of the obelisk. Reaching for his duffel bag, he withdrew handfuls of green glow sticks and passed them round for everybody to crack. They were frequently used for night FARP operations, so plentiful supplies were always available in the Avionics Maintenance Shelter, and he'd figured a few would be no great loss to the US military.

The neon green light from the sticks they dotted around only added to the eeriness of the cave, seeming to illuminate and emphasize the etchings and give them the appearance of an almost supernatural self-luminescence. It also tinged each face with a light hint of ghoulish green once they turned off their flashlights. They made short work of getting the music playing, the familiar sounds of modern compositions going some way to dispelling the ancient and taboo feel of their surroundings. Once again, the whiskey bottles began circulating, and snacks were munched on as they talked and joked.

They all had at least a pleasant buzz going by the time George picked up his guitar. Joey reached over to stop the music from the laptop, shutting it down to preserve the battery. George had already begun to play and, recognizing the song; Joey joined in while the others guys listened and drank. When they played a rock track that everybody knew, they all sang along, yelling out the chorus at the top of their voices, JDub chair dancing – much to the amusement of the others. Joey smiled at their antics. This wasexactly what they all needed, especially DJ. Reaching the end of the current song, Joey turned to George.

"Do you know any CCR or Eagles?"

"Not off the top of my head, but I might be able to pick it up and join in as we go. What you got?"

"This one's probably the easiest," Joey replied, starting a well-known riff, much to the delight of his audience who whooped and cheered his choice.

"Yeah, Bad Moon Rising, go Joey!"

As he played, Joey began to sing, calling out the chord changes to George as he did so, adding them into the lyrics. When the two guitarists reached the chorus, the guys went wild, singing along to the point where Joey had to yell for George to hear the chords. After the second verse, George had the chords and Joey didn't need to call them out anymore, just sing with the rest of them.

He paled as he sang the words of the final verse, a fact that went unnoticed by the others in the green light of the glow sticks. He hadn't given the lyrics much consideration, only thinking that it was a popular song with an easy riff and simple chord changes for George to pick up. Recalling the unnerving words spoken by DJ only a few short days ago, the final line of the final verse held poignant significance that chilled Joey to the bone. As he followed George's lead and played two encores of the rousing chorus, he glanced at the Specialist. To his relief, DJ appeared to be applying no special significance to the lyrics, simply waving one of the whiskey bottles around wildly as he belted out the chorus with the others. Joey brought the song to a hurried close and quickly moved on.

"That was great, man," George exclaimed. "Thanks for teaching me that one. What's next?"

Joey proceeded to teach George a few more of his favorite songs, mentally recalling the time when he'd been the student, and someone was teaching them to him. He felt a sense of pride at passing them along, almost as if he were honoring the man by doing so.

The thought made Joey smile and memories of the man flooded his thoughts as he played. Larry was one of his father's best friends – an ex-army badass if ever there was one – and the only time he ever opened up about his thoughts and opinions on the army, love, and life in general, was after he'd had a few choice adult beverages. At all other times, he was a stoic man who would hold his tongue on most issues. He was the one that had introduced Joey to many things as he'd grown from a boy to a man; things such as Wild Turkey 101, Army lifestyle, living life on the edge, and best of all, acoustic guitar.

With the guys all cutting loose around him – more than a little buzzed now by the Iraqi booze – and George having mastered the current song, Joey laughed aloud as he relaxed and let the memories overtake him. When Larry and his wife Diane came to visit, or when he and his Dad would call on them, the couple would both get shit-faced, Mamma Diane's preferences being Hot Damn Cinnamon Schnapps or Busch light, both mixed with a blend of classic rock that she would beg the boys to play. They would happily oblige with a selection from The Eagles, Bob Seger, or Creedence Clearwater Revival. Her voice drunkenly belting out the lyrics over the twin acoustic guitars playing classic rock was what was missing from the gathering tonight for Joey. He recalled how he had to strain his ears over the sound to hear the chord transitions that Larry would call out to him as they played, just as he had done for George. Those were some of Joey's happiest memories.

He recalled how Larry – at least ten years before any producer even had the glimmer of an idea for a television show – used to talk about his time as a King Crab fisherman in Alaska. He closed his eyes and let the memory of the man's voice wash over him. *It was the most dangerous job in the world at the time, and probably still is. We had to stay awake for days on end, our faces numb, our muscles aching from the cold, fingers ready to drop off in spite of our heavy gloves, beating the side of the boat with whatever we*

183

could find to keep the ice from freezing and capsizing us. Still, it was one of the best times I ever had. Never stop living on the edge, son.

To Joey, it wasn't just advice. He'd adopted the phrase as a creed, and it was one he still lived by today, at least when he wasn't trying to keep a bunch of green teenagers alive or prevent them from being thrown in the brig. He snorted with laughter at his last thought. He wasn't exactly doing a good job of that tonight. Being caught out here, or even staggering back to their housing units in this state, would have them all in deep shit. *What the heck,* he thought, *when you spend a year, or more, with death loitering in every shadow just waiting for his chance to claim you, everybody deserves a night like this now and again.* He decided then and there that he would gladly take the rap for this party if anything negative came of it. There was no way he would have denied the guys this opportunity, nor his friend the chance to express himself and get it all out while they were all too damn drunk to even remember it. Deciding that he and George had some catching up to do, and they'd better make it quick before the booze was all gone, he put a limit of two more songs on their playing, letting George chose and took a turn to teach him something he didn't know. When they were done, he booted the laptop back up and returned to the playlist he'd selected earlier.

"So, any of that booze left for us?"

"Oops."

Billy giggled as he held up the whiskey bottle he was holding, less than a finger remaining in the bottom. He grinned sheepishly as he passed it, Joey. The other was already dead in the water, so Joey passed it to George instead.

"We've still got that rocket fuel," Justin said, almost falling off his crate as he reached for one of the cans of Russian vodka that lay at his feet. He managed to snag one and sit upright, looking decidedly dizzy as he did so. "Oh, head rush."

They all laughed at Justin, unaware that their own condition was no better. Joey stood and took the can from him, preventing Justin from leaning over to hand it to him and hitting the deck. Popping the top by ripping the pull-ring, he took a sniff, grimaced, and took a tiny, tentative sip.

"Holy shit, my throat is on fire," he said, coughing and laughing at the same time.

"Here, we got plenty of this left, in fact, no one's touched any of it yet," JDub said, handing him a can of the fizzy orange he'd brought along.

"Thanks."

Joey placed the can of vodka on the ground, holding it between his feet. He opened the soda and took several long gulps, allowing it to soothe the burn in his throat. He then placed the soda can on the ground and poured a decent measure of the vodka into it, filling some of the space he'd created. Picking up the soda can, he took another swig. "Much better," he announced.

"Great idea!"

"That looks good; I'm going to try that."

The cans of soda were passed out and the vodka passed round as everyone copied Joey's rough screwdriver, much of the vodka soaking into the sand beneath their feet as they missed their target by unsteady hands. Protests of wastage and insults were traded among hoots of laughter until finally everyone had a new drink in their hands. The vodka can empty; JJ closed one eye and held it aloft, wavering slightly as he did so.

"It's a difficult shot," Craig mock commentated, his voice deep and hushed. "But if anyone can make it, our man, Jacob 'Jet engine' Johnson is the one. He takes aim…"

JJ launched the can forward, and it hit the obelisk just left of center before ricocheting off the side where it landed in the sand with a soft plop.

"He shoots, he scores," Craig yelled as JJ ran a half lap of honor around the guys and back again, arms open wide to receive the adoration of the imaginary fans while the guys mimicked the sound of a crowd going crazy.

"What the heck is in this stuff?" George asked Joey, holding up his can and shaking his head.

"No idea. Anyone read any Russian?"

"Not me, I'm Irish American," JDub said.

"Well, doesn't that explain a lot!" JJ said, retaking his seat with some difficulty.

"Oh yeah, and what's your heritage then, string bean?"

"German actually," JJ replied with a smug smile.

"Hey, me too," DJ added, volunteering to join in the actual conversation for the first time that night.

The guys glanced at him in surprise, but Joey's warning glare soon dispelled any thoughts of commenting.

"Bet you'd never guess, but I'm part Choctaw," Billy said hurriedly, covering their faux pas.

"You're kidding, right, weren't they supposed to be one of the civilized tribes?" George said. "What went wrong with you?"

"Now that's funny!" Justin said, giggling wildly.

"Cherokee here," Joey said, bumping cans with Billy.

"Well, you know I'm African American, and we know Justin is of Polish descent, so that leaves you, George," Craig said.

"Guess," George said with a grin.

They all studied George through screwed up eyes and began to guess. Twenty minutes later, George declared them all losers.

"Put us out of our misery then. I don't think I'll sleep tonight unless I know," Craig muttered.

"Filipino and Italian," George declared, laughing at the stunned expression on their faces.

"Shit, how were we supposed to get that?" Justin grumbled.

"My Clara had Italian in her blood line."

The men fell silent. The moment had come.

"Yeah?" Joey prompted softly. "How far back?"

"Her great-grandparents made the journey, but the whole family loved to make the claim, passing down the family traditions, not to mention the recipes. God, the meals she used to make for my homecoming! She sure could cook."

DJ dropped his head, staring at his can, which he dangled loosely between his knees. When he raised it again, he had tears in his eyes. "How could she do this to me? How could she send me a Dear John when I'm on deployment? How could she just *leave* me?"

Murmurs of sympathy came from the guys. They'd all expected this moment to come, had organized the party mostly so that it could, but that didn't make it any easier to deal with.

"You know what got me the most? That line, that one fucking line where she said, I think you'd actually like him. I mean, what the fuck, right? She thinks we're gonna be hanging out or something? Having cozy little get-togethers where I pat him on the back and tell him he's a better man than me and to take good care of her, well fuck that! I tell you something else; I do know the bastard."

"You do?" Joey asked; surprised that this was the first he'd heard of this.

"Yeah, was stationed with him for several months back in Hawaii, and he was a smug, self-satisfied, arrogant, uppity prick even then. I don't know what she sees in him."

The Armament Dogs let DJ talk for another hour, joining in and taking his side through his angry rants, sympathizing when he broke down and cried. In their drunken state, they were there for him as much as anyone can be there for someone suffering such intense personal pain. Joey was relieved to see the light in DJ's eyes again, the love and passion when he spoke of Clara, the depth of pain through

188

the shininess of his tears, and the burning rage when he spoke of her new man. It was normal, natural, and light of any kind was good. It meant his friend was still in there.

DJ wound down, his emotions spent, his face drawn and exhausted. Joey couldn't let the night end there; it needed to end on a high. He picked the most upbeat, hard-rocking tracks he could find on the playlists and cranked the volume, returning the men to their earlier exuberance. They carried on that way until the laptop battery had died, the last of the glow sticks had burned out, and the booze was all gone.

"We'd better tidy this mess up and head back," Joey said with a resigned sigh, "before we pass out, or our flashlights give up the ghost on us."

In a stupor, they staggered through their task, gathering their belongings and the rubbish that was strewn around.

"Should we take the crates back up?"

"Nah, leave them down here. We might do this again sometime."

"In another six months maybe, after I've had time to recover."

They made their way up through the levels of the bunker, some clinging to the back of the other's jackets for support and guidance as they navigated the sets of stairs. Once at the metal door, Joey inspected them all, ensuring their battle rattle was correctly in place.

"For God's sake, keep it down on the way back," he instructed as he led them outside. "And close that door behind you whoever's last."

Once outside, the fresh air hit them hard, making them dizzy and turning their legs to flimsy rubber. They weaved their way along behind Joey.

"How come Joey's suddenly got a twin?"

"Shhhh."

"Who are you shushing? You shush."

"Shhhh, both of you."

The drunken, exaggerated whispers had them all laughing and shoving each other and Joey, although amused, wondered how he was going to get them back without being caught. He quickened the pace, hoping a march would help sober them up before they hit occupied areas of the base. One look at them would give the game away right now.

"I don't know, but I've been told…" Craig began at the top of his voice.

"Don't you dare," Joey warned him, "and keep your voice down."

Giving Joey a sulky look, Craig instead hummed a tune just under his breath, tailing off as Joey's plan worked and the brisk pace and cold, desert night air began to clear their heads. By the time they reached the hangars, they were able to walk in some sort of resemblance of a straight line and keep their faces serious until they'd passed.

Their high spirits returned once they'd averted the danger point without being contested, and their capering antics resumed all the way to the CHU's, in spite of Joey's numerous and futile attempts of quieting them down. Their noisy arrival home in the early hours of the morning, along with their inebriated state, wouldn't be missed by other sin the nearby trailers. It was only a matter of time before they found out if it would be ignored and accepted or reported to top. Entirely unconcerned, they dragged their drunken asses to bed with just enough time to catch an hour's sleep before they needed to be up and preparing for their next shift.

Chapter Twelve: Normandy

Joey sat inside the Black Hawk with his eyes closed and his earplugs firmly embedded. In spite of this, he could still hear and feel when the pilot switched from running idle to powering up to fly. He wasn't actually afraid, but his body was already anticipating the takeoff, his stomach lurching and his mind expecting and psychologically creating the light-headed dizziness he would experience when it happened.

The Black Hawks had unlimited torque and power, with the ability to lift straight up from the runway. It was an ability that no pilot would refrain from using during deployment as every aircraft was at its most vulnerable during takeoff. In fact, there probably weren't any circumstances where the pilots wouldn't want to delight in the sheer brute force of the twin turboshaft engines of the machine and shoot it straight into the air. The negative G-force created by the maneuver was worse than the craziest roller coaster ever constructed and no matter how many times Joey traveled in a Black Hawk, he couldn't quite get used to the sensations that ripped right through his insides and left him reeling.

The Hawks were used mainly as troop carriers and logistical support aircraft. Therefore they were lower, longer, and sleeker in design than the birds Joey worked with on a daily basis. It had some safety features such as low detectability and resistance to small arms fire and medium caliber projectiles, but it came nowhere close to the combat-ready and muscled fighting machine that the Kiowa Warrior was. After seeing what had happened to two of those recently, Joey knew that getting out of base and over the surrounding mountains would be touch and go, and if they went down it might well be the end in spite of the energy absorbing seats and crash resistant, self-sealing fuel system.

It was the only reason he could assign to the lack of his battles around him. Specifically designed to carry up to eleven fully equipped troops, and at least three crew members at any one time, the pilot and copilot up front and the crew chief back in the cabin, there was no explanation why his particular team of eight had been split over two birds and that DJ wasn't flying with him, except that they didn't want to lose them all in one go if anything went wrong. His group of Armament Dogs had quickly gained the reputation of being the fastest and most efficient team at turning around the birds and he guessed that the army wanted to try and preserve at least some of them if they came under fire at any point during transit. George and JJ were with him, but the others, minus Justin, were in the second Black Hawk with DJ.

193

"Don't put all your eggs in one basket," Joey muttered, knowing that no one would hear him over the deafening sound of the rotors and engines.

As with most things military, the marching orders had come at short notice. Joey let his mind drift back over the events that had led him to where he was now. A few days had passed and business as usual for the Armament Dogs, the only negative outcome from their party being their blinding headaches and queasy stomachs at work the next day. If anyone had noted their late return and less than sober condition, no one had reported it and caused them any trouble. DJ had been better since he'd had the chance to open up, although Joey wouldn't yet consider him back to his usual self. They'd been gathered in his and DJ's room as normal when a knock had come at the door. Billy had opened it, expressing his surprise as Sergeant Heard had marched in. Joey reached to hit pause on the music, and they all looked at him expectantly, knowing this wouldn't be a social call.

"New orders from the top," the Sergeant had informed them. "Tomorrow you ship out to Camp Normandy for two weeks. There's a large offensive scheduled for that sector, and we need a jump FARP team. You're all on it. That's all except you," he'd added, pointing at Justin. "You've been selected for your two-week mid-tour leave. The rest of you; be ready to move out a moment's notice. Travel time is unconfirmed as yet."

"I'm sorry, guys," Justin had said when the Sergeant had left. "I know most of you have more need to go home than I do."

Joey had silently agreed, but not for his own sake. DJ was the one that needed to go home right now to give him a chance to sort out his personal life, and himself.

"You almost seem disappointed," Billy had commented.

"I am. I've got nothing to go home for. You guys are my only family. Besides, I'll miss all the excitement."

"You won't be missing much," Joey had said. "Jump FARPS are the same old routine, just in a different place."

"I wish they'd picked someone else, though," Justin muttered.

It was only one more thing in a long list that they had no control over.

Joey couldn't help but think that Justin would have been in his element as the Black Hawk carried out its first jolting lift then rose cleanly into the air, the force of the downdraught kicking up a mini sandstorm below them. His stomach flipped, and he opened his eyes – keeping them closed was increasing nausea and dizziness he couldn't help but experience. His stomach lurched again as the bird changed from rising to moving forward with no gentle easing into the motion. He closed his eyes again, knowing that everything would settle down now that the worst was over, and soon managed to drift off into an uneasy sleep through sheer exhaustion.

He hadn't been asleep for long when he was jolted awake by the sound of the door gunner firing his 240-H fully automatic weapon. Fear clutched at him with icy cold hands and every hair on the nape of his neck stood up. He glanced around at the other faces, hoping to see calm acceptance of something he'd missed while he was asleep, but all he saw was his own panic reflected back at him. Whatever was going on, they were as frightened as he was. The only assumption he could make was that they were under enemy fire, and there was every possibility that the helicopter would be shot down in the next few minutes or even seconds.

I'm not ready, Joey thought frantically. I *still have so much I want to do and there's so much that I need to say.*

Trapped in his seat within the confines of the helicopter, he was helpless, unable to stand and fight; even his own weapon unloaded as the safety rules during flight for passengers demanded.

All he could do was wait, listening to the gun's rapid report as the gunner held the trigger depressed, sending a spray of ammo down towards the desert below.

He saw the soldier sitting closest to the crew chief tug on his arm and lean in close to lifting one side of his headphones and yell in his ear. The crew chief turned his head to shout back at the soldier. Joey ripped out one earplug to hear what was being passed around the cabin at high volume, fighting against his restraints to lean as close as possible.

"He's only test firing the weapon."

A wave of pure relief washed over Joey, and he breathed out a long, slow breath, slumping back down in his seat. Others did the same, almost seeming to deflate in front of his eyes. The crew had obviously been aware that a test fire of the door-mounted weapon would occur at some point early on in their flight, but they had neglected to inform the passengers. He tried to relax, his hands trembling slightly as he folded them in his lap. Death was an acknowledged part of his job description that he was well aware of when he signed on the dotted line, and its expectation hovered over him on a daily basis. He'd thought he was prepared. Those brief moments had been a serious learning curve. He didn't want to die yet, not even for his country and especially not while defenseless in the air. If he was never to return home, he wanted to go at least taking a few of the enemy out with him.

The rest of the trip passed uneventfully, and he, and his companions managed to endure it, although he could feel the tension that still inhabited the cabin. Joey had no doubt that a few of them would be having some serious words with the gunner when they landed about the lack of notice. He wouldn't be one of them. They had transported him safely and despite scaring the pants off of everyone, that was all that really mattered.

Night had fallen when they touched down at Camp Normandy just outside Muqdadiyah, Iraq. The village itself was approximately eighty klicks northeast of Baghdad and about one-hundred-and-twenty klicks from their normal base of operations at Camp Speicher. As the birds touched down, the men were given the signal to move out. There was a scramble to undo their shoulder straps and waist buckles and to gather their gear. Black Hawks could cruise at an average of one-hundred-and-fifty kph depending on conditions, and therefore, the journey had only lasted half an hour or so, but Joey was as keen as the rest of them to vacate the helicopter and have his feet back on solid

197

ground. He barely had one foot out of the bird when they came under heavy AK-47 fire from outside the camp perimeter.

In the darkness, Joey could see the rounds streaking orange across the sky towards them and heard them crack right next to him. His instinct was to dive back into the helicopter for cover, but his common sense and training overcame the desire – the pilots needed to get the hell out of here, and fast. Pushing aside the fear, he stood his ground and reached for the men closest to him, grabbing the sleeves of their uniform and pulling them free of the bird as the sounds of the rounds hitting the outer shell of the helicopter surrounded them. Together they ran, making a dash out across the flight line towards the metal shipping containers that served as the FARP, the area an almost replica of the setup used back in Speicher. Diving for cover, they crouched there, watching the Black Hawks take off in a hurry as they took on more rapid fire. Only when they had made it out apparently unscathed, or at least without sustaining serious damage, did Joey turn to the men around him.

"Anyone hit?" Joey asked, the slight waver in his voice giving away his inner reaction to the unexpected and extremely intense situation that had just occurred.

The answers came in the negative; all had avoided a direct hit.

"Just as well they can't shoot for shit," George said, a nervous laugh in his voice.

"I'll second that. Is everyone here, did we all come in the same direction?"

A quick check confirmed that all the men from both helicopters had run in the same direction, coming together as one as they found shelter.

"Okay good. That's twice I thought my time was up in the last hour, I don't want a third. Let's get inside somewhere."

They had barely stood up and dusted themselves off when they were met by three escorts from the camp.

"There you are; we wondered where you'd gotten off to. Sorry, we weren't out on the flight line to meet you, we were, but had to retreat. Welcome to Camp Normandy."

"Wasn't exactly a friendly welcome party," JJ muttered.

The three soldiers laughed. "You're not in your cushy environment now, boys, you're at the front of the fight. What else did you expect, a red carpet?" one of them replied, his strong accent intimating that he was probably native to or a long-time resident of the Brooklyn area of New York.

"Well, ain't that just peachy," Billy said, deliberately playing up his mild mountain twang to get a rise from the sneering city soldier. "Nothing I love more than a pepperoni roll but to be in the middle of a good ol' gunfight."

"Just stick to the job you're here for and leave the hard stuff to us," the guy replied, taking the banter as less than light-hearted and stepping forward to get in Billy's face.

"You want to make something of this?" DJ snarled, stepping closer to the pair. "Because if you have a problem with my battle you have to come through me first."

Joey looked at DJ in surprise. They were both fiercely protective of the young soldiers they'd taken under their wing, but he'd never heard him sound this way before. He normally reacted to any situation with a calm head and used it as a learning curve or a chance to set a good example. Seeing that the situation could quickly escalate into a brawl, Joey sidestepped DJ and pushed his way in between Billy and the other soldier. "We understand we're here as a jump FARP team. What aircraft will we be dealing with and when do you need us to start?"

"I don't see why we need you at all."

"That's enough, Eric. These boys didn't book this excursion as a package vacation; they're here because they've been told to be here. Let's all simmer down and be friendly. Don't mind him; he's just grouchy because his coffee mug broke this morning."

"I can see how that could affect a man's disposition. Specialist Joey Stevenson, at your service," Joey said with a smile, holding out his hand.

"Private Mike O'Connell," the man replied, gripping Joey's hand firmly in his.

Introductions were made all round, and then Mike got back to business. "We actually don't have much of a flight line here; the base is pretty much organizedaround a Tactical Operations Center. Our main use is as a radio transmission station to extend out the radio communications range; our main objective is to send and receive communications from the ground troops and units that are out of antenna range. How many birds are you used to handling?"

200

"We've been handling twenty-two Kiowa Warriors, flying in teams of two."

"You won't find anything like that here. We only have four Warriors, and one of them is currently out of action, and another has some issues that need to be fixed. Besides, the flight line can barely handle two."

"I'm sure we'll be able to repair the issues, and maybe we can get the fourth one back in the air for you."

"Yeah, that'd be great. You can take a look at her tomorrow. Nobody's looking for you to jump into action tonight and to be honest, I think you'll find it pretty quiet here regarding workload, although maybe not in other respects."

"Okay, if we're not needed tonight, maybe you can show us to our accommodation, and we can get settled in."

"I'm afraid you're not far from it," Mike said with a grin. "Cots have been set up for you in the FARP container."

"That's fine, nothing we're not used to."

Mike pointed out the latrines then escorted them inside the huge metal shipping container that had a corner cleared for cots for the visiting soldiers. Before leaving them to get settled, he promised that he would be back for them at first light to show them around the camp.

"We're back to square one," JDub said as he stashed his duffel beneath his chosen cot.

"Hey, don't complain. Isn't it great being all back together this way, I bet you've missed us, right?" Joey said, an innocent expression on his face.

"I haven't missed anyone, especially not their snoring and farting in their sleep."

"Consider yourself lucky there aren't nearly three hundred of us this time."

"Yeah, I guess, but I wasn't just referring to the cots in a container. We're back to being the new kids, the outsiders, where no one knows us and no one respects us."

"I agree that we're back to no one knowing us, but it's not true that they don't respect us. Don't let that one guy color your view of the place or the people here. We're all brothers, the same blood in the same mud. Would you not hold respect for someone wearing the uniform?"

"Not unless they'd proved unworthy of it," JDub was forced to agree. "I might think they're an asshole, but it doesn't mean I don't respect the job they do and trust them to have my back when the chips are down."

"Exactly. Give the place a chance. That guy might have had a bad day, and out here, a bad day can be a really, really bad day. We didn't exactly help the situation."

"I was only trying to be funny," Billy muttered. "The guy was being a condescending asshole. I was just trying to get some light-hearted sparring going."

"I know that, and the guy shouldn't have kicked off the way he did, but you've got to remember that while most of us know that wise-ass comments are meant to be funny, some guys will need time to get to know us before they can accept that kind of shit from us. Just try and judge the situation better next time."

"Yeah, okay. I'm sorry."

Joey nodded, accepting Billy's apology. He waited, expecting DJ to step in and apologize for his own outburst or at least try to justify his actions, but his fellow Specialist remained silent. He shrugged. DJ would come around when he was ready.

"I just had a thought. Since we're actually sleeping in the FARP, does that mean we're on duty twenty-four-seven?" JJ asked.

"I guess the sixteen of us will be split into two teams working twelve-hour shifts, although with our accommodation being in the FARP we're pretty unlikely to get any sleep anyway, so we may as well be."

"At least we can have some serious R & R even when on shift," Craig said, swinging his legs up onto his cot and settling back. "You can just wake me when you hear something coming in."

"We'd better wait to see what morning brings before we make any assumptions. I'm going to get some sleep if I can, you should do the same."

***

Morning brought Mike rousing them at 0600 hours. "We've got less than an hour before sun up, so get ready, and I'll take you over to the chow hall for breakfast then I'll give you a tour of the place. It shouldn't take long; there's not a lot to see."

203

Most of the soldiers had opted to remain mostly dressed while they slept – a precaution for unknown routines and unknown expectations from an unfamiliar place – so it didn't take them long to be assembled and ready to follow Mike.

Compared to the large and sprawling Speicher, Camp Normandy appeared tiny. The chow hall was small, but at least it served hot prepared or fried food, allowing the guys to have a hearty breakfast that wasn't an MRE or a shop bought snack.

"I wonder if they'll have the chow hall completed on base by the time we get back," Billy mused. "I've got to admit; this is pretty great."

"You're kidding, right? The food here is far from great."

"We've been living on MRE's and whatever we find in the local-run bazaar," Joey explained. "It seems our chow hall barely made it onto the bottom of the requirements list. We've been there over six months and only recently got CHU's and showers."

"No wonder this seems good to you. Just wait until you get used to it, then you'll realize just how bad it really is. I'm probably being unfair. This chow hall is the best part of camp. We've got the most advanced and top of the range comms equipment you could ask for, but practically nothing in the way of amenities. We're just here to make sure that the TOC stays safe."

"Well, you can be sure we'll do all we can to help while we're here."

"Thanks. Is everybody done? If you are, let's roll out and I'll give you the guided tour."

Mike hadn't been kidding when he'd said the camp was sadly lacking. Other than the TOC and tiny flight line, the camp basically consisted of the small chow hall and a few concrete structures that were being used for accommodation. The camp was situated in the flattest and most barren area that any of them had ever encountered – the landscape wide open as far as they could see.

"Must make it easy on the checkpoint guards," George said.

"Not as easy as you'd think. That beige everywhere you look really takes a toll and gives you eye strain. Approaching vehicles are easy to spot as they kick up a dust cloud that is better than smoke signals, but they also prevent you from seeing who or what is coming. Come and say hello to our guys in the guard shack."

As they entered the guard shack, they were greeted by a small group of men, and Mike made introductions having to check the names of some of the newcomers.

"Sorry, I'll get them all eventually."

"No problem, it's just nice to have a few friendly faces around here. Do I detect accents that are definitely not from any part of the US that I know about?"

"You noticed?" one of the men chuckled. "We're South African military, proud to be assisting."

"Well then, thank you for your continued support."

"Yeah, I don't know what we would do without them," Mike said. "There isn't really enough of us on base and without these guys, I don't know how we'd man the checkpoint and still cover the rest. They're a godsend."

Noticing the small stack of rifles in the corner of the shack, Billy's curiosity was piqued. "How come you guys don't have to have your weapons on you all the time?"

"Technically, they're not our weapons," one of the South Africans replied. "They belong to the South African military, but we're not assigned personal weapons the way you are. These belong to the checkpoint, not us, so they stay here for whoever is on duty."

"Wait a minute, so what do you do when you're not on duty? Are you telling me you're unarmed?"

"That's correct."

"Holy shit, that's not good. Not in a place where you come under fire the minute you step off the bird. You've got nothing to protect yourself with."

"It's not ideal, but it's what we're used to."

"I don't know what I'd do without Angeline on my shoulder. I'd feel naked," Craig said, giving his rifle a pat.

"Angeline? Your rifles have names?"

Joey laughed subconsciously. "It's something a lot of us do. I guess we often name things that are important to us, like our first car or first guitar. Out here, the most important thing is our weapon, so she's the thing that gets the name."

The men chatted for a few minutes more before Mike informed them they needed to move on.

"Nice meeting you guys. I'm sure we'll see you around the base," Joey said as they took their leave.

The rest of the tour didn't take long as Mike hadn't been downplaying the camp; there genuinely wasn't much to see. They ended up back at the FARP where Mike talked them through the layout and procedures; although it was so similar to their own, they could have figured it out themselves within seconds. He then led them to the hangar where the four Warriors sat.

"This is the one that's grounded, and this one is the one that has a few issues that the pilots are concerned about. There are full reports on both of them in that cabinet over there. The three that can fly will probably be going out at some point today. No doubt top will send down word on when."

"We'll have them ready," Joey confirmed. "And we won't do anything major to this one at the moment. We'll take a look at her and the reports but if she's going out on a mission, we won't strip anything until we know what time frames we have to work with."

"I'll try and make sure you know as soon as possible. I'd better leave you to get to work."

"Thanks for the tour, Mike. Hopefully, we'll catch you later."

"Sure of it," he agreed as he left.

DJ had already moved over to the cabinet and removed the paperwork for the helicopter that had faults.

"He's a nice guy isn't he?" Joey asked as he stepped close to DJ to peer at the report over his shoulder.

"Huh? Oh, Mike, yeah, he is. Look, there are things here that I'm pretty sure I know exactly what's wrong. One or two of these issues we could fix in twenty minutes to half an hour each."

Joey looked at where DJ pointed and had to agree. Years of working with the birds had given them an insight into many of the things that could go wrong and their fault-identification was usually spot on. "If we do them one at a time and don't have her in a position unable to fly, I don't see any reason why we can't make a start on her and give the pilot a better flying experience today."

"Let's do it," DJ said, offering Joey the first genuine smile he'd seen from him in a while.

They busied themselves with the helicopter, using the other guys to help and move the process along, instructing them as they worked. Their instincts turned out to be correct, but the repair job more complex than originally expected due to the current state of the avionics equipment. When the word came down the line that the three helicopters needed to be armed and ready to go within twenty minutes, they had plenty of time to finish what they were working on but were disappointed that they'd only repaired one of the issues in the pilot's report.

Joey shook his head as he watched the birds leave the base. "They just haven't had the proper care and maintenance in a while. If they had, lots of these problems could have been prevented."

"Maybe we can give them all a full overhaul while we're here," DJ replied. "Sounds like FARP duties are going to be pretty slow."

"We can try, as long as we're kept up to date with their mission schedule. At least there's one we can work on anytime we want."

"What are we waiting for?"

Joey and DJ threw themselves into the task, working until well after 0100 hours on the grounded bird. They took a short break for a late dinner that the other guys brought back from the chow hall for them, but were too enthused by the project to stop there. Joey found working this closely with DJ was rebuilding some of the bond that had been lacking between them as of late. He admitted to himself that he'd missed the camaraderie and support of the other Specialist. He was willing to do anything it took to regain that and have his battle back.

When they finally decided to call it quits for the night, they found the other guys sitting around on their cots, talking softly amongst themselves.

"What's the hot topic?" Joey asked as he sat down and accepted the bottle of water handed to him.

"This place," Craig replied. "We complained about the lack of basic human requirements at Speicher, but at least we knew it was coming eventually. This place really blows."

"Yeah," JDub added. "Did you see that crappy defense perimeter? Nothing but three rolls of razor wire, two on the bottom and one stacked on top. That shit wouldn't keep out a raccoon."

"Let's hope the Virginian raccoons are more resourceful than the Hajis then."

The comment elicited some chuckles for the guys but didn't dispel their dreary mood over the realization that they actually had it lucky on Speicher.

"Listen up, guys," Joey said. "Don't feel too bad. This place is fucking Disneyland compared to my first tour in Iraq on Camp Taji in '03 to '04."

"You were on Taji?" JJ asked, his face displaying an expression of awe. "Tell us about it."

Joey chuckled as he saw the guys settling down for a story. He took a swig of water and cleared his throat. "The place was only about thirty-two clicks from Baghdad. It was originally an Iraqi Republican Guard airfield and base in the Saddam era, right in the heart of the volatile Sunni triangle. The word was that it was once a facility where they actually manufactured chemical weapons."

"No shit?" Billy breathed.

"Nope. UNSCOM reported that they found over six thousand empty canisters just waiting to be filled and loaded into rockets."

"Filled with what?"

"I don't know; just whatever deadly crap they were manufacturing there. We heard some horror stories passed on from the guys that had been there right at the start. They said one building was full of barrels and dead birds. When they tipped the barrels to roll them out, some of the contents leaked. It wasn't long before they were disoriented and spewing their guts up. At least twenty were Medevac'd out."

"What happened to them? What was it?"

"Like I said, I never heard anymore and I've no idea what it was. I never encountered anything like that while I was there, but I

210

don't doubt the stories are true, and whatever it was, it was pretty damn nasty."

"No wonder Desert Fox bombed the shit out of the place. Whatever you think about how various governments handled everything, nobody can say that chemical warfare doesn't come under the banner of mass destruction."

"You can't forget that the place was also the largest and most advanced military base in Iraq. It was the one that dealt with tank repair and maintenance and was a central point for weapon caching. There was no doubt they were planning for an invasion of some sort. Anyway, I arrived there in 2003, shortly after the base came under American control after the invasion. I was stationed in Kuwait at the time, and we had to convoy for fourteen hours straight from there to Taji, driving our own vehicles. You've got to remember that this was before the army had put any up armor or steel plating on the trucks," he reminded them, referring to the extra upgraded armor that the Army had deemed a necessity after the bitter experience of loss during the Iraq invasion. When put to the test during tactical situations, the standard fortification of the trucks had been found to be sadly lacking.

"At the time, their idea of up armor was two sheets of plywood screwed together with a layer of sandbags between them. It wasn't worth jack, not against the kind of weapons we were facing."

"That must have been one hell of a journey."

"It was. I was given center position in the LMTV, so I had to stand there with my head sticking out of the top of this truck's gunner door with just my usual weapon to protect us all. It was January, so it was freezing, never getting above fifty-five degrees even at the hottest time of day. You couldn't relax for a minute. The rural areas were littered with IEDs and the cities, well; driving through the cities scared the crap out of me. Eyes watched you from every corner of every street as we made our way through. People would just stop to stand and stare as we passed by; it was damned eerie. No matter how vigilant I was, you wouldn't have seen an attack coming until the very last minute. Everyone covered up, long robes ideal for concealment; the buildings all like rabbit warrens and a million tiny side streets and alleyways for threats to hide. A lot of the buildings were flat on top and made use of the roof space as outside space, so you were trying to look everywhere at once. All that kept going through my mind was that I didn't want to have to shoot anyone, but at the same time, I was damned sure I didn't want to let my guard down and let my friends be killed instead."

"How did you know who the bad guys were?"

"You could never tell; that was the problem. DJ and I were talking about this before. It's not as if they wear a uniform that marks them as an easily identifiable target. Your enemy could have been the farmer coming back from the field, the woman walking with her kid, or the teenager hanging with his friends. Any one of them reaches for anything; you have to hold on and see what's going to appear. The last thing I wanted to do was make a mistake. I wasn't ready to shoot anybody, never mind an innocent civilian."

"Did you have to, shoot anyone I mean?"

"Not during that particular trip," Joey replied.

"So what was the camp like when you got there?"

"The first thing I remember was that it had been raining, and the place was a mud bath. The buildings were mostly concrete, and there was a lot of Iraqi graffiti, even some Saddam artwork on the walls, huge murals of him and his army. Most of the buildings had already been cleared and secured, but the stashing and cataloging of the weapons, mortars, and vehicles was still a work in progress; and the outlying areas hadn't been searched. We ended up with an extensive Captured Enemy Materials warehouse by the time we were done. As you probably know, around 2008, the word was out to the public that they'd found huge caches of mustard based chemical weapons buried all around the surrounding peninsula. None of us that were there really know what we might have been exposed to."

"Wow, okay, I'm not going to complain about this place ever again. I'm starting to think smaller might be better, and we're still further away from the action than you were then."

"I thought Taji was supposed to be one of the better ones?"

"It got to be that way eventually," Joey agreed. "Or at least, better regarding facilities. It's got the largest PX in Iraq, with a Subway, Pizza Hut, and a Burger King, and the new chow hall built at the tail end of '04 was three times bigger than the previous one with about twenty times the food choice. They had to start slow, serving only twice a day because our stomachs just weren't used to the food. After living on MREs and rations, the temptation to gorge was too much, and we needed time to adjust. Later on, air-conditioned and heated living conditions, four meal services per day, hot showers, and fully equipped gyms were all part of the service. But you know yourself that while it helps to have comfortable surroundings with familiar things around you, it doesn't make your actual job any easier, or take away from the fact that you haven't seen your family for a year and aren't sure when or if you'll ever see them again. Besides, none of that was there at the time, and it was a hard slog to get it that way. All we had was the remnants left over from previous tenants, and believeme, Saddam didn't care much about the living conditions of his army; he had his mansions to stay in."

"Didn't training take place there?"

"Yep. By '04, we were training the Iraqi National Guard battalion. To be honest, they didn't have much of a clue, and their weapons were worse than their skills. Still, by the time I left they were shaping up into something pretty decent."

"Didn't you worry? Having armed Iraqis on the base I mean?"

"Well, sure, it was a concern. You never knew if someone was going to turn out to be a plant and would turn on the trainers, butto give the people a fighting chance, it was a risk we were all willing to take. We always have to believe that the good outweigh the bad and the fanatics and insurgents were in the minority, or there would be nothing worth fighting for. We were there to help free the people, and we never forgot it."

Joey's words gave the guys a lot to think about, but still they were keen for more. The question and answer session went well into the wee hours of the morning, with DJ being begged to share some of his previous experiences from tours in Afghanistan. He relented, telling tales from his past as they made comparisons and absorbed all that the two Specialists could teach them as they swapped war stories. As the first time out soldiers listened, they all understood why they had instinctively looked up to DJ and Joey and accepted them as their leaders and mentors. It had less to do with rank and more to do with their quiet confidence and quick thinking in certain situations, as well as their ability to cope with whatever life threw at them. It was a way of being that could only come from the combination of knowledge and experience, and it was one that they all admired and aspired to attain for themselves.

DJ groaned as he glanced at his watch. "You've done it to me again. We've only got a couple of hours before we're due on shift."

"At least we don't have to work through the mother of all hangovers this time," Joey chuckled.

"Yeah, that was rough," JDub said. "I thought I was dying that day."

"Did you do the whole I'm-never-drinking-again speech?" Craig asked with a grin.

"Hell no! As soon as I get home, I'm packing a six-pack on ice and going fishing, and this time, I'm not sharing."

The Armament Dogs laughed, all able to visualize JDub on a camping chair, his feet up on the cooler and his cap pulled down over his eyes, fast asleep with the empty cans scattered around him.

"On that note, I think we should all get some shut-eye."

"I wouldn't worry too much, from what I've seen today we can sleep through most of our damned shift anyway."

"Not DJ and I, we've got a bird to strip and fix."

"Yep! No matter what, I'm determined to have that bird repaired and cleared for missions by the time we leave this place."

"You betcha," Joey said, enthusiastically returning the fist bump offered by DJ.

Joey curled up on his cot with a small smile on his face, happier than he'd been since the day they'd received the first mail run.

Chapter Thirteen: D.A.R.T.

While some of the guys had looked forward to being away from Camp Speicher for a while, they soon found that their time in Camp Normandy wasn't quite what they'd expected it to be. They tried to keep as busy as possible working on the downed bird, but fetching and carrying for DJ and Joey wasn't keeping them as occupied as they'd hoped it would, and they were beyond bored. The downtime and waiting around for something to do turned out not to be so relaxing and peaceful after all, but more of a source of irritation. Having nothing to occupy themselves was a huge drain on them mentally as they stared into nothingness, too much time to think about their situation and the reasons for them being where they were. DJ and Joey had experience enough to have expected it, but it came as a surprise to the younger guys, who still had a lot to learn about overseas deployment.

"Man, if anyone had said to me back home to go and sit around for two weeks and do nothing, I'd have been happy as a pig in mud," JDub said. "Why does this suck so much?"

"Because back home we've got things we can do. Internet, TV, pick up the phone and call friends or family, jobs and chores around the house, books to read, church to go to; you name it. It's all things we take for granted and don't even really notice we're doing until they're not available anymore," Craig replied.

"Yeah, like when you're doing something online and have a power outage and think to yourself that it doesn't matter, you'll go and watch TV instead," Billy said. "Then it dawns on you that you don't have TV either."

"So you think, no problem, I'll watch a DVD instead. I've had that moment," JDub added.

"And don't you feel like a real dumb ass! Been there too," JJ added. "But you know what else gets me about this place?"

"What's that?"

"How small it is. Back at camp, it was weird having hundreds of guys around at first, but now that I don't have them, I realize how secure it made me feel. It's especially bad this close to the action. I keep having thoughts of being outmanned and outgunned unexpectedly by a large group of Hajis. They could appear from anywhere, and there aren't really enough of us to fight back."

"I hadn't actually thought about that, thanks a lot," Craig said with an eye roll.

"I had," George said. "Thought about it pretty early on, too."

"What conclusion did you come to?" JJ asked with genuine interest, keen to discover what helped his battle cope with his nightmare scenario.

"Just that if it ever happened, we'd fight as hard as we could, shoulder to shoulder, and pray we made it out the other side."

"That's it?"

"That's it."

"Well, at least it would give us something to do and some excitement," JDub said. "This place is making me nuts."

"Be careful what you wish for," Joey called over, having been listening to their conversation in spite of his head being buried in the bird. "The universe has a funny way of answering, and it may not be in the way that you wanted."

Joey shrugged as the guys scoffed at him, more than happy if he was proved wrong on this occasion. This was an easy assignment, and they should be thankful. Complaining about it was asking for trouble.

It wasn't until the next day that they had to revisit the conversation and eat their words. In the hangar, tinkering as usual, the monotony was broken by a breathless Mike, bursting inside.

"Kit up and get ready to move out guys; you've got your marching orders from top. We just had an urgent radio call and need a D.A.R.T. team."

The Armament Dogs leaped to their feet while DJ and Joey scrambled down from the bird they were working on, hurrying to grab the pieces of their full battle rattle they'd removed. Having been left unsupervised and uninterrupted for days in the hangar, they'd seen no need to be sticklers for the rules. As long as weapons were attended at all times, they'd gone easy on the rest of the guys and themselves, allowing them to remove helmets and Kevlar for comfort. They knew they would need everything they had at their disposal now. Being a Downed Aircraft Recovery Team was usually a very dangerous occupation, the enemy as anxious to gain control of the military equipment and survivors as the US army was.

"What's down?" Joey asked, adjusting his helmet strap.

"Two Kiowa Warriors," Mike replied.

"Our guys?" DJ asked sharply. Being responsible for the aircraft they flew, he'd already adopted the pilots from the camp as his own.

"No, the birds are from FOB MacKenzie up in Samarra, but they're down in Jazira, a small city about seven clicks from here. We're closest. You've got to report to head shed for the full brief, follow me."

Minutes later, the Armament Dogs stood to attention in front of the Commander for the first time since their arrival at Camp Normandy. He repeated the information that Mike had already given them before adding vital information.

"I'm only sending four of you out, partly for safety and partly because we can't spare more than two Armored Troop Carriers. Specialists, David Jones, and Joseph Stevenson will make up one team, and Privates George Ates and William Knowles the other. The rest of you are dismissed."

"Yes, Sir."

The four not chosen turned to leave, giving their battles pointed looks as they left. The remaining four understood the silent order to watch their backs and come home in one piece. The commander continued as soon as the others had left.

"You'll be accompanied by four of my own men who are already briefed. The birds are close together but city center. We have infantry troops on the ground surrounding them and so far, they're managing to hold the enemy back. We don't know how long that situation will last. When you get there, download the Hellfire missiles, rockets, and machine guns as well as the radio equipment. Your mission is to retrieve those items. That is your one and only objective, do you understand?"

"Yes sir," they responded in unison.

"If all else fails, the infantry in the hot zone have what they need to do what's necessary, but only as a last resort. They'll take the instruction from you on my orders if you think it's the only way, and you can't complete your task. They'll be dealing with it when you're done regardless. Pick up a D.A.R.T. kit on your way out; they're waiting for you at the door."

"Yes, sir."

"Good luck. Dismissed."

They moved single file out of the head shed, Joey and George grabbing the kits on their way. They knew the medium sized, square, yellow tool boxes would contain just about every tool needed to remove the weapons and radios within the protective foam cutouts inside the sturdy outer box. In addition, the Armament Dogs already always carried a Gerber brand, plier multi-tool, which could perform just about any task in a pinch. It was a multi-functional go-to tool, and no decent army mechanic was ever without one.

Two Humvees were already waiting for them outside, engines running. Each contained two men from the camp occupying the front seats. George and Joey loaded the D.A.R.T. kits into the back of each Humvee and nodded to each other before separating and climbing into their respective vehicles, barely having time to close the doors before the drivers sped away, anxious to reach the crash site so they could complete their mission and let everyone get out of the hot zone.

"I wonder what their original mission was," George muttered.

"Who knows, probably something in Baghdad," Billy replied. "Why does it matter?"

"It doesn't, I suppose. I'm assuming that the two birds were air support for the ground soldiers on whatever mission they were on, but it just seems odd that they were carrying what's needed with them. Must be a bad situation if they travel prepared for the complete annihilation of equipment thrown in there as an option."

Sitting close to George in the rear of the Humvee, Billy considered his battle's statement carefully before replying. "I suppose it makes sense to be prepared for all eventualities. Then again, if the vehicle carrying it was captured, it's not a good thing for the Hajis to get their hands on. I don't know, I think he should have just given us the materials to do what was needed, just in case, we're more than qualified. What if the scene is already overrun by the time we arrive?"

"Not our call. We're the action, not the brains, but it would have made sense for us to have some as back up," George agreed, referring to the explosives that would be used to destroy the military equipment if there was no other way to prevent it from falling into enemy hands. Their own equipment and weapons being used against them was not a good scenario, and prevention was attempted whenever possible. Only if it was damaged beyond all usage or if the enemy completely overran the D.A.R.T. team would the decision be made to blow up the equipment in situ without recovery.

"Having said that, we're not his unit; maybe he didn't trust us yet not just to take the easy option and blow it all the hell up before we'd even tried to get it out," George suggested.

Billy snorted. "Yeah, maybe, as if we would. Well, whatever, we wanted something to do, and here we are getting it."

"Yeah. Joey warned us to be careful what we wished for."

"And we didn't listen, and here we are."

The two men looked at each other, neither required to express the trepidation they felt at that moment with words. They could see their own fear reflected back at them in the other's eyes.

In the second Humvee, the journey was passed in silence. The information that the birds were down in an occupied city had given the two Specialists more than enough information to have a good idea of what to expect once they reached the outskirts of the city. The enemy would want to prevent backup from reaching the site as much as they wanted to get their hands on the downed birds and any survivors. Already, the two men were mentally preparing themselves to be thrust into a desperate and chaotic situation and were doing their best to accept it, push it aside, and focus only on their objective. They knew it wasn't going to be easy. They didn't need the updates that blasted across the Humvee radio system to tell them how difficult the conditions already were or how much would be resting on their shoulders once they arrived.

It took less than ten minutes for the teams to reach the small but heavily built-up city. As they moved cautiously towards the center, the streets were lined with typical three story buildings and peppered with side streets and small alleyways between the houses. Laundry hung heavy on ropes on rooftops in the breezeless air, and the occasional burst of loud and rapid conversations was caught as they passed by open windows. The anticipated attacks as they moved through the streets never came, adding to their growing unease. The outlying areas seemed unnaturally quiet, alerting them to the fact that the scene of the crash was already the main focus and would be even more heavily attended than they'd first thought.

"This is the worst possible place for a bird to go down," Joey murmured as the sound of distant gunfire reached their ears. "We must be getting close."

DJ nodded. "I've got your back, battle."

"Thanks. Same goes for you. We got this, right?"

DJ smiled faintly, recognizing that Joey had picked up the expression as a kind of catchphrase for them, an utterance of reassurance filled with fake confidence. "We got this," he replied.

Soon, the smoke from the smoldering wreckage came into view and the sounds of weapon fire increased, so constant it was almost a loud and intrusive barrage of white noise assaulting their eardrums. The remains of the two crashed birds were in the middle of the street, surrounded by tall buildings on either side, the usual maze of alleyways and side streets leading a path straight to them. Muzzle flashes seemed to come from every direction and every window of every building as the ground infantry attempted to stand their ground from the cover provided by the fallen helicopters and their vehicles. They were under heavy fire; the enemy determined to push forward and claim the birds as their spoils of war, eliminating the men who protected it in the process.

As the Humvees pulled up as close as they could, the infantry increased their fire, hoping to provide some cover for the D.A.R.T. teams exiting the vehicle. Joey estimated there were around ten of them, nowhere near enough. He knew the odds would worsen by the minute as more and more people arrived to join the fight on the wrong side, the downed helicopters already a reason for excitement and celebration. Fueled by the success of bringing down the two powerful and feared combat aircraft, their bloodlust was high, and it would trigger a pack mentality, a fevered, frenzied desire to keep on killing and then rejoice in their victory, something akin to rioters claiming police vehicles and dancing on their roofs, only with so much more macabre display of their conquest. If they had the opportunity, they would parade the dead bodies – probably separate from the heads – of the pilots around the city, a stark reminder to non-supporters of exactly

225

who was in charge and what they could achieve against the massive war machine that was the United States Forces.

Quickly assessing the two birds, Joey already knew there was little to no chance of any survivors. There was barely anything left of the aircraft. As one, the four of them leaped out, DJ and George grabbing the kits from the rear of the Humvees before dashing over to the wreckage and joining the infantry. The man closest to them leaned over to shout to them.

"They were taken down by intense RPG and AK fire, so everything's pretty mangled. You haven't got an easy job ahead, but we'll give you as much cover as we can for as long as we can."

Joey nodded in response. "Any survivors?" he yelled back.

"All four dead."

"The bodies?"

Joey knew he'd been ordered to concern himself only with the weaponry and sensitive communication equipment, but he was damned if he was going to leave men behind to be used in some sick and twisted celebration. The soldier made eye contact for a fleeting few seconds, understanding Joey's train of thought and silently thanking him for the consideration. "We've already got 'em in the back of our Humvee. Nobody gets left behind on my watch."

He's barely old enough to shave, Joey thought as he motioned for George and Billy to take the nearest bird. *He's stepped up and taken charge of this situation. God willing, he'll make it out. He'll have a great career in the military if he wants it, he's a born leader of men.*

"We'll work as fast as we can," was all he said to the soldier, glancing at the nametag and insignia on his chest. It was important for him to know and remember this young man's name, whatever happened.

The boyish face was set with grim determination as he raised his weapon, ready to keep the enemy busy while Joey and DJ made their way around to the second bird. The charred remains were still smoldering, but at least the acrid smell of smoke and hot metal covered the stench of blood and flesh, outside of the aircraft anyway. It didn't mask it quite so much as the teams dived inside to remove the radios. They were held onto a metal shelf at the rear with four Philips head screws and some electrical connectors behind them. The only way to retrieve them was to climb inside and scramble to the back of the bird.

"Let's hope the screws haven't melted so much there's no head or thread left on them," Joey said as they crawled their way through the hot, twisted metal to the rear where the radios were positioned.

They figured that the radios were the most important pieces of equipment to remove and the ones the army would regret the loss of most if it all went to hell in a hand basket and they lost control of the crash site. The situation they now faced was an almost replica of the one they had encountered in the hangar back at Speicher, with blood and pieces of flesh coating the inside of the cockpit. Joey silently sent strength to George and Billy, hoping they'd be able to deal with the gory sight and the stench without losing it, willing them to ignore it and get the job done.

Hearing the heavy fire hitting the outside of the aircraft and the agonized scream of at least one of the infantry as he was presumably hit, they worked as quickly as they could, knowing their skills had never been more necessary nor put as much to the test. DJ and Joey had the radio disconnected and out in record time, having to hack away the melted electrical connections rather than removing them. Once they had it in their possession, DJ ran out to throw it into the back of a Humvee belonging to the infantry, ignoring the four twisted, blackened, and bloody bodies that already lay there. Having disposed of the radio, he made his way to back to the bird to the rocket launchers on the outside where Joey had already begun working.

He had flipped the metal foot at the rear of the rocket containment pod by the propellant side, releasing the two small teeth located inside the pod at the back that gripped the actual rockets within. Once they were released, the rockets could be manually pushed from the back with a short wooden stick until they were close enough to the front to be grabbed and pulled from the pod, allowing for easy disarmament. DJ reached in to snag the first and ran with it to the Humvee. Joey pushed some more, concern masking his face as he did so. DJ not only braved the fire they were under, but he seemed completely unconcerned, not even ducking as bullets rained down all around them. Before he could think about it any further, his attention was taken by spotting the other team leaping out of the first bird with the radio, George bending low and racing to the Humvee to dump it in the back. Joey had to admit they both looked a little sick, but they seemed to be holding up okay. Relieved, he figured he could concentrate on his job and not have to worry about them too much.

The second remaining rocket was much more difficult to move, almost completely melted onto the inside of the warped metal rocket pod. Joey rammed it repeatedly from behind, but it refused to budge. Sweat was pouring down his face, stinging his eyes and blurring his vision, the intense heat from the burning fuel and RPG's almost too much to bear. He thought he could feel his face starting to blister on one side. DJ peered into the pod from the other end then looked at Joey, shaking his head. Joey tried again but still nothing was budging. By silent agreement, they abandoned the rocket pods, knowing that the last remaining rocket was as good as useless anyway, and moved down to about half way down the metal launcher rail when the locking arm for the Hellfire missiles was located. DJ flipped it forward to release the tension from the spring that held them in place. Together, they slid one of the one-hundred-and-nine-pound missiles forward until it dropped down from the rail into the small opening in the track. Heavy and awkward to handle, it took both of them to carry it to the Humvee. DJ, once again, seemed to ignore the firefight around him, unflinching as bullets whistled past their ears and clanged against the sides of the birds and the Humvees. His blank face frightened Joey. This was more than the battle hardened and focused, his attitude bordered more on blatant disregard for his own personal safety. It flashed across Joey's mind that his friend might be suicidal, seeking the hand of another to end his life and absolve him from blame and recrimination. To die at the hands of the enemy during such an important mission would provide an easy way out and assure DJ would be remembered with honor and respect, and Joey would be left as probably the only remaining evidence of the bleakness that had haunted his battle buddy for the past few weeks. The others believed it had passed. While in Camp Normandy, DJ had seemed more like his usual self again, and the period of blackness had all but been forgotten by the others. Joey still saw flashes of it, and it had never been more evident than it was now.

As much as the thought worried him, there was no time to dwell on it at the moment. As Joey had suspected, more and more weapons had joined the siege against them. The empty streets and lack of attacks on the way in had been the result of exactly what he thought, everybody was racing towards the two birds, knowing that the army would send in men to reclaim what belonged to them. The sheer volume of firepower aimed at them was keeping the infantry practically pinned against the birds, going through the motions of firing, reloading, firing, and reloading. There was no way they could cover every direction and keep all the shooters taking cover at once; the number was too overwhelming, and they had already come close to being overrun. The desperation of the situation was affirmed when the two teams of two men commissioned only to drive the Humvees in and out of the hot zone leaped from the vehicle and added their personal weapons to the suppressive fire in an attempt to allow the D.A.R.T. teams to make it back to the birds.

DJ and Joey only had the fifty-caliber machine gun left to deal with, while George and Billy were working their way through the rockets, the pods less damaged on their bird and giving up more of their ammunition. The machine gun was an optional attachment that could be released from the Weapons Pylon by loosening four metal alignment arms with a small wrench. Joey and DJ were working on one each when a double tap on his shoulder alerted him to someone requiring his attention. He turned to see the teenager he'd spoken to before standing beside him; his cheeks covered in sand and dirt that stuck to the sweat that coursed down his face.

"Any idea how long you need? We can't hold this much longer! Three of our men are down, and we're close to being overrun. We need to move out fast."

Joey looked at the alignment arms. DJ had already removed one and was working on his second, Joey's side looked to be in not too bad a shape, considering. He couldn't foresee any unaccounted for problems. He glanced over to Billy and George, seeing they hadn't yet moved on to the Hellfire missiles. "Ten minutes, maximum."

The young man shook his head. "Never make it. I'll try and call for air support, but I don't even know if they'll make it in time to help us, even if the request is granted."

"If you have to go, just go, get your men to safety. Just leave us with what's needed to finish up."

DJ had moved closer, having finished with his two arms and starting on one of Joey's while he was occupied talking to the soldier. "Leave it with me," he growled, "then you can all get the fuck out. I'll take care of it."

"And leave you behind to have your head mounted on the end of your rifle and carried through the streets?"

"I'll make sure I'm inside, so there's nothing left to parade."

"Over my dead body," Joey snarled back.

"Could be all of our dead bodies," DJ said with a shrug, "if that's how you want to play it."

The young soldier had been watching the conversation between them, looking back and forth from one to the other. "I'm radioing in," he called. "Just get a move on so we can all get the fuck out of here."

He blasted off a few more rounds before screaming into his radio and running around to help a soldier that had taken a shot to his calf limp further under cover of the fallen bird. Joey pushed his argument with DJ to the back of his mind and helped him loosen the final arm. Once done, DJ delved into the kit and removed an Allen key and a large ratchet. He fitted one to the other, slipped it into the hole in the ejection rack, and cranked it to the left. The small movement was enough for the metal feet at the bottom of the rack to release the metal hooks on the top of the machine gun, letting it go. Once again, this was a two-man job, one at each end being required to lift the machine gun off and carry it. They made it to the Humvee against the odds and piled it on top of the other weapons already inside.

"Help the others or try to help out with the cover?" DJ asked as they unloaded it.

"Don't think we can make much difference. Finishing up quicker is the best option."

Despite their earlier conflict, they moved as a team to the other bird, DJ still walking in a straight line and upright while Joey weaved and ducked, making himself as difficult a target to hit as possible. Several times, he felt the whoosh of air on his head and cheeks as bullets whizzed past him, missing him my fractions of inches. The other guys were removing the Hellfire missiles, so DJ and Joey left them to it and made a start on the machine gun. This one was trickier, the arms buckled and warped, much harder to loosen. They were struggling with the task, listening to the excited cries of the enemy that screamed out as frequently as the AK47 rifle fire. Soon, the sound of rotor blades was added to the unholy cacophony of war.

"I hope to God that's air support," Joey yelled.

DJ paused to peer up into the sky, waiting until two AH-64 Apache helicopters appeared in his vision. "Looks like it," he yelled back, renewing Joey's hope that some of them might make it out of there alive. "They're definitely ours."

They continued to work, relieved by the sound of the thirty-millimeter chain machine guns firing from the front of the helicopters that swooped in to assist the ground troops, halting the bullets that zinged around them for a few precious moments until they'd passed over, the enemy having the sense to dive for cover. The fire that resumed as they passed over was significantly reduced, the spray of bullets have successfully eliminated many of the rooftop and high window shooters and sending others scurrying for better protection. As they flew, the ground crew heard the whoosh of 2.75-inch rockets being launched from the pods, taking out large chunks of the further away buildings. George whooped as the rockets hit and the resulting explosions took out entire floors at a time.

"We got everything else, want us to take it from here?" he yelled to DJ.

"No, we'll finish up. Either take up a position and add your guns or get into the Humvee, ready to move out."

While DJ and Joey continued to struggle with the damaged rail and arms holding the machine gun in place, the helicopters returned for a second pass. Knowing they were the only thing preventing everyone from moving out, the two men gave it everything they had, finally liberating the gun and getting it clear of the helicopter. After depositing it in the Humvee, they joined the infantry, adding their assistance to the cover for the two that made their way over to the helicopters to plant them with several blocks of military-grade C-4 explosives. Once the men were clear, they helped the injured that were still fighting to their Humvee and made a dash for their own. DJ and Joey climbed into the back at the same time as the men from camp climbed into the front, and the Apaches made another pass overhead.

With everyone inside the armored vehicles, they began to roll out in a convoy, attracting a swarm of rebel fighters out from the buildings to chase after them, firing frantically as they ran, unwilling to give up their spoils. The vehicles came under heavy, concentrated fire as the enemy tried desperately to prevent their departure. DJ and Joey glanced at each other as the radio crackled, then sprang to life.

"Detonation in place."

They peered out to watch the Apaches make a hasty departure from the scene just as a man rushed out from a side street with a hand-held rocket launcher, taking up position in the middle of the road to shoot an RPG in the direction of the leaving Apaches. The rocket whizzed into nothingness; their target went from range. All eyes were back on the launcher as he loaded another, preparing to fire, his target now the retreating Humvees. Suddenly, an explosion blasted behind him, sending him flying through the air as the two downed military aircraft were taken out of enemy hands for good. A massive fireball rose up into the sky and filled their vision as the occupants of the Humvees felt their vehicles being rocked by the concussion of the blast. The drivers held the vehicles steady, ignoring the raging mayhem behind them. As the old diesel engines hurled the Humvees down the street – both now riddled with fresh battle wounds – the men looked back at what had moments ago been a fully-fledged war zone and now felt like staring into the burning mouth of hell itself. Body parts of those that had been caught in the blast were scattered beyond the greedy consumption of the hungry flames while others screamed as they burned. The men inside the vehicles were still pumped full of fear and adrenaline, their bodies shaking and uncontrollable, simply marionettes under the control of a cruel and merciless puppet master. Joey forced himself to slow his breathing, trying to bring his extremities and his racing heart under control. When he finally managed to speak, his voice was a trembling, forced hiss of air through a slit of a grimacing mouth.

"Fucking A, battle! Those bastards almost punched our ticket this time."

Chapter Fourteen: Dancing in the Desert

Shaken up by their recent near miss in the firefight, the Armament Dogs were less concerned about the boredom that infiltrated every day on Camp Normandy. They could now see it for the blessing that it was. Those that hadn't been involved had been regaled with stories from both Billy and George, as well as the four others that had been driving the Humvees. Acutely aware that they'd nearly lost some of their friends and both their mentors, they were more than happy to put up with the endless hours of nothing to do. Still, when they were informed they'd be heading back to Speicher five days later, they were all relieved. They didn't look down as the Black Hawks lifted them up and away from the place, and breathed contented sighs as they touched down back on Speicher just after 9 pm.

"Home sweet home," George said.

"Yep, it's good to be back. I can't wait to have a long hot shower," Craig agreed.

"I wonder what's been happening in our absence."

"Probably not a lot, JDub, but we can hold out some hope for even more improvements if you like disappointment."

The seven of them climbed into the waiting LMTV that had been sent to transport them back to their CHU's. They chattered excitedly throughout the short drive, all of them anxious to see their tiny rooms that had become their sanctuary in this barren wasteland. As soon as they jumped out, Justin came barreling out the door of the trailer that housed his room, a huge grin on his face.

"Heard you guys were landing tonight. I've been waiting for you."

"Hey, Justin, good to see you, when did you get back?" JJ greeted him.

"Just this morning."

"You actually look happy about it. Aren't you bummed out?"

"Nope, nothing for me back there, not even anyone to visit. Everything I have is here."

Most of the guys thought that was pretty sad, but none of them voiced their feelings, instead greeting Justin in a way that they hoped fulfilled his expectations and made up for the lack of welcome home at the beginning of his leave. Without being asked or offered, they all made their way to DJ and Joey's room.

"I guess you wouldn't have had time to find out any of the news of what's been happening back here while we've been gone?" Joey asked.

"Not a lot, but some. Did you happen to notice the big top on your way in?"

"Big top? Has the circus come to town?"

"Well, okay, it's not actually a big top, but it's shaped like one. The only difference is it's a dull khaki color instead of nice, bright stripes."

"Nope didn't see it, but that's not surprising since it's already dark."

"Well, it's our new chow hall!"

"Finally!"

"At last."

"Thank God. It was going to be hell going back to MRE's after two weeks of proper food."

"It's supposed to open sometime tomorrow. The fridges, freezers and cookers and stuff all got delivered and put into place yesterday apparently, and the supplies arrived a couple of hours ago."

"That's some good news to come back to then. Anything else?"

"Not much. There's another bunch of guys here that were shipped out from Hawaii."

"Typical. We get put out here with nothing, suffer through the lack of basic amenities, do all the hard work, and then they waltz on in when everything's set up. Seen any of them yet?"

"No, not yet. I just hung around here for most the day waiting for you guys. Without the team, they didn't bother assigning me anywhere. We're back on Armament duty tomorrow."

"So that's it? It doesn't sound like we missed much."

"There is one other thing," Justin said with a sly grin. "The doctor brought back a little souvenir from his trip home. Something to ease all your troubles."

Justin reached inside his field jacket and removed a large glass vial containing a clear liquid. A small dropper was suspended inside, attached to the screw on lid.

"Just what the hell is that?" Joey asked, not liking the look of what Justin was gleefully waggling in front of them.

"The finest LSD money can buy. I thought we could have a little reunion party back out at the bunker. Celebrate being back together again."

"I really don't think that's a great idea, Justin."

"Chill out, Joey. We don't have to go crazy with the stuff. If we're careful, this could last all of us the rest of the tour. It'll just take the edge off of everything and make it a night to remember."

"Count me in," JJ said, accepting any opportunity to break the rules.

"Hell, after what I went through back in Normandy, I'll give anything a shot. I swear I haven't stopped shaking yet," Billy added.

"Yeah, I'm in too, that was scary shit that went down. I could use a blowout, but I hope it's a night to forget, not remember."

"Good, that's four. What about the rest of you?"

"I'm up for the party," JDub said. "Not sure about the drugs, though."

"Don't be such a pussy. It won't kill you, and even if it might, it's only something else to add to the list."

"Yeah, what the hell. Okay, I'm in."

"Count me out, guys. Sorry, but I don't want to have anything to do with that stuff."

"Suit yourself, Joey; it's your loss." Justin's tone was petulant, aware that his attempt to ingratiate himself had failed on one of the most important members of the group. "What about you, DJ?"

"I'm not in the mood for a party."

"Fine! We don't need you two anyway. Craig?"

Craig hesitated, wanting to follow the lead of his two superiors but unwilling to be ostracized by his peers for his refusal. "Just name the time and place and I'm there," he finally said.

Justin's grin returned. "Tomorrow night, back at the same bunker. We can meet behind the shower block as soon as it gets dark and the base settles down. You two are welcome to join us if you change your mind."

"We won't," Joey said firmly.

"Anyway," Justin said, tucking his prize back inside his jacket. "What happened on Normandy that was so bad? I want to hear everything."

They stayed up for several more hours, filling Justin in on the events and shooting the breeze as they sipped on cans of beer from their small fridge. When they'd run out of things to say, they headed for their separate rooms to catch a couple of hours sleep.

Their morning started with bad news. Due to the current volatile situation, the President had put out the order that all tours were to be extended to fifteen months minimum. Instead of being half way through as they had originally thought, they now had another nine months to go. It was a bitter pill to swallow and it had put a damper on the anticipation they had felt over their impending celebration. They were sullen and uncommunicative on their way out to the hangar for their shift. Three more months added to the year away from home would feel like a lifetime. They had no way of knowing that more bad news already awaited them.

On arrival, they found their hangar already occupied. A tall man with blond hair, blue eyes, and a chiseled jaw sauntered confidently over to them as they entered.

"Hello girls. I hear we have to share our space with you while we're here."

"And you are?"

"Saddler, *Sergeant* Saddler. I'm in charge of this team of aircraft mechanics. We arrived last week, so we've made ourselves at home, but I'm sure you can just work with us. Well, well, Specialist David Jones. Good to see you."

Joey saw DJ clench his fists and noted the tight, pinched look on his pale face. He clawed around in his mind, trying to figure out what was happening here. Then it came to him. The words in a letter that felt as if it were read a lifetime ago. *His name's Sgt. Greg Saddler and he's a good man, David; he makes me happy. I think you would even like him if you got to know him.* Then the revelation that followed. *I do know the bastard, I was stationed with him for several months back in Hawaii, and he was a smug, self-satisfied, arrogant, uppity prick even then.*

"Oh shit," Joey murmured.

He was hoping this wasn't the same Sgt. Saddler. He could tell immediately from DJ's reaction though that it was. Besides, the guy was obviously a prick, just like DJ had said. He could have recognized him from that description alone.

"DJ, I need to talk to you immediately about something important in private," Joey said, grabbing DJ by the shoulders and practically pushing him back out of the hangar.

"Going so soon?" he heard the asshole call. "I didn't get a chance to give you the message from Clara. She said to tell you she's come more in two months with me than she did in two years with you. She said she always had to fake it before!"

His team guffawed, obviously in on the details of their Sergeant's relationship with another soldier's wife. The muscles in Joey's arms strained as he struggled to hang on to DJ and stop him from charging back in and beating the man to a pulp. He wouldn't blame him, but he couldn't let it happen. He was pleased to see his entire team followed, encircling DJ in a protective shield.

"What the fuck? Don't tell me *that's* the douchebag that your wife's seeing?" Justin spat. "What a total loser."

"Let me go! I'm going to go in there and rip that smug head off his shoulders."

"No! DJ, I get it, and I'd want to do the same, but this isn't the way. Why give him the satisfaction of you ending up in the Brigg."

Joey still had DJ in an arm lock while he wriggled and squirmed, fighting against the firm hold.

"Yeah, man, that's what he wants you to do, what he's hoping for. Don't let him see that you give a shit. He'll get what's coming to him; we'll make sure of it," George added.

"Like how?" Craig asked.

"I don't know yet. Give me some time to think. We'll come up with something, something good."

"Something that'll make him look like a prize chump if he ever tells anyone about it," JJ added, "with no witnesses and no way of tracing it back to us. We can figure it out tonight."

DJ still hadn't stopped fighting Joey. "Come on, man. What do you say? Can you rein it in, just for today until we figure out a plan? You know he's only acting like this because he's threatened by you and your relationship with Clara. That can only mean one thing, she must have spoken about you a lot, and it must have been obvious how much she loved you. He wants to make sure you hate her, and he wants to see you in trouble to keep you out of his hair. Don't let him win, DJ, you're better than that."

He felt DJ go limp in his arms and exhaled with relief. He hadn't been sure if he could have held him much longer, he was stronger than he looked. DJ's eyes were still blazing with hatred, but Joey could see the spark of interest. He didn't release him, though, not yet, although he did loosen the hold he had on him.

"You think so?" he asked.

"Absolutely! Why would he care about her past if she didn't? Why would he want to torment you unless he wanted to make sure there was no chance of you trying to win her back?"

"And we can work on payback? Something good?"

"You bet, or even lots of little goods, make his life a living hell," Justin said. "Come along tonight and we'll start working on ideas."

"Okay, I'm in, but I don't know if I can work alongside that asshole all day and hold it together."

"You can," Joey said. "You have to, or let him take your career away, too. You can be the better man."

"How can I listen to him talking about my wife that way? This is the woman I've loved since high school."

"The woman he's talking about doesn't exist. It's all bullshit, lies to get to you where it hurts the most. You were childhood sweethearts, and that's special. She isn't going to be blabbing about you and her, and you can't ever wipe away all those feelings completely. Even if you have changed, she'll still love the man you were, and she'll always care about you. She won't sully those memories with the kind of shit he's spewing out, trust me."

"You really think so?"

"I'd stake my life on it," Joey said, aching inside at the hope that now shone from DJ's eyes. "Do you think you can hold onto that and not react?"

"I don't know, but I can try."

"Goodman. I know you can do it. Let's go back inside before we all end up in trouble from slacking on our shift."

"I take it you're both on for tonight after all then?" Justin asked.

"We'll be there," Joey said, giving DJ a pat on the back as he finally released him completely.

"You guys go on in, I'll take another minute or two to cool down, and I'll be right there."

"Want me to stay with you?"

"No, I'm good. I need a moment to myself. I won't let anyone see me out here without a battle."

"I'll wait right by the door where I can see you."

"We've got your back."

The rest had muttered their agreement and reassurances before they went inside, Joey taking up position by the door as promised as the rest of them prepared to get to work, ignoring the knowing smirks from the newcomers to the hangar. It was going to be hard on all of them to ignore their presence, but for DJ's sake, they needed to practice what they preached.

***

"Man, that was some shitty day," Craig said as they began their trek out towards the out of bounds area that contained the forbidden bunkers.

They'd gathered behind the shower block as agreed, laden down with items for their party. Joey had packed for DJ, taking his laptop and speaker as well as his camera. Ever since the letter, DJ had abandoned his idea of documenting his tour since it had been mostly for Clara's benefit, but Joey thought it would be good for him to pick it up again. This tour was probably going to be one of the worst he would ever have in his life, and the reminders of all that he'd managed to overcome would serve him well in the future. It could only help to make him even stronger. If he could cope with this shit, he could cope with anything. He also had the feeling this was going to be one wild and crazy night, and the resulting pictures could help them all to raise a smile when things were tough. With the way this tour was playing out so far, he couldn't fail to know that it was only going to get rougher. No tour ever got easier as the months passed.

With Justin already providing the main goodies, the others had clubbed together for snacks and booze, and Billy had snagged a large bunch of the green glow sticks from the hangar, far more than needed to light the place for several hours.

"Tell me about it!" George said, reacting to Craig's comment. "Can you believe we lost the chow hall before it had even opened?"

George was careful to keep the conversation away from the touchiest subject, the arrival of Sergeant Saddler. His turning up on the camp and working in such proximity to them on a daily basis was worse for the group than learning of their deployment being extended.

"Stupid Haji, he's lucky they escorted him off base. I know a lot of the guys were looking for retribution."

As they'd come off shift the guys had headed back into camp, anticipating a decent dinner at the newly opened chow hall. Instead, they'd found a pile of blackened ash and charred and sooty appliances.

"What the heck happened?" Billy had asked two soldiers that happened to be walking past when they reached what was once a source of grateful anticipation but was now no more than a burnt out husk.

"One of the locals was put in charge of filling up the diesel tanks ready for them to start up and be ready with hot food by mid-morning. I don't know how he did it, but he managed to start a fire. The truck exploded and the whole thing pretty much burned to the ground in seconds," one of the soldiers had informed them, his tone filled with disappointed disgust.

"Well that just sucks big, hairy balls," had been Billy's response, causing the others to laugh hysterically.

It seemed to be either that or cry.

It was the last straw in a day of disheartening events and bad news. Anyone that had misgivings about their excursion that night was now convinced that they needed and deserved this, and those that were already sold on the idea were looking forward to it more than ever.

Seeming to sense that the team of eight were all on edge and if pushed, he would have them all to deal with; Saddler had backed off a little for the rest of the day, making no more direct references to Clara. DJ had managed to keep his cool over the occasional snide comment or sneering look, making it through his shift without incident. He didn't know how he'd done it and didn't know if he could repeat it. He only hoped that they could come up with something tonight that satisfied his need to inflict a similar amount of humiliation and pain on the home-breaking sergeant. If not, he'd have to take matters into his own hands and damn the consequences.

About three-quarters of their way to their destination, Joey stopped in his tracks.

"Oh shit."

"What is it, what's wrong?"

"Look over there."

They all looked in the direction he was pointing.

"I can't see jack," Billy said as he peered into the blackness.

"Exactly. Where did the skyline go?"

It had been a clear and starry night a moment ago, the undulating land and the outline of the mountain ranges clearly visible. Now they were gone. Suddenly, it dawned on George what was happening.

"It's a haboob, run for it!"

They didn't need any encouragement. Laden down with their kit and their supplies for the party, they ran as fast as they could, trying to outrun the intense and violent sandstorm that was approaching rapidly in an almost solid wall. If it hit while they were outside and exposed, it would plunge them into complete darkness and while thirty miles per hour winds weren't that drastic, being battered by gritty sand moving at those speeds was no picnic. Caught in it, they would be blind and disoriented, and any exposed skin would be stripped raw.

"Get your sand goggles on," Joey screamed, fumbling in his attempt to rearrange his load to free up a hand as he ran.

While Joey succeeded, others couldn't manage the task, having to stop and lay down some of their bags to pull the goggles down from the helmets over their eyes. Joey stopped, waiting for them impatiently while Justin, DJ, and JJ ran on, either oblivious or uncaring of their plight. Glasses on, Joey grabbed another two of the bags they carried, allowing them to redistribute the others between them and move faster.

"Go, go," he urged them, taking up the rear as they moved forward together.

It had already begun to darken further, the sandstorm blocking out more of the light from the night sky as it hurtled towards them. Hoping the three front-runners had found the gate still unlocked, they ducked their heads and concentrated on moving as fast as they could. When they reached it, they found the others holding the gate open for them.

"Sorry, didn't realize you'd fallen behind, come on, we might just make it," Justin gasped as he shut the gate behind them.

They moved on as a team, heading for the same bunker as before, knowing they had to take advantage of its three levels to shelter them from the storm. Just as they reached the entrance, they were blasted by the first wall of sand and buffeted back by the wind, staggering as it hit. Ploughing forward, Justin maneuvered himself into the corridor, finding relative shelter from the wind, but not the debris contained within that were spinning and twisting around him. He reached out and grabbed the nearest body – no longer able to see whom it was – and pulled them in, pushing them towards the door. One by one, he guided them all inside, and they slammed the door shut behind them. Inside, they found little shelter, the open guard tower above allowing the elements to reach them.

"Down, everyone, get down to the lowest level."

They clicked on their flashlights and negotiated the two sets of stairs, soon finding themselves back down in the third level, the one that contained the strange writing and weird obelisk. The crates they had used as chairs were right where they had left them, scattered in an untidy semi-circle around the small, pointed monument.

"That was close," Billy said, collapsing down onto one of them and dropping the bags he was carrying before removing his goggles and backpack.

"Too close," George said. "What if we can't get out again?"

They all knew that these storms could span for miles, last more than three hours, and often deposit huge piles of sands against the sides of buildings or other obstacles that were in its path. It wasn't unheard of for them to bury vehicles and block entrances and exits.

"Then we spend the rest of the tour holed up here and getting high," Justin said, making them all laugh in spite of the very real concern.

"We'll cross that bridge when we come to it," Joey said. "We need to shelter from the storm here for a while anyway, so we might as well make the most of it and do what we came to do."

Billy began opening his kit bag, removing handfuls of green glow sticks. He began cracking them, placing them around the room to illuminate it. When he was done, there was a significant pile remaining at his feet.

"Why did you take so many," JDub asked.

"We've got acid, right, so this isn't a party; it's a rave!"

Billy grabbed another two sticks, cracking them both before dancing to imaginary music, raising his arms high above his head and waving the sticks, then dropping them to form figure eights in front of his body, reducing the rest of the guys to hysterics as they found seats and unpacked their party goods.

"If I'd known, I'd have brought some string," George said. "You can do much more complex moves if they're on the end of a piece of string, arms wraps, leg wraps, neck wraps even."

"Listen to the city dude. You think we country folks only have square dances and hoedowns?"

Joey had been busy setting up the laptop, ready to play some sounds.

"Hey, DJ, any rave music on there?" JDub asked.

"I think you'll find the genres were dance, trance, and techno," George said.

"Whatever, man! Who cares what it's called as long as it's loud."

"I think there is," DJ replied. "My aim was to have music for all occasions. Try under the 'Beats' folder and see what the subheadings are."

Joey did as instructed, grinning as he found one named 'Techno Old School Club Mix'. The file was a large one and he figured it would provide several hours of nonstop music, just what they needed for their impromptu rave. He clicked to open and play the file, the fast-paced, bouncing, bass beat that started up eliciting a loud cheer from the guys.

"Let's get this party started!" JDub yelled.

"Never fear, Dr. Justin is *on* it, boys. Did you bring the candies, Craig?"

"Yeah," Craig replied, rummaging in his bag. "Is this the kind of thing you need?"

Justin took the bag of Sweet Tart candies and grinned. "Freaking perfect!"

Sitting down, he opened the bag of candies and sat it between his feet. Removing the glass vial from inside his jacket, he carefully twisted open the cap and filled the dropper. He laid the bottle down gently and pulled one candy from the bag. Expertly, he dropped two small drops onto the center of the candy. "Who's first?"

"Me!"

JJ leaped off his seat and took the candy, popping it into his mouth while Justin prepared the next. One by one, they each took the laced treat. When it was DJ's turn, he grabbed at it, stuffing it into his mouth, his reservations long gone. Joey hesitated as Justin held a candy to him, still unwilling to participate.

"Come on, man, live a little," Justin urged.

"Yeah, just go for it. We never know which night will be our last night, enjoy it while you can."

"Don't be a party pooper."

"You chicken?"

Giving in to the pressure from his battles and not unaffected by the far-reaching effects of the day they'd had, Joey took the offered candy and popped it into his mouth. The guys cheered and congratulated him, Billy slapping him on the back. "There you go, wasn't so hard was it?"

"How long will this take to have an effect?" Joey asked Justin, the concern evident in his voice. "And what exactly can I expect?"

"Don't fret, just chill, go with it. Take two and call me in forty-five minutes; all will be right in your world," Justin said with a chuckle.

He took one himself, then began passing out round two.

"Might as well have a beer while we're waiting," George said, removing two six packs from his bag and handing them out.

JDub spotted the digital camera in DJ's half-open bag, lying at Joey's feet where he'd left it after removing the laptop. He snatched it and proceeded to snap pictures of them all as they raised their cans or pulled faces at the lens. The camera was passed around as each tried to find a more inventive or embarrassing pose to outdo the others. As the music picked up the pace, the frantic, high-pitched weird and wonderful electronic sounds laid over the jumping bass beat had them all bopping around in time in their seats. Soon, they were all up on their feet, unable to resist the sounds that called to something deep within, affecting them on a primal, instinctual level. It was impossible not to move. They grabbed glow sticks from the pile, cracking them in the middle to produce the eerie green glow that they proceeded to wave about, creating mystical patterns that hovered in the air for a split second before dissipating. Joey had upped the volume and soon they were all jumping to the beat, kicking up the sand beneath their feet as they moved harder and faster as the music all but possessed them, controlling them like puppets as the pounding rhythm penetrated into their very core.

Soon, the LSD had begun to take effect, the patterns from the sticks swirling around in their vision as if created by kaleidoscopes, no longer disappearing. Billy reached out a hand to grab one, laughing as it danced away from his hand, playing with him, toying with him.

"I'm flying!" George cried as he spun round faster and faster, his arms spread wide, his feet moving at an impossible rate.

Just then, the playlist mix hit on Darude's Sandstorm, the composition from the late nineties a blast from the past that they all recognized; be it from clubs, video gaming, or as one of the most widely used pump up songs before sporting events.

"Wooooohoooooo," Justin screamed. "Dancing in a sandstorm to Sandstorm, battles."

"Cosmic," Billy replied, his eyes wide, his mind blown by the seemingly epic fateful timing.

They danced, they drank, they tripped; all while the sandstorm raged outside, never touching the depth of the bunker where they sheltered and partied. None of them noticed the obelisk begin to glow as if illuminated by its own light source from deep within.

Chapter Fifteen: Mortar Bob

As with last time they'd broken the rules and made their own entertainment on Camp Speicher, the guys had suffered no fallout or backlash from their illicit party that they were aware of. Apart from a few of them having crushing hangovers from the cheap booze they'd consumed and a lingering sense of emptiness and mild depression that they all attributed to the coming down period from the extreme high of the LSD, nothing seemed amiss.

For most of them, it was their first experience with drugs of any kind other than alcohol, tobacco, or the occasional prescription or over the counter medicine as kids. They hadn't known what to expect from the acid trip, so they definitely didn't know what to prepare for during the aftereffects. Justin had told them in advance that the trip would probably last four or five hours if they were lucky, and that the drug would have metabolized and been excreted from their systems within twenty-four hours at the outside. They either had believed him or hadn't cared at the time when he'd assured them that it had no long-term effects or addictive properties. George had been the only one that had sought out Justin the next morning before their shift began in order to question him.

"Hey man, can I have a word?"

"Sure, come on in."

"Where's Billy?"

"Over in the shower block. He's only just gone, so if you're looking for him he might not be back for a few minutes yet."

"No, it was you I wanted to see. I just wanted to know if we had some privacy for a while to talk."

"We have. What's on your mind?"

"I'm worried about something, Justin, and I'm feeling a bit jittery about it this morning. I've heard some stories about acid, like it staying in the spinal cord forever, and how it can cause hallucinations and flashbacks weeks, months, or even years later."

"You didn't worry before taking it last night," Justin said with a wink. "You're probably just having a mild paranoia attack. There are hardly any side effects, but that can be one of them. Look, that spinal cord thing is just a myth with absolutely no scientific evidence to support it. We're all young and at the peak of our physical fitness, our bodies will get rid of it quickly. In two days max, we'll be completely clear of any traces of it in our system."

"Two whole days? What if we get random drug tested?"

"Chill, dude. We haven't been drug tested since we got here so why would they suddenly start now? Besides, they don't include LSD in standard drug tests anymore. Why do you think I chose it? That and the epic trip of course."

"What about the flashback thing?"

Justin sighed. "Look, I'll be straight with you. It can happen, but you'll be talking within days, maybe weeks at most, and it'll be really mild, just a lingering perception you experienced during the trip. The decades after the thing is mostly just an urban legend, and serious cases of Hallucinogen Persisting Perception Disorder only really affect long-term users or seriously heavy users, especially those that have had really bad trips. You're worrying over nothing; it's not going to happen. Where did you hear about that anyway? I thought you were an acid virgin."

George glanced around, checking the room was empty and that no one was loitering around the narrow hallway outside. "Can you keep a secret?"

Justin raised an eyebrow, surprised that George wanted something kept from the rest of the group and that he'd chosen him to confide in. "Sure."

"I had some trouble a while back before I joined the army. Had myself a little heroin problem and ended up in rehab. That's where I heard peeps talk about their acid trips and flashbacks."

"Wow, didn't expect that from you, Georgie-boy. You clean now?"

"Been clean from the day I signed myself into the place, until last night, I guess."

"Good for you. You did the right thing coming to me, and I'm glad you told me. I'll be mindful of that and be careful what I choose to get my hands on for your sake. There isn't any such thing as a little heroin problem, and if you have an addictive personality, it could cause issues. Still, you're fine with LSD and last night was a blast wasn't it?"

George shook his head at Justin's wide grin. "I have no idea; I can't remember a darned thing about any of it after we ate those candies."

Justin laughed and patted George on the back. "Trust me, you had a ball, and so did everyone else. No one had a bad trip, and no one will suffer any lasting effects. We're all golden, battle buddy, absolutely golden."

"And you won't say anything about this or what I told you to the other guys?"

"Secret's safe with me."

"Morning George, what's up?"

They both turned to see the toned body of Billy wearing nothing but a towel around his slender waist and unlaced combat boots that flapped around his ankles as he walked into the room. His hair was wet, and his skin glowed pink from the scalding shower.

"Hey there, Billy. Nothing much, just thanking our man here for last night. You shower with your boots on?"

Billy looked down at the heavy boots from which his slim legs protruded. "I don't wear them in the shower exactly, no, but I'm not taking a single step more than I have to without them, so I leave them right outside the stall. Didn't you hear about Sergeant Suazo a couple of nights ago?"

George shook his head, and Billy was more than content to fill him in. "He went to the latrine in the middle of the night and got stung by a scorpion, right in the arch of his foot."

"No way! Is he okay?"

"Yep, he's fine. Quick thinking son-of-a-gun clubbed the thing to death with a rock and took it with him to the medical tent, so the doc knew exactly what he was dealing with and how to treat him. I don't know if it was one of the deadly ones or not but thanks to being able to identify it, he's absolutely fine. Still, I'm not taking any chances; these boots go wherever I go."

George and Justin glanced at each other, the plan to steal Billy's boots at the next available opportunity being formed in their minds simultaneously. George turned his head to hide his grin. "Well, best get ready for the shift. See you guys soon."

Other than George's minor and quickly dispelled fears, there were no repercussions. It seemed as if no one else knew or cared about their nighttime excursion to the bunker in the forbidden area of the base or their contraband goods.

The day after the wild night, Saddler and his cohorts had attempted to get an even bigger rise out of DJ, determined to see him either crumble or retaliate and land himself in serious trouble. Everyone had been so tired or so hung over that day; they couldn't find the strength to so much as a glance in his direction, concentrating only on trying to make it through the shift without keeling over, throwing up, or dozing off. As a result, the Sergeant had been left confused and angry, looking pathetic in front of his team as the Armament Dogs acted as if they didn't hear him or he didn't even exist. It was the biggest insult they could give to a man such as him, who needed validation through seeing their pain and anger while exploiting DJ's one weakness. The team barely even noticed the effect their action, or rather their non-reaction, had on him, not realizing they'd hit upon the perfect way to deal with him without even trying.

During the party, they'd completely forgotten about the discussion they were meant to have on ways to pay the Sergeant back, not only for stealing DJ's wife but also for the way he'd treated both him and his entire team since his initial arrival. War was its own kind of hell, and they didn't need men like him adding their pettiness and making it worse. This was no kindergarten schoolyard, but he seemed to have forgotten that fact. However, they'd been so engrossed in the music and so unable to sit still, talking had been the last thing on their minds. DJ either hadn't remembered or didn't care anymore, as he hadn't mentioned it the next day, or for several days after. None of the others felt inclined to bring it up just yet, waiting to see if it could be possible that DJ had somehow made peace with the situation within himself. If he had, they didn't want to be the one to kick-start the trouble, at least not yet.

Two weeks passed, and the status quo remained. Sharing their hangar with the other team was uncomfortable, but had become bearable since Saddler had kept his distance and his mouth shut, still trying to work out why his insults and taunts had failed to have any effect on them. Joey was certain they hadn't heard the last from him but for now, it was quiet.

There wasn't much happening on base exceptthe normal routine of shifts, mortar attacks, and vehicles and aircraft coming and going at all hours. Locals were still being taken onto base to carry out mundane tasks. Quite frequently, there would be a flurry of excitement as yet another was caught with a cell phone or camera on his person once inside the fences, often after working among them for several hours. Some were even caught trying to count paces as they walked across the base, trying to mark distances between things like the control post, equipment stores, and sleeping quarters. They were obvious attempts by the terrorists to gather intelligence regarding the inner workings of the base, and a constant reminder that you never knew whose side these people belonged to, or where their loyalties lay. On interrogation, it was often found that those who committed these transgressions had wives or children that were being held hostage or threatened, forcing them into committing the required acts against the U.S. military against their will. It made the soldiers even more certain that the Hajis were nothing but cowards, afraid to come here and do their own dirty work.

Some of the guys that were eventually considered good guys – hard workers who turned up every morning and never attempted to gather intel to pass along – earned themselves nicknames, a badge of honor in the eyes of the soldiers. There was Crazy Eye, the man who had a scar running from the center of his forehead down over his left eyelid and disappearing into his heavy sideburns at the side of his cheek. Then there was Whiskey Pimp, a man that professed to all that would listen that he loved 'beer.' He would back this statement up by making exaggerated drinking motions with one hand. He was also a self-professed ladies' man. No one doubted him on that. These faces and names became as familiar around the camp as those of the soldiers stationed there did, as welcome as any other member of the team on the base fighting for what they all believed was a worthwhile cause.

One of the duties the locals were given was to build a new chow hall since the unfortunate and still unexplained tragedy had stolen away the first. While it would be a welcome addition, the ongoing work was a reminder of what had been lost. Joey had attempted to talk to the guys about it, although not in the hangar where their every word could now be overhead by Saddler and his crew.

"I don't know guys, there seems to be something weird about this tour," he'd said on a rare night where they were all gathered together in he and DJ's room.

That wasn't such a regular occurrence recently, and Joey had no idea why. Their room had been 'party central' from the day it had been allocated, the place they all made their way to after their shift, no questions asked and no invitation needed. The first night after the party, it hadn't happened, but it was no surprise that everyone just wanted to crawl into bed at the end of their twelve hours and do their best to catch up on as much sleep as they could or suffer through the remainder of their hangover in some resemblance of comfort.

Joey had expected everything to be back to normal the night after, but he had been mistaken. Somehow, things were never the same after that night, although nothing had happened to cause the small rift that seemed to appear between them. The guys now came and went at various times, not hanging around as long as they used to, and never all there at the same time, or if they were, not for long. They must have all noticed this change – even if they didn't deliberately or consciously contribute to it – but none of them voiced their observations or concerns. They merely seemed to drift apart.

"What do you mean?" George asked, curious about Joey's statement regarding the tour.

"I don't really know what I mean," Joey admitted, running a hand through his hair. "It's everything and nothing. It just seems as if we've had more bad luck on this tour than I've ever seen before."

"Its war," Billy shrugged. "Bad things happen, right?"

"Well, sure, and a lot of things are exactly what you'd expect, like the deadly creatures, the sandstorms, the constant attacks, the helicopters getting shot down right in front of us, the shit living conditions and the work to make it better, heck, even almost being overrun while reclaiming our equipment from those two Warriors was pretty normal. It's all the other little things that bug me."

JJ looked at Joey with a condescending expression. "So the really big stuff is normal, but the small stuff is weird? People are being killed and injured every day by the mortar attacks. We almost got shot to pieces arriving in Normandy. Four of you almost came out of a situation in body bags and riddled with more holes than Swiss cheese after having to climb inside choppers filled with the baked blood and guts of your fellow soldiers for the *second* time, and you don't give a rat's ass about any of that?"

Joey held his gaze. "I do, but it doesn't surprise me. That's about what I would expect during deployment. No one ever said it would be a picnic."

"So what it is exactly that's upsetting you, *Specialist* Stevenson?"

"Hey, don't talk to Joey that way," Craig said.

JJ turned on him, his eyes blazing with anger. "I'll talk to him any damn way I please. In fact, I'll talk to anyone anyway I like. You got a problem with that?"

"As a matter of fact, I have."

JJ rose to his feet, taking a step towards Craig. "So what are you gonna do about it?"

George leaped between them. "Come on guys, you two are roomies, battles, don't fight."

"You going to stop us?"

"If I have to, yes."

JDub was quick to join in. "If anyone wants to start on my battle, JJ, they're going to have to come through me first. If you want to go at it, George, I'm more than ready."

Soon, all the Privates had joined the argument, taking sides, standing up for various battles, dividing the group in a way that had never been seen before. Joey, shocked and confused, turned to DJ for assistance. Instead of being horrified and surprised at this turn of events as Joey was, DJ was sitting cross-legged on his bed, a faint smile upon his lips, his eyes shining with what looked suspiciously like glee

265

and excitement, almost as if he was enjoying the chaos that was playing out before him.

"DJ? DJ? DJ!"

DJ finally snapped out of his trance-like state and looked towards Joey with a questioning expression. The sounds of the melee appeared to filter through, and he slowly turned his head away from Joey, his eyes widening as he saw the guys yelling at each other, up in each other's faces, the occasional shove on a shoulder being dealt out to punctuate a statement.

"Guys! Quit it. Calm down. I said that was ENOUGH!"

The roar from DJ silenced them in an instant, all turning shocked faces towards their usually mild-mannered, easy-going, and soft-spoken superior. Craig and Billy hung their heads in shame, the rest of them shuffling back to their seats and sitting down, the odd narrow-eyed glance still being flashed at those they'd been arguing with only moments before.

"I don't know what this is all about, but this isn't some dive bar, and we don't brawl. Whatever is up with you can be talked over and resolved like men. We might be soldiers, but that doesn't mean we resolve everything with violence and can't use our brains. Now, one of you – and I mean just one of you – tell me what happened here. JDub?"

"You were right there, man; you didn't hear?"

"No, I was spaced out for a bit. Must have been daydreaming or dozing, I don't know. Just answer my question, and the rest of you, keep your mouths shut."

JDub nodded, accepting DJ's explanation. "Okay. Joey said that he felt this tour seemed different from the others; that it seemed to be doggedwith bad luck. He tried to explain further, saying that it wasn't the big stuff, which he kind of expected, but the accumulation of all the smaller stuff that was making him uneasy. For some reason, JJ seemed to take exception to that, and it all kicked off from there."

DJ glanced at Joey, who nodded and shrugged, half an apology and half a 'beats me' gesture. He turned to JJ. "Okay, so why did what Joey said upset you?"

JJ stared at the floor, poking at it with his foot. When he spoke, his words were muttered. "It sounded as if he didn't care that you guys almost died, or that seeing death every day was no big deal. It was like he was showing off that he was so used to it and had done so many tours before."

"Does that sound like Joey to you?"

"No."

"So was there something else?"

JJ remained silent for quite some time, refusing to raise his head. They all knew that DJ had hit the nail on the head. Something else was bothering JJ, but he didn't want to voice it. When the words came, they came out in a rush.

"He was scaring me, okay! I don't know why but I've had a real bad feeling recently, and him talking about this tour being plagued by bad luck and being different from others just made it seem like I really did have something to be afraid of, something apart from agreeing to certain death when I signed on that dotted line. Happy now?"

Joey's face filled with pity. "I'm sorry; I didn't mean to frighten anybody. I had no idea you were feeling that way, or I wouldn't have said anything."

"No, Joey, you were right to speak up," DJ said before JJ had a chance to respond. "JJ, fear isn't always a bad thing. Fear keeps us alert, sharp, and cautious. A soldier without fear is a danger to himself and his battles and has no place here."

"Doesn't it just make me a coward?"

"Hell no! A coward is someone who lets fear stop him from living his life, and having no fear isn't bravery. What's brave is being afraid of something,but doing it anyway, that's a real hero in my eyes."

JJ swallowed and nodded; only slightly pacified by DJ's words. "I guess I owe you and everyone else an apology, Joey."

"I'm as much to blame."

"None needed, man."

"Don't sweat it; it's all good."

Reassurances came from all directions, along with back pats and apologies in return. Joey watched, having the feeling none of them were as sincere as they appeared to be.

"So back to what Joey was saying, care to explain further?"

"It's nothing, forget it."

"No, come on. You're an experienced soldier and you know to trust your gut. Whatever you say might save our lives."

"I doubt it. It's not that kind of feeling. I'm probably just being dumb, letting everything get to me. Maybe it's just coming down off the high from the other night, lingering paranoia, yeah, that'll be it."

DJ was like a dog on a bone, unwilling to let it drop no matter what Joey said. In the end, he gave in to DJ's insistence and cajoling. "I didn't really mean much by it, just that all the extra stuff on top of what we have to face is making me a little uneasy."

"Like what exactly?"

"Well, the accident at the checkpoint when we'd only been here five minutes, the local having the freak-out, the little girl that was brought in not making it, the chow hall burning down, Saddler not only showing up on base but assigned to our freakin' hangar, and now this thing with the water. It all just seems like a lot on top of the expected stuff, that's all."

"Yeah," Billy agreed. "The water was a shocker true enough."

That morning, a frantic message had been sent out all over base. The bitter tasting bottled water with the Arabic writing that they'd been supplied with and drinking in copious amounts for several months had now been banned. Curious about the strange taste, someone, somewhere, high up in the chain of command had decided to have it analyzed. The results were frightening. Although it didn't account for the strange bitter taste, the water was found to contain high levels of arsenic, a tasteless and odorless poisonous metalloid that could cause acute illness – including cancer – either in high quantities or from long-term exposure. Everyone had been warned to drink as little as possible until a safer alternative could be sourced and supplied. In the heat of the desert sun, it wasn't easy to limit fluid intake. Already, three soldiers had collapsed due to dehydration in their reluctance to take even one more sip.

"Not that unusual, really," DJ said. "Arsenic shows up in groundwater all over the place. It doesn't surprise me that no one bothered to check the source before bottling it and selling it."

"You're right. I'm being stupid. It was a lot in a short space of time, and somehow it just seemed like too much. I'm on edge for nothing, forget I said anything."

"Must be the Cherokee blood making you believe the land has gone bad or something," Justin joked.

The other guys joined in, making fun of Joey and his possible superstitions and irrational fears. Most of them decided to call it quits for the night, leaving while the mood was light. In the doorway, Craig turned back to look at Joey. "Tomorrow's Easter Sunday. I'm going to pray for us all."

Joey nodded to him, acknowledging his unspoken insinuation that he thought Joey might have a point. Craig nodded back and left, not needing to say anymore. Once they were alone, Joey turned to DJ. "Did you ever see a team turn on each other so quickly?"

"Only in the very beginning when they were still having their pissing contests to establish their place in the group. I've never seen a close-knit team with an established bond break down like that, especially over what was essentially nothing."

"Do you think we can fix it?"

"I don't know, man, I just don't know. Best to sleep on it and see how everyone is come morning."

***

There was an unusual hush among the Armament Dogs as they worked the next day. Normally, the hangar would be filled with chatting, banter, and wise-ass remarks, but now they worked in silence, abandoning small talk and speaking only when necessary. JJ and Craig had decided that after last night's argument – in spite of their apologies and forgiveness – that the air had not been completely cleared between them and that they were no longer comfortable sharing a room. Craig had confessed this to Billy, who in turn had a long talk with Justin. After receiving Justin's blessing and approval, Billy offered to take JJ's place in Room Two. JJ had readily agreed, packing quickly and taking up his new residence in Room Four with Justin. When the others had learned of the switch the next morning, a few of them shrugged it off as unimportant while others, including Joey, had a sense of foreboding, feeling it somehow marked the beginning of the end of something great. With the argument not as over as they'd all hoped and the tension palpable between the two groups forced to share the hangar, they had all remained locked within their own thoughts. It was only when an abnormal amount of rockets whistled across the sky that they made eye contact with one another.

"Sounds like Mortar Bob is here again," George said.

No one really knew if Mortar Bob was one person or several. All they knew was that on a daily basis, the same truck would appear, flying around the perimeter of the base at breakneck speed while a crew of two in the back would drop rockets into tubes mounted on the rear of the truck and fire them at the base. The truck driver knew his weapons, always remaining just out of reach of the short range of personal and guard tower weapons, and disappearing before anyone had time to pin him down with longer-range artillery. The only comfort was that the speed he traveled didn't allow for any accuracy from the pair in the rear. The base made the assumption that it was always the same driver and so Mortar Bob's visits to the base became part of their usual routine. The nickname had almost become affectionate.

"This sounds different," Joey commented. "Too many of them."

The group rushed out the large, open doorway of the hangar to see what was happening. They soon realized this was no ordinary duty call from Mortar Bob; this was a massively orchestrated attack on the entire base. Overhead, the sky was streaked with blazing orange burn trails heading in from every direction, often crisscrossing each other in midair, creating a stunning, flaming portrait – a beautiful and deadly work of art. With light traveling faster than sound, the almost blinding trail of light appeared before the accompanying whooshes and whistles caught up. It was both disorienting and mesmerizing.

"Craig, if ever there was a time to pray, this is probably it," Joey said, his voice awestruck.

They watched as the rockets began to land, some safely far away from any target, others wreaking their intended havoc. One of the airfield guard towers exploded and collapsed, a place that was occupied at all times with men assigned to duty there. Sorrow filled them as they thought of the plight of those inside, unlikely to be alive but badly injured if they were. It could have been any of them, from any section, any platoon. One of the larger tents across base was hit, the resulting explosion and fire no doubt killing everyone inside. Medical trucks were setting out across the base in an attempt to reach injured survivors. There was no guarantee they would make it intact. They veered and swerved, trying to avoid the weapons falling from the sky in a heavy barrage.

Shocked beyond belief at the intensity and ferocity of the surprise attack, the armament dogs stood with open mouths, almost frozen to the spot. Sounds other than the spine-chilling whistles and booms reached their ears – screaming, yelling, the squawking of the radio – and frantic activity was apparent in front of their eyes, yet it was as if they were encased in a bubble in which time was standing still. The illusion was shattered as two rockets came from behind, streaking over the hangar, dropping and whistling low over their heads before exploding on the flight line before them. They winced and ducked as more came and the two Kiowa Warrior helicopters that had been taken out to the flight line, fueled, and fully armed that morning and ready for flight at a moment's notice, were instantly disintegrated. One moment there were two beautiful combat machines, and the next, nothing but flying shrapnel and a huge ball of fire that roared up into the air. It was carnage. The Armament Dogs scrambled back inside the hangar, taking cover and manning the radio, awaiting any instructions that might come their way.

**

The aftermath of the attack from the day before was still being measured. The flight line had taken seven direct hits and the rest of the base too many to even count. The number of lives lost was still being calculated, many on the edge, their fate uncertain. Medevac had been in operation as soon as the skies had cleared enough for them to make it out with their wounded cargo, and the medical tent was full to maximum capacity.

As Renewal Monday is celebrated by Christians as the day after Christ's resurrection, the US military rose from the ashes of destruction. The first hint of dawn had only begun to make itself known when the Armament Dogs received their marching orders to be part of the Quick Reaction Force Team. They scrambled into their full battle rattle, jumped into the already waiting LMTV and headed for the hangar, finding the fuelers already there and pilots and gunners milling about awaiting further instructions. If an attack came today, they were going to be prepared. Also, the powers that be had decided they'd had enough of Mortar Bob. If he dared to show up again today, they were determined to take him out.

Two helicopters were prepared immediately, ready for action as soon as top gave the word. The Armament Dogs huddled around the radio, an air of trepidation mixed with excitement so thick it could be cut with a knife. When the guard tower announced an approaching truck, the tension increased to almost unbearable levels. The first mortar fire was spotted and announced before it was heard. The Armament Dogs flew to the hangar door, watching as the pilots and gunners ran full speed from their tent just off the flight line to the waiting birds. Within moments, the helicopters were rising gracefully into the air and flying overhead.

"Go get him, boys," DJ murmured. "Blow him apart."

Each helicopter was armed with fourteen rockets, and as soon as the pilots and copilots got a fix on their attacker, they let loose, sparing nothing. The men watched in awe as the rockets ripped through the sky, that odd delay in the sound fooling their brain into thinking they'd gone deaf until it caught up, making their ears ring. Clouds of sand exploded at ground level as the rockets hit and exploded, then a detonation louder than the others and filled with the scent of diesel assaulted their senses. The radio that they had turned up to maximum volume confirmed their suspicions as the pilots gleefully reported that their target was acquired and destroyed. Humvees that had been waiting at the gates were immediately let loose to gather the remains and ensure there were no miraculous survivors.

After an agonizing wait, the report came, the voice metallic and static over the radio.

"Target confirmed and retrieved. No survivors."

The team of eight cheered and whooped, some leaping to their feet and high-fiving or fist bumping each other.

"We got him!"

"Way to go guys! Let's hear it for the Warriors!"

"We finally nailed that little fucker!"

They celebrated, feeling that moment of closeness that had been missing, all of them reveling in it even though they all suspected it was fleeting.

The rest of the day was busy for them, if not quite as exciting. Mortar Bob's truck was brought in and word quickly spread of his makeshift welding job that had attached the launch tube to the back. He had always fired as many rockets as his truck could hope to hold, and his speed of return had long since alerted those on base to the fact that he must have ammunition cached nearby. With the man himself gone, they launched a full out search, infantry troops heading out in droves in Humvees and circled by Kiowa warriors lending eyes and air support should they need it. The Dogs were on constant alert for the birds coming back in to be refueled and rearmed if necessary, ensuring the fastest possible turnover to keep the ground troops covered at all times.

Not only did they locate several rocket launchers placed in strategic places around the surrounding mountains in a pattern designed to cover the majority of the massive base, but they also made a shocking and revealing discovery. That Easter Sunday, the infantry uncovered a huge cache of weapons stashed in quite close proximity to the camp, a cache that included both mortars and rockets as well as spare or backup launchers. Along with the find came a revelation and understanding that they didn't know whether to be furious with it or admire it for its sophistication and ingenuity. The weapons had been frozen in ice, presumably placed into containers of water, and then chilled until frozen solid within a deep layer. Once frozen, they had been buried deep into the ground where the sand was damp and cold. The result was a sort of rocket Popsicle, one that could be chipped away just enough to rest the mortar on top of the launch tube, creating

276

an ice timer system. The enemy could prime all the launchers scattered throughout the mountains and know exactly how long the heat of the desert sun would take at any given time of day to melt the ice enough for the rocket to drop into the tube and launch into the base. Not only did it provide a way for them to be long gone before the mortar attack even began, but also it explained how the all-out attack had been carried out with such stealth and no warning. If each launcher had to be manned, they would have had a higher chance of being spotted. This would have possibly led to the alerting of the lookouts in the guard towers, that something major was afoot.

It rocked every single person on the base to the core to discover that the perfectly orchestrated and devastating multi-directional attack on Easter Sunday had probably been planned and carried out by one man more or less acting alone. Mortar Bob. It was unthinkable that this single person, with his homemade version of a mounted gun and team of two loaders clinging precariously to the back of the truck while it flew around the base at high speeds, could plan something so clever and complex, and be solely responsible for the loss of so many lives, and so many injuries. He had been given a nickname, been spoken of with amusement and derision, considered nothing more than an annoying fly buzzing around the base that they'd made efforts to swat but hadn't been overly concerned when they'd failed in their attempts. It was a costly mistake and a deep and resonating lesson for them to learn, one that would stick with them and alter their perception of any similar circumstance for the rest of their lives. Mortar Bob was a name that would be remembered forever, raised whenever any small niggle or problem was about to be brushed off as unimportant. In some bizarre and unforeseen manner, the insurgent had achieved a version of the end goal he believed would be his final reward for his actions. In the minds of many that had been on Camp Speicher that day, and those whose ears the story reached, he had gained a form of infamous immortality.

-

Chapter Sixteen: Sleep Eludes

The following weeks were a drudgery of extra shifts and duties as everyone pitched in to help rebuild the base after the damage done by the Easter Weekend attack. Extra locals were employed to assist, and the base was teamed with unfamiliar tongues and faces. The additional shifts on top of the long months of little sleep left every person in uniform looking tired and pale, their appearance disheveled and haggard, in spite of the new facilities.

With the situation as it was, the black circles, red-rimmed eyes, and gaunt, tense faces of the Armament Dogs went unnoticed, blending seamlessly with the other exhausted men on base. No one noticed anything untoward; no one guessed that all eight of the team were finding what little sleep they caught plagued by nightmares; nightmares filled with guttural screams and dark images. None of them spoke of it, assuming the horrific dreams were simply a reaction to the terror and ferocity of the recent attack. Had the group still been as close as they'd previously been, they might have opened themselves up, talking through their experiences and having the images fade in the laughter and derision of their battle buddies. Instead, they remained silent, keeping the darkness they experienced to themselves. It might have soothed the less experienced soldiers to know that even the two Specialists were not immune, that even they were being haunted in spite of having seen similar things many times before. Then again, it might have concerned them even more.

There were a few moments of light relief and cause for celebration, particularly when the base finally received a phone center, and a new chow hall had been erected. This time, the mess hall was more substantial than the first, more of a proper construction than the large tent that had not survived until opening day. The signs that adorned it were solid and professionally printed. One, in particular, was a source of many conversations and mirth. It was a massive sign out front that reminded the soldiers of the basics of Army Regulation 670-1, which detailed Wear and Appearance of Army Uniforms and Insignia. It caused much hilarity on the base when someone actually bothered to read it and found that one of the instructions read 'Nothing shall be 'pertruding' instead of 'protruding.' Since the signs were made back in the good old US of A, they couldn't even blame the error on the Hajis. There were many a comment made over the skills and knowledge of military intelligence. In a place where there was little to laugh over, amusement was taken whenever it could be found. Everyone was glad when the sign stayed, even once the error had been blatantly pointed out and mocked.

JJ was still chuckling over it for the third time when he climbed into bed, trying to keep the happy thought of someone's idiocy in his mind in the hope that it would keep the dark dreams at bay. He had just come from the midnight meal in the chow hall, wanting nothing more than to collapse and sleep a dreamless sleep. With the extra work, there was no time or energy for socializing or hanging out. He fell asleep almost instantly, and almost as quickly, the dark dreams began. He tossed and turned, moaning in his sleep, twisting the thin blanket around him. Something was coming for him, but he couldn't run, there was nowhere for him to go. In his dream, he reached for his rifle, even though he knew in his heart it would be useless against his unseen enemy. To his horror, his faithful weapon – the only thing that would have offered some comfort and sense of security – wasn't on his shoulder. He looked around for it as he backed away from whatever was coming, but his eyes couldn't penetrate the blackness that surrounded him.

Suddenly, JJ awoke, his eyes snapping open to find himself lying on his back, a massive pressure on his chest. In his panic and confusion, he thought he might be having a heart attack. He tried to open his mouth to yell for Justin but found it was already open and gasping for breath. His throat was frozen, couldn't get the muscles there to move and form any sound, never mind coherent words. He wanted to clutch at his throat, but his arm wouldn't move. Then he became aware of what was causing the crushing sensation on his chest. Something was sitting there. A dark mass, a figure, only discernable by the deeper black than the normal darkness of the room. *It's just a dream,* his mind screamed. *You're still asleep; it's only another nightmare. You think you woke up, but you didn't.*

He squeezed his eyes tightly shut, willing himself to wake up properly, relieved that at least his eyelids still seemed to work, even though this was just a dream and wasn't actually happening. Opening his eyes for the second time, there was no denying he was fully conscious. He couldn't ignore the fact that the dark presence still occupied the room with him, squashing the air from his lungs, making it impossible to breathe. He panicked. In his head, his arms flailed, and his legs kicked as he frantically tried to free himself from underneath the unknown enemy, but in reality, his muscles didn't even twitch. He was completely paralyzed. He desperately tried to convince himself that it was only a lucid dream, one where he felt he was completely awake, but his consciousness knew it was a dream within a dream. As he lay there helpless and afraid, he could hear the sounds of mortars in the distance, the rough diesel engines of the trucks out on perimeter patrol, the AC unit humming, Justin snoring beside him. He tried to cry out again to wake his battle, but all that came from his throat was a pathetic mewl. A single tear ran from the corner of his eye down into his hairline. It tickled, but his arm wouldn't react to brush it away. He couldn't deny it any longer. This was real. This was really happening.

For more than twenty minutes, he lay there, unable to move, unable to speak, unable to react physically to his abject terror, although his mind was a screaming, gibbering mess. It felt like an eternity. As suddenly as it had happened, the paralysis broke. JJ leaped from the bed, not pausing for a second. In only his boxers and t-shirt, he fled the room. Barefoot, he ran outside, desperate to escape whatever lurked within his trailer. His senses appeared heightened. He felt he travelled the short distance at lightning speed, yet his ears caught the sound of the scurrying camel spiders and the chatter of those still on shift; his nose picked up the acrid scent left behind by a discharged mortar and the lingering scent of a recently taken shower, his body reacted to the arid desert heat. He burst into DJ and Joey's room, sobbing uncontrollably.

"What the fuck!"

Joey leaped from his bed and reached for his rifle, his befuddled brain taking a few seconds to come fully awake from his own nightmare and recognize the figure in his doorway as one of his own. "JJ, is that you? What the hell's wrong?"

He fumbled for the light and turned it on, shocked to find JJ in a state of undress and trembling violently as he sobbed. Joey grabbed his still-warm blanket and flung it around JJ's shoulders, leading him to a chair. JJ was trying to speak, his words jumbled, panicked, and completely indiscernible through his terrified tears.

"Calm down, JJ; I can't understand you. I need to know what's wrong before I can help. Deep breaths, come on, with me. In...out...in...out, that's it."

"What's going on?"

The groggy voice came from the bottom bunk, the commotion finally having penetrated DJ's deep sleep.

"I don't really know. JJ's here, and pretty damn upset over something, but I can't make out what's he's saying yet."

"Is it Justin, has something happened to him?" DJ asked, scrambling out from his bunk.

JJ shook his head and pointed to his chest, indicating the issue was his own. Joey wrapped an arm around him and carried on the slow breathing with him, in through the nose, out through the mouth, until JJ's crying finally subsided and he was almost calm enough to speak rationally. He retold his terrifying ordeal in explicit detail to the two Specialists, leaving nothing to their imaginations.

"Are you sure you weren't still dreaming?" DJ asked; his uncertainty obvious.

"I thought I was too, but I swear on my own life I wasn't. It really happened. I couldn't move, not a single damn muscle. What's wrong with me, guys? What's happening?"

"I'm sure it's nothing serious. Look, we're all stressed, overworked, and overtired. You say you've been having nightmares for a while?"

JJ nodded his glum affirmation to Joey.

"Well, there you go then. We're getting precious few hours of kip as it is and the nightmares just mean it isn't a restful sleep. Sleep deprivation can cause some pretty strange things. The problem is that if you allow the fear to take over, you never get a decent night's sleep, and things only get worse. You need to relax, accept it for what it is, and get some quality rest."

"But why am I having nightmares in the first place?"

Joey gave JJ's shoulder a squeeze. "This is your first time out, and it's been a pretty shitty tour for a first deployment. No one expects you guys to handle everything like a pro from the outset, but you've all done a pretty damn good job so far. Some cracks were bound to show eventually, and this is it."

"You think that's all it is?" JJ asked, sniffling and wiping his nose and eyes with his arm.

"I'm sure of it," Joey said. "So the best thing you can do is tell your own mind to shut the hell up and leave you in peace, and go and get some decent sleep."

"You're right. I'm sorry to have disturbed you two."

"You didn't. You know we're always here for you, anytime of day or night."

"Thanks. I should get back to bed and leave you in peace."

JJ stood and removed the blanket, handing it back to Joey. "Any chance I could borrow a flashlight to go back. I'd kind of like to scare off any scorpions or snakes that might be hanging around."

"Sure thing!"

When JJ had departed, and Joey had closed the door behind him, he puffed out his cheeks, letting out a deep exhale. "Well, that was pretty traumatic."

"Do you really think it was just due to lack of sleep?"

"I have no real idea. It's plausible, and it seemed to be the right thing to say."

DJ looked at him, opened his mouth as if he were about to say more, but snapped it closed instead. "Well, since that little drama is over, I'm going back to sleep."

Joey waited until DJ had turned to face the wall and settled before turning off the light and using a flashlight to climb back up to his top bunk with his blanket in his hand. He was about to click the light off when a piece of paper laying on his bed caught his attention. Surprised and curious, he picked it up, the possibilities of what it could be running through his mind. Maybe an earlier note from JJ with some scuttlebutt he'd obtained, or details of another party from Justin. Maybe even something that someone wanted to address but couldn't bring themselves to do so in person. He was even more surprised when he aimed the flashlight and saw it was in his own handwriting. That was odd. As far as he could remember, other than filling in endless military paperwork, he hadn't written a word since his arrival. Brows furrowed, he began to read.

> *In the end, I've danced a broken dance, sifting through the*
> *remnants of translucent beings.*
> *Filter out the thick fluorescence, leaving whispers of truths in*
> *the king's mind.*
> *The souls of weary travelers twisting and tormented as the*
> *broken dreams of children throw*
> *themselves into endless constellations, echoing, though unheard*
> *throughout eternity's forest.*
> *The fear of the unmatched soul, heavy laden with suffocation,*
> *takes hostage the child and*
> *leaves the mother exiled in her thoughts.*
> *The offerings aside, and the fire of the souls resting on a*
> *thimble beneath the dragon's scales.*

In crowded halls and deep within chasms, the indifferent

march, collecting youth and drunken

with laughter.

Into emotionless hell, the spiders battle truths and leave the

heroes thoughts uncovered.

Before the great assembly, the man is secured and contently

drinks the poison offered

without expense from the heart.

In the face of madness, tossed upon the enchanted seas, the

ancients bleed, completely

At peace with their sins … and so must I. For, in the end, I

have danced a broken dance.

"What the hell is this?" Joey muttered. "I didn't write this."

Joey slid down from his bunk and flicked on the light. "DJ, wake up, I need to talk to you," he hissed as he shook his shoulder.

DJ turned his head around; his eyes screwed up against the light. "What is it now? Can't a guy get any peace around here?"

"This is important."

"Okay, okay, I'm awake."

DJ clambered out of bed and sat down again on the side of his bunk. "So what's so important?"

"I want you to take a look at something and tell me if you think it's my handwriting."

"Why are you asking me, you should know your own writing?"

"I know, just do it."

"Fine."

DJ took the proffered piece of paper and squinted at it. "I'm no expert, and I've only really seen your writing on work reports, but it looks like it, yeah. So what's your point?"

"The point is, I'm certain it's my writing, but I didn't write it, or at least I don't remember writing it. Heck, I'm not even sure if I understand it."

"It's a bit out there," DJ agreed. "But you have to have written it since it's your writing. Where did the paper come from?"

"I dunno. It looks like it could be that notebook JDub keeps in the drawer by the fridge. The one where he made everyone write down what they'd taken and what they'd bought so we could keep it all fair."

Joey went to the drawer and pulled out the notebook, flicking through until he found the jagged edge of a torn out page close to the back of the book. He showed it to DJ.

"There you go then."

"But I didn't do this," Joey said, flinging the book back in the drawer and slamming it shut in frustration and confusion.

"You must have. There's no other explanation. So let me get this straight. JJ's paralyzed in his sleep, and you're sleepwalking, sleep writing, whatever."

"It seems that way."

"Then it's got to be the stress of this particular deployment."

"I'm not so sure now that's all it is. Anything strange happening with you?"

DJ froze, startled by the question, a rabbit in headlights. Joey nodded knowingly. "Out with it."

"Yeah okay, but it's nothing as weird as what happened to you guys. It's only dreams, but man are they vivid! For the last three nights, I've dreamt that I'm alone in the hangar after dark. Out of nowhere, this chick appears–"

"Oh yeah?" Joey raised his eyebrows and gave DJ a suggestive leer.

"No, it's not like that, and she's no ordinary woman. She's just a dark and blurry silhouette, and she rushes towards me as if she's floating above the ground. I can feel the whoosh of air as she comes at me. For some reason, I just stand there, even as she reaches out and grabs my face. Then, with her face all up in mine, she starts screaming at me. Amanda, Amanda, over and over again, only it's not a high pitched screech, her voice is deep, gravelly, and it comes out more like a growl, even though I know she's shouting. It sounds almost demonic."

"Oh wow. So what happens next?"

"That's when I wake up."

"That sounds pretty scary."

"It is. I wake up terrified, and even once I get a grip, I can't help but feel a lingering dread that I just can't shake."

"I'm not surprised. Do you know any women named Amanda?"

DJ shook his head. "There were a few Amanda's back in school, but nobody I knew more than in passing or part of our crowd, nobody close, and no one I kept in contact with."

"That makes it all the weirder. Why didn't you tell me before now?"

"Why does anyone keep things like this to themselves," DJ said with a shrug. "Fear of ridicule, thinking they're making something out of nothing, finding things to explain it away in the light of day."

"Yeah, you're right. I've been having nightmares too, on top of this whole sleep writing thing. With JJ saying the same tonight, I think it's time we speak to all the guys. I don't like this, DJ. It's creeping me out. If we're all experiencing similar things, we might learn more about what's going on. At the very least it might do us all good to talk about it."

"I guess so. I suspected this day was coming anyway. Tomorrow then."

"Tomorrow," Joey agreed.

***

The next morning, Joey ensured that the guys all sat together at early breakfast, choosing a spot as far away from any other occupied tables as he could find. After he'd rounded everybody up, he pulled the crumpled piece of paper from his pocket. He knew he would have to go first, or no one else would feel comfortable opening up.

"Will everyone read this, please?"

Justin shrugged and took the sheet of paper, his eyebrows raising as he read. Once finished, he passed it along. Joey waited until it had gone full circle and come back to him before glancing at all the expectant faces turned his way.

"Song lyrics?" George asked.

"You're a poet, and you didn't know it?" JDub said with a grin.

"I don't know," Joey replied. "I know it's my handwriting, I even know where the page came from, but I have absolutely no memory of either ripping the page out or writing a single word of this. The only explanation I have is that it was some form of sleepwalking."

"That sounds a bit freaky, especially out here. If you're sleepwalking, you could go wandering off around the base and walk right into an incoming rocket. I think you should go and see the doc."

"I might have to do that, Craig, but I wanted to talk to you all first. I've been having really bad nightmares too, and last night, JJ and DJ admitted the same. DJ?"

DJ told them all about his recurring nightmare, leaving nothing out, opening himself up to the usual harassment he would expect from soldiers after such an admission. It didn't come. Instead, there was a lot of throat clearing and uneasy glances. JJ, looking nervous, added his own frightening experience to the mix. There were a few moments of silence as they all looked pale and wide-eyed, then the floodgates opened, all of them admitting to their nights being disturbed by horrible nightmares that they struggled to wake from and couldn't leave behind when they did. The more they revealed, the more frightened they became. Their own instances, they had been coping with and passed off, but learning that the others were sharing the experience rocked them to the core. They were on the verge of panic.

291

"Hold on, hold on," George said, holding his palms up to quieten them. "Couldn't this just be some sort of mass hysteria, all of us afraid and on edge out here, the fear feeding itself from the others, amplifying as it's passed down the line until it reaches fever pitch. I've heard that can happen."

"Sure it can," Joey agreed," but those situations usually need someone to pull the trigger. For one person to initially voice their fear so that the others' can take it and run with it. Not one of us has said a damn word about what we're experiencing."

"Maybe we can just sense it from one another because we're so close and spend so much time together."

"You felt close to these guys recently, JDub?" DJ asked. "Have we spent any time hanging out together in the past month?"

JDub slumped in his seat. "No, I guess not. Well, I got nothing."

"Could it be, you know, the stuff," Craig hissed, waving a hand at Justin.

"Not speaking about that here, but no, absolutely not. I'm betting my life on that."

They fell silent, their breakfast mostly untouched. With no explanations and no comfort to be drawn from their peers, they felt lost and afraid. It was a relief when it was time to start their shift, a return to normality and practicality where they could push this aside. They moved together as one, almost like the old days but missing the camaraderie and connection they'd felt back then.

Saddler gave them a smirk as they walked silently into the hangar together, not having spoken a word to anyone since their conversation in the chow hall. "Morning, ladies. What's up with your faces, somebody die?"

"Its war, you asshole. Somebody dies every freaking day."

"Shame it wasn't some of you. I'm sick of sharing this space with a bunch of clueless grunts. Maybe I'll put in a request for leave, go home to my fine woman who's waiting with open arms and legs."

Joey and Billy grabbed DJ, holding him back from the Sergeant. "Not worth it, remember?" Joey whispered.

Saddler laughed as he turned and walked back to his own section of the hangar. "Oh, by the way, top left marching orders for you. I know most of you can't read so if you've got any trouble, bring it over and I'll help you out."

"What a dick," JDub said with a shake of his head as Saddler's mocking laugh echoed around the hangar. "One of these days he's going to open his fat mouth to the wrong person and get his lights punched out."

"But not by any of us," Joey said firmly. "Come on; let's see if he was telling the truth about orders or if he's just yanking our chains."

They found that Saddler had at least been telling the truth about the orders. The commander was sending the Kiowa Warriors out on a upcoming special mission and had ordered the reconfiguration of their weapons systems. Joey let out a low whistle as he peered over DJ's shoulder to read the document that had been attached to a clipboard and left for them.

"Flechette rockets, huh. Things are getting serious."

"Remind me," Billy said from behind Joey. "It's ringing bells from lectures, but I can't quite recall what they are, and we haven't come across them for real yet."

"I'm not sure if you'd want to know the details, but I guess if Armament is where you want to be then you have to. The Flechette is pretty similar to your regular 2.75-inch rocket that gets loaded into the pods on the side of the bird, so they load the same way, except that they have a small wire, called the fuse, on the front of them that connects to the rocket pod in a small hole. This fuse allows them to air detonate."

"Oh yeah, the Hydra 70 range of rockets. They can be used to create illumination over an area, or smoke screens and stuff. It's coming back to me now. We used the signature smoke ones in training."

"Good. The Flechette has a slightly different purpose, though. It's used primarily for anti-personnel operations. Inside, there are over twothousandsixty-grain Flechettes – or tiny, hardened steel, razor sharp little darts – and it has a pretty impressive burst radius."

"Hot damn! I think I've heard of these things. Are they even legal?"

"I'm not sure if their production is legal anymore under the Geneva Convention, but the army has large reserves of them, so maybe it's a loophole, George. Anyway, when these things detonate, these tiny nails, or darts, fly out at high velocity, cutting their targets to ribbons, hence, the very reason they are used for crowds of people."

"That's pretty gruesome."

"That's not the worst. Before it's all put together, every single Flechette is dipped in a long-lasting anticoagulant. Being shredded by one of these would be absolute agony, but it wouldn't necessarily kill you. What makes it a death sentence is that the wounds won't stop bleeding as the blood can't clot."

"So you would feel like a hundred razors cut you and then slowly bleed to death?"

"Pretty much, only depending on the severity of the wounds, it might not be that slow."

"That's downright barbaric! No wonder they didn't go into detail about these."

"They're an absolute atrocity, but you can't deny their effectiveness in dispersing a crowd or taking out a large number at once. If you were stuck inside a building, surrounded by the enemy with no way to execute your extraction plan, could you think of a better sight to see coming to your assistance than a bird loaded with these?"

"No, I guess not."

"Exactly, and orders are orders, no matter if we agree with them or not. Lesson over, time to get to work. We stashed these right at the back, so we'd better hustle and dig them out."

The group followed Joey to the rear of the hangar where they set up an effective production line to move the crates of ammo to locate the weapons they needed. Once the crates were freed and the rest stacked neatly back in place, they carried them to where they were needed. They were busy rearing the birds detailed on their list when they heard approaching footsteps. A broad grin spread across DJ's face as he recognized the figure walking towards them.

"Hey, guys. I'd like you to meet Specialist Larson Curtis. He's a friend of mine. We toured together in Afghanistan and were stationed together back in Hawaii. I had no idea he was here so he must have come out with the second wave. Hi man, how are you?"

The man didn't smile or acknowledge the others. Instead, he walked straight up to DJ, his face serious. "Hey man, I was just at the phone center talking to my friend, Amanda. She says she's been trying to contact you on the astral plane. She's a psychic, so she's into all that stuff. She's been trying to reach you because she says she has to warn you. Your dark soul is calling her to you; you're in some sort of trouble."

Eight faces paled, eight pairs of eyes went wide with a mixture of fear and amazement. DJ's jaw dropped open, and he gaped at his old friend. He knew he was a no-nonsense, no-bullshit guy. This friend of his had to have really pressed home a sense of urgency before he was relaying a message such as this. The fact that her name was Amanda stunned him beyond words. His mouth opened and closed like a goldfish until he finally found his voice.

"What do you mean, what sort of trouble?"

Specialist Curtis shrugged. "No idea, that's all she said. The rest was just about how urgent it was that I get the message to you, so I hotfooted it out here as soon as I got off the phone. Sorry, man, I'm late already, so I'd better go. Maybe we can catch up later."

As Curtis departed, DJ turned angry eyes on his team. "Who's been blabbing about my personal shit?"

"No one, dude."

"We haven't said a word."

"We wouldn't do that."

"Somebody must have said something! How else could he have come up with that name?"

"DJ, think about it! You only told me in the privacy of our room a few hours ago. Since then, I haven't been out of your sight, and apart from the guys, the only person I spoke to was Saddler, and you were there when I did. You heard what I said so you know it definitely wasn't me. We told the others at breakfast, and they haven't been out of our sight or spoken to anyone since either, so how could they have told anyone?"

"Maybe someone overheard us at breakfast," Craig offered.

Joey shook his head. "You saw the chow hall. We were so early it was still practically empty. There was no one else around for at least three tables. Unless some of us are bugged, no one heard."

DJ gripped Joey's arm, his eyes frantic. "There has to be an explanation. There just *has* to be!"

A moment of silence followed as they all wracked their brains, trying to find some normal, everyday explanation. As they failed to debunk the revelation, their fear and agitation only grew.

"DJ, I'm sorry, man, but I can't think of anything to explain this other than he was telling the truth. You told us yourself that it was as if she flew towards you, and that she was a shadowy figure. I don't know much about this astral plane thing, but it seems to fit that it would be in a kind of spirit form, right?"

"What you're talking about, JDub is commonly called astral projection, a sort of out-of-body experience where the body and soul separate but the body doesn't die. Supposedly, the soul can go traveling on its own," Joey informed them. "She might have been doing that, or maybe just creating some sort of psychic link with you, a sort of spiritual visitation which you perceived as a dream. Maybe your brain just created the whole shadow figure part to help make sense of what was happening."

"There's no making sense of any of this! This is crazy," JJ exclaimed. "You're trying to tell me that some weird chick crawled out of her body and hopped over here to visit DJ in his dreams, scream her name at him, and scare us all half to death? Not only is it impossible, but it doesn't add up. What was the point?"

"I don't think the whole thing is quite as creepy as your making it sound. That really isn't helping. Try to think of it more like a shifting of consciousness into another realm."

"And what about you with your dark spirit on your chest suffocating you? This isn't any creepier than that!" Craig admonished JJ. "So you think this could be real, Joey?"

"Joey thinks anything's possible with enough peyote, right man?"

"Sure, Justin, that's right," Joey said with a shake of his head and a roll of his eyes. "Look, I'm no expert, and I believe that many of the so-called psychics are charlatans, but that doesn't mean there aren't genuine people out there that have tapped into something the rest of us have chosen to close off. As to the point, who knows? Maybe she couldn't get enough of her message through to DJ because he's not open to this stuff, or maybe she just wanted him to get her name so that when she could use traditional methods to pass on an actual message, it would be like a confirmation that it was genuine and couldn't be easily dismissed as BS."

"I consider myself a very spiritual person," George said quietly. "I fully believe this is absolutely undeniable, and you're all missing the most important point."

"Which is?"

"That she said DJ has a darkness in his soul and that he's in trouble. I'd say that's spiritual trouble. I think you should go and see the Chaplain. If you don't do that, maybe you'll pray with me?"

"I don't think I can take anymore of this," DJ said, covering his face with his hands. "It's too much."

"That sounds as if a bit of escapism is required," Justin said with a grin. "A cue for another party!"

***

Once again, green glow sticks illuminated the dark cavern and techno music blared from the Bose speaker. It felt natural and right to the group of eight to be there. It no longer felt menacing and creepy to them; it felt welcoming, a sanctuary from the horrors and madness above. Two rounds of Justin's doctored candy had been passed round, helping the guys to forget all they were experiencing. They were dancing, unable to sit still even though physically and mentally exhausted, grinning at one another, having nothing but a good time.

Without warning, DJ's demeanor changed. His eyes are filled with rage and he reached for Justin, grabbing him and throwing him to the ground. Before Justin could react, DJ was on top of him; his hands clamped around his throat, squeezing tight. Justin kicked and punched at the man on top of him, gasping for breath. His eyes tried to plead where his voice couldn't, his throat too constricted. There was no recognition on either side. Justin saw no remnants of the man he knew as his terrified eyes stared into the dark and soulless face above him, the eyes empty and blank. They were the last thing Justin saw before he blacked out.

"DJ, let him go. Get off him!"

The drug-slowed reactions of the others had kicked in, and they grabbed at DJ, trying to pull him off their battle.

"Fuck, he killed him! He killed Justin!"

"Oh my God! What are we gonna do?"

They were panicked, frantic. It took all eight of them to hang onto DJ as he struggled and fought with them, trying to get back to Justin. With oxygen returning to Justin's system, he came round, groggy, disoriented, and very high. He coughed, his throat raw as he tried to gasp more air into his lungs. DJ began to scream at him.

"Wake up, Justin! Come on! You have to get out of the car. You've just wrecked it, and it's on fire. Hurry!"

Justin's confused eyes filled with terror once more. He fought to remove himself from the imaginary, burning wreckage of the non-existent car. The others fell afoul of DJ's hallucination, letting him go to help pull Justin to safety and scrambling away from the danger.

JDub was on Justin as soon as they'd reached their perceived safety. "What do you think you were doing, driving like a lunatic like that? You almost killed us all!"

"Yeah, Justin, you moron!"

"It wasn't his fault, leave him alone!"

Chaos ensued, arguments breaking out between them all. Everyone was screaming at one another, punches were thrown, vicious fights broke out, the intention not to harm or subdue, but to kill. Only their evenly matched physical prowess, their lessened abilities due to the booze and drugs, and their failure to think about the loaded rifles that sat propped up against the wall prevented any of them from achieving their intended goal.

Justin was the first to come down from the trip, blinking away the confusion as his arm was pulled back to hit Craig again. He released the chokehold he had on his battle and began to laugh, a wild and hysterical cackle that cut through the trip of the others and brought them back to awareness. Battered and bruised all over, those on the floor scrambled to their feet, their befuddled minds unaware of what had happened or the injuries they'd inflicted upon, and received in turn from, their battles.

"Holy shit that was intense!" Justin cried through his laughter. "I had no clue! Again!"

Joey was the only one who heard the low, throaty chuckling that echoed around the cavern, blending with Justin's manic giggling. He looked around at the other men. None of them were laughing.

Chapter Seventeen: Boys Will Be Boys

Joey sat in his room, DJ's laptop open in front of him, one hand placed gently upon it. Apart from the occasional twitch of a finger, he was completely still, his expression sad.

It had been a few days since the last party, and he was struggling to shake the uneasy feeling that had dogged him ever since. The cuts and bruises were beginning to heal, and none of them had much to say about what had happened between them. They couldn't remember much about it, nor did they want to dwell on it too much. Maybe it had been a way of releasing the tension building within the team while their inhibitions were lowered, or maybe it had just been a bad, crazy trip. Either way, the silence seemed appropriate, and they hid what they could of their injuries, keeping as much of their bodies as possible concealed to cover the revealing marks, cuts, and deep, purple bruises; particularly those that displayed perfect handprints low around Justin's neck. Once again, they'd gotten away with it, explaining away their damaged faces and grazed knuckles by way of a friendly, impromptu boxing match after shift. Torn muscles and broken ribs were being disguised by a stoic refusal to wince or limit movement in any way.

Joey had already convinced himself that the laughter he'd heard was simply an acoustic anomaly created by the bunker itself – Justin's hysterics altered and echoed back at them – or his own little acid trip in his head. No one else had reacted to it, so they obviously hadn't heard it. His conviction didn't stop the sound from appearing in his dreams, though. He'd heard it there every night since; that deep, malicious, mocking laughter haunted him whenever he closed his eyes.

He didn't glance away from the screen when DJ entered the room, his top half-naked except for a towel around his shoulders. DJ stopped just inside the doorway, assessing the mood of his roommate.

"Who pissed in your cheerios?"

Joey glanced up. "Oh, nobody. I'm just looking at the pictures I uploaded from your camera. You don't mind do you? You said I could use the laptop anytime. Shouldn't you be covered up?"

"Its fine, no problem, on both counts," DJ replied, coming over to stand behind Joey and take a look. "It's pitch black out, and the bruises are finally starting to fade. I'm mostly a sickly yellow color now. Shit, look at the face on JDub in that one. I'd forgotten we'd taken pictures that night."

The picture in question was of JDub, Billy, and Craig, arms around one another, mugging for the camera, their crazy expressions emphasized by the green glow from the sticks they held. It provided the comfort that Joey had sought, showing nothing but guys having a good time, everything normal apart from the glassiness of their eyes caused by the gear.

"Shuffle up and let me see them."

Joey did as he was asked; shifting over on the bed and resuming his clicks on the tracker pad, going slow so DJ could see each one in detail before moving on. While DJ laughed and exclaimed over the images of their wild night, Joey made the occasional comment, but his smile never reached his eyes. Once they were back to the beginning, DJ rose and went to look for a T-Shirt.

"So why the long face, don't like the way your hair looks?" he asked as his head momentarily disappeared then reappeared as he tugged the shirt down over his broad shoulders and taut abdomen, wincing a little as he hit a still tender area.

"Haha, very funny. No, I was just thinking about how happy we all were, how close we were. Even in these pictures, high as kites, you can see the bond we shared. We've lost it somehow, and I don't know why, or how to get it back. We're falling apart, man, as a team and individually."

DJ shrugged. "Guess it doesn't matter, as long as it doesn't affect our jobs."

Joey frowned. That wasn't something the man he knew would normally say. A bond with men on your team was an essential part of making it through a deployment, and they all knew it.

"So the memory card in the camera's empty now?"

"Huh? Oh no, I only uploaded the ones that had the guys in them. Want me to grab the rest?"

"May as well keep them all together in one folder. I don't really have much use for the camera now so I doubt I'll be adding any more."

"Okay, I'll get that done for you."

A few minutes later, Joey called DJ back over. "Take a look at these."

DJ watched as Joey flicked through some pictures that had been taken of the bunker itself without any of the partying subjects. He chuckled. "Place sure does look creepy in these. Doesn't feel so bad when you're in there, but if anyone showed me this, I'd say it was somewhere I'd never want to go."

"No arguments from me there, but look as these last few." Joey pointed to the obelisk on screen. "Damn thing seems to be glowing by itself."

"Nah, it's just the glow sticks."

"But it's not doing it in the earlier ones, only these."

"So someone threw a few more sticks over there, or accidentally kicked one over to where it was going to get caught right by the camera to give that effect. It's nothing, Joey; don't go all Spooky Mulder on me."

Joey let out a laugh. "You're right, I'm becoming dumb, just ignore me."

"Already was."

Joey gave DJ a playful punch on the arm. "Asshole. Hey, do you mind if I copy this folder onto the flash drive and take it over to the computer lab? You've got some great shots of the journey here and the scenery, and I'd love to send everything to Carrie."

"I don't know why she'd want to see all our ugly mugs."

"It's good when she can put faces to the names I talk about all the time; it helps her picture everything."

Sadness flashed across DJ's face. "Yeah, I know."

"God, I'm sorry, I'm becoming an insensitive ass, aren't I?"

"No, no, it's fine. That's why I took them in the first place so it's good that they'll still serve a purpose. You go ahead and send her my love too. Just make sure she doesn't post any up anywhere where it could get us in trouble. We've gotten away with it so far, but I keep getting the feeling that our luck's going to run out soon."

"I'll make sure of it. I'll go on over and email her now."

"Okay, I'll catch you in the morning then, I'm heading to bed."

***

The next day passed quietly, a conversation between the Armament Dogs practically nonexistent and when it occurred, it related directly to their current task. The jocularity and easiness were gone. Joey had initially explained it away as being due to the presence of Saddler and his crew, the risk that anything they said could be overheard and subsequently used against them. Had it been anyone else sharing their hanger, they would have done everything in their power to make friends and expand their group. As it was, every twelve-hour shift was depressing as hell, and with everything else that had been going on, Joey was having a hard time attributing it all to Saddler. He was more of a convenient scapegoat than a genuine reason. Joey couldn't talk to the guys about his fears; they were on edge enough as it was. He'd considered talking it over with Carrie but was afraid of worrying his wife unnecessarily. There seemed to be nothing else to do except keep his mouth shut and his thoughts to himself.

At the end of the grueling shift, the team headed for the chow hall for a late evening meal, sitting together more out of a sense of duty than desire. Halfway through the meal, Justin threw down his fork, causing his mashed potatoes to spatter the table around him.

"This is bullshit! I don't know what the fuck's wrong with you all. You used to be fun to be around, you were better than any family I'd ever had the pleasure of knowing, now look at us, we barely even say good morning. What the hell happened?"

"I don't know, Justin, why don't you tell us?" George hissed. "Nothing's been the same since you brought that shit back here."

"That's got nothing to do with it, and you know it."

Justin's tone was angry, his brows raised, daring George to push him. Afraid of his secrets being revealed, George backed down.

"It was just a suggestion. We keep going round in circles with this and every time we explain it away, more stuff happens. JJ, have you had any more of those nightmares?"

JJ nodded. "Happens every night or every second night now, only they're not nightmares. I'm awake, but I can't move, I'm completely paralyzed, the life being crushed from me by something sitting on my chest. I know how it sounds, but it's real, something's there, in the room with me, in my bed, on top of me."

"I wish you guys would agree to pray with me. I really think it would help."

"I don't really go in for group prayers and stuff, George, but even I've been considering it. Anything that'll stop those dreams of that crazy chick."

"You're still having those, DJ?" Joey asked, surprised.

"Yep, and just like JJ, it's getting more frequent and more intense. I know she's saying more than her name now, only I can never remember what it was when I wake up."

"Maybe you should talk to her directly, for real I mean. Can't you ask that Curtis guy for her number?"

"Larson Curtis," DJ corrected. "I could, and I've thought about it, but I'm afraid to."

"Why afraid?"

"Lots of reasons. I guess part of me doesn't really want to hear what she has to say, and part of me thinks that if I give any of this any credence at all, I'm opening myself up to a whole can of worms. Better to tell myself it's all bullshit, just freaky coincidence than to think it might hold any truth."

Murmurs of agreement spread across the table.

"I've got an idea," Joey said. "DJ, your laptop has a built-in video camera. Do you know if it has the ability to record onto the hard drive?"

DJ's smile was one of fond remembrance riddled with sadness. "Yeah, it was originally supposed to be Clara's laptop. I remember the day we went shopping for it as if it was yesterday. Clara was determined at the time that we were getting a puppy. She got it into her head that she wanted a new computer that she could use to watch the puppy during the times she wasn't with it, like when we went to bed or when she had to go out. I thought it was cute that she wanted to be able to keep an eye on it that way, and figured it might be a good idea in case it got any ideas of wrecking the house while we were asleep. If it got up to too much mischief, we'd hear it, and it would wake us up. She said it would all be good practice for when we started our own family and would need to monitor the baby, teaching us to respond quickly to sounds. I told her that a baby monitor would be the best solution, but she wanted something that could record, said she would be making keepsakes and storing memories, not just keeping them safe. How could I refuse that, it was so damned sweet? We thought about a home CCTV system with a hard drive recorder, but the thought of running cables all around the house and fixing cameras to the walls didn't appeal. Too inflexible and too invasive, so she came up with the idea of a laptop that could be carried around and placed wherever.

"We went to the store, and after finding out that they didn't really do what we wanted the camera to do, she told the guy in the store she wasn't going to part with a single dime until it did. He told her it was impossible, but she told him that was rubbish, nothing was impossible. Boy, was she feisty and determined when it came to getting what she wanted?I don't know if the guy was afraid of her or afraid of losing the commission, but at the end, he told her if we bought the one with the highest grade camera. He could fix it for us and install the software we'd need, for an extra fee paid in cash direct to him, of course. So we bought the thing and left it with him, with instructions to meet him at the coffee shop down from the store in two days' time.

"Clara thought the whole thing was an absolute hoot, treated it like some undercover operation. To be honest, I just felt like we'd lost the money, that the guy wouldn't show and when we went to the store; he'd claim we took the laptop with us."

"What happened?"

"Did he show?"

"Well, obviously, dumb ass, he's got the laptop hasn't he?"

"Oh yeah! Stupid me."

The others were engrossed in the story, glad of the change of subject. They were tired of going round in circles with things they couldn't make sense of and didn't understand. This was a moment of light relief, and it felt nice to have DJ talking so much again, and even better to see him laugh.

"Yeah, he showed, with the laptop. I zoned out when he talked about what he'd done, something about taking it apart and removing filters I think, whatever. Clara kept him there for nearly an hour, getting him to explain how to use everything before handing over the money. I'm pretty sure he was late for work and pretty pissed off with us, probably thought it had been more trouble than the money he made was worth. I remember him making some snide comment, wishing us luck with our power bills or something when we left. In the end, we never did get that puppy, and Clara found she didn't really like the new laptop, too different from her old one that she was comfortable and familiar with, so she insisted I have it."

He was quiet for a moment, the laughter gone. Joey thought he was probably thinking of the family he would never have with her either, and felt sorrow for his friend as well as guilt for bringing back so many memories. Finally, DJ gave himself a shake. "Anyway, I never really used that side of it, but as far as I remember, it'll pretty much do whatever you want."

"I'm sorry, DJ. I didn't realize it would be such a painful question."

"That's okay. I guess there'll be a million questions that bring back memories like that one. I might as well start getting used to them. I guess I owe you all an apology, too. You didn't need to hear all that, a simple yes would have done it, but it felt kind of good to talk about her and remember stuff we did together."

"We enjoyed hearing it. You can talk about her anytime you want; it'll probably be good for you. We're all happy to listen; we're all here for you in any way you need us, and want to help any way we can."

"Thanks, I'll keep that in mind. So what did you have in mind for the camera?

"I was just thinking, what if we set it up to record JJ while he's in bed?"

"You wanna perv over him, Joey?"

"Shut up, Justin. Look, we're all sitting here wondering if we're going crazy or what. We set up the camera, and we've got eyes and ears in the room. If this has a simple medical explanation, we'll see and hear nothing except Justin's snoring and JJ having a nightmare or some of

312

sort of panic attack. Then we know this is all just down to stress and our overworked imaginations."

"Okay," Billy said with a nod. "That makes sense, but I have a question."

"What's that?"

"What the hell do we do if we actually see or hear something else?"

"Then we get down on our knees in front of George and beg him to pray for our sorry asses."

There was a moment's silence while they allowed this to sink in.

"Okay," JJ said. "I'm in if you all think it will help. Maybe we should do the same for you too, DJ, and you Joey. Any more nocturnal poetry?"

"Not that I know of, and I haven't woken up anywhere except in my own bed, so I don't think I've been sleepwalking."

"Maybe you should sleep with your boots on, just in case."

"Might be a good idea," Joey said with a chuckle, feeling better now that they had something to focus on, some small action that they could take that might provide answers.

"Let's start tomorrow night," Craig said, rising from his seat, yawning and stretching. "I'm beat. All I want to do is crawl under the blanket and forget about everything."

Everyone followed his lead, tidying up their half-finished meals and pushing their chairs in. Joey had a final word of warning for them.

"Don't speak about what we're going to do again, definitely not in the hangar or in the rooms, not even while we're setting it up. We bring it in ready to rock and roll and don't even mention it."

"Why the hell not?"

"Because whatever it is might be listening, and we don't want to give the game away."

JDub shuddered, but Justin snorted. "Seriously? You really think this is some ghost or something that's creeping around and listening to our conversations?"

"That's what we're trying to find out."

"Okay then, Gypsy Rose Lee, let's just say it is. Won't they see the computer anyway?"

"They might be from the 1800's or something," Craig said with a grin. "They might not know what it is."

"Give me shit as much as you want if it makes you feel better," Joey said with a shrug as they left the chow hall and made their way to their trailers. "I'm hoping I'm ridiculous just as much as you are."

They walked in silence until they reached the area that served as their homes.

"Thanks for walking me home, ladies. If you don't mind, I'll pass on the coming in for a coffee and don't expect a good night kiss on the first date."

"Justin, has anyone ever told you you're an A-grade ass hat?"

"Sure, JDub, all my life. At least I got an A for something, but I'm trying for A+."

"Keep going; you're almost there."

"Go to bed," DJ said with a shake of his head. "All of you."

The group split up and headed for their respective rooms. DJ cocked his head as he opened the door and flicked on the light.

"What is it?" Joey said from behind him.

"Thought I heard scuttling or scuffling as if the light had disturbed something."

"Oh shit, a big bug or something must have gotten in. We'd better have a look for it in case it's a scorpion. I'm not going to bed until I know what kind it is."

A quick scan over the floor showed no sign of any intruder. Although not really expecting to find anything, DJ flipped back the blanket on his bed. His scream was an instinctual reaction as he dropped the blanket and leaped back, crashing into Joey.

"What the hell, what ..."

Joey trailed off as he saw what had caused such an extreme reaction. DJ's bed was crawling with not only various types of scorpions but also with large camel spiders. Many of the scorpion's tails were raised as they fought against the large spiders that were trying to devour them. Some of the other spiders gladly made the small leap from the bed to the floor, seeking out the brightest patch on the floor caused by the overhead light. They were notorious for loving shade throughout the day but seeking out any patch of light at night. The Scorpions, however, disliked the light and tried to find shelter from it, burying beneath DJ's blanket and pillow, or scuttling off the bed to scurry beneath the few items of furniture.

DJ and Joey backed up a few steps, their brains barely processing what they saw before shouts and yells could be heard from the other rooms. Craig's panicked face appeared in the short, narrow hallway.

"Snakes!" he said. "My bed's full of snakes!"

Soon, all eight of them were huddled outside the trailer, having each found their beds to be crawling with insects of some variety or another and mostly the nasty kind. They'd been joined by the four other guys that shared the trailer with JJ and Justin and six guys from the next trailer along who'd come to see what the commotion was about.

"Well, shutting off the lights inside and putting up a big work light out here will get rid of the camel spiders, they'll run to the light," one of them offered, scratching his head. "Won't work for the scorpions or snakes, though. What the hell did you guys have in your rooms to attract them all in like that?"

"Nothing. Any food we've got is sealed in the fridge, and we're really careful with crumbs. They didn't get in there on their own," DJ replied, his face grim.

"So how did they get in?"

"Someone had to have put them there, and I've got a pretty good idea who – Saddler and his boys, it has to be."

"Son of a bitch!" JDub exploded. "Wait 'til I get my hands on him in the morning!"

"Hold up there; we don't know that for sure," Joey said. "How would he have gathered them all up, and how did he have the balls? I suggest we ask him first. If he knows anything about it, he'll be too smug to hide it. If he gives himself away, then we kick his ass from here to kingdom come, agreed?"

"Yeah, I guess so, but I've been itching to let loose on him since the day he arrived."

"We all have, but we don't jump to conclusions, we're better than that. Just concentrate on how the hell we're going to get these things out of our rooms."

"My momma used to sprinkle cinnamon around the doors and windows to keep scorpions out, must have worked, I don't remember ever seeing any hanging around near our house," Billy supplied.

"Good thinking. Go and find Sergeant Heard and see if he'll sign a requisition for us to have some, they'll probably have catering size cans of the stuff. Also, see if we can have his permission to borrow some long grill tongs or something and see if they've got any deep, plastic storage containers or sacks that we can stuff them into."

Billy ran off to summon the Sergeant for his assistance and Joey turned to the other guys that had joined the group. "Any chance any of you will stick around to help?"

"You bet, you'll be here all night otherwise, and there's no way I'm going back to bed with all those things so close."

The Sergeant not only agreed to give them whatever they needed but also came to help, rustling up some additional assistance on the way. There were about twenty-five of them in all, and they worked together using a variety of methods and suggestions until they were satisfied that each room was clear.

"That's it," Joey said after a final check. "The creepy crawlies are either loaded into these crates or have left of their own accord. If we could have an LMTV, Sergeant, I'll run them out to the far side of the base as far from CHUville as possible and set them free."

"It's okay, I'll have some of the boys that are on patrol do it, you've all lost enough sleep as it is. I hope to God this wasn't you playing pranks on each other."

Joey held Sergeant Heard's stern gaze. "I can assure you it wasn't any of us. A prank's a prank, and none of us are above that now and again, but this was several steps too far."

"Fair enough. Any ideas as to who was responsible?"

"Maybe, but I'm not willing to say until I've spoken to that person and judged his reaction for myself."

The Sergeant looked at Joey long and hard, considering the unspoken as much as the words he'd said. "Okay then, I'll leave it with you. If you want to report anything, you know where I am, otherwise, just don't let it get out of hand or go too far."

"Understood."

Joey knew the Sergeant had given them the go ahead to deal with the situation, however, they saw fit, accepting that this was far from a friendly prank and that retribution would be called for. Provided they didn't half-kill Saddler, anyone who went whining to their superior would be sent away with a flea in his ear. It was a good end to a horrible night.

The next morning, the guys agreed to let DJ take the lead in the questioning while they watched for telltale reactions from any of

Saddler's crew. They walked in together and marched to where Saddler was working.

"First question, how did you get in?"

Saddler's smirk of greeting was nothing out of the ordinary. "Through the big door, same as always. Did you forget how they work? You just open them up and walk right through."

"You know I'm not talking about the hangar."

"Then I don't know what you're talking about. Go away; I'm busy, and you should be too."

DJ took a step closer. "Not so fast. I want answers. How did you gather them all up then set them loose inside, and how did you get into our rooms."

Saddler paused in his work and looked at DJ. The puzzled expression was genuine. "I really haven't got a clue what you're talking about."

"Don't give me that BS! You know exactly what I'm talking about!"

"Whoa there, princess, don't get your silky panties in a knot. It sounds as if someone messed with you guys pretty good. I don't know what was done, but since you're all so riled up about it, it must have been good. I wish I could take the credit, but I can't. Hats off to whoever it was, though; I'm pretty jealous of them right now."

"So you don't know what happened last night?"

"Nope, although no doubt I'll hear about it soon, it sounds too juicy not to do the rounds. I'll look forward to hearing about it, unless of course, you want to tell me now. Nothing like hearing it from the horse's mouth. Maybe you'll even cry."

DJ turned away in disgust, and the men followed, disappointed. They'd all been eager to have a piece of the smart-mouthed Saddler.

"He really didn't have a clue, did he?" JDub muttered.

"It certainly looked that way," Billy agreed.

"I still don't trust him, and if it wasn't him then who the heck was it? We don't have any enemies here, and that could have turned pretty serious. No matter how mild the venom is, if we'd received multiple bites or stings, it still could have been really bad, and some of them around here are fatal anyway."

"It was a dangerous stunt, and if not Saddler, I can't think who'd do something like that to us. I guess we need to put it aside and get to work; it looks like we've got a busy day ahead of us."

Three Kiowa Warrior helicopters were lined up in the hangar, waiting for attention. After studying the report sheets, they knuckled down and got to work. It was nearly the end of the shift when DJ finished the last job on the list, reassembling a 50-caliber gun on one of the birds. Putting the finishing touches on it, he double checked his work then signed the paperwork to say it was done, adding it to the pile. Seeing him do so, Saddler wandered over. Much to the Armament Dogs' chagrin, he'd been appointed one of the shop's Technical Inspectors, and he made good use of the position, painstakingly checking over their work with accompanying tsks and shakes his head before finally signing off on it with a sly grin. It was a practice that he never failed to find amusing but drove the Dogs' crazy. Still, there was nothing much they could about it. They stood through it once more, willing him to hurry up and get it over with, have his laugh at their expense, and let them go. With last night's debacle, they were tired, grouchy, and just wanted to get out of here.

After having his usual fun, Saddler checked over the 50-Cal, inspecting it closely. "This is shit. Whoever did this needs to do it over."

DJ knew that Saddler could tell at a glance who'd completed the work; his signature was against it on the paperwork. He stepped forward. "The work's fine."

"No, it isn't. The rest of you can go if you want, but you're staying here, stripping this down, and starting again. I'll be back in fifteen minutes to check it again."

"I'll help," Joey volunteered.

DJ shook his head. "It's okay; you guys go on and get out of here."

Joey looked from DJ over to where Saddler loitered around chatting with his team. "If you're staying, I'm staying."

"Yeah, we're all staying," George said.

"Okay fine, but nobody touches this thing, just stand around and make sure he can't see me."

Joey grinned, figuring out what DJ had in mind. Fifteen minutes later, Saddler re-inspected the machine gun. "Much better. Why you didn't just do that in the first place, I'll never know."

"I did."

"No you didn't," Saddler said, signing the paperwork.

"Yes I did, you prick. Seven witnesses can verify that I didn't touch the damn thing. What you're looking at now is the same work you refused to sign off on last time."

"Watch your mouth when you speak to me. It's not my fault that you're shit at your job and needed your fuck buddies here to help you do it right."

DJ snapped. It was long overdue.

"You bastard!"

Before any of the others could intervene, he flew at Saddler, slamming him hard with his shoulder and knocking him to the ground, landing two good punches to his face before Saddler managed to throw him off and leap to his feet, delivering a hard kick to DJ's lower abdomen. DJ was winded but got to his feet and advanced, his hands up in a defensive position, ready to strike at any available opening. He took advantage of several, enjoying seeing Saddler's nose explode in a flurry of red as he got in a perfect right hook after two short, sharp body jabs. Saddler staggered back, and two of his team stepped forward. George and Joey blocked them.

"You get involved in this, we're all in," George growled. "Take one more step."

The man looked from George to his suffering superior who was obviously losing the fight. DJ was relentless, the pent up frustration being released through his flying fists. He was pummeling Saddler to a pulp, giving him no time to recover between hits. The man stepped forward. George swung. It was carnage.

As much as they'd fought each other in the bunker, they now fought together against a common enemy. Only one of Saddler's crew refused to join in, fleeing the hangar. The rest threw themselves into the fight with gusto, and the Armament Dogs did the same. They were outnumbered and already in pain from previous injuries, weak and tired from lack of proper sleep, but they were driven. Driven by the righteousness of injustice, driven by the torment of keeping their mouths shut and their heads down, driven by frustration, confusion, fear, and rage. Saddler's team took the brunt of it all. It didn't take long for some of them to be down and in no hurry to get up, for others to back off and raise their hands in defeat. Saddler himself was a curled ball of agony and misery on the ground. DJ got in one last kick to the broken man's kidney area before Joey gripped his shoulder.

"It's over, man, it's over." He could feel the muscles beneath his hand trembling with adrenaline and anger, DJ's bloodlust far from sated. "DJ! That's enough."

Reluctantly, DJ took a few deep breaths and turned away, allowing his body to relax. He ran a bloody hand through his hair. "Yeah, if you say so."

"I do. Come on; the shift was over half an hour ago, let's get out of here. These assholes can clean up the mess unless they want to tell the whole base that they got beat up by a bunch of fuck buddies in silk panties."

Those in Saddler's crew that had backed off before they were too badly hurt or winded glowered at the Dogs as they put their arms around one another and assisted each other out of the hangar.

"Damn, my ribs hurt," Craig said. "But that sure felt good."

"It was a long time coming," JDub agreed. "Do you think we're going to get in trouble?"

"I doubt it," Joey said. "I think they'll want to keep their defeat quiet, probably use the same excuse we did."

"We absolutely kicked ass," Billy said with a smile before wincing as his split lip opened again. "Ouch. I think I'll skip dinner tonight; I don't feel much like eating."

None of them did. They agreed that all they wanted to do was crawl into bed and try to get some sleep; give their aching bodies time to recover.

"I'll get things set up and stop by the room as we agreed," Joey said to JJ when they reached their trailers. "It'll only take me a moment."

"See you soon then," JJ agreed. "Although if anything sits on my chest, tonight I'll probably pass out from the pain, I ache everywhere."

"We're all going to feel this in the morning," Justin agreed. "Might be time to pick up one of those fine hookah pipes the PX has on display and partake of their finest herbal remedies to get us through the day."

"Herbal my ass! Just do what the rest of us do Justin, man up."

Justin flipped George the bird.

"Don't make me laugh," Craig wheezed. "It hurts too much."

Groans of agreement came from the others as they made their way to their rooms where they gingerly undressed, checking out their injuries, and comparing wounds with their roommates as they did so. JJ sat on the end of his bed in his shorts and t-shirt, waiting for Joey. As promised, Joey arrived within minutes, the inbuilt laptop camera software already up and running, ready to start recording straight to the hard drive. He put his finger to his lips as he walked in, reminding JJ not to say anything and gave him a wave, indicating that he should go ahead and get into bed.

As JJ settled, Joey spent a few minutes trying to work out where best to place the laptop. Like DJ and Joey's room, the furniture had been placed in a layout that was different from the usual preferred method of setup for the small rooms. Whether it was a remnant of the old closeness the guys had shared back when they'd first been allocated, or whether it had been altered when the swap had taken place, Joey didn't know, but it made his life a lot easier right now. Justin's bed was jammed lengthwise along the far back wall, his tall metal locker close to it on the left wall. JJ's locker was on the right, the foot of his bed against it and the head almost at the door. The small, cheap, flimsy desk was directly across from the bed, providing an ideal place for the laptop to sit.

He angled the lid and checked what he could see on the screen. Ideally, he would have liked a wider angle, but the narrowness of the room made it impossible. He wasn't familiar enough with the supplied software to know if the camera lens was adjustable other than simply zooming in, and he was too tired to play around with it tonight. He'd learned enough to know how to activate night vision mode where it would see in infrared and wouldn't need any external light source, and he knew how to get it to record continuously rather than simply stream or be motion activated. He'd thought he'd done pretty well in the short time he'd had. He checked the screen again. He had all but the bottom few inches of JJ's bed in the shot; it would have to do.

Satisfied he'd done everything he could, he gave the watching JJ the thumbs up and hit record before taking the short few steps to the door where he paused, flicking off the overhead light and plunging the room into pitch darkness. *Night, night, sleep tight; don't let the bed bugs bite.* He snorted, wondering where the old rhyme had come from. He hadn't heard it since he was a toddler, so it had no reason to come unbidden to his mind right now. Closing the door, he left their trailer and went to his own. He undressed and climbed into bed, where he lay wondering just what the hell morning would bring.

Chapter Eighteen: Something Dark and Wicked

Unable to do more than fitfully doze, Joey rose well before dawn. He gathered up clean clothes quietly so as not to wake his sleeping roommate. Although he never mentioned it, he often heard DJ crying into his pillow well into the early hours of the morning, only to be plagued by dreams that caused him to moan and thrash when he finally did fall asleep. The last thing Joey wanted to do was to wake him when he was finally peaceful and getting some much-needed rest.

Clothes bundled in his arms, Joey slipped out and across to the shower block. The water in the tank was icy from the plummeting temperatures of night, but he braved the shower for as long as he could, actually enjoying the alertness it brought. It dawned on him that he hadn't felt that awake for a while as if he'd been in some sort of lethargic fog. Under the harsh, neon strip lighting, he dried himself briskly and dressed before heading straight to the computer lab. One of the few plus points of deployment was that with everyone working different shifts, most things were available to them twenty-four hours a day, every day.

Logging into his email account, Joey was pleased to see one from Carrie's username. He smiled as he clicked on it and settled down to read, hearing her voice in his head as he made his way through the opening words telling him how much she loved and missed him. He enjoyed her updates on what she and the family had been up to, liking the upbeat tone and humor that she always applied, knowing that any communication should be a heartening and uplifting lifeline to a soldier away from home. As he reached the fifth paragraph, he sat up in his seat, his brow creased.

Thanks for sending the pictures; it certainly looks as if you're managing to have some fun out there! They look like a good bunch of guys, but ugh, that place you were in! I won't ask any questions right now, but I want to hear all about it when you get home. Anyway, a weird thing happened. It was so downright creepy, but interesting at the same time, you know that I couldn't resist putting a couple up on my page. Don't worry! No people in the pic nor did I didn't mention where it was or where the pictures had come from, and you know my screen name is pretty obscure so I doubt anyone would ever make a connection. Anyway, within half an hour or maybe even less, I got a private message about them. It kind of scared me a bit, so I haven't replied, but I've copied and pasted it for you here to see what you make of it.

Joey read the following words twice over, with increasing excitement mixed with a sensation of dread. He couldn't help but wonder about the validity of what Carrie had copied and pasted if it was somehow linked to all the weird shit that had plagued this particular tour. On the other hand, it could just be more mumbo jumbo to mess with their already over-stressed heads. He read it once more, ensuring he had everything committed to memory before typing a hastily constructed response to Carrie, thanking her for her email, and asking her not to reply to whoever had contacted her and not to mention any of it to anyone. He finished off by promising to write properly soon and telling her how much he loved and missed her and the kids.

Once that was done, he deleted the message he'd originally sent with the attachments and their subsequent responses. He didn't examine his motives too carefully, only acted on his instinct that it wouldn't be a good idea to have those pictures traced back to him. Someone, somewhere along the line and up the military chain of command, might be mighty pissed about them.

Shutting down his email and logging out of the computer lab, Joey dashed to the chow hall, thankful that the days of being on a meal card were long gone. He waited in line then requested eight boxed up breakfasts to go, selecting random choices that he hoped would please everyone. His request brought him an odd look, but he just grinned and told the contract server that his team was all hung over, and he didn't want them to miss a meal even though they could barely drag themselves out of bed. The server shrugged and complied with his request.

Laden down with take-out food, Joey dumped it all on his desk and roused DJ. "Wake up, man, I've got something I need to talk to you all about. Get dressed; I'm going to get the guys."

Joey practically jogged from room to room, banging on doors, yelling out names, telling them all to meet in party central in five minutes. Soon, bleary-eyed, yawning, but perfectly presented, they were all gathered in Joey's room.

"Here, I got us all breakfast. Fight it out amongst yourselves, mix and match, whatever, but I need to talk to you all while we eat."

He waited until the packed up breakfasts had been examined and various swaps and exchanges had been made.

"So what's this about," Billy asked, before shoveling a large forkful of omelet into his mouth.

Joey swallowed the mouthful he'd been chewing then began. "Remember we took photos with DJ's camera the night we partied in the bunker? Well, I sent them to Carrie in an email, and she put a couple up on Facebook, anonymously, before you ask, and she didn't say where it was or where they came from. It was only a couple that showed the close up of the bunker wall and the obelisk; we weren't in any of them. I got an email back from her this morning, saying that within half an hour of putting them up, some scientist guy got in touch with her via private message."

"Oh yeah? He knows something about that weird pillar thing?"

"He did, George, or rather; he knew a colleague of his would be really interested in seeing it. He said he downloaded the pictures and sent them on to someone he knows who specializes in ancient writing and symbols, and apparently, this guy almost blew a fuse when he saw the pics. He called him up straight away, all excited, demanding to know where it was. Of course, he didn't know so couldn't tell him. He wrote back to Carrie, explaining what the guy had told him, as well as asking for the location, saying the specialist wanted to visit the site immediately."

"I think he'd change his mind about that one once he found out it was in a restricted area of a military base in Iraq," JDub said.

"He's not going to find that out from any of us. I've asked Carrie not to reply to him at all."

"So what did he have to tell her?"

"That's the interesting part, and the reason I dragged you all out of bed. He said that the writing and symbols actually predate Ancient Sumerian – which is the oldest language in existence – so this stuff is older than anything that had ever been previously recorded. The specialist has been working with a small group on this for a couple of decades, examining these symbols whenever and wherever they show up, trying to trace them throughout history. Apparently, they've shown up on similar obelisks discovered on sites that were the home of ancient civilizations such as the Mayans, Incans, Egyptians, Sumerians, and even as recently as medieval Europe. They've no idea where they come from and no evidence that any of those civilizations actually created the scriptures or even understood it. From what he can determine, they were all just discovered by those cultures, pretty much the same way as the US army stumbled across this one, and probably the Iraqis before them."

"That's all fascinating, but couldn't you have told us this later?"

Joey shook his head. "I wasn't going to talk about the obelisk where we could be overheard, and besides, I haven't gotten to the point yet. He said that although no one has ever been able to decipher the writing, over the years, they've established a pattern. Now that experts can pretty much read or interpret nearly all of the ancient writing known to man–"

"Except the stuff in the bunker."

"Yeah, Craig, except that, they've found that the discovery of the obelisk has always coincided with some terrible cultural event. He gave some examples, like war, famine, severe drought, plagues, uprisings, floods, things that wiped out thousands of people, if not eradicating the civilization entirely. Never has one been recorded where it hasn't been followed by loss of life in massive numbers."

"Holy shit," JDub breathed. "So do they think this thing is some sort of warning system, hidden away and somehow allowing itself to be discovered just at the right time?"

"That's actually one of the most favored theories by the group he mentioned. Carrie said that his message frightened her a little, and I can see why especially when I consider the other theory he mentioned. If you haven't already guessed it yourself, the other is that it actually somehow orchestrates the situation that causes all the deaths."

"Bullshit! It's just a piece of rock with some stuff engraved on it. Don't tell me you guys are buying all this?"

"This did come from a scientist, though, Justin," Billy said, biting his lip.

"So what? These guys think they're all so clever, figuring out all these ancient civilizations, understanding their languages and inscriptions and shit, thinking they know how they thought and lived just by finding a few old foundations and broken pieces of relics. There's *nothing* to say that anything they think is actually right, no way to prove any of it. I could speculate as much as the next man, and give perfectly sensible, valid reasons why I think what I do, but it doesn't make it truth or fact. Even if they are right, they only see fragments, little hints with no way to see the bigger picture. That's easily misinterpreted."

"You've actually got a point there, Justin," DJ agreed. "And how do we even know this guy is what and who he says he is?"

"Exactly! This guy might just be some weirdo, trolling the internet, having a sick laugh at Carrie's expense by frightening her, just some creep getting his rocks off. I bet if she replied, he'd ask to have a video chat to discuss it further, and when she agreed, the only thing she'd see on the screen would be his dick in his hand."

"That could be true too," Joey replied. "Then he'd have me to deal with when I hunted him down, intent on chopping it off so he could never flash it around uninvited again. I'm not vouching for the validation of any of this; I'm only passing on what he told her, and I haven't even told you the creepiest part yet."

"You mean it gets worse?" Billy said with a shudder.

"Yep. These specialists have traveled the world searching for these things in every location that one was ever recorded, and never found them, not even a single trace that they ever existed. Either they get destroyed during the disaster they predict – or cause – or they simply disappear once it's over, popping up somewhere else years later."

"Geez, that is creepy," Craig said.

"I still call bullshit," Justin declared. "I've got a pretty good radar for it."

"I don't doubt it. Obviously, you're free to think and believe whatever you want, but what if there was something more to it. None of us can deny that this tour's had more than its fair share of bad luck. Can all this just be coincidence and circumstance? Oh, and you haven't seen the pictures yet."

Joey glanced around before remembering that DJ's laptop wasn't in its usual place. "Oh yeah, how did things go last night, JJ?"

"Shit, sorry, should have brought the laptop back with me, still half asleep I guess. I'll get it."

Before Joey could prevent him and press for an answer, JJ dashed out of the room. The others sat in awkward and uncomfortable silence, concentrating on the congealed remains of their breakfast that had been forgotten during Joey's revelations.

"Do you want me to set it up?" JJ asked as he burst back into the room with the computer tucked under his arm.

DJ glanced at his watch. "No time right now. Anything else will have to wait. We need to get to the hangar; we're almost late for a shift."

"Time flies when you're having fun."

"Button it, Justin."

***

334

The day had passed in blessed normality, less the usual taunts and snide remarks from Saddler and his crew. The other team had displayed a variety of emotions as they'd arrived, from burning anger, to meek contrition and even a hint of grudging respect from one man. Saddler himself had strutted in, head held high, shoulders back, pretending they didn't even exist when the Armament Dogs had snorted and laughed at his bandaged nose, swollen eye, and bruised cheekbones. They knew they didn't look a whole lot better themselves, but better than the other team, which was a source of great satisfaction and mirth, particularly when it came to Saddler.

Nobody had been pulled up for disciplinary after the fight, so they felt it was safe to assume that the men hadn't made any formal complaints and had used some excuse to pass off their obvious injuries. When Sergeant Heard had stopped by to check in with them, he'd glanced from one team to the other, his face shrewd. In the end, he'd simply nodded at Joey, assuming that his men had found the culprits of the overblown and dangerous prank that had been pulled the other night. He didn't exactly approve, but since everybody was still walking and working, it wasn't worth making a huge deal out of it. With this many men living in such proximity, the occasional fight was something the army was used to, as were pranks and pissing contests. Sergeant Heard had a fierce sense of pride for this particular team, and since the prank had been seriously out of line, felt they deserved the opportunity to handle it alone. It appeared they'd done so, and had shown a certain amount of restraint while doing it. Provided this was the end of it between these two teams, he felt he was justified in making no further inquiries into the matter. No formal complaints had been made from either side, and it saved him a whole heap of time and paperwork. His decision made, he'd left without another word, but vowed to keep an eye and ear on the two teams in case the situation escalated.

The shift had ended, and the Dogs had left, unhindered and unchallenged, making their way to the chow hall and sitting down together for their meal.

"Did you notice Saddler didn't even pull his usual stunt of pretending our work wasn't good before signing off on it?" George asked. "I don't think we're going to have any more trouble out of him."

"That's something I guess, although I still don't think he pulled that scorpion stunt," Craig said. "That must mean someone else has it in for us, so we'd better watch our backs although I can't think of anyone else who has anything against us."

"Maybe it was Joey's obelisk," Justin chortled, breaking into the theme tune of The Twilight Zone. He stopped abruptly when JDub threw a sausage at him, leaving a wet, greasy mark on his field jacket. "Hey! This was clean this morning."

"It'll be good if Saddler does back off from now on, it'll make the rest of this tour a whole lot easier to take," Craig said quickly, hoping to steer the conversation back to a common enemy and prevent the argument that was about to break out between his battles.

"He's still won," DJ murmured, too low for the rest of them to catch.

"Huh?"

"I said he's still won. No matter what happens out here, I go home to an empty house, and he goes home to my wife, my Clara."

They dropped their heads, unsure of what to say, ashamed that they'd almost forgotten the initial reason for the animosity between them and Saddler. When he spoke of her, it was in the past tense, treating her loss almost as a bereavement. They'd all begun to think of her that way as if she no longer existed as opposed to being shacked up with some other guy.

After what felt like an eternity, JDub cleared his throat. "So what's the plan, are we all heading over to party central to watch the video from last night?"

He felt sad as he said the words, knowing that DJ and Joey's room didn't really live up to its nickname anymore. He couldn't remember the last time they'd hung out there and had a good time, forgetting their troubles, relaxing and enjoying the company of their battles. Now it was more like a conference center, where they gathered to talk in hushed tones about things they couldn't share with anyone else on base. The name was nothing more than an ingrained habit.

"Oh yeah, JJ, you never answered earlier. Did you have one of your experiences last night?" Billy asked.

"Let's just see what we see," George cut in. "The human mind is very prone to suggestion. Best if we don't view it with any preconceived ideas of what we might or might not see. I'd say we'd be best to keep our mouths shut too while we're watching, just compare notes at the end. We're trying to rule out certain things, and mass hysteria is one of them. Let's try and do this as scientifically as possible."

"You've got a point there, good thinking," Joey agreed.

"Yeah, well, I gave it a lot of thought throughout the day. I was itching to know if it had happened to JJ, but of course, couldn't ask, not with those assholes listening in. Then the more I thought about it, the more I decided I didn't want to know in advance."

"Well, I'll watch, but not because I think anything's creeping around in my room at night, but because I want to figure out what's happening with my roomie and help him."

"So does everyone agree we'll still watch it together as planned? Nobody changed their minds?"

They all agreed that they were in, and their conversation turned to more mundane topics until they'd finished their meal. When they were done, Joey led the way and opened up the door, allowing them all to troop past before entering himself. There were a few moments of scuffling, jostling, and laughter as they tried to arrange themselves where they could all see the laptop screen where Joey had set it up on the desk. When they'd all found a place, Joey keyed up the stored video, ready to hit play. "All set?"

The room settled into silence after their murmurs of confirmation, the air thick with anticipation. Nobody looked at JJ, afraid that his face would give something away, ruining George's strategy. Joey hit play.

The image that appeared was grainy, comprised of various shades of grey. It took a moment for their eyes to adjust and be able to recognize the scene in front of them fully. Occasionally, the image would pixelate in parts of the screen, particularly where the shadows were darker.

"Was that movement there?"

"No, just the camera trying to get a fix on things."

"Oh, okay."

It didn't take long for their brains to adjust to vision in this unfamiliar light spectrum, and learn how the upgraded and modified camera handled it. Soon, the image appeared clear to them provided they didn't look away and back again.

For the first fifteen minutes, all they saw was JJ tossing and turning in bed and occasionally fitfully dozing for a few moments before awakening again. The soundtrack to their home movie was the buzz saw of Justin's snores from the other end of the room.

"I think we've hit on your problem, JJ. You can't get any sleep with that racket," Craig said.

"I remember it well," Billy agreed. "Even I had a hard time with it once it was just him and me, even though we'd slept close to each other in the hangar. It was easier to handle in the bigger space."

"Shut it, you two. I can't help it."

"I know what it is!" JDub exclaimed. "You're dreaming you're logging, and a tree falls on you."

Even Justin couldn't help but join in with the laughter at that one. Still chuckling, Joey hushed them and asked them to concentrate. Another ten minutes passed, and the guys were beginning to get bored and restless, fidgeting where they sat.

"I think we're wasting our time. Sorry, man, but you're obviously just losing it."

JJ didn't comment.

"Give it some time, guys; it's only been just over half an hour."

"Come on, Joey; we're not going to see anything."

"Please, just give it a fair chance. You can insult me all you want if we see nothing by the end. Until then, just watch."

There were a few huffs and sighs, but they did as they were asked, continuing to watch the screen. They looked on as JJ finally fell into a deep sleep, lying on his back, one arm by his side; the other flung casually up behind him, bent at the elbow, so it lay on the pillow above his head. Joey concentrated harder, knowing that if they were to learn anything about JJ's possible experiences or condition; it was most likely to happen when he was in the deepest sleep. Expecting audio and visual evidence of the beginnings of a nightmare, he was momentarily confused as he saw a small patch of black mist begin to form at the very left-hand edge of the screen. At first, he passed it off as more pixelation, a subtle change in light reflection causing the camera to struggle to focus on the area. Still, he leaned forward, hoping to get a better view, unaware that the others had done the same, their faces now frowning and intent.

The mist continued to expand, growing and taking on density. Soon, it filled one-quarter of the entire frame, too big to be contained by the lens angle. It was a solid, dense, black mass, clearly displaying what looked like a torso standing side on, an arm, and the top of a thick thigh. If it had legs and head, they were out of shot. All of them struggled against the instinct to yell, point, or scream, remembering George's words, determined to prove once and for all if any of this was real, or just some wild craziness being transmitted through the group like a rampant infection, feeding and mutating as it went. They relied heavily on their army training to enable themselves to watch on in silence.

What they saw rocked them to the very core. Slowly, and with clear intent and purpose, the thing straddled JJ's legs and began crawling up the bed. It was large, dwarfing his six-foot-two-inch, two-hundred-pound frame. They could clearly see the depression of the mattress as it added its mass to JJ's on the bed, as well as the specific impressions made there by its hands and knees as it crept along. Reaching JJ's chest, it sat there, placing its weight on his sternum. It leaned over; it's face close to his, taking hold of both his wrists and holding both arms down against the pillows at either side of his head.

In the video, JJ's eyes snapped open, the abject terror on his face obvious even in this grainy scene. He opened his mouth wide, but no sound was emitted; a silent scream, his eyes pleading and begging with the shadow creature above him. They could see JJ's chest struggle to rise and fall beneath the weight, his throat muscles working as he tried to cry out, the muscles in his arms straining as they attempted to break him free. The scene grew more shocking and more terrifying as time went on, his efforts failing, the attempts growing weaker as his body began to give up, oxygen deprived and weakened by the second. They could see tears running from the corner of his eye, glistening on the side of his face. He managed to make some kind of noise, a desperate, rattling, choking sound that made Joey think of a catfish out of the water, trying to suck in enough air to stay alive. Lost in the horror of what they were witnessing, they had no concept of the passing time, no idea how long the scene lasted. Just when Joey believed he couldn't take watching another moment of this, the thing turned its head towards the camera.

There were no discernable features, only blackness where a face should be, but they were all frozen to the spot by the knowledge that the thing was looking right at the camera, playing to whatever future audience it would have. Although they could see no mouth, they heard it chuckle; a deep, menacing, and mocking sound, the same one Joey had heard in the bunker.

Then it was gone.

One minute it was there, laughing at them, the next, JJ was hanging off the side of the bed, his arms limp, gasping for breath, tears streaming freely off the end of his nose and pooling on the floor in front of him. When he regained some strength, he raised his head to the camera, staring straight into the lens.

"Help me; please help me."

The voice was barely a mewl, a desperate plea that made them all want to turn to JJ and comfort him. Once again, they restrained themselves, knowing what George needed from them, what they all needed. They watched the rest of the video in silence, their own chests constricting as they watched JJ curl up in a fetal position and stay that way, crying until the dawn broke, when he rose and turned the camera off.

The video turned to a black screen, and the room descended into silence. The Dogs sat, heads bowed, lost in shock, confusion, fear, and pity, so blown away they couldn't think of anything to say, and didn't even know where to begin. It was George who eventually broke the long, stunned silence.

"O to the M to the F and the G. Did I really just see that?"

"Fuck yeah."

"Holy crap."

"You saw it too?"

"Jesus, battle, what the fuck did we just watch?"

"I can't believe it, this can't be happening; it can't be real."

"What the hell was that?"

"Okay, hold on. I know we're all shaken up, but try to keep it calm and do this as rationally as possible. Everyone, fix your own words in your mind, be honest, and don't let what anyone else says influence you. Billy, you first, tell me what you thought you saw?"

"A demon, I saw a demon preying on JJ."

"JDub?"

"A shadow man, squeezing the life out of my battle."

"Craig?"

"A ghost or something, some nasty entity that's learned to manipulate his environment."

"Justin?"

"Some black mass, something that shouldn't have had any substance, but it did. It was suffocating him, man, squashing the life out of him! This can't be possible!"

Justin, the biggest skeptic, was taking this the hardest, unable to deny the evidence but also unable to accept it as the truth. His mind was in turmoil, a whirlwind of conflicting thoughts and emotions. He clasped his hands to his ears, trying to shut the commotion out.

"Easy there, buddy, deep breaths. Don't wig out on us."

"I'm not crazy."

The words were a mere whisper. Joey turned towards the source. "You holding up okay there, JJ? That must have been pretty fucking traumatic for you to watch."

"Yeah, but I'm not crazy. You all saw something; this isn't just in my head. As fucked up as it might be, it's real, it's actually happening, and I'm not losing my mind. I'm scared out of my wits, but I'm relieved too. This was the moment that might have proved I'd lost it, turned into a total nut job, unfit for duty, a danger to my fellow soldiers and useless to my country. Whatever this is, it has to be better than that. You can't fight crazy, but whatever this is, we can fight it, right?"

"Are you freaking kidding me? Did you see the size of it? Did you see the way it looked at us, didn't you hear it mocking us. It knew the damn camera was there all along, knew that we would be watching. We don't even know what it is, but it's big, strong, and smart. How are we supposed to fight it? Everything we've got is useless; all the training in the world can't help us now!"

"Calm down, Justin. Let's try to stay rational here and take it one step at a time. Despite different interpretations of what it actually might be, we all saw the same thing, right? A big black mass building up at the edge of the screen, taking on a humanoid form, crawling up the bed, then onto JJ, crushing him and paralyzing him?"

Everyone agreed that that was exactly what they'd seen. "You could even see the depressions where its weight was on the bed," Craig added.

"I saw that too," JDub agreed. "And they moved up the bed at the same time as the shadow thing did."

"Yeah, and did you see the size of it? JJ's a big guy, a strong guy, yet he couldn't move a muscle."

"He was trying to scream. That was so freaky, his mouth was open, but no sound was coming out. That's gonna haunt me forever."

"I don't think any of us are going to forget this in a hurry, but the point of it was so we could learn something, so let's see what we've got. I think we're safe in saying we can rule out imagination, stress, sleep deprivation, mass hallucination, and everything else we've used to pass all this off as coincidental and insignificant. We have to admit now that all the weird things are actually happening to us, that they're all connected. We have hard evidence that *something* is going on, something we really don't understand. What we need to figure out is what we do with that evidence from here on in."

"Maybe we should go and speak to Sergeant Heard, tell him what's going on," Craig suggested. "He's a good guy, a straight shooter."

"Sure, Craig, and we'll all end up medevac'd home in restraints and taken straight to our local psych ward," DJ said. "No one's ever going to believe us, not even with this video. They'll just think we rigged it. You can do so much with software these days; you can't prove anything's real."

"Shit, this is so fucked up," Billy said. "I haven't got a clue what we should do."

"We should sleep on it, wait until our heads are clearer, and see if anything comes to us then. We're all pretty shaken up and not even thinking straight. We're also dealing with an area we know nothing about. Arming ourselves with information instead of guns might be a good start."

"Umm, Joey? I really don't want to sleep in that room tonight. Is there any chance I could crash here?"

"Its fine by me, and I don't blame you. Okay with you, DJ?"

"Sure, go ahead."

"Well I'm not going back there alone," Justin said. "Who can I crash with?"

"Actually, I don't want to go out there at all. Can I stay too?"

"Me neither, I'll just crash here if it's okay."

In the end, they all decided that a night spent crammed into DJ and Joey's room on the small, uncomfortable, folding chairs would be preferable to leaving the companionship of the others to go to their own beds. No one wanted to leave behind the safety in numbers, the warmth, or the light, and venture out into the dark trailer hallway. No one wanted to open the doors to their rooms, afraid of what might be lurking behind them. Therefore, they stayed together, none of them getting a wink of sleep but taking some comfort in knowing their battles were beside them. The horrors of the night had brought them closer again.

Chapter Nineteen: Night Shift

In the week that followed, the team stuck close together, sharing their down time again as well as their shifts. The buddy system ingrained in them by army training prevented them from being alone for any length of time but even in pairs, they felt uneasy. Like pack animals, they instinctively sought the safety of the entire group, gravitating together and remaining that way unless circumstance absolutely forbade it. They huddled together in party central, although there was little partying going on. Occasionally, Joey or George would pick up their guitars and strum gently, a quiet backdrop to the subdued conversation or silence. After three nights of no more strange activity, the others had finally plucked up the courage to return to their beds in their own room but did so only once their drooping eyelids, jaw-cracking yawns, and nodding heads dictated that they couldn't stay awake a moment longer.

In spite of the urging of the team, DJ still resolutely refused to approach his friend to discuss the medium that they all now believed was genuine and finding some way to reach out to DJ in his dreams.

What had seemed fantastic and ridiculous before now seemed almost normal in the face of everything else they'd recently experienced. They begged him to speak to her directly, find out how much she knew and ask if she could offer any assistance. They knew they needed all the help they could get. DJ wasn't sure what was holding him back. Their request was logical, and it might even prove to be very useful, but he couldn't bring himself to do it. He still attributed his reluctance to simple fear. The less he knew, the easier it was to bury his head in the metaphorical sand and hope it would all just go away. He couldn't help but feel that the more he delved into this, the more he poked and prodded, the worse things would become, like some infected abscess. Every instinct he had screamed at him to leave it alone, to keep his head down, and hope that whatever it was would forget about them and move on.

Although they had previously agreed to record in various rooms through the night, the laptop still lay on the desk, untouched since the night they'd played their shocking home video. They'd been too frightened to repeat the exercise, far too afraid of what they might actually see. JJ hadn't improved any since the experiment; in fact, his terrifying nighttime visitations were even more frequent and intense. If anything was paying any of the rest of them a nocturnal call, they'd all come to the conclusion that they would be better off not knowing about it.

Even George had dropped his insistence that they pray with him, having seemingly lost interest or faith in his own spirituality in light of the recent events. The Bible that he had brought with him and occasionally read from had been shut away in a drawer, pointedly ignored the same as the laptop. It was as if a sense of hopelessness had fallen over all of them as if they'd given up already; surrendered without even making a stand.

Joey was itching to do some research online, to learn all he could, feeling that knowledge might be the only thing that could give them some power in this situation. He had no idea what he was dealing with but knew he would feel better if he had some clue or even a few suggested directions to go in. He'd given it serious consideration, but had decided that the fact that any internet browsing he did would be monitored, it would attract too much attention and maybe even some awkward questions. The last thing he needed was for word to spread across base that he was some sort of paranormal-loving nut job. He could hear the jibes and smart-ass comments from the other soldiers already. He had also considered asking Carrie to reply to the scientist to see if they could learn more about the obelisk, but Justin's warning that he might just be some sick, internet troll had blocked that avenue of exploration. She was at home alone with his children, he didn't want her to be afraid, wouldn't put her at risk when he wasn't there to protect her. For now, he was as stumped as the rest of them, feeling stymied at every turn he tried to make.

It was top that finally forced the group to separate, exactly seven nights after they'd viewed the terrifying video. Craig, JJ, and George were given marching orders to return to duty in the guard towers at Checkpoint 00 for a full week; and worse still, they were all assigned to night shift. A feeling of dread and foreboding accompanied the order for the three assigned to the checkpoint, far more than the normal anxiety that might afflict a young soldier at the responsibility placed upon him by the duty of keeping the base safe. It was an intense and exhausting experience with all that watching, peering into the gloom, all that waiting. The tension could be unbearable. Now they would have to cope with it when they were already jittery and on edge, jumping at shadows. It was a recipe for disaster, and it was with trepidation that they headed out to the tower for their first shift.

George was assigned to tower two with another soldier that they were unfamiliar with while Craig and JJ were assigned to tower one together. George glanced back at them over his shoulder as he walked away, his expression pained and pleaded, but there was nothing they could do for him except offer a grin that was meant to be reassuring but failed miserably, more of a grimace than a comforting smile.

"This sucks," Craig muttered as they climbed the stairs of the tower together to relieve the soldiers on post.

"I dunno, maybe being here will be better than in my bed," JJ replied in a quiet murmur. "And think of poor George. At least we're together; he's alone, vulnerable, separated from the herd."

Any further conversation regarding their current assignment was prevented as they reached the top. The other soldiers chatted to them for a few minutes after the official handover, pleasant small talk that made the atmosphere light and welcoming. As soon as Craig and JJ heard the door shut below them and they were alone, the feeling in the small area instantly changed; their own fears seemingly tangible in the air around them.

"I'm going to say it again, this absolutely sucks. The timing couldn't have been any worse for us. I've never had an issue with the dark before, but I sure do now, and I'm forced into twelve hours of being awake in it and out in it. What's worse is that I have to be stuck up here in this tower, away from everyone else, and given no choice but to stare out at it, hour after hour. I can't even close my eyes for a second to shut it out. You have no idea what my mind is already conjuring up, what it's thinking I might see creeping across the base or down from the mountains. Why, when so much of the base is lit up, and lots of guys are still on shift, does the place feel so damn creepy at night?"

"It's probably just psychological. I think deep down, we all have a small fear of the dark. I don't know; maybe it goes way back to when we were prey for animals but look at big cities. Often, their main drags are as brightly lit by streetlights and neon as they are by daylight, yet they don't feel half as safe after dark. I guess we just associate the night with the natural time for the Predators to come out and hunt."

"Well, gee, thanks for that. That helps a lot," Craig said, peering through his goggles at the surrounding area. "If the only predator that might come for us was a bunch of Hajis, I wouldn't worry so much. Those I can handle. Those I can fight. We can't fight what we don't understand, or maybe can't even see half the time. What if we can only see it when it wants us to, have you thought about that?"

"I'm actually trying to think about it as little as possible, and to be honest; I don't think we should talk about it tonight either. It feels so isolated and cut off up here, and it's so damn quiet, it's eerie anyway. There's no point in spooking ourselves even more. We're not kids telling ghost stories around a campfire. Besides, what if talking about it actually attracts it, you know, like the old saying, speak of the devil and he shall appear?"

"I don't think we're actually dealing with the devil himself, but you might have a point. So what do you want to talk about then?" Craig asked, lightening his tone when he saw how deeply his words were affecting JJ.

"Well, since DJ's not around to overhear us, how about Saddler? I've been itching to talk about him to someone, but I'm always afraid to bring it up in front of DJ. The guy has been so damn annoying to all of us since he got here, I sometimes find myself forgetting about the whole Clara situation. I don't want to be an insensitive ass, so I've just been biting my tongue whenever I want to bring him up."

"Yeah, I get where you're coming from. I admit that I've momentarily forgotten that part on occasion too, then feel disgusted with myself for not being a good friend. The thing is Saddler started the fight the minute he set eyes on DJ, not the other way around. If DJ had gone for him, we'd all have remembered exactly what it was about and what started it. I'm not sure if I can explain this, but it seems as if Saddler just has it in for DJ, and it actually has nothing to do with

Clara, almost as if he just used her as another way to get at him. Am I making sense?"

"Yeah, I get you, but I've asked a few discreet questions around base and couldn't find out anything much. Almost everyone I spoke to hated Saddler, and they'd all seen him be a bastard to DJ and everyone else back in Hawaii, but there was nothing to suggest that DJ did anything for him to be singled out for such special treatment, not even a whisper of anything big between them before this tour."

"Well, if there were gossip to find, you'd be the one to find it, JJ. You're like Spy Thirty Nine, the nickname my Mom gave to the nosy old bat in our hood. She knew everything about everyone, always watching, always hanging around outside, sidling up to people and whispering someone else's secrets in exchange for whatever they'd seen or heard. She had a knack for wheedling things out of everybody. Damn, now that I think of it, the army should employ her and put her undercover."

"Hey! I'm not like that; I just know the right people to talk to at the right time, and I never exchange anything, only gather intel."

"Fair enough, I believe ya. So what did you specifically want to talk about in regards to Saddler?"

"What I wanted to ask was, do you really think the ass kicking we gave him and his crew will be an end to his sneering and jibes? I'm not sure if any of us could take it if he starts winding DJ up again. Some of his comments were pretty damn nasty."

"I think it'll keep him quiet for a while, but I've got no doubt he's plotting and planning something. He's too much of a prick not to

354

be. Losing the fight must have infuriated him, he'll be thinking about his revenge already."

"That's what I was afraid of, but I thought so too. I've even been trying to think of how he might do it so we can be ready."

"Yeah? What did you come up with?"

"Not much, to be honest. I don't think he'll try another prank like the scorpion thing, it kind of backfired and just got the Sergeant and the other guys on our side."

"You still think he was responsible for that? I didn't see any evidence of guilt when we confronted him. I think that was something else entirely."

JJ glowered at Craig. "Taboo subject, back to Saddler. So, he tried rattling DJ, goading him into physical violence. He got it, but he didn't win as he probably hoped he would, and DJ didn't even get into any trouble because Saddler retaliated, and the Sergeant was already expecting us to do something about that prank. So far, the tables have pretty much turned on him. I think that next time, he'll try to use army regulations against us, get us into trouble with top somehow. That way he won't be directly involved, and we won't be able to fight back."

"That makes sense. In other words, we should all try to keep our heads down and our noses super clean right now?"

"Exactly."

With nothing more to say on the subject of Saddler, the pair fell silent, concentrating only on the duty they were required to do. The radio checks were made and responded to by the book, and the surrounding area they were watching was still and quiet.

At exactly 0300 hours, the radio burst to life and JJ reached for it to respond. At the same time, Craig turned from the window, laid down his field binoculars and walked purposefully out of the small room at the top of the tower. JJ gaped at him; wondering what the hell he was doing leaving his post. He completed the radio check as quickly as possible, hoping that the operator on the other end couldn't hear the dismay in his voice or the rhythmic thud of Craig's boots as he went down the stairs. If anyone knew he'd left the tower during his assigned hours, his battle would be in serious shit. As soon as he'd completed the check and announced himself out, he ran to the windows, checking first that they hadn't missed anything while he'd been occupied. If a bunch of the enemy had crept up on them while Craig had been walking out on their duty, they were either dead already or in the brig for insubordination and putting the entire base at risk. Seeing nothing moving outside, he ran to the top of the stairs, calling down them.

"Craig, what the fuck are you doing? Where are you going? Get your ass back up here right now!"

The only response was the slamming of the bottom door.

***

At the same time as a good soldier was inexplicably abandoning his post, the other five Armament Dogs were hard at work in their hangar, arranged in various positions around and inside a grounded Kiowa Warrior. For the most part, the night shift assignment had been a relief to them, providing a much-needed respite from sharing their

356

workspace with Saddler and his team. DJ wondered if their Sergeant had anything to do with the change up, being aware of the tension between the two groups. If so, he silently thanked him. He was a good guy, fairer than many, but also a natural leader, his squad was inspired by him to follow his example, do their best for him, and to not abuse the trust he placed in them. They were lucky to have him on this tour.

The downside to Saddler's absence was, of course, the isolation of the hangar, accentuated by the reduced number of their team. They all felt small and vulnerable in the huge space far away from the occupied area of the base in the dead of night. One pair of Warriors had been out on a night mission early on in the shift but had long since returned and powered down, the pilots and copilots now off duty and had gone to catch some sleep. As far as the team knew, nothing else was scheduled for tonight. Things could always turn on a dime, but for the moment, they were alone out here for the remainder of the twelve-hour shift, and it wasn't a comfortable feeling.

"Pass me up that wrench, please, Billy," DJ said from three-quarters of the way up a ladder, holding out a hand behind him without looking, expecting the tool to be placed into it.

He and Joey were taking a look at the main rotor speed sensors on top of the bird, the pilot having reported a possible problem, mainly but only partially attributing to the grounding of the aircraft. The other issue was that one of the weapons had failed to respond during a mission, and until the rotor was thoroughly checked and the cause of the weapon failure was established and repaired, the helicopter would remain out of service.

It wasn't their job to maintain this part of the helicopter, but with Justin and Billy working on the arms systems, and JDub inside the bird waiting for the go to power up and check that all systems were responding as they should be, they'd decided they might as well take a look. It couldn't hurt, and if they saved someone else sometimes even just by running a diagnostic, then it was a good thing. They were both pretty much of the opinion that if it had moving parts, they could fix it.

Suddenly, the heavy wrench clanged against the side of the bird, bouncing off and hitting DJ's shoulder before it fell back to the ground.

"Hey! I said pass it, not throw it, you just missed my head."

"I didn't throw it; I was still looking for the damn thing. It wasn't where we left it," Billy said.

"Justin, if you're messing around again, I'm coming down off this ladder to kick your ass."

"Nice. How come I automatically get the blame?"

"I call busted," JDub said, sticking his head out from inside the copilots' area. "I saw a shadow dart past on the other side of the bird a few second before the wrench hit."

"Well, it wasn't me, I haven't moved. I was right here beside Billy, helping him look for the wrench."

"It's true guys, he was. He didn't throw it."

"Then who did?" DJ scrambled down off the ladder and put his hands on his hips, looking around the place. "Whoever's in here better quit playing games and come out right now," he called, his voice echoing around the space.

They all whipped their heads to the right as they heard the soft, telltale sounds of furtive movement, catching a fleeting glimpse of a dark shadow darting out of view.

"Stop running and hiding. Show yourself, you pussy!"

***

JJ banged frantically on the window of the guard tower, trying to attract Craig's attention. From his high perch, he could see him now; walking purposefully across to where a handful of Humvees were parked, ready for emergency use should they ever be needed. He was desperate to go after his battle, but there was no way he could leave one of the towers completely unmanned. He rapped harder on the glass, yelling Craig's name.

Craig either didn't hear him or chose to ignore him, instead jumping into one of the vehicles and cranking the engine. Without turning on the headlights, he slammed it into reverse, engine screaming and tires kicking up sand as it shot out from between the others. It stopped abruptly, turning in a tight turn and shot forward, heading straight for the towers.

JJ was frozen, could only look on, confused and frightened. If it had been anyone but a member of his own team, he might have got behind the spray and pray and obliterated the driver behind the wheel before the vehicle could reach the towers. It was moving at speed with purpose and intent; he probably had all the justification he needed to request permission to engage, even though the threat was from inside the base perimeter, but knew he could never bring himself to do it. His thought made him glance in horror towards the other tower. If he'd had the thought, maybe the occupants there had too. He could just make out the two shadowy figures. He grabbed the field binoculars for a better view.

With his enhanced vision, he saw the panicked face of George, who was struggling to restrain the other soldier and prevent him from being able to reach the radio. *Shit, we're all in so much trouble now. At least the guy isn't going straight for the machine gun.*

JJ turned his attention back to the vehicle, knowing that if Craig had intended to ram the towers, the impact would have happened already. He could still hear the engine screaming and protesting, high revs in a low gear. He stared down, seeing the vehicle in the dirt lot next to the towers, going around and around in tight little circles. JJ had no idea that the Humvees were that maneuverable, or that Craig could drive that way; the handling of the damn things was more akin to a tank than an Aston Martin.

His relief that his friend wasn't trying to take down the guard towers soon turned to fear as he watched the Humvee turn in circles for five minutes solid, kicking up a sandstorm around it. Craig had clearly gone nuts, the pressure of the tour too much, the intensity of guard duty the final straw. He exhaled a deep, relieved breath as the engine eventually stuttered and died, either clogged with sand, damaged by the harsh treatment or maybe simply out of gas. Whatever the reason, it had to be a blessing.

Craig jumped from the vehicle and made his way towards one of the lower buildings that were dotted around the checkpoint. He tried the wooden door, and on finding it locked, he began to kick it. Once again, it was as if he were stuck on a loop, kicking the door over and over. With each resounding pound, the door rocked and buckled in the jamb and dust and sand flew up around it. JJ couldn't take it anymore, couldn't just stand up here and watch, having no clue what his battle would do if he gained entry to the building.

He flew down the stairs and out to Craig, grabbing him by the shoulders and turning him around to face him, screaming at him.

"What the hell are you doing?"

Craig's face was contorted and twisted to where it no longer bore any resemblance to his own, his brown eyes so dark they were almost black, unblinking as they stared at JJ. Craig opened his mouth, but it wasn't a response that came. JJ let out a scream and stepped back as a deep, guttural voice spewed from Craig's mouth. The words made no sense and was either gibberish or in another language JJ had never heard before. They felt angry, rage-filled, and they felt powerful. Bracing himself against the torrent, he stepped forward and gripped Craig's shoulders again, shaking him hard.

"Snap out of it! Craig! Craig! Come back to me. Come on, soldier, pull yourself together!"

His commands held no authority, delivered more like a petrified screech, but they were relentless, both them and the shaking driven by abject terror and horror. Finally, Craig blinked, and when he looked at JJ, his face was his own. He was like a limp rag in JJ's hands. JJ stopped the shaking, turning his grip to supportive hands on his battle's shoulders.

"Craig?"

Craig looked at his friend and teammate, his face a mask of confusion. "Why are we out here? Aren't we supposed to be on guard duty?"

JJ began to laugh, close to hysteria. "Fucking hell, dude, what did you think you were doing?"

"What do you mean? We were in the tower, watching. Why are we out here?"

"You scared me half to death! What were you playing at?"

"I don't know," Craig said, miserable. "I don't know what you're talking about. I don't understand anything."

"You don't remember leaving the tower?"

Craig shook his head.

***

Just as DJ called whoever was messing with them in the bunker out, the entire team turned their heads in different directions, all seeing shadows darting around in different places.

"I bet it's some of Saddler's team. They probably heard we were going on night shift and hid back here to try and scare us," Justin said.

362

Joey hoped that Justin was right. One of the other possibilities was that the enemy had infiltrated the camp and hid in the aircraft hangars, hoping to take out the one thing they couldn't fight effectively against, no matter how many of them amassed on the city streets. The Warriors had a reputation similar to that of the Apache, their armor and weapons systems making the sight of them pretty much a sign of oncoming death. Nothing sent the enemy scurrying for the perceived safety of their houses faster than the appearance of a team of Kiowa Warriors on the horizon. Taking them out when they were nestled safely in their resting places would give them a distinct advantage back out in the war-torn streets. He couldn't quite figure out how it would be possible for the base to have been breached, but his experience had taught him never to rule anything out, never to let his guard down, even inside a perimeter fence or in a supposedly safe zone. The insurgents didn't play by the rules of engagement. It did seem unlikely that they would play such stupid games or reveal themselves in the manner that they were doing, but perhaps it was their idea of a mind game, a psych out to draw them away from the bird they have crowded around and essentially protecting. The other possibility was one that Joey didn't want to think about too much.

"What have we taught you, Justin? You should never assume it's a friendly, even an unfriendly friendly. Gather your weapons; two of us need to guard the bird. The rest of you spread out and search the place, every inch of it. Keep your eyes peeled and be ready to act."

As always, their rifles were within arm's reach, loaded and ready. Each man grabbed theirs, and JDub and Billy took up defensive positions on either side of the helicopter. None of them questioned Joey, no matter how unlikely the scenario. He, DJ, and Justin spread out and began to search methodically through the vast hangar, leaving no crate unchecked and no dark, shadowy place unexplored.

"There's no one in here," Justin said as they completed the task and gathered together back beside the Warrior. "Joey, what the heck? There's no one here."

"I know, Justin, I know."

Joey's voice was soft, soothing, although he was equally concerned. The other remote possibility had just become the top explanation, and Joey didn't like it one bit.

"It's the shadow man, isn't it? That thing we saw on the video?"

"Even if it is, JDub, I wouldn't worry too much. The wrench only glanced off my shoulder," DJ said. "Whether it's a ghost or whatever, I really don't think that the dead can harm the living."

As if in response, the radio inside the Kiowa Warrior gave a sudden burst of static, the white noise at a deafening level. They all jumped, turning to face the bird, weapons drawn. Seeing no one inside, DJ chuckled.

"Damn, that gave me a fright. You should have turned the power off before you jumped down, JDub, it's an important point that you shouldn't have forgotten about."

"I didn't. I didn't even turn the power on."

"What?"

"I might be country, but I'm not dumb! Sure, my job was to power up far enough to test the weapons indicators inside, but did you seriously think I'd do that while guys were still working on the weapons and you two were up working on the rotor system, what do you take me for?"

DJ scratched his head. "Yeah, sorry, man, but how could the radio come on if there's no power? That's impossible."

As if to mock him, the radio burst into life again, the hiss of white noise and static interference making them wince. This time, the radio didn't immediately shut off. Instead, the static cleared and the white noise lowered, allowing them to hear clearly the maniacal and guttural laughter being broadcast across the airwaves.

It echoed around the hangar, seemingly on a loop, the same sound repeating over and over again, the slight metallic tone adding to its menace. It was the same voice that they'd heard a week ago through the laptop speakers, still mocking, still deep and dark, only instead of the low, mocking chuckle, it sounded like the laughter of a mad dictator, filled with psychotic glee.

DJ jumped up into the bird, trying to switch the radio off, finding everything inside already turned to the off position. The guys all crowded around, peering in, their faces pale and frightened. DJ powered up the bird and flicked the radio on. Instantly, the laughter cut out. DJ engaged the radio.

"Armament Three to Saber One Nine."

"This is Saber One Nine to Armament Three; we have you, Lima Charlie. Go ahead."

"Saber One-Nine, this is Armament Three. Can you tell us if anyone was broadcasting on this channel approximately thirty seconds ago?"

"This is Saber One Nine; that's a negative, Armament Three."

"Saber One Nine, did you pick up any unauthorized broadcasts across the channel or pick up any radio interference from an external source?"

"This is Saber One Nine; we can confirm that's also a negative, Armament Three. Do you have something you need to report?"

"No, Saber One Nine, nothing to report, just a small glitch with one of the systems. Thank you for your assistance. Armament Three out."

"Okay Armament Three, Saber One Nine out."

DJ looked down at the upturned faces and shrugged. "I don't know what to tell you. The power was definitely shut down, the radio was off, and you heard radio control, no one was broadcasting, and they didn't hear a single goddamned thing."

"But that can't happen; it's absolutely impossible."

"Impossible or not, it just happened."

"It wasn't coming over the radio."

The faces all turned towards Joey. "Huh?"

"Think about it. No power source, radio off, no broadcast. The only explanation is that although it came out of the radio speakers, it was something using its own energy and coming directly to us, not actually broadcasting across the radio frequency."

Justin brightened. "So it was just a fault, an electrical surge that caused the speaker to malfunction? Must be an electrical short somewhere in the bird's system."

Billy frowned. "At a push it could explain the burst of static, but it doesn't explain that damn laughter, and it isn't the first time we've heard it."

"No," JDub agreed. "This is the second time; the first was on the video."

"Actually, it's the third time for me. I've heard it before."

"What! Joey, why the hell didn't you tell us this before? Where did you hear it?"

"It was in the bunker, just as we'd all come out of our trip and stopped beating the crap out of each other. I didn't mention it because I thought it was either the acid or the acoustics. It was laughing right along with Justin."

"No way, no, no, no. Don't tell me shit like that. I don't wanna hear it, especially not out here, and not in the dead of night."

Justin was visibly trembling. He glanced over his shoulder nervously, and his body froze. He turned slowly, his mouth gaping open. He managed to raise a hand, tugging on Billy's sleeve. One by one, they all turned and looked in the direction he was now pointing. There, in the center of the floor, it appeared as if every single tool in the hangar had been arranged into an impossible pyramid, each one perfectly angled and placed.

"What the actual fuck?"

As if in a trance, they walked towards the construction, gathering around it. It was almost six foot high and incorporated multiple examples of every type of tool you would expect to find in any shop. It was as if every tool chest and each personal tool kit in the hangar had been raided, sorted into length and width, then carefully placed one at a time to form the perfect shape. Each tool looked precariously balanced, almost defying the laws of gravity to hold the next, but the overall feel they got from the thing was that it was remarkably sturdy and secure. They moved around it slowly, awestruck, the engineering side of their brains taking control as they examined it.

"This is amazing. It would take days to build this."

"Yeah, and a lot of false starts and mistakes along the way, that's even if it could be done at all."

The more they looked, they more they realized the impossible nature of the structure. As that reality sank in, so did the fear.

"What the hell could have done this?"

"More to the point, what could have done it so fast and without making a single sound? We'd just searched this hangar, the entire thing, and apart from the tools we're using, everything was exactly where it should have been. We only turned our backs while DJ was checking out the radio, just a few minutes at the most."

They hadn't realized it, but they'd instinctively huddled together in a defensive position, backs together in a circle so they could watch the bunker from all directions.

"What are we going to do?"

"I don't think there's anything we can do."

"We've got to call someone out here to see this!"

"Like who? The local ghost hunter or demonologist, the resident alien abductee? Then what? Everyone has a good ol' laugh at our expense, and we end up with disciplinary for wasting valuable army time doing shit like this?"

"But we didn't do it, probably couldn't even if we tried."

"And who's going to believe that?"

"So what then? You expect us just to ignore everything that went on here tonight. Things are escalating, DJ, things are getting worse. I'm scared, man, really scared."

"We're all scared, but I don't know what to do about it, can't you see that? I'm lost. It's my duty to mentor you guys, to protect you, to guide you, but this was never in the remit. I don't know what to do, where to turn. I don't know what's happening, and it terrifies me that I don't know how bad it might get. I'm as out of my depth as you are. It's the blind leading the blind."

The desperate admission made by one of the strongest and bravest members of their team floored them and devastated them. They all looked to Joey, hoping he would be their salvation.

He looked at them helplessly; wishing there was something he could say, anything at all that could make it better. He shook his head, shattering their hope. He had nothing to offer.

DJ glanced at his watch. "We've got a little over four hours left of our shift. My suggestion is that we get this down and everything back in place before someone sees it then if we've got time, we make a start of trying to find an electrical short somewhere in that bird."

Joey knew that it was a lame attempt to occupy and reassure the guys, hopefully keeping them calm and sane until the dawn broke, when they would all feel a little better. He also knew that no matter how long they had to check, they'd find nothing wrong with the electrics in the chopper.

Chapter Twenty: Blow Back

The Armament Dogs huddled in party central, glad that their nightshift was over; glad it was daylight outside, and glad to be together. In spite of just having finished a twelve-hour shift, none of them felt inclined to eat or sleep. The two groups had shared their separate experiences with each other, both of them shocked that incidents had occurred simultaneously at almost opposite ends of the base. JJ had asked them three times to confirm the time that events had begun to unfold in the hangar, unable to believe it was the exact moment that Craig had begun to act oddly. They'd been sitting in stunned silence ever since, all engrossed in their own private thoughts, almost afraid to voice them. Each knew that the other would be thinking similar thoughts, asking the same questions. How could one entity be in different places at the same time; just what exactly was it that they were dealing with here?

"Joey, DJ, what's going to happen to me?" Craig finally asked, his voice small, the subject an unpleasant one but preferable to the other.

"Well, George might have persuaded the other guard in his tower not to radio in at the time, but I don't suppose we can count on his silence for long," DJ said.

George shook his head. "The guy was freaking out. I did my best to restrain him then spent the rest of the night trying to talk him down, downplaying everything as much as possible, trying to pass it off as harmless fun, cutting loose. I think he kind of bought it, but he wasn't one bit amused. No doubt he'll be making his report sometime today, and no doubt, it'll include me holding him back and JJ running out after Craig."

"That's what I was afraid of. What the heck am I going to say to explain it all and get us off the hook? I only know what happened because you've told me; I don't remember a thing about it."

"I've given you the order of events, but that doesn't mean I understand what actually happened any better than you," JJ said. "One minute you were on watch, the next you were out the door. I can tell you this much, though, when you turned around to look at me, it wasn't you. I can't explain it, but it was like there was another face inside yours, trying to push its way out. Then you opened your mouth, and the words came spewing out, in no language I've ever heard, and I swear to God that it wasn't your voice, it was much deeper, much more throaty and raspy. If it weren't for my nightly visitor, I'd say it was the creepiest and scariest thing I'd ever seen in my life. If ever there was a moment when I thought I might wet my pants then that was it."

"Gross!"

"Shut up. You weren't there. I guarantee if you were you'd have felt the same way."

"Come on guys; this is serious. Is that what I tell them when I'm called intotop or whoever, that I was possessed by something and not acting of my own free will? How can I go with the truth when it sounds so ridiculous?"

"You can't," Joey agreed. "They'll probably just think you've had enough and are playing at crazy for a medical discharge, and believe me; they'll give it to you faster than you can blink. Either that or they'll believe that you are actuallycrazy, and that'll be worse, discharged and committed straight to a psych ward. You don't want a record like that. Nothing frightens civilians like a trained soldier discharged with severe mental issues. You'll find it really hard to move on from that, not accepted in either world. For your own sake, I'd urge you to keep your mouth firmly shut when it comes to the truth."

"Yeah, I can see that. If I talk, I'll drag all of you down with me too, and I won't do that. So I just go with the cutting loose thing that George said?"

"I think it's probably best. Sure, they'll tear you a new asshole, but they'll see it as being honest, owning up, and taking responsibility for your actions. They can't help but find that an admirable quality and it'll probably bring about the least serious consequences, for you, and JJ and George."

"Okay, that's what I'll do, and I'll take whatever they throw at me. Thanks, guys, I feel better now that we have the official story worked out, although I don't know what to do about the actual events.

I don't think anything could frighten me more than not being responsible for my own actions when I walk around with a loaded rifle and have access to countless weapons day in and day out. What if I hurt someone, or worse, kill them?"

"I don't know if it'll come to that," DJ said. "Things have been happening for a while now, and although JJ comes close most nights, none of us have actually been hurt yet, or caused harm to anyone else."

"You mean apart from when we kicked the shit out of each other in the bunker?" George snorted. "That was pretty darn serious; I still ache in some places."

"Yeah, and apart from the time when you might have actually killed Saddler if Joey hadn't stopped you?" Billy added.

DJ looked surprised then ashamed, dropping his head, unable to deny any of it.

"It's playing with us," Joey said.

"Huh, what was that?"

"I said it's playing with us, toying with us, cat and mouse. It's having too much fun and getting too many kicks out of us to get rid of us yet."

"So you think it does have something in store for us later, something bad?"

Joey gave himself a shake, his tone returning to normal from the hushed voice he'd spoken in earlier. "I don't know. I haven't really got a clue what I'm talking about; it's just how I feel. Maybe it just wants to watch us thinking we're going crazy."

"We're all beyond that now," George said. "I don't think there are any of us left that don't believe. Isn't that so, Justin?"

"Yeah," Justin muttered from his position on the floor where he sat hugging his knees to his chest. "This is real all right. Doing stuff to us is one thing, but getting inside us is something else entirely. I think I'll be paying my friend at the bazaar a visit a little later. I'm close to tapping out; I need something to take the edge off, something to protect my mind from slipping over the edge."

"That's it," Joey said, snapping his fingers. "Not your way, Justin," he added, catching the surprised looks on their faces. "But protection of some sort. Something that can stop it from taking us over and controlling us. That's the biggest threat and the biggest concern, so that's where we need to start."

"So what, we go around chanting like Buddhists or something all day?"

"It wasn't what I had in mind, but feel free if you believe it'll work, Justin. Again, I don't really know what I mean, but I know someone who might. Look, DJ, I realize you don't want to do this and have been avoiding it like the plague, and I honestly do get why, but I really think you need to speak to this Amanda. She's a medium, right? She spends her life being able to see and hear spirits, entities, whatever. She must have methods of protection in place for herself, and she's already been trying to reach out to you, so we have to assume she's willing to help. It's quite possible that she could give us some advice, teach us some of her methods, or tell us something that could offer us some protection, how to make ourselves strong enough to keep it out."

"It makes sense, DJ."

"Yeah, we don't have anywhere else to turn."

"It could work."

DJ looked at the expectant and hopeful faces. He ran a hand over his eyes. "Yeah, yeah, okay, you win. I'll go and find Larson later today and ask him for her phone number and give her a call, okay?"

"Thanks, DJ, we all appreciate that. I could make the call to her if you really don't want to."

"No, that's okay, Joey. It was me she reached out to, maybe through some connection that I don't know about, so I guess it should be me that talks to her. I'll do it as soon as I'm awake, but right now, I'm going to hit the hay. You're all welcome to stay, but keep it down."

They decided that they did want to stay, curling up in the folding chairs or on the floor while DJ and Joey climbed into their bunks. They'd been asleep for approximately three hours when a loud rapping on the door stirred them from their uneasy slumber.

Billy rubbed his eyes and staggered to the door, tripping over Justin on the way. He pulled open the door to reveal Sergeant Heard standing there. He stepped into the room without an invitation, looking confused.

"What's this, sleep over?"

"Uh, no Sergeant. We were hanging out after shift and must have just dozed off."

"Never mind. Hardwell, I've been looking for you. It seems you had a little excitement on guard duty last night. Might have been nice if I'd heard it first hand, or even first. It would have given me the chance to be the first one to talk to you, but the report went in over my head. Our little chat will have to wait until later, but believe me, it'll be happening at the first opportunity. Johnson and Ates, I'll be talking to you too. Right now, Hardwell, you're wanted in Commander Martinez's office, so move it. I'll be in there with you, but unless you've got anything you want to explain to me on the way, I'll be keeping my mouth shut."

Craig hustled, taking one final glance at Joey as he left. From his bunk, Joey gave him a reassuring nod, the gesture speaking a thousand words. Craig walked in silence with the Sergeant, nothing he could say to him that would make any sense or help his cause. He caught the Sergeant's occasional sideways glance from the corner of his eye. He was possibly hoping that he would offer him some reasonable explanation, something tangible that he could pass on to the Commander in his squad member's defense. Craig knew he would want to stand up for him, but he had absolutely nothing to offer. Keeping his mouth shut during proceedings would be better for the Sergeant anyway. He already knew he'd let him down badly; he didn't want to make it any worse for him. He took one last deep breath before stepping inside the office, giving the Commander a sharp salute.

"Private Hardwell reporting as ordered, Sir."

Commander Martinez returned the salute to both men. "At ease."

Craig dropped his salute and repositioned himself into the at ease position, keeping his eyes on Martinez. Sergeant Heard adopted a similar stance, remaining beside the entrance out of the way but prepared in case he was needed. This team was the best Armament Dogs he'd ever had, and he was prepared to fight for this soldier if he had to. For the moment, he let the Commander take charge as was his right.

"A report made its way up the chain of command to me this morning, Private, a rather worrying report in actual fact. Any idea what I'm talking about?"

"Yes, Sir."

"I see, and are you also aware of the utmost importance and seriousness of guard duty?"

"Yes, Sir."

"So you're not denying that without authorization, you left your post unattended, commandeered a vehicle, and proceeded to drive said vehicle around the base before abandoning it and attempting to kick in the door of one of my buildings?"

"No, Sir."

Martinez took a step towards him. "Then what the hell were you thinking!"

This was the moment Craig had dreaded. The urge to spill the truth rose in him like bile, the idea of lying to his superior abhorrent, the desire to share and not be alone with his terrifying secrets almost too great to ignore. How good it would feel to talk to an outsider, to bring in some additional help. He looked at the Commander's face and saw the truth of the matter. No matter how good a man he was, no matter how compassionate, how understanding, he simply wouldn't believe. The help they needed wouldn't come from anyone in command, not from anyone else in the military. *The medium,* he reminded himself. *DJ's going to talk to Amanda.* The thought calmed him, allowing him to do what needed to be done to prevent being kicked out of the army and sent home in disgrace.

"Sir, I just needed a little something to break the monotony."

"So you thought tearing ass around in one of my vehicles was the proper outlet!"

"No, Sir. I apologize. It was a momentary lapse of good judgment. It won't happen again, Sir."

"Damn right it won't. I have something far better to break that monotony for you. I take it you know what the UCMJ is?"

"The Uniform Code of Military Justice, Sir."

"Well, at least you learned something in basic training. I take it you're aware that the UCMJ gives Commanders full authority to impose non-judicial punishments for infractions. Don't answer that; I don't care. I know it, and that's all that counts. I'm imposing the maximum punishments permitted under Company Grade Article 15 in terms of restriction and extra duty. Fourteen days of extra duty and restriction should ensure that you're too damn tired and too locked down to get into any more trouble, so I hope that will be a nice little change of pace for you, something to break the monotony." The commander was furious enough to allow the sarcasm to drip from his voice. "On top of that, I'm ordering weekly visits to the post psychiatrist until I feel you've been cleared as a hazard. Anything to say?"

"No, Sir."

"So you don't want to plead your innocence, and you're waving your right to refuse Article 15 and push for a trial by court martial?"

"Yes, Sir. I'm accepting my guilt and will accept any fitting punishment you deem it appropriate to administer under the circumstances."

The anger left Commander Martinez, turning instead to disappointed resignation in his soldier's conduct. "Fine, I need you to sign this counseling to confirm your agreement. Your Article 15 packet will be sent to JAG for approval. You should think yourself lucky I'm not applying the pay forfeiture or grade reduction. If Sergeant Heard hadn't spoken so highly of you, this could have been a heck of a lot worse."

Craig nodded, stepping forward to sign the paperwork as requested. After doing so, he stepped back and snapped to attention. Commander Martinez saluted Craig, and he returned the gesture.

"Dismissed."

Craig dropped his salute, performed a perfect About Face maneuver, and marched out, Sergeant Heard following behind him. As soon as they were out of earshot of the Commander, Sergeant Heard steered Craig to a quieter area of the base.

"Well, that could have gone a lot worse. When you've done something wrong, the best thing is always to confess, apologize, and take your punishment like a man. Commander Martinez is a good man, but he was pretty riled up by what you did. The fact that you were so accepting took the heat out of him a little."

"I'm sorry I let you down, Sergeant."

"You let yourself down, Private, and I must admit I'm pretty surprised at you. Is there anything you want to tell me, anything you couldn't say to Commander Martinez?"

Craig dropped his eyes, his chest constricting. "No, Sergeant. It all went down exactly as you heard it. I was an idiot, but I'll do everything in my power to ensure it never happens again."

The Sergeant shook his head. "That's a pity. I could have sworn that there must have been more to it than that, but if you say there isn't, then there's nothing more I can do except to be really disappointed in you and agree with the Commander that he actually let you off lightly. Your perfect record to date helped, but you've lost that buffer now. Any further misconduct would be taken much more seriously."

"I understand."

"I hope you do; I'd hate to lose you, and so would your team. You guys need to pull yourselves together and keep your noses clean. If it comes to light now that I've ignored certain behaviors in the past, I'll be considered as much to blame as you, and it won't go well for any of us. I'd stand by my past decisions, of course, but others might not share my opinions so don't let anything like this happen again. Oh, and by the way, it probably won't surprise you to learn that you've been removed from guard duty for the foreseeable future, at least until the shrink clears you. You'll spend the rest of your nightshift allocation back in the hangar with the rest of your team. They can keep an eye on you. Tell Privates Johnson and Ates that I'll speak to them later, I've had enough of this for one day. It took a lot to convince the

Commander to leave them out of this, that they acted impulsively to protect a member of their team and were probably already regretting it, and had learned their own lessons. Go on and get some sleep. With fourteen days extra duties, you're going to need it."

"Yes, Sergeant."

Just as Craig turned to walk away, Sergeant Heard gripped his arm. "If you ever need to talk, about anything at all, you come to me, you hear? Don't let things escalate to the point where it's too late for me to help."

Craig looked the Sergeant in the eye and nodded. Sergeant Heard released him and watched him walk all the way back to the CHU's, still unsatisfied. Something was going on with his boys, but he was damned if he could figure out exactly what it was.

Craig arrived at party central, surprised to find all the guys awake and waiting for him, anxious to hear his fate. At their insistence, he recounted both conversations word for word.

"Lying to them was so hard," he finished. "I was itching to tell the truth. If they were both asses, it would have been a lot easier, but they're not, especially the Sergeant. I don't know how I managed to look him in the eye and pretend I willingly broke the rules and made him look bad. It was killing me."

"You did great. I don't know if I'd have done half so well. My mama always says I'm the worst liar ever, that my face is an open book," Billy said.

"As hard as it must have been, you did the right thing," Joey said. "All in all, it probably went better than I was expecting. Your convo with the Sergeant is actually worrying me more than the Article 15. Do you think he might know something?"

"I think he strongly suspects that I wasn't just messing around, but there's no way he has any idea what's really going on. He probably thought that someone was putting me up to it, or maybe even forcing me into it by threatening me somehow. He's going to be keeping a much closer eye on me from now on, maybe all of us, but I can't see how he would get to the bottom of it unless we give it away."

"Then we have to make doubly sure we don't. We don't discuss it outside this room, we stay well away from that bunker, and we do our best to protect ourselves. We can't afford to bring anyone else into this, not ever. Not only would we all end up with a discharge, but we might be putting them in danger too."

"So what if top ever decides to do something more with those bunkers? Do we keep our mouths shut then?"

"I guess we'd have to cross that bridge when we came to it. They haven't so far, not since the local laborer had his freak out. All we can do is hope that it stays that way. In the meantime, we concentrate on containment. Right now, all we have to work with is army training, so until we learn anything more, we approach it like any other military situation; contain and minimalize risk as much as possible. If Amanda can tell us more, then so much the better, but for now, it's instincts and training. We can't let the fear get to us, have to prevent it from consuming us and leaving ourselves wide open."

"Easy to say and much harder to do, Joey, especially when you're face to face with something impossible."

"I know, JJ, I get that, but we have to act as normally as possible at all times. I'm sure we'll all feel better once DJ makes contact with outside assistance."

"Yeah," George agreed. "I think talking to her will be like when you're part of a ground troop, surrounded and overrun, and someone manages to call for air support. She's our equivalent of a Kiowa Warrior appearing on the horizon and swooping in to rescue us. Let's hope she makes the enemy scatter in the same way."

"I get the hint, guys," DJ said with a laugh. "I don't think I'd manage to go back to sleep now anyway so I may as well go and see if I can find Larson. I know which platoon he's assigned to; they might well be having lunch right now. I'll go take a scout around the chow hall."

"Want some help or company?"

"No thanks, JDub. You all get some sleep if you can; it's going to be a long hard shift tonight."

DJ stretched as he stepped outside, the desert heat slamming his body like a tangible force after the air-conditioned comfort of his room. He knew that no matter how long he stayed here, he would never get used to it. It was just something else that added to the oppressiveness and strain of deployment. He headed for the chow hall, believing it was the most logical place to begin his mission. Still early afternoon, the place was pretty packed. DJ roamed up and down the aisles between the tables and along the serving line, searching for the familiar face of his friend or any others he might recognize from Larson's platoon. A complete sweep failed to produce the required result; Larson wasn't here. He walked back outside and strolled around aimlessly, hoping to come across them. He knew he could just start asking; someone would know exactly where the platoon was at this precise moment, but he didn't want this task to be over too soon. Although it was ultimately related, he was glad of having something else to think about and do other than his job or recent events. He also wanted to delay having to make the call as long as possible, the whole idea of speaking to someone he'd only met in a dream was making his skin crawl. The longer he took to find Larson the better.

He'd walked around various parts of the base for just under two hours before he finally spotted him. Larson was standing in full battle rattle in a less occupied part of the base. He was on the sidelines, watching a group of soldiers who'd stripped down to far less than regulation allowed to play a five-a-side game of soccer. Piles of their gear marked out the field perimeter and goalposts. Larson appeared transfixed by the game, staring intently at the makeshift playing field several feet away. DJ watched them as he approached, grinning at the amount of illegal tackles and blatant cheating going on, the game rowdy and frantic. Each player was dripping with sweat; having to wipe it out of their eyes almost constantly. He wondered where they got the energy. He reached Larson and tapped him twice on the shoulder.

"Hey there, battle, how's it going?" He didn't wait for an answer, anxious to get the question out now that he'd found him; afraid he would lose his nerve. "I'm hoping you can help me out. You know you came to me a while back and said that a friend of yours spoke about me, the medium, Amanda? Well, I think I might need to talk to her and was wondering if you'd give me her phone number or email address so that I can get in touch with her. I know it's a lot to ask, and you might need to check with her first, but it's important and pretty urgent. I was hoping I could maybe speak to her today."

Throughout DJ's rushed request, Larson hadn't taken his eyes off the game. As DJ stood, waiting nervously, Larson turned his head towards him and smiled, not a friendly grin, but a smile full of regret and pity. He shook his head slowly, pursing his lips before giving the soccer players one last glance and turning to walk away.

"Larson? Larson?"

DJ scratched his head as his friend didn't acknowledge his call, ignoring him completely. "Well, thanks a lot, buddy," he muttered. "You could have least said you'd think about it."

DJ marched back towards his CHU, annoyed and frustrated, too soon for the realization of what this meant for his team to have sunk in. He flung open the door to party central, and seven pairs of eyes looked hopefully in his direction. He shook his head, wanting to let them know immediately that he'd failed before they built their hopes up any higher.

"You didn't find him?" Craig was obviously disappointed.

"Oh, I found him all right."

"So what? He needs to check with her first before he passes along her contact details?"

"No, JDub, worse, he won't give them to me at all."

"What! How come? What did he say?"

"That was the thing, he didn't say anything, didn't give me any explanation, or even a lame excuse. He just looked at me with a 'sorry but not a chance' expression, shook his head, and walked away."

"Wow. Has something happened between you, anything that could have pissed him off? How was his mood before you asked?"

"I don't know. I didn't give him a chance to speak so I guess that's my own fault. Maybe that was it; I only sought him out to ask him for something. I guess I haven't been a good friend this tour; I've hardly seen him."

"With different assignments and shifts, it happens," Joey said with a shrug. "Every soldier knows deployment's different from just being on base back home. I can't see why he would be pissed at that."

"Well then, I don't know what his problem was, I can't think of anything else."

Joey bit his lip. "You said he looked kind of sorry about his refusal right?"

"Yeah, but him being sorry doesn't help us any."

"I realize that, but what if it was because something's happened to Amanda?"

Billy let out a gasp. "You mean, like, maybe she died or something?"

"Well, I'm not going as far as that, but maybe she's sick or something. It could account for both his refusal and being sorry about it, as well as maybe not wanting to talk about it."

"You're right," Justin said. "Or he could blame us. Maybe her being sick has something to do with what she encountered when she reached out over here in her dreams."

"Oh come on! Mr. Skeptical to Mr. Dark and Creepy all of a sudden. Who do you think you are, Stephen King?"

"Give him a break, DJ; we're only tossing ideas around. We don't actually know anything. Amanda is most probably fine, and there's always the possibly that she's explicitly asked her friends not to hand out her contact details. In her line, she must get enough whack jobs popping up without adding to them."

"Yeah, sorry, I'm just on edge. The last thing I need is worrying that we've inadvertently caused someone else harm, especially someone we thought was trying to reach out and help. No offense meant, Justin."

"None taken, but I can't see how you could find my turn around surprising when you've all seen what I've seen."

"We don't, I swear. I guess one definitive experience turns a skeptic into a believer, and after everything we've been through you probably held out longer than most. If I'm honest, I reacted badly because you were scaring me. I'm sorry."

"Apology accepted. At the risk of being called Mr. Dark and Creepy again and getting my head bitten off, you do all realize what this means, don't you?"

"Yeah," George said. "It means we've been denied air support."

"She was our only hope."

"Where do we go from here?"

"I don't know guys. Look, I'll try again in a day or two, okay. Maybe he'd just had some bad news or something and didn't want to talk today, or maybe he wasn't feeling too well. There could be a million and one explanations so let's not panic yet. Let's say air support's been delayed, not denied, for the moment at least. Anyway, if we're going to eat before shift tonight, then I suggest we head over to the chow hall. It's getting late."

Cheered by DJ's promise to try again and afflicted by rumbling guts since they'd missed both breakfast and lunch, DJ received no arguments. They scrambled to their feet and headed to the chow hall where they all ate heartily, their appetites healthier than in the last couple of weeks. They even laughed and joked over the meal, reminding them of the old days. Whether it was relief that nothing too drastic had happened to Craig or the renewed prospect of expert help, none of them knew and didn't much care. They were simply glad to be feeling better, lighter somehow. They were still laughing and joking as they piled out of the LMTV at the hangar to begin their shift. Saddler and his team were just leaving as they arrived. The last man hesitated before climbing into the waiting troop truck. With one hand on the side, he looked from Saddler to DJ, then back to Saddler. Making his decision, he let go and jogged over to the Armament Dogs, surprising them all when he tapped DJ on the shoulder. They all stopped and turned to face him. The soldier was nervous, shuffling from foot to foot. None of them said a word, waiting for him to speak. Eventually, he did.

"Look, I know we haven't been on the best of terms and to be honest, I hate the atmosphere it creates, but I have to go along to fit in, you know?" He didn't wait for an answer, needing to say what he'd come to say. "Anyway, I just wanted to say I'm really sorry about your friend. You probably won't remember me, but I was stationed with you both at Hawaii. I know you were close, so, you know, I'm sorry."

DJ's expression was confused, his mind torn between trying to place the man in Hawaii, and figuring out what the hell he was talking about. "What friend?"

"Curtis, Larson Curtis."

Like a striking snake, DJ was up in his face, his hand twisting a handful of field jacket beneath the man's chin. "What about Larson?"

"Aw shit. I thought you would have heard by now. I don't want to be the one to break it to you, but I guess I've got no choice. He's gone, man, killed by an IED while he and his team were out on patrol outside the wire. There was nothing anyone could have done. I'm so sorry, but at least it was quick and over in an instant. He wouldn't have suffered; he probably wouldn't even have known about it."

An image of Larson standing in full battle rattle watching the match from the sidelines flashed into DJ's head. The sad smile, the shake of his head, his silence.

"When" His voice was a hiss.

"It was just a little after 0600 hours this morning, that's why I figured you'd already know."

DJ's blood turned to ice in his veins, freezing him in place. Joey stepped forward, loosening DJ's fingers from the handful of jacket.

390

"Thanks for letting us know, we appreciate that. We'll take it from here."

The soldier nodded and ran to his waiting team while Joey put a protective and comforting arm around DJ, steering him inside the hangar. "I'm sorry," he said softly.

DJ looked at him, his face pale and pinched. "Then who the hell did I talk to, Joey? Who the fuck did I tap on the shoulder and speak to?"

"It was your friend, DJ. I guess in his ownway; he was saying goodbye. To the army, to you, to life."

"But I touched him! He was solid; he was real!"

Joey pulled DJ in towards him as he began to sob, gathering him up in a bear hug. He could feel his hot tears soaking through the layers of his clothing. For fifteen minutes, they remained silent as DJ cried; the shock of the loss equal to the shock of his realization that he'd seen and spoken to his friend around ten hours after he'd died. When his sobs subsided, he pulled himself out of Joey's arms and wiped furiously at his traitorous eyes, still leaking hot salty tears. The others stepped up, offering condolences but saying nothing more. They would talk only when DJ was ready. He walked to one of the cots that served as a makeshift bench and sat down heavily, his head in his hands. Finally, he raised his head and looked at them, fear and panic in his eyes.

"What if he was killed because he could help us?"

A frisson of fear touched them all, causing a few to shiver visibly. They'd been too stunned to think beyond the fact that DJ had conversed with what could only be described as a ghost.

"No." Joey's voice was firm. "It's just war, man, just war. People die every day out here. The odds are it's going to be people we know now and then. It's bad, but it's the facts. Don't twist it to make it worse than it is; don't find a way to make it our fault."

"It seems kind of a coincidence, though," Billy said.

"I agree with Billy, but if it is the case, then we're saying that it knew that Amanda could help, that it knew in advance that DJ was going to find Larson today like it's been listening to us all along. What level of intelligence does that convey?"

Joey put a hand on Justin's shoulder and shook his head. DJ was in no state to hear this stuff right now. "It was an IED. Nothing unusual, nothing unexpected, and certainly nothing paranormal. Got it?"

"Yeah, I got it, but it doesn't change one simple fact."

"What's that?"

"Air support hasn't been delayed or temporarily denied, it's been blown out of the fucking sky. Nobody's coming; no one's going to help us. We're completely cut off, isolated, out here all alone."

Chapter Twenty-One: A Reckoning

Somehow, they'd managed to get through the rest of their week on night shift. They'd began to notice a pattern; that the strange and frightening events would often come in waves, escalating and building until they came crashing down, breaking in an explosion of frenzied drama and then fizzling out. All would be quiet for a while, but they felt no relief, only the trepidation that came with the wait for the next wave to begin to rise and form, looming ominously on the horizon. They were constantly on edge, jumping at every shadow, ready to snap at the slightest provocation.

The death of Larson had affected them badly, both the loss of the information they needed as well as his subsequent unexplained appearance. DJ had taken it worst of all and not only because he was the one that had the strange encounter. He'd already lost so much on this tour, and the death of yet another friend pushed him into an even deeper depression that he couldn't find a way to break free from. He'd become increasingly withdrawn, and none of them could seem to reach him. They'd given up trying, hoping he would come round on his own as he'd done last time, simply waiting for the moment when they would have their friend back.

They still felt the instinct to stay together, to converge as one for safety and comfort, but their ill temper made them unwilling to do so. They all felt that they weren't fit company and that they would only drag the others down with their fear, despair, and increasingly short tempers. They ran the risk of breaking bonds forever with one wrong word, and they didn't want to take that chance. They didn't drift apart completely as they did before, but they held themselves in check, biting back the sudden exasperation, irritation, or even anger they would suddenly feel over something trivial and unimportant. They would hang out together after shift only until they could take no more; then they would retire to their rooms before they could do or say something they would later regret.

Craig spent less time with them due to the extra duties he'd been assigned, and if he was honest, they came as something of relief. With what was happening, talking about anything else seemed absolutely pointless, yet he didn't want to talk about it any longer. No matter how a conversation began, it always came back to the same thing, and he didn't think he could take much more.

As well as the extra duties, his restriction occasionally prevented him from joining the others. It meant he was confined to his CHU, his place of work, the chow hall, and the shower block and latrines. If the team decided to go anywhere such as the computer lab, the PX, the gym, or any of the other places set up for recreation on base, he couldn't go with them. It was the military version of being grounded by parents. He knew that the Dogs would refrain from going to the out of bounds areas if he asked them to but he never did. He told himself that it was only because it wouldn't be fair, that they shouldn't be denied just because of him,but it was the perfect excuse for when he didn't feel he could handle their company. He even used it to leave party central on occasion, although with his room being in the same trailer, that wasn't really an issue. No one would ever know and even if they did, he believed his trailer would be enough to satisfy the conditions of the restriction.

He had another reason to be thankful for the outcome of that fateful night, and that was that George and JJ hadn't suffered any serious repercussions for their actions. Sergeant Heard had pulled them both aside for a quiet talk, and although it had been intense, they hadn't received any punishment, only a warning. Then he'd exposed them to the same coaxing that Craig himself had been subjected to, where the Sergeant had tried to encourage them to talk about what was going on. They'd both held firm and had come away with their secrets intact. Evading or omitting the truth or even outright lying was becoming a way of life for them all outside of their own small group, and they didn't like it.

After finishing three extra hours of duty, Craig decided he could handle a little company for a few minutes. Instead of his own room, he knocked and popped his head inside party central to see who was around. Only Joey, George, and DJ were there. DJ was lying on his back on his bunk, fully clothed, his eyes closed while Joey and George gently strummed their guitars, playing a soft, soothing, melody.

"Hi Craig, you coming in?"

"Yeah, thanks, Joey, maybe just for a few."

Craig closed the door behind him and pulled out one of the folding chairs. "Where's everyone else tonight?"

"In their rooms. I think. Justin left first, and the others gradually followed, drifting out in ones or twos."

Craig nodded. It had been a common occurrence since they'd gone back onto day shift.

"So how was extra duty?"

"Not so bad. I'm still grateful things weren't a lot worse for all of us. I'm handling it fine."

"Good to hear. Fourteen days will be over before you know it."

"Probably."

Craig couldn't think of anything else to say. Joey went back to his strumming and plucking, his fingers joining George's in seamless perfection. They'd learned a lot from each other, the result being that they were both much-improved musicians. Craig allowed the music to wash over him, finding it soothing. "What's that you're playing?"

"Just something we put together ourselves, nothing special."

"It's good; I like it."

Joey smiled and continued to play. Craig stayed for another twenty minutes, simply listening to the soothing swirl of notes. Feeling sleepy, he yawned and rose. "Your lullaby's relaxed me. I'm going to hit the sack before it wears off. If anyone else drops by say goodnight from me."

"I will," Joey said, although he was sure everyone had gone to their separate rooms already and wouldn't be back. "See you in the morning."

Joey kept on playing, not failing to notice that DJ hadn't greeted or said goodbye to Craig, and hadn't even opened his eyes once during his short visit. He was worried about him again, seriously worried.

Over in the next trailer, JJ and Justin had prepared for bed but hadn't yet gone. Ever since learning that the medium was now out of their reach, Justin had been relying heavily on items he could pick up from the local bazaar on base. The owner spoke little English, but knew Justin well, always greeting him with a wide smile and a wink. Provided no one else was around, he would disappear for a few moments, always returning with a well-wrapped package that he would hold out towards Justin.

"For you," he would say, his words heavily accented. "Special for you, not much dollars."

Justin would smile, and they would haggle over the price, Justin always knocking him down while also knowing the man started high. It was a ritual. He never knew what he was buying, but it didn't matter, the guy knew what he liked, what he wanted, what he needed. Sometimes it would be local booze, firewater with a crazy proof level that would burn like molten lava all the way down and in his belly for hours afterward. Other times, it would be an unnamed herb or occasionally a sticky resin. The man would let Justin know what he should do with it in manner of code and sign language. If it needed to be mixed with tobacco and smoked, he would wave a packet of cigarettes at Justin.

"You pay," he would chortle. Other times he would mimic lighting a pipe. "Hookah, hookah, hookah."

Justin would laugh at his antics and hand over his money, knowing that whatever he got that day would be good, something to calm his terrified mind and see him safely through yet another night. He also knew that they might not always be illegal substances and that he could be paying inflated prices for simple, natural plants and herbs that could be picked on any mountain. Maybe if he'd been raised in a home with a mama who cooked, he would recognize some of the scents and textures, but he hadn't, and he didn't really care what he was buying as long as it worked; and they always worked.

Today, he'd received a bottle that claimed it was whiskey but smelled more like paraffin when he broke the seal and unscrewed the top that night. He took a drink regardless, grimacing and coughing while handing the bottle to JJ.

"Shit, that's really rough this time."

JJ had gingerly taken a small sip. "No arguments there. They obviously haven't had enough practice at making booze."

"Maybe they'll get better in time, but I don't really care. As long as it does the trick, I'm happy." He took another guzzle as JJ passed the bottle back.

"You've been hitting shit from the bazaar pretty heavily recently; maybe you should think about cutting back."

"Nah, nothing I can't handle. Besides, I'm sure he rips me off most of the time, sells me oregano or basil or something."

"Well, maybe you should try sprinkling it on a pizza instead of smoking it."

Justin snorted and choked, sending a spray of the dark oaken liquid across the room from his mouth. "Now look what you made me do," he laughed. "I'm wasting it."

JJ grinned back. "Just don't light a match in here tonight; the whole trailer will go up in a blaze. I'm sure you're right about him ripping you off, though. You know he speaks perfect English, right?"

"No way, I've heard him talk."

"Don't be fooled. It's all an act so that people talk freely in front of him, thinking he can't understand them. You wouldn't believe the stuff he hears."

"JJ, I think you've just revealed one of your secret sources of intel."

"Yeah, I have, but it doesn't matter. You won't get a word of sense out of him."

"So how come you do?"

"He understands our group dynamic. You get the gear; I get the info."

"That's how we roll," Justin agreed with a laugh.

They continued to chat, keeping their conversation to light banter. After three more sips, JJ couldn't take anymore. "No thanks, I'm out. I feel buzzed already; I'm going to get my head down. Justin?"

"Yeah?"

"Don't drink too much more; that stuff's going to pickle your organs."

"That's good isn't it? It preserves them."

"It's only good if you don't need them anymore. Call it quits soon and go to bed."

"Yes, mom."

JJ rolled his eyes and climbed into bed, the alcohol doing a lot to prevent the normal terror that accompanied the action. As much as he tried to talk Justin out of overindulging in his own particular coping mechanism, he couldn't deny that it worked. Five minutes after his head hit the pillow, he was snoring loudly.

Justin sat for a while longer, watching his battle sleep, hitting the bottle just a little harder. When he finally felt he'd reached the stage of being able to sleep, he recapped it and shook what was left, pleased to see that there was just over half a bottle remaining.

"You'll live to fight another day my friend," he slurred before setting it down on the floor and crawling into bed. His stomach lurched, and a wave of dizziness accompanied the motion.

He knew he was well and truly bombed, and it was exactly what he wanted. He lay down, only having to wait a few seconds before the desired effect overcame him. He passed out before the room had even stopped spinning.

JJ's fuzzy mind began to panic as he half woke to a familiar pressing sensation. With relief, he realized it wasn't that awful crushing sensation on his chest accompanied by the terrifying paralysis; it was simply an urgent need to empty his bladder. He glanced at the luminous hands of his watch, seeing it was just after 0400 hours. Damn booze, he knew he shouldn't have drank that stuff right before bed. He never needed to visit the latrine in the middle of the night. His body was obviously desperate to expel the stuff, and he couldn't blame it, it was toxic.

Fumbling in the dark, he grabbed the boots that always sat waiting by the bed, turning them upside down and banging them against the frame. Even the tightly sealed CHU's weren't a guaranteed safe zone from the sneaky spiders and scorpions – even when they didn't have insider help to invade. He didn't try to be quiet, knew his battle would have consumed enough of the gut rot to knock him out cold for several hours. Certain that anything that might be nesting inside his boots for the night had been evicted; he slipped them on before planting his feet on the floor and standing up. He wouldn't bother dressing; the sight of soldiers in nothing but shorts and a tee was a common one within CHUville, especially on the latrine route. It was against regulation, but it was a rule that wasn't that strictly applied to soldiers that were off duty and sleeping. He doubted that he would run into any sticklers or jobsworths out there tonight. Besides, his need was greater than the desire to follow the rules.

He snagged his flashlight just in case any of the base lights had failed or had been shut down due to mortar attacks and dashed outside, steeling himself against the blast of frigid air that would hit him as soon as he opened the external trailer door. He'd only jogged a few steps when he went sprawling, skidding over the rough sand to come to a stop just before the rock perimeter they'd built when they'd first transferred to the trailer. His flashlight had flown from his hand as he'd landed and he'd heard it shatter against those very rocks.

"What the hell!"

In a flash, JJ was on his feet, turning to see what had tripped him. He could hardly believe it when he saw that it was Justin, sprawled in the dirt on his stomach, his face barely turned to the side enough to avoid inhaling a lungful of sand with every breath, if he was even breathing.

"Jesus H. Christ. Justin, Justin!"

He kept his voice to a frantic whisper, not wanting to attract any unwanted attention. He held two fingers to his battle's neck, relieved when he felt the throbbing beat of a pulse beneath his fingers. "Oh, thank God."

Assuming he staggered out here in a drunken haze then passed out, JJ rolled Justin onto his back, intending to check his airways and roll him once more into the recovery position before attempting to bring him around. As he pushed him over, he half expected to find a pile of puke beneath him but instead, something fell from Justin's hand, rolling a short distance across the sand. JJ reached for it, horrified to discover that it was the vial of acid Justin had brought back out with him after his leave, the stuff they'd shared in the bunker. He couldn't really remember, but he had the gut feeling that it was a good bit emptier than the last time he'd seen it. He went to stuff it deep into a pocket before remembering he didn't have any.

"Shit!"

He ran inside with the gear, returning it to Justin's hiding place before dashing back outside, leaving the doors open on the way. "Justin, wake up, Justin."

He gave him a few gentle slaps on the cheek. When they failed to work, he tried again, sharper slaps that echoed in the night. Still nothing. With a shake of his head, he slipped his arms under his battle's armpits and clasped his hands over his chest. Unceremoniously, he dragged him across the ground and into the trailer. He dumped the dead weight onto the floor then hurried off to attend to his original desperate need that had been momentarily forgotten, hoping that Justin would have come round by the time he got back. No such luck.

He reached for the bottle of water on his nightstand and splashed the entire contents into Justin's face. That did the trick, barely, but enough for Justin to wave a hand half-heartedly in the direction of his face and blink in confusion.

"Wassup?" he muttered.

"I don't know, why don't you tell me?"

JJ's angry growl cut through the fog, and Justin struggled to roll onto his side and prop himself up on one elbow. "Why am I on the floor and why are you mad at me?"

"I asked you not to do this, told you to call it quits and go to bed, but what do I find when I get up? You sprawled face down outside, passed out cold. You scared me, man; I thought you were freaking dead!"

"I did quit and go to bed, not even half an hour after you; wait a minute, did you say *outside?*"

"Damn right I did."

"No," Justin said with a shake of his head, emitting a pained groan as he did so. He clutched at the floor as the room began to spin and he swallowed hard to push back the rising stomach acid. "I feel like shit, that whiskey must be full of more crap than I thought, but I swear I didn't drink much more before I went to bed. I remember lying there waiting to pass out, and then I don't remember anything else. I couldn't have been outside."

"You definitely were. I face-planted and went sliding when I fell over you. Look."

Justin stared at the raw scrapes on JJ's hands, elbows, knees, and chin in confusion. "Where was I?"

"About four or five feet from the front of the trailer. You were face down, and I was all prepared to perform CPR, but your pulse and breathing were fine, your airways were clear, but I couldn't wake you up. I had to drag your sorry ass back inside before someone else saw you in that state."

"Thanks, I appreciate that, but I still don't understand how I could have been out there. I clearly remember getting into bed, and sure, I was totally hammered, but I've never gone walkabout before. You know me, I just pass out."

"Well, how about you just pass out again now. You're still at least half ripped and need to sleep this off in a hurry, and I'm cold and tired and want to go back to bed. We'll talk about this again in the morning."

JJ helped Justin to his feet and into bed. He was right; his friend barely had any control over his own legs, and his speech, although coherent, was slow and slurred. Once he had Justin settled, he crawled back into his own bed, but sleep wouldn't come. Instead, he listened to Justin's snoring, the sound comforting for once instead of irritating. At least while he could hear him, he knew his battle hadn't gone into cardiac arrest.

***

Unable to sleep well, George had risen early and decided to tackle the pressing issue of laundry. His Army Green laundry bag was growing full and his metal closet growing empty, reminding him that he hadn't dropped off or picked up clothes for a while. Working by touch and familiarity in the dark, he hauled his dirty clothing from the canvas bag and stuffed it into one of his two provided mesh bags. Once the bag was ready, he quietly slid open his one drawer and fumbled inside for the paper receipt he'd received from the laundry last time that would allow him to pick up his clean clothes. After stuffing it in his pocket, he slung his mesh bag and guitar over his shoulder and headed out.

No matter what the hour, the laundry facility was always a bustling hive of noisy activity. Soldiers came and went, and the male Pilipino laundry workers were kept busy taking in or handing out mesh bags, writing receipts or checking them against the piles of clean mesh bags to find the appropriate one to hand back. Others were busy cramming the mesh bags of dirty laundry into the machines, as many as they could possibly fit. It was a never-ending cycle.

George handed over his receipt, waiting until he'd received the mesh bag he'd handed in a couple of weeks ago before handing over the second mesh bag of dirty clothes and receiving another receipt in return. He watched as it was thrown onto a pile, ready for someone else to stuff into a machine. He knew he shouldn't wait so long. The way the mesh bags were crammed into the machine, it was a small wonder that the clothes inside got clean at all. If the mesh bags were tightly packed in the first place, there was little hope that the items inside would receive a thorough wash. He promised himself he would do this more often. The fastest service they offered was a four-hour turnaround; he didn't have any real reason for waiting until he'd practically run out of clean stuff to wear.

With his dirty bag swapped for his clean bag, he walked around to the back of the laundry facility and sat down cross-legged. The idea for a new song had come to him through his restless night, and he wanted to work on it immediately. It was too early to disturb his roommate with his playing, so instead he sat there and strummed and plucked, working out chords, making changes here and there until it began to flow and soar, sounding just right.

It had still been dark when he'd sat down, but it was daylight when he left with his bag and guitar over his shoulder. There was no sign of JDub when he entered their room. He assumed he was either in the shower or already set for work and hanging out in party central to pass the time before shift. He busied himself with folding each item from the bag and putting it away in its proper place, still humming the new song that was swirling around in his head. As he delved into the bag again looking for another item that needed to be folded on the shelf he was working on, he felt that prickling sensation on the nape of his neck, the one that alerted him that someone else was in the room and watching him. His first thought was that it was JDub and wondered why his roommate hadn't spoken as he'd come in. It only took him a second to realize that this wasn't his battle and that whoever was there wasn't friendly.

He whirled to face the intruder, his Golden Gloves winning fists raised, muscles in his arms bulging with power and tension, his stance prepared to defend and fight. Anyone who dared to sneak up on him with ill intent would end up sorry. He'd expected to see Saddler or one of his cronies. Instead, he saw nothing. Nobody was there. He dropped his raised fists, staring around in complete confusion, scanning every corner of the room. His senses never failed him, and his body was still telling him danger was close, yet his eyes were telling him otherwise.

"What the hell?"

As soon as the words were out of his mouth, George felt himself being grabbed and slammed against the CHU wall, so hard it knocked the wind from him. His body instinctively wanted to double over to relieve the pressure crushing his lungs, but he was pinned, the hundred-and-ninety pound boxer was as helpless as a live bug on a mounting board. The pressure released for a split second, enough to allow George to grasp in one deep breath and raise his fists again before the invisible force reappeared around his throat. He swung and jabbed, but his punches failed to connect with anything, swiping through the empty air in front of him.

Impossible!

His mind screamed, his body struggled, but it made no difference. Impossible or not, the life was being choked from him, and there was nothing he could do about it. His arms dropped, his muscles weak and aching from lack of oxygen, black spots beginning to appear in his fuzzy vision. He was on the verge of passing out. Then the grip loosened, not by much, but enough for George to get thin slivers of precious air into his lungs. The grip was icy cold, yet he was subjected to what felt almost like static electricity jolting through his body, the invisible hands the source of the disconcerting sensation. Just as George thought things were better, a malevolent laughter filled the room. It didn't come from an external source; he didn't hear it with his ears. It was inside his head, bouncing around his synapses. *I'm going to go crazy; my mind is going to snap.*

The laughter stopped, turning to a sharp hiss of hatred. Then George was flying through the air before being slammed against the ceiling. He opened his mouth to scream, but nothing came out. He could feel the hands still around his throat, yet his whole torso was being pressed against the internal roof of the trailer, his arms, and legs dangling, kicking and flailing in sheer panic and terror. Once again, the stranglehold tightened, cutting off his air supply, making his vision fuzzy and spots dance as he stared wide-eyed at the floor below him, light-headed, beginning to drift. He knew this was the moment he was going to die. He stopped struggling, accepting as he allowed the darkness to wash over, resignation and relief his last emotions as he slipped into unconsciousness.

He wasn't aware of being yanked from the ceiling, had no knowledge of being thrown across the length of the CHU, felt nothing as he hit the wall and slid down, folding into a crumpled heap in the corner.

That's where he was when JDub strolled back into the room from party central, coming to see if George was ready to go for breakfast before shift. He didn't see him at first; mildly puzzled that he wasn't in the room when his mesh laundry bag lay on the floor only half-empty. He strolled over and bent down, fingering the items to see if they were still warm from the dryer, trying to pick up some clues. That's when he noticed his battle in the corner behind the door.

"George, what are you doing down there?"

He received no answer. JDub rushed over. "George, George! What happened, buddy?"

Nothing.

JDub opened his mouth wide. "Help! Guys, help, something's wrong with George!"

Without waiting for assistance to come, he scooped his battle into his arms as he would an injured animal on his Daddy's farm and ran with him, finding an inner reserve of strength he didn't know he had, rushing him to Joey and DJ. They were already in the short hallway but doubled back when they saw JDub approach with George in his arms, ushering him in and urging him to lay George on the bottom bunk, where they both quickly checked him over.

"He's fine, it's okay, he's fine, just unconscious."

Joey tried to calm the frantic JDub. The others had heard the cry and had come running, even the half-awake and hung-over Justin, who had been slouching out of his trailer with JJ breaking into a run when he heard the cries. They gathered around George, who was slowly coming round with each gentle tap DJ was administering to his cheeks.

"Come back to us George, come on, man, wake up."

"Huh?"

"That's it. He's coming round, guys, give him some space to breathe."

They all backed up, anxious expressions on their faces.

"Jeez, I feel like I've been hit by a truck. Where am I?"

"You're in party central; you're safe. Here, have some water."

George sat up and drank gratefully from the offered bottle.

"How do you feel?"

"Better, thanks, but sore, like I went ten rounds with Tyson."

"Holy shit," Joey exclaimed. "What the hell is that on your neck?" He pulled aside George's field jacket, allowing them all to see the deep purple bruises on George's neck, formed in perfect handprints.

"Who did this to you?"

DJ was angry, his fists balled by his sides. To his utter amazement, the tough alpha male that was George Ates put his hands over his face and began to cry. Not just cry, but sob, his body shuddering, wailing as the tears gushed through his hands. The others looked on, uneasy to see such a strong man so utterly cowed and overcome.

Eventually, George recovered enough to recount his story to the group, his voice trembling with delayed shock and fear as he verbalized it, turning it into stark reality although his mind still fought to deny it. They were stunned, but not as horrified as they should have been, strange events so commonplace now that they'd almost come to expect them. That thought frightened Joey as much as the experiences did, their acceptance of this as their normality a red flag to the fact that they were ready to let their guard down and give in.

"You tried to fight physically, but did you try to fight with your mind as we spoke about?"

"No. My mind refused to believe what was happening, even after everything we've seen and heard. Then I just gave up, I was dying, and I just rolled over, almost wanting it to kill me and get it over with, and put an end to all this." George sniffed and wiped at the tears that threatened to spill over yet again. "I just wanted to fucking die."

"How do you feel now?"

"Ashamed and embarrassed as hell. I don't remember ever crying in my life, not even as a kid."

"Don't be ashamed of that, not with us. But do you feel more normal now, you feel like yourself?"

"At the risk of sounding like a girl, I feel cleansed, as if the crying helped. Now I'm just mad and want revenge."

"You're definitely back to normal then," Joey said, making them chuckle half-heartedly. "On a serious note, though, we've got to learn a lesson from this, all of us. It can't be fought with our hands and bodies; we can't touch it that way. It somehow gets inside our heads, and that's where we need to fight. Put up barriers, push it out, take control, and visualize what we want to happen."

"You mean like the T-wall and sandbags, except inside our head?"

"Exactly, Craig, if that's a familiar visualization that you think will work. Imagine it all around your head, don't let it pass, and don't let it find a way in. If it gets through, push it out, remember who you are, latch on to your favorite memory or something, I don't know, just try anything."

"What if you can't? What if you're unconscious or asleep when it slips in?"

They all turned to look at JJ, so he explained what had happened with Justin in the early hours of the morning.

"I don't think that was anything spooky. No offense, Justin, but it sounds like you were just messed up."

"No, I mean, yeah, I was, but not to that extent. All I had was maybe half a bottle of local firewater at most. You've seen me drink much more than that and still be standing."

"Justin, I checked the bottle first light, it's empty, and it wasn't just the whiskey."

"What are you talking about, JJ?"

"When I found you, you had that vial in your hand, you know, the one you brought back."

"Nope, I didn't touch that."

"It rolled out of your hand when I turned you over."

"So where is it now?"

"I put it back first in case someone came along; it's where you usually keep it."

"So you can't prove it then."

"Why would I need to? I know what I saw. You'd been dropping acid on top of drinking almost that whole bottle on your own. I only had a few sips."

"Wait one minute here! I already told you, I went to bed shortly after you did, and the damn bottle was still half-full at least. Next thing I know, I'm on the floor, and you're splashing water in my face. I didn't touch the acid; I wouldn't. I know I have an addictive personality, but I only like tripping with my battles, I know better than to do it on my own without a babysitter, and flying solo is no fun anyway. Besides, I brought that back for all of us to share; I'm not going to hog it all for myself. The other stuff is just to make sure I sleep 'cos I'm sick of the damn nightmares, and I know better than to mix that shit with too much booze. I know we drink beer and maybe pass around a bottle of spirits between all of us, but I'm not dumb enough to drink that much then indulge; not unless I was deliberately trying to kill myself."

Joey looked around at the group. "He's making sense. I believe him. I don't think this was just his usual idiocy."

"Thanks for the support there, Joey."

"Sorry, but when it comes your little habits, it's the truth."

"I didn't see any of you complaining while we were having a good time."

"You're right, I apologize. Can you remember how much was left after last time we used it?"

"I've got a rough idea, why?"

"Go take a quick peek, see what you think when you see it."

"Yeah, sure, good thinking. That'll prove I didn't take any."

Justin hurried off, and once he was gone, JJ spoke up. "Just for the record, I'm admitting that I can't recall all that clearly, and I was already stoned before Justin gave us that last second round, but thinking about how many drops we used on each occasion, I've got the distinct impression that there's less than there should be although I think he's telling the truth about not remembering."

"Fair enough, JJ, we'll see what he says when he comes back."

Justin returned with his face pale and sweat beading on his forehead. "You're right; some's missing, and more than one person should ever take at once. No wonder I feel like crap; I'm surprised I woke up at all. How could I be that stupid?"

"So you definitely believe now that you dropped acid last night?"

"Yeah, I must have been so drunk I don't remember it. There's no other explanation."

"Maybe there is." They all turned towards JDub. "Maybe you were being manipulated. Maybe it was inside your head and making you do it, just like it did to Craig."

"That's exactly what I've been thinking about all night after I brought him round and he really didn't seem to know," JJ agreed.

"Shit. That means it was an attack on me too, a deliberate attempt to take my life but one that would just look like my own stupidity. No one would ever see anything different."

"Possibly, but it doesn't explain why you were outside," said Craig. "You could have overdosed in your room just as easily, and it would be a more realistic place to be found."

"Maybe it wanted you to go somewhere and do something first," Billy said. "But your body gave out on you, or on it, depending on how you look at it."

"Do what?" Justin asked, his face going paler still.

"I guess we'll never know, but thank God you didn't do it," JDub said. "It could have been something really horrible, and they'd have blamed everything they found in your system after analysis."

"Justin, you need to cut this out. You need to be more aware."

"You think that will make a difference? George was aware, and it didn't stop him from being attacked, nor any of us. We don't even know what this thing is, but it's not a ghost or spirit. It can be everywhere at once; can come at us at any time and in a million different ways. We never know what to expect or when to expect it. We've been played with, laughed at, physically attacked, and made to attack each other or do things completely against our will. What the hell is next?"

"Joey," George said, speaking for the first time since the telling of his ordeal. "I think you need to ask Carrie for that scientist's details. I think we need to speak to him."

"You're starting to believe this has something to do with the obelisk in the bunker?" Billy asked.

"I reckon it might. As Justin pointed out, this is no simple haunting, we're not dealing with a dead soldier or Haji here; this is something far greater and far worse."

"We can't communicate with him from here; you know that stuff's all monitored. We mention that bunker once, and we're all in the brig," JJ said.

"Then we have to use Carrie as a go between."

"I'm really not comfortable with that. What if the guy is some nut job like Justin said? I don't want to put my wife and kids at risk."

"I want to let it be known that I'm completely retracting anything I said before all this went down. I'm no longer hanging onto my skepticism. You guys said way back that something wasn't right about this tour, and I don't need any more convincing of that. All this stuff started happening to us personally after we went to that bunker. It ties into what this guy said, so I now think it's extremely likely that he is who he says he is. We need to know more about this thing, hear the stories and find out what they know. That way, we can decide if there really is a connection, and if there is, what can been done about it. We're out of any other options."

Joey bowed his head, taking a moment to think everything over. Finally, he raised his head and looked around the group. "You're right, we've got no other choice. I'll do it."

Chapter Twenty Two: Last Resort

"Hey honey, how are you?"

"Joey! This is a surprise."

"A good one I hope?"

He could hear the smile in Carrie's voice as she answered. "Oh, definitely a good one."

He ran a hand through his dirty blond hair, his heart filled with longing as he imagined her face, her full lips curved upwards, and the sparkle in her hazel eyes. It was just before 1200 hours in Iraq, so if his rough calculations were right, it would be coming up on 2300 hours back home in Hawaii. Depending on how hectic her day had been with the kids, she might even be in bed by now. He almost groaned at the thought of snuggling up beside her on the soft bed, buried beneath the comforter, safe, the protected and the protector.

"So what are you up to?" he asked instead, hoping to distract himself from his desire to be home with his family.

"Not much, kids are asleep, and I'm about to head up soon myself, I'm just waiting to move clothes from the washer to the dryer. Your son forgot to gave me his football gear again and needs it in the morning."

"He's your son too."

"Not when he's done something dumb, then he's all yours."

Joey couldn't help but laugh, knowing she was teasing. His mental image of her shifted, knowing that if she were tired but waiting for laundry, she'd be sitting at the kitchen table, either reading or watching TV with the volume down low, so it didn't disturb the kids.

"Fair enough."

"So to what do I owe this unexpected pleasure? Where are you?"

"I'm in the phone center on base."

He heard her disappointed sigh. "For a moment there I thought maybe you were on your way home and calling en route to surprise me. I know you don't call from base that often because of how expensive the prepaid cards are from the PX."

"Sorry, hon, no such luck."

"Is there something wrong? Is that why you called instead of emailing as usual?"

"Nothing in particular, but I really needed to hear your voice."

"I'm always here for you; you know that. Is it just me or has this tour lasted forever this time?"

"It's definitely not just you. I feel the same way."

"Any word of leave?"

Now it was Joey's turn to sigh. "No, no word at all. Only one of our team has been selected for leave since we arrived. The rest of us seem to be stuck here."

"Is it bad?"

The question was simple, but it was laden with sympathy and understanding. It was one of the million things he loved about Carrie; neither of them needed many words to say the deep stuff, the bond between them allowed unspoken communication, even from this distance and along telephone wires. He'd heard many soldiers say that they were wary of calls with their spouses as words could so easily be misconstrued without the assistance of body language or facial expressions, so they often ended in arguments due to miscommunication. That had never happened to Joey with Carrie, nor did she ever spend the time whining and complaining as he'd heard of a few other army wives doing.

"Oh, Joey, I'm sorry."

He realized he'd taken too long to answer the question and from his silence, Carrie had figured out for herself how hard this tour was on him. She wouldn't know the specifics, but she'd know that whatever events were taking place, they were affecting him deeply.

"It's tough, but I'm okay."

"Need to talk about it?"

"Yes and no. I actually need a favor."

"I knew you would have an ulterior motive!"

He heard her laugh and could imagine her rolling her eyes. He appreciated her attempt to lighten his mood. "What were you hoping for, a dirty phone call?"

"A booty call would be better, but since that's impossible, I might settle for phone sex. Not ideal but better than nothing. Shall I start?"

"Don't you dare!"

She giggled, knowing full well that others could easily overhear conversations that take place in a phone center. "Okay then, I'll let you off. If that isn't it, what's the favor?"

Joey's face turned serious. He had a few seconds to change his mind. Otherwise, Carrie would wheedle it out of him anyway, judging by his pause that there was something he wasn't bringing himself to say. He thought about his beautiful wife and precious children home alone, then thought about the terrified faces of his battles, all looking to him to find answers and solutions. He thought about the hundreds of soldiers on base, protecting the USA and trying to protect the innocent people caught up in the middle of this fight. He thought about the danger they might all be in. He strengthened his resolve and slouched in the uncomfortable folding metal chair provided, ducking low to ensure he was hidden by the half plywood walls on either side of him that at least tried to give the illusion of privacy. He kept his voice low.

"You remember those photos I sent and the guy that got in touch?"

"Yes?"

"I need to speak to him, or even better, the specialist he mentioned."

"You do?"

Her surprise was obvious. He'd specifically told her not to reply to the message, and now here he was saying the exact opposite. "Yeah. There's been some... developments. I really need your help to get in touch with him."

"What kind of developments? Joey, you're scaring me, what's going on?"

"It's okay, baby, nothing for you to worry about. The guys and I just really want to know more about the... historical background, that's all."

"Okay, I get it; you don't want to say too much. Just tell me this, are you in any danger, apart from the obvious and usual I mean?"

For the first time in his life, Joey lied to his wife. "No."

"Fair enough, I trust you. So you actually want to get in touch with either of them from there, is that a good idea?"

"I figured maybe a video call, nothing before that, no record."

"Okay, so you want me to act as a go-between and try to set that up? I can do that."

"That would be great, thanks, honey. Just one thing, still make sure you don't tell him anything about you. He doesn't need to know your name or anything about us. He just needs to know the guy that took the picture wants to talk."

"I'll be careful. What shift are you on over the next week or so?"

"As far as I know at the moment, we're on 0600 hours to 1800 hours for at least the next week, but they could change that at the drop of a hat; we never get much notice. I'll call you back later tonight and see how you managed to get on. If anything's changed with my schedule, I can let you know."

"That sounds great. I'm not going to pass up the opportunity to speak to you twice in such a short time. Since I'm up anyway, I might as well send a message tonight. If he doesn't get it tonight, he should see it in the morning, so I might know something by the time you call back. Don't expect too much though on the first day. Even if you wait until midnight to call, it'll still only be mid-morning or something here."

"I know and I won't. Thanks, honey, this means a lot to me."

"I can tell."

"I'd better go. I ducked out of the half-way point food run to call, so I'd better get back before I'm missed. The guys are covering for me."

"You mean you're shamming? I'm shocked."

"I know right? I'd better go. I'll talk to you again soon. I love you."

"I love you too. Joey?"

"Yes?"

"Be careful."

"I will."

When he walked back into the hanger laden down with lunch, seven expectant faces turned towards him. He nodded. He'd made the first move.

***

Carrie rose and walked into the living room where her laptop sat on the coffee table, already shut down for the night. She drummed her fingers on the table while she waited for it to boot up. She knew there was so much that Joey wasn't telling her, but she also knew there was nothing she could do about it. He either couldn't or wouldn't talk right now, and she just had to trust him and be patient. She would find out what this was all about eventually. It didn't stop her from worrying, though. The first message from that scientist guy had scared her, and she wasn't sure she really wanted to hear any more about that creepy pillar thing than she had to. Still, she needed to do this; Joey had asked, and she would refuse him nothing.

With her laptop now ready and waiting for further instructions, she logged into her social media account and went into the message section, looking for the private message she'd received. She was glad she hadn't deleted the conversation, because even though she could remember much of what he'd said, she couldn't remember his name or the institution where he worked. She was sure he'd told her, but couldn't recall the details. She reread the unanswered message over again, reminding herself of all that it said, her concern for her husband and his battle buddies growing with every word. *Why did Joey need to speak to him now? Why are they even interested in this thing?* She had no answers, and with Joey stuck right in the middle of whatever this was about, that made her even more nervous. With a feeling of trepidation mixed with determination, she placed her fingers on the keyboard and began to type.

Hi there

Thanks so much for getting in touch regarding my photograph. I'm sorry I took so long to reply, but your message gave me a lot to think about, and I wanted to do that before getting back to you. I have some questions for you, but rather than message back and forth, it might be easier if we spoke on the phone. Would that be something you'd be willing to do? If so, please let me know how I can get in touch with you.

Regards

C.

She read over what she'd written, stalling the moment when she would have to hit send. It seemed to hit the right note, polite but unrevealing, curious but not desperate, and hopefully enough to catch his interest. She pushed the button.

She walked back into the kitchen and cocked her head, listening for the sound of the washer in the laundry room. It was coming to the end of the final spin cycle, so she headed through; leaning against the dryer while she waited out the last few minutes, deep in thought. Her mind continued to race as she moved the clothes from the washer to dryer and turned it on.

From what she could read between the lines, this pillar, or obelisk or whatever the guy had called it was obviously somewhere on Joey's base. They were partying in the other pics, and they wouldn't do that off base. Outside that fence was all hostile territory; no way would they let their guard down that way if they weren't somewhere safe, or at least as safe as anyone could be during deployment. According to the scientist, a similar thing had shown up throughout history before large-scale death or destruction. That made sense; war in the Middle East had been ongoing for a few years now so if that didn't constitute death and destruction, she didn't know what did. If everything he said was true its presence followed the pattern, so why the big mystery and the interest? She tried to tell herself it was only an idle curiosity for the guys, just a way of passing the time. She didn't really believe it, but it worked as an excuse for now.

She went back to the living room, fully intending to shut down her laptop and head to bed. She was surprised to see a notification of a private message. She knew whom it would be from before she even opened it.

> *Dear C*
>
> *Thank you for contacting me. I would very much like to talk on the phone with you regarding your pictures. You can call me at home right now, but if that's not convenient for you or if it makes you uncomfortable, you can call me at work. I'm usually there from around 8 am until at least 7 pm and apart from a half hour to an hour commute; I'm usually at home all*

other times. I'll give you all my contact numbers and extension
number below. I'll very much look forward to your call.
Sincerely
James Grimes

She hadn't expected such a rapid response. She checked out the phone numbers, easily determining that they were all within the United States so wherever he was, it was getting late. The fact that he was so keen to talk right away made the situation all the more worrying.

"What the hell is it about this thing?" she muttered.

There was only one way to find out. She reached over and snagged her cordless phone from the side table. Remembering the words of caution from Joey, she used her blocking feature to hide her number before making the call.

"Hello?"

"Hello, is this Mr. Grimes?"

"Yes, speaking."

"Umm, Hi, I messaged you a few moments ago regarding some pictures, and you said it would be okay to call?"

She heard the sharp hiss of breath through teeth. When he spoke again, his tone was excited. "Yes, hello. Sorry, I don't know what to call you; do I just call you C or ConstantBattle321?"

Carrie smiled at hearing the screen name she used for almost everything. Joey had pressed home the importance of internet security when they'd first gotten married, and more so when she was expecting their first child. Everything she'd set up wouldn't easily reveal anything about who or where she was. The name she'd chosen was a playful one, partly because it was an expression she'd often used when Joey was gone. Whether it referred to dealing with the loneliness, her pregnancies, and the babies when they were little, keeping the house tidy, or keeping the kids in line when they were at the most awkward ages, she'd joked that it was a constant battle having to do it all alone. The other side of the expression was that it was what Joey had called her, his constant home ground battle buddy, always by his side, always backing him up. The 321 was added later as an in-joke, something she used for the kids when she issued them an order she expected them to obey, as in they had a three-secondcountdown in which to comply or they were in big trouble. Pulling herself from her reverie, she realized the man on the other end of the line was waiting for an answer.

"It's Cece," she said, coming up with the first thing that came to mind. "My name's Cece."

"Okay Cece, please call me James. So you want to talk about the obelisk?"

"Yes, well actually, it's my husband that's developed a bit of interest in it, but I was better placed to get in touch."

"I see. Well, I'm not too sure if there's much more I can tell you other than what I said in the original message, especially as I don't know the location of the artifact."

"Artifact? So you genuinely believe it's something ancient, something that's existed for a very long time."

"I do."

"I'm struggling to understand how that's possible. If these things are dotted all over and have been for centuries or whatever, how come they don't just get discovered at random times, how does it always coincide with a disaster?"

"That's the million-dollar question, isn't it? It's why I'm leaning towards the belief of my friend, who's a specialist in this matter."

"And what belief would that be?"

"I see you very neatly avoided the subject of the obelisk's location. Perhaps we should make this conversation more mutually beneficial. I'll tell you what my friend believes if you reveal the location."

Carrie hesitated, wishing she could consult with Joey before she spoke again. He'd said little, but she'd picked up the desolation and desperation behind every casual word he'd spoken. Whatever this was about, it was urgent. She needed to take control.

"I don't suppose you'd be willing to give me contact details for your friend?"

"He's a very busy man and travels extensively for his research. It might take a lot to convince him to take the time out to speak to you."

"Perhaps a lot as in the location of the most recently found obelisk?"

"Tell me where the picture was taken and I'll call him as soon as we hang up and ask if I can pass on his details."

"I don't know how safe it would be to reveal that to you, and I'm not sure it would do either of you any good. It's in a place with absolutely no access."

"You'd be surprised at how many places our credentials can gain access to. I don't want to play guessing games all night, Cece, although I probably could work it out from a few careful questions."

"All right. It was found on a military base."

"In the U.S.?" The tone was sharp.

"No, Iraq."

The relief was palpable even down the phone line. "That narrows it down, but there are a lot of occupied military bases there right now. Which one?"

"Look, I don't know all the details, but I do know my husband could get in a lot of trouble over this. This has to be kept quiet."

"I'll do my best to keep it to a select few. Which base?"

"Speicher."

"Thank you. I'll go and make that call. If he's agreeable, I'll message you his details."

"Wait! You said you'd tell me his theory."

His impatience was clear. "He believes there aren't several obelisks waiting to be found. He thinks there's only one."

The click and dial tone were loud in Carrie's ear. She hung up and sat waiting by her computer.

***

Joey sat nervously in front of the computer and glanced at his watch once more. The computer lab wasn't that busy. Carrie had done well setting up the appointment with the specialist, Dr. William King, at a time when she'd hoped it would be quiet. The call was scheduled for 0300 hours in Iraq. He'd tried to nap beforehand, but it had been impossible, he was too keyed up and so were the rest of the guys. When he'd left his room, they'd all been camped out in party central, dozing in chairs or on the floor, wanting to be on hand for his return and hear what he had to say immediately.

He'd arrived thirty minutes early to ensure he snagged one of the machines and was ready to take the call. Once seated, he'd removed all his insignia from the front of his field jacket, hoping that it would help him keep a certain anonymity. Like Carrie, his video call account was personal and set up with a screen name only, the privacy settings shut down as much as possible, so only the bare minimum was revealed. He'd also borrowed DJ's set of ear buds for the occasion. He couldn't help being overhead, but at least if anyone around listened in to his conversation it would be one-sided and hopefully, wouldn't make much sense to them.

He checked his watch again. Five minutes to go. He plugged in the ear buds and put them in place before signing into his account and ensuring he was showing as available.

At 0300 hours exactly, the incoming call tone sounded in his ears. He hit accept.

On the screen in front of him, a man appeared. His face was lined, the leathery, tanned skin emphasized by the bright white lab coat he wore. He had a full head of thick, silver-grey hair and his blue eyes were bright and intelligent. Joey guessed that he wasn't as old as his complexion made him appear.

"Dr. King?"

"Yes, call me Bill, it's easier. So you want to talk about the obelisk?"

"Yes."

Joey saw him narrow his eyes and pay full attention to the screen in front of him for the first time. He recognized the flash of understanding that crossed the man's face.

"Right, okay, you're still in situ at the base. First off, is the obelisk situated somewhere highly populated or frequently accessed?"

"No."

"That's good. Is its existence common knowledge?"

"Not that I'm aware of, but perhaps among top."

"I have aerial pictures of the camp here, by your answers I'm guessing that it's probably in the farthest outlying hangers, the more ramshackle ones?"

"How did you get those?"

"Doesn't matter. Am I right?"

"No, further out."

"In the bunkers? Yes, of course! I should have known that. Which one?"

" The third one in from the fence on the right."

He saw Bill pick up a sharpie pen and mark something on the desk in front of him, presumably one of the aerial pictures. When he raised his face again, his expression was animated. "So was it discovered during the initial recon, or a clear out mission?"

432

"I don't know if it was either of those. A cleanup was ongoing but a local refused to enter, and the project was abandoned. That's when the fences went up. Initial search, maybe, maybe not. It's three floors down, and the stairs are simply but cleverly disguised."

"So how was it discovered?"

"Curiosity and recreation."

"I'm getting the picture now. It looks like it appeared while the base was still in Iraqi hands and perhaps some of the native people experienced effects or recognized it for what it was, but as far as the U.S. military goes, it's entirely possible that no one knows about this except you, and presumably a handful of your friends."

"Correct."

"Has it started?"

"I'm sorry, what?"

"Sorry, I'm getting ahead of myself. I forget that others don't know what they're dealing with when they come across this. From my extensive studies, and believe me, they're as extensive as any studies can be considering it always disappears, I've seen the pattern of events that build up around it and know what to look for. Have you noticed anything odd or out of the ordinary on base, accidents, runs of bad luck?"

"Yes, definitely."

"What about you and your friends?"

"What about us? Aren't you supposed to be the one giving me information?"

"True, but I want to know how far things have progressed before I do. It makes sense that it would turn up in the middle of war, and it may have first arrived during the Afghanistan crises. That would very much match the pattern, and I know how horrific things are over there, and the amount of bloodshed and death that occurs on a daily basis. What concerns me is what might be to come."

"Can you explain further for me please?"

"Typically, events begin slow and small then build and build until they culminate in one massive event. I have a feeling that this ongoing war might not be it. I'm trying to establish where the obelisk is at in regards to its timeline."

"What could be worse than this war?"

"I don't know, and that's what's worrying me. So, you and your friends, any bad dreams, unusual experiences, mood swings, personality changes, blackouts?"

"All of the above."

"But you're all still there?"

"On base, yes. One went on leave but has been back for a while."

"That wasn't what I meant, but it answers my question nonetheless. It would seem my suspicions are right; it's only getting started."

"That's what I was afraid of too. What can we expect in the future? Can you tell me more about the history of the others?"

"First off, I don't think there are others. This might sound far-fetched, but believe me, everything I'm about to say is based on years and years of study. Today, for example, right before this call, I was running more tests on ground samples taken from around each known location. As techniques and equipment advanced through the years, I've learned more and more. Based on my findings, I'm convinced that there aren't several of these; I believe it's always the same one."

"But I thought it was always destroyed during the disaster it foretold?"

"That was a theory, yes, but one that I'm close to discarding as I've found evidence to suggest otherwise. Not only do I think it's the same one, but I also don't believe it foretells disaster, it creates it."

Joey ran a hand over his face. "A few months ago I would have said you were crazy and ended this call. Now, I have no choice but to listen and accept what you're telling me. So what exactly do you think it is?"

"According to my studies, it appears that the obelisk itself is completely dormant when it first appears. It's only when it begins to attract attention that things change. The more it's examined, looked at, touched, or even just passed by, the more things happen. The faster that occurs, the quicker events escalate. Its concealed location is possibly the only reason things are happening more slowly this time. Let me tell you about one account I managed to transcribe. It's a rough translation, but the main gist of it was very clear. It described the obelisk as a living entity that feeds on negativity, so any fear, anger, frustration, or any other negative human emotion felt around it acted like a trigger and gave it power. Then it used that power to create more negativity, essentially creating its own food source if you will, which in turn made it even stronger. This pattern continued until it was strong enough to wreak complete havoc. The last line of the transcription says that it laughed as it fed upon the very souls of the people it killed."

Joey shivered, suddenly feeling icy cold. "And you believe this account?"

"Mostly yes, except for it being the obelisk that's in control. I've come to the conclusion that the obelisk itself is merely a housing, perhaps even a containment chamber. I believe that thousands of years ago, some civilization created the obelisk as an entrapment device for whatever was threatening them."

"Containment to minimize the risk."

"Exactly, and it worked to a certain extent, but not as well as they'd hoped."

"Somehow it found a way to draw people to it and then used their energy to get out."

"Correct again, you're a quick study. Once it had achieved its goal, it could continue the pattern, using the stored energy from mass destruction to move, then lying dormant until it felt like or was able to start all over again."

"Let's just say you're right and I buy all this. What exactly is the 'it' we keep talking about?"

"That, I don't know. It's the one piece of the puzzle I've never been able to guess even at, never mind solve. All I can say is that it's something ancient, powerful, and to all intents and purposes, pure evil."

"How can you be so matter of fact?"

"I'm a scientist; I'm matter of fact about everything and tell me, in the face of something like this what other way is there to be?"

"Terrified, panicked, devastated."

"That wouldn't do anyone any good, and I would suggest you try to keep those types of emotions in check too. It sounds as if you and your friends were the initial trigger so it's already attached to you and any negative emotion only makes it stronger."

"Okay Doc, here's the million dollar question. What can we do to free ourselves, and what can we do to stop this thing?"

"If I'd learned of this much sooner, maybe I could have tried some things, but it's active now. It's out, and there's nothing anyone can do about it."

"Bullshit! There must be a way!" Joey caught himself and lowered his tone to a murmur. "There are thousands of soldiers here, good men and women all trying to serve their country. We can't just sit back and wait for one massive disaster to wipe out the base, the country, whatever. We have to stop it. What the hell has been the point of all your research if that's not what you're working towards?"

"The exact nature of my research is not for you to know, soldier, but if I'd found anything to suggest it could be stopped I'd be talking to higher ranks right now."

The snub was an obvious one, but Joey believed this man would help if he could. He was an American; there was no way he would sit on this and let events play out if he had any choice in the matter. "So there's nothing we can do to protect ourselves or anyone around us?"

"Absolutely nothing that I'm aware of."

"And you're the top expert in this particular field?"

"Yes."

"So if you can't help us, no one can."

"I'm afraid not."

"Well, thanks for your time I guess."

"I'm sorry."

Joey's screen went blank as the call ended. He thumped his fist on the desk, frustrated and afraid. "What the hell do I tell the guys?"

With a heavy heart, he made his way back to party central, knowing he had to tell them the truth but dreading the looks upon their faces.

***

In a lab somewhere in the United States, Bill King picked up a phone and dialed a number he'd had memorized for years. Inside the Pentagon, Colonel Frank Cooper pulled his cellphone from his pocket and glanced at the screen.

"Excuse me; I have to take this call."

The other man in his office nodded and left, leaving Colonel Cooper in private. He accepted the incoming call.

"Bill?"

"I've found it again."

"Talk."

Bill King talked, spilling everything he knew about the most recent discovery of the obelisk.

"So what do you want?"

"Access, as soon as possible."

"Let me see what I can do. I'll get back to you."

The line went dead and Bill hung up. He checked on the tests he had running but found he no longer had any enthusiasm for them or whatever results they might produce. He slumped in his chair, replaying the conversation with the soldier in his head. No matter the actual nature of his grant funding, the research into the obelisk had always been exciting, a treasure hunt almost. He and his team had traveled across the entire globe, gathering evidence at every site they could find, spent hours in labs studying and collating that evidence, but it had all been historical. The events were over and done with, and nobody could turn back time. This was different. This was real; it was happening right now, and so many lives were at stake, so many people were in grave danger.

He'd spoken the truth when he said it couldn't be stopped, and to be honest, he didn't know exactly how much power it could contain or how far reaching the effects could be, but maybe, this time, things could be different. What if there was a way to decipher the inscriptions on the pillar and the bunker walls and recreate whatever had been done originally, possibly reinstating the barriers that had once been put in place? What if it could at least be slowed down until the war was over? It was unlikely, but if he could only have access to the thing, he might at least be able to try. If the war ended and the troops were pulled out, it would lose its main energy source. By the sound of it, that was probably a vain hope. It was gathering momentum fast, and the war was far from over, the death tolls would be supplying an enormous amount of power. His only hope of helping was getting in there.

He jumped when his phone rang. He snatched it up.

"King."

"Bill, Frank."

"Yes?"

"Access denied."

"But–"

"No buts, Bill. You might as well drop it. I went to the highest authority; there's nowhere else to go. We're old friends; you know I did my best for you. It's never going to happen."

Bill King dropped his head into his hands, desolation overcoming him. He didn't have much hope before, but all was lost now. It was out of his hands, and everyone out there was on their own with this.

Chapter Twenty- Three: The Plan

When Joey returned to party central, he found the team fast asleep in their makeshift beds. He knew they'd wanted to wait up for him, but exhaustion had overtaken them, the sense of security at all being together too much for them to resist closing their eyes. He sighed a deep sigh of relief, glad of the temporary respite before having to deliver the crushing news. As quietly as possible, he slipped past them, using his natural stealth to climb to his bunk without waking them.

He didn't bother undressing or getting under the covers; he knew sleep wouldn't be an option for him tonight but a couple of hours he had before the shift started could at least be spent resting. What he should have done was call Carrie immediately at the end of the video call with Bill King, knowing she'd be waiting anxiously for word, but he couldn't face it, couldn't face hearing the love and concern in her voice. He knew their bond would allow her to pick up on his desolation no matter how jocular his tone or how light he kept the call. What the hell was he going to tell her? How would she and the kids cope with getting over the loss and getting on with their lives? How would she cope financially? Leaving them he couldn't bear thinking about, yet he knew there was nothing he could do. He passed the time with his head filled with memories of his life with them, not quite knowing which day could be his last on this earth.

When he heard the guys rousing an hour later, he kept his eyes closed and his breathing slow and steady, pretending to be asleep and ignoring their efforts to wake him to go for breakfast.

"Leave him be," he heard DJ say. "He had a late night. We'll take something from the chow hall with us and pick him up afterward."

Only when he heard them leave did he sit up, his legs dangling over the edge of his bunk, his head in his hands in an attempt to ease a pounding headache brought on by concern and the lack of sleep. The lack of privacy for the next thirteen hours would buy him more time, but he knew it wouldn't help him find a way to put any sort of good spin on the news he had for the team. He couldn't decide if he was doing them a favor by giving them one more day of hope or not. Maybe it was being cruel to allow them to believe a solution might have been found. He imagined their crushed faces and decided he'd made the right decision. When stripped down to the basics, his news was that they were all going to die; he might as well give them as much time as possible before they had to hear it.

He jumped down from his bunk and grabbed a clean uniform, heading for the shower block, intending to make his way immediately to the hanger and ensuring he avoided the guys until they were in a place where they definitely couldn't talk. Under the running water, he did his best to wash away his anguish, but it didn't help; nothing could.

***

At the end of the shift, Saddler checked off the last item for inspection, having bypassed his usual pretense of being unhappy with their work. He gave the Armament Dogs his smug grin as he signed the paperwork with a flourish. "I thought I'd give you guys a break today since I have some good news for you all."

"We don't want to hear any news from you, Saddler, good or otherwise. Shift's over, and you've signed off on everything, we're out of here."

"That's Sergeant Saddler to you if you don't mind, but don't be so hasty DJ, this news affects mostly you. I've been dying to tell you all day, but I thought it might affect your work, and that's crappy enough as it is."

"Then I definitely don't want to hear it," DJ replied, turning to walk away.

"Oh, come on, don't be like that. It's a cause for celebration. I'm going to be a daddy."

DJ froze, his blood running cold in his veins. He turned slowly. "What did you say?"

"I said I'm going to be a daddy."

DJ's fists clenched by his sides. "No."

"Oh, but yes. Clara's pregnant. Isn't that great? I got her letter this morning, along with pictures of her with the testing kit. She's so damn excited she sent me about twenty of 'em. It must have been our frantic farewell fucks before deployment, damn, that girl's insatiable sometimes; no wonder you weren't enough for her. Anyway, she wanted to wait until after the three-month mark to tell me, you know, in case anything went wrong, then her damn letter was held up somewhere so I only just got it. Stupid, dumb military can't get anything right."

"I don't believe you, you're a lying bastard," DJ said, his voice hushed, his head shaking in denial.

"You don't? Here, I'll show you. I took a couple in with me especially for you, the ones where she looks the prettiest. You know she isn't very photogenic." Saddler rummaged through his pockets, taking his time to savor the moment. "I'm sure it'll be a boy. I can't wait till there's a mini version of me running around. Of course, she's all fat and bloated by now but with a bit of luck, I'll miss all that. She'll look absolutelygross, so I hope she'll have popped by the time I get back."

"You fucking prick!"

The Armament Dogs leaped on DJ, wrestling him to the ground before he could react further, knowing that Saddler's words were designed specifically to make DJ snap. He could just about handle hearing him talk about being with her, but insulting her and being so unfeeling towards her was something completely different and the exact thing that would push DJ over the edge. They'd been poised and ready ever since Saddler had first opened his mouth.

DJ struggled and fought but with the seven of them holding him down; he didn't stand a chance of getting up, no matter how enraged he was. Saddler laughed, delighted with the effect he was having. He pulled out the photographs, obviously having known exactly where they were the whole time, and waved them at DJ tauntingly. DJ's face turned red with his effort to break loose, the veins in his neck and arms bulging.

Saddler looked down at the photographs and sighed happily, shaking his head. "Who would have thought it, going home to a new addition to the family, amazing right? Of course, if you were half the man I was then maybe it would have been you who knocked her up, and she'd still be with you."

The guys increased their grip on DJ as he struggled even harder to free himself, trying to lash out, kick, bite, anything to get away and get at this hateful man who was delighting in torturing him. Saddler laughed again, throwing the pictures in their direction. They fluttered and spun in the air before falling to the ground, discarded like worthless litter. He turned and strode out of the hangar, motioning for his team to follow.

JDub, seeing the others had DJ under control, freed himself from the melee on the ground, and hurried to pick up the photographs. He was hoping that they were of nothing in particular, not what the douche had said they were, desperately pleading for Saddler to have been lying through his teeth just to get a rise out of DJ.

He glanced down at the two prints in his hands. What he saw was a very pretty woman looking thrilled, holding a home pregnancy testing kit up towards the camera, her smile absolutely beatific, her eyes sparkling with delight and excitement.

"Damn," he said quietly, shoving the photographs deep into his back pocket.

"Let me see," DJ growled.

"I'm not so sure that's a good idea, man."

"Let me see the damn things, and let me up for fuck's sake."

JDub checked outside, making sure the truck had left with the other team. "Saddler's long gone," he informed the others.

Slowly, they all clambered to their feet, ready to jump on DJ again if he made any sudden move to try to follow. He just stood there, holding out his hand to JDub, his arm trembling with suppressed rage, his cheeks and forehead still flushed red.

"Let's wait until we're back in CHUville. It might be better to be somewhere private before you see them."

Joey nodded approvingly at JDub. It was a smart move. "Yeah, come on battle; let's get back to party central. Maybe Justin can bring over something medicinal for us all; God knows we need it and deserve it."

"Sure, no problem. I have vodka or whiskey. I'll bring them both, and you can take your pick. I've been trying to cut down like you told me, so they're both unopened."

"Good man."

Keeping DJ surrounded at all times, they headed back to DJ and Joey's room. Justin detoured to his own room to pick up the two promised bottles, his hands shaking a little as he anticipated taking a long swig. The cutting back had been harder than he'd expected and he had to admit that the guys had been right, he didn't have it as under control as he'd believed. Pushing his own thoughts and needs aside, he hurried over to party central and joined the others. It was harder to get inside than usual, and he couldn't help but notice the others had more or less blocked the passage from the bunk to the door with the folding chairs. They'd positioned themselves deliberately to easily stop DJ from leaving at any point until he was calmer. Justin clambered over them to the last free spot set up for him and sat down, holding the bottles out to DJ.

"Thanks," DJ said, choosing the vodka and cracking the seal.

He took a short drink and kept hold of the bottle, not passing it around. Justin shrugged and opened the whiskey, taking a drink to steady himself before handing it to George on his left. DJ looked at JDub. "So, is it true?"

JDub really didn't want to answer, but he knew he didn't have an option. DJ had to find out eventually so it might as well be here and now, and with his battles around him. "Well, it's a woman with a pregnancy test for sure, but I can't say if it's Clara. I don't know what she looks like."

"Is it positive?"

"Huh?"

"The test in the picture, it is positive?"

"Why else would she take pictures of herself with it?"

"Could be celebrating a false alarm, I've been there," JJ said.

"Yeah, I guess," JDub agreed, "but I don't know. I don't know a thing about these tests."

"Let me see," Joey said.

JDub fished the pictures out from his back pocket and handed them to Joey, who studied them for a moment, happy memories flashing through his mind, playing like a video. He wanted to zone out and get lost in them but needed to keep his focus and remember how bad this was for his battle. "I'm sorry, DJ. Carrie used this same brand; it's showing a positive result."

DJ held out his hand. Joey placed the pictures into it, and DJ took another deep draft from the bottle before he glanced in their direction. He closed his eyes, letting out a deep sigh. "That's Clara alright."

"Aw shit, we're sorry," Craig said.

DJ opened his eyes. "Why him? We spoke of starting a family so many times, why did she have to do it with him and not me? I was more than ready; it was her who held off saying the time wasn't right."

"I guess if you really wanted to know you'd have to ask her, I think she would feel she owed you an answer at least. What you would have to decide is if you really want to know and if the answer is that important. Would it make any difference?" Joey asked.

"No, I guess not. She's with him, and now they're having a baby together. It's final. There's nothing I can do, I can't even fight for her, not when there's a kid involved."

"Maybe it's a good thing," Joey said quietly.

DJ glared at him angrily. "What the fuck? How can you say that?"

Joey held his gaze. "Because of what I know, that's how. There's no easy way to say this guys, but from what I learned last night, that baby isn't going to have a daddy, but Clara will be well looked after. She's still married to DJ, and she'll be able to prove paternity so she will have a claim on Saddler's estate. She'll be entitled to two lots of benefits, and that should set her up in a good position to raise the kid."

"Joey, what the hell are you talking about?" Billy asked. "You're making no sense."

"I'm making perfect sense; you just don't know it yet."

"Oh yeah, the call last night," George said. "Funny, it's been on my mind all day, and I've been itching to ask you about it, but it clean went out of my mind after Saddler's little speech. How did it go?"

"Not well at all, and I'm not even sure how to tell you. I hate to be the one to deliver bad news, especially on top of what's just happened. It just seems so unfair. None of you deserve this."

"Just give us the truth and give it to us plain and simple," Craig said. "Tell us the conversation word for word if that makes it easier."

Joey did, the words of the scientist burned into his brain so he could recite them verbatim. He'd expected hysterics, denial, panic, and fear. Instead, the guys sat still and silent, contemplating their fate. It seemed as if they hadn't held out much hope after all as if their subconscious had already come to the conclusion that it was over for them and now they just needed their conscious minds to catch up. It was Billy who finally broke the silence.

"Well, I guess it was no more than I expected."

"Hang on," Craig said. "Let me just get this straight in my head. The obelisk contains some sort of demon thing or whatever, and humanity's own negative energy releases it, is that right?"

"From what I understood, that's it in a nutshell."

"So it's like some sort of divine retribution, something we bring upon ourselves by being evil and cruel?"

"Are you kidding? You've seen the way it's been playing with us. Whatever this thing is, it's the furthest thing from divine I've ever seen in my life," George spat.

"Yeah, I've got to agree with you there, George, and we have to keep in mind that it's not necessarily anger, rage or any bad emotion that awakens it and gets it all excited, just a negative one. It could be fear or grief, a sense of loss, depression, anything like that."

"Those are things that we were all feeling in abundance when we went down there, considering the way this tour's gone," Billy agreed.

"This is all our fault or more specifically, mine," JJ said.

"How do you make that out?"

"I was the one who insisted JDub, and I check out the third bunker. He wanted to use the first one, but I wanted to see what the Haji freaked out about, and I was the one that insisted we use that one for our party. If we hadn't gone down there, then we wouldn't have released this thing."

"We don't know that for sure. Maybe the Iraqis already released it."

"Think about it, Joey. Those bunkers hadn't been touched for years, and the local risked being shot down to run from it; he knew, they knew, and they buried it and hid it. It was us blundering around down there that set it off. None of this weird shit started until after we went down the second time and beat the shit out of each other!"

"Okay, okay, calm down, just take it easy. Even if you're right, it doesn't change anything, and if it hadn't been us, it would have been someone else eventually. You heard what Bill King said; it has a pull; it draws people to it without them realizing it to kick-start the whole process. It's unfortunate that we were the suckers this time, but it was going to happen no matter what, it's never been avoided, not once in its entire documented history. You probably weren't even acting of your own free will when you chose that bunker."

JJ went silent, still feeling the overwhelming guilt and responsibility but unable to argue with Joey's logic.

"So we're dead already, that's it, game over?"

"Seems that way, JDub. If Bill King says it can't be stopped, then I guess it can't. The only question is what's going to happen, when, and how many lives it takes when it does, but I think we can be pretty sure going by the past records that it'll be at least the whole base, if not the whole damn country. The war is feeding it, fattening it up like a turkey for thanksgiving."

They sat in silence, each one lost in thought, contemplating what their death meant to them and any loved ones they had.

"This is bullshit," DJ finally said. "We can't sit by and do nothing at all. Why don't we blow the thing up, just blast it to smithereens, destroy it once and for all."

Joey shook his head. "You're forgetting that it always survives whatever disaster it creates. I'm sure it's been buried, blown up, ended up underwater; you name it; it just moves right on along and gets ready for the next time."

"Maybe, but it's never come across us before," DJ said with a manic grin. "Listen up, you said it feeds on the souls of the dead after the major disaster it creates, and you're talking thousands, if not hundreds of thousands. That's what gives it the power to survive, move, and lie in wait. The disaster hasn't happened yet, so maybe there's a chance it wouldn't be strong enough yet to survive an attack, and couldn't fend off whatever we throw at it."

"What exactly would we be throwing at it and where would we get it?" Billy asked.

"We're Armament Dogs remember? We can lay our hands on pretty much anything and everything."

"You're talking about stealing the army's weaponry? Shit, DJ, we'd all end up court-martialed and kicked out for good if we do that," Craig said.

"What does it matter if we're all dead anyway? I don't give a shit anymore. We have to try something. I can't just sit back and see all these people hurt or killed. I've had enough of being held hostage by this thing and have had enough of cowering in fear. It's time we took a stand. If we're going to die, I want to die fighting, not sitting and waiting for it to get me. If we succeed, we've saved countless lives, if we fail, then being kicked out and sent home might save our lives. It's a win-win situation, but if you pussies are too chicken to help, I'll do it alone."

"I think DJ might have a point," JDub said. "We've got nothing left to lose."

"Yep, I think I might have to agree," Billy added.

"Now just hold on," Joey said, raising his hands. "Even if we do decide to do this, you're all forgetting the most important thing. The obelisk isn't anything but the transport; even if we did manage to blow it up, all we would be doing is making sure the thing stays free, walking around loose forever. You might just increase the amount of destruction it can cause. If that inscription holds it, even temporarily, we'd be dumb to destroy it."

DJ wasn't about to be dissuaded. "So we make sure it's inside when we do the deed, that we destroy the thing as well as the obelisk."

"And how the hell do you propose we do that?"

"I really don't have a freaking clue, but anything we come up with is better than nothing."

Billy and Craig slumped back in their chairs, seeing how the plan could backfire. JDub bit his lip, deep in thought. "Okay, so the scientist said that the inscriptions on the obelisk were some sort of spell or something to trap it, right?"

"Yeah, so?"

"So why don't we recreate that? Couldn't we carve them on another side of the stone, enhancing it and trapping it again before we destroy it?"

Joey scratched his head. "Maybe, yeah, maybe, but they must have had a ritual or something to get it inside in the first place, and we can't recreate that because no one knows what it was and no one can read the damn inscriptions."

"So we come up with our own ritual," Justin offered, his excitement rising. "George, you're a spiritual guy, you could say a prayer, evoke all that's good and right to come to our aid and send this thing back inside or down to the pits of hell, right?"

"I'm afraid my faith's been sadly lacking recently."

"Yeah, but that's probably just its influence over you. It's all still in there; you just have to fight a little harder, dig a little deeper to find it."

George nodded slowly. "I could see that being true, sure. Yes, I'd be willing to give it my absolute best shot. As we've said, what have we got to lose?"

"I don't know guys. What if we do more harm than good?"

"How much more harm *can* we do, Joey? We let it out; now we need to put this right or die trying," DJ said.

"Maybe I should talk to Bill King again."

"Forget him; he's in love with this damn thing. If you forewarned him that we were going to blow up his precious obelisk, he'd be straight onto whoever he could to have us all thrown in the brig to stop us. His research means far more to him than our lives. He probably can't wait to see how it plays out this time."

Joey grabbed the whiskey from Craig and took a swig, giving himself another second or two to think. This sounded absolutely crazy; eight soldiers standing around a stone pillar, one chanting some sort of incantation to entrap a demon and then recreating some ancient inscription before blasting it to kingdom come. It was ridiculous, would be hysterical if he didn't already have the proof that it was so damn serious. He couldn't help but think of all the things that could go wrong with this plan, but his battles were right. It was already about as bad as it could possibly be and probably nothing they did could make it any worse. Even if they ended up blowing themselves up instead of the obelisk, at least it would be a quick end and would deny the dark shadow thing the satisfaction of finally killing them. That alone made it worthwhile. With one more swig, he made his decision.

"Fine. If we're all agreed, then I'm in."

"Good. George, can you write down something and copy it for all of us. In movies, you always see people chanting together when they're saying spells or invoking, or whatever. Maybe the chanting joins our intent or something and gives it more power. Anyway, we can start by chanting then you can adlib over the top of us and say whatever's in your head or heart."

"Sure, DJ, I'll do that. When do you want to do this?"

"As soon as possible. I know weird shit has happened through the day or at least early morning, but mostly it happens at night. Night would be better for us to sneak into the bunkers with the stolen goods, but maybe it would already be in there during the day, sleeping, or resting or whatever it does. I think we should go for it straight after shift tomorrow, while it's early evening and still light out."

"Okay, so what are we going to use?"

"Everything we can get our hands on, let's make a list of what we know is in the hangar and come up with an arrangement around the obelisk and a means of setting it off."

They plotted and planned for another two hours, debating the issue back and forth until they were satisfied with what they came up with, their final plan laid out in writing in a notebook. When they were done, they grinned at one another, happy to be able to be proactive in this situation, finally more than ready to make a stand together, even if it were their last. They all went to their separate rooms, feeling more at ease now that their decision was made. Come what may, tomorrow they would fight like the soldiers they were. Each one of them collapsed into bed and fell into the first deep, peaceful, and dreamless sleep they'd had in months.

Chapter Twenty-Four: The Last Stand

None of the others awoke as DJ suddenly sat up in bed a little over an hour later. A sleepwalker with perfect night vision, he grabbed his uniform and weapon and navigated silently through the disarray of chairs and bodies to the door. He closed it softly behind him, dressing in the hallway before stepping outside the trailer into the dark chill of the night. Mortars streaked and boomed overhead, but he paid them no heed.

He walked purposefully but not animatedly or hurriedly, ignoring everything around him as he made his way through CHUville, a specter, a shadow. He stopped outside Saddler's trailer, waiting. Saddler appeared in the doorway and stepped outside, just as DJ had known he would. Side by side but certainly not together, they continued through the base, never glancing in each other's direction and paying no attention to anything that was going on around them or any of the soldiers that greeted them along the way. Their boots marched in unison; their steps equally matched as they walked.

Saddler showed no surprise, dismay, or anger as they reached the fence surrounding the forbidden section of the base, nor when DJ opened the gate and stepped through without hesitation.

Saddler followed, pausing to close the gate behind him before catching up with DJ and following him inside the third bunker. He immediately walked down the first flight of steps and then slid through the disguised opening, going down the hidden set of stairs as if he'd been there a million times before as if he'd done it every single day of his life.

In front of the obelisk, they both stopped and turned to face one another. Their faces were blank, expressionless, and their eyes were empty. They both removed their rifles from their shoulder and tossed them aside.

What's happening, where am I?

The thought was faint and fuzzy; a cry from a distance but DJ struggled to clutch at it, hanging onto it as if it were a buoy thrown to him in a stormy ocean. He looked around and recognized the bunker, but it looked different as if he were seeing it from the altered perception of a dream.

Then, as Saddler exploded into enraged animation, DJ knew that this was no dream. Saddler's mouth was opening and closing and at first, DJ heard nothing. All of a sudden, it was as if he snapped out of a daydream and his brain was assaulted with sharp clarity.

"What the fuck did you do to me? You fucking drugged me!"

DJ threw his hands over his ears, Saddler's voice deafening after the muted haze. He ducked his head, screwing up his eyes against the harsh beam of the flashlight that Saddler had clicked on and pointed in his direction. "I didn't do anything, man," he said. "This wasn't me."

"Then how the fuck did I get here?"

"I don't know. I don't even know how *I* got here, let alone you."

Saddler had begun to pace, examining his surroundings. "Where the hell am I?"

"We're in one of the bunkers."

Saddler stopped and turned back to DJ, pointing the flashlight beam directly at his eyes. "You took me to a restricted area of base?" His voice was a hiss, his red rage fueled by fear now turning white hot and dangerous. "Do you know how much being caught here could cost me?"

"I already told you, it wasn't me! It was the obelisk. It did this."

"What the fuck are you talking about, you crazy bastard?"

"I know it sounds crazy, but please, listen to me. The obelisk has power, it's been fucking with us, and now it's fucking with you too. We have to get out of here, get as far away from it as possible. We can't be angry aroundit; that'll only feed it."

Saddler stared at DJ then slowly began shaking his head. "You've lost it. I pushed you too far, and you've snapped. I don't know what the fuck you did to me to get me down here, or what you planned to do with me once you did, but whatever it was has worn off, and I'm fucking outta here. I'm not sticking around to listen to your lunatic ravings."

DJ wanted to tell him *good; that's exactly what he should do*. He hated this man with a passion, but he didn't want to see anyone else affected by the madness he'd experienced, not even his worst enemy. He opened his mouth, but before he could form the words, it slammed shut, and all that came from his throat a deep, guttural growl forcing itself out through his clamped lips.

A flicker of fear flashed across Saddler's face at the unholy sound, but he quickly caught himself and turned it into a mocking sneer. "You don't scare me."

DJ had no control over his response. The words were the last thing on his mind, but he spoke them anyway. "I should."

Unable to stop himself, DJ advanced on Saddler. He hated the fear and confusion he saw on Saddler's face and could only imagine what he was seeing in his own to cause such a reaction, but once more, he had no control. There had been moments recently where he'd lost his self-control, but he knew this wasn't one of them. He was urging his body to stop with every ounce of strength he had, but it was refusing to obey. A million synapses were firing in his brain, but somehow the signals weren't reaching his limbs. Saddler was backed into a corner, and DJ felt his mouth smile as his arm raised, and his fist flew.

Saddler's head snapped back, bashing against the wall of the cavern. He rubbed his jaw and shook his head, trying to clear the bright white spots that clouded his vision. "Okay, I guess I deserved that, I'll give you that one. Now let's get out of here."

He made to step forward, but DJ's fists prevented him, slamming into him repeatedly to force him backwards. Saddler held up his hands in supplication. "I don't want to do this, especially not tonight and not here." His words were slurred through a swollen and bleeding lip. "Don't push me. I *will* fight back, and I *will* beat your sorry ass to kingdom come."

I don't want to do this either, can't you understand that! It isn't me. I'm not doing this!

Another punch slammed into Saddler's stomach, and the Sergeant had had enough. Doubled over from the blow, he came up swinging with an uppercut that caught DJ firmly under his chin. Pain exploded throughout DJ's jaw and face, and he knew that the obelisk's entity had given him the level of awareness this time for a reason. It wanted him to suffer.

He stared at Saddler, stunned to find that he could also see himself standing there, could see the redness on his skin, the bruising and swelling already beginning to form. He was wide-eyed with fear and astonishment, except he wasn't. He was standing still, absolutely stoic as Saddler threw another punch that shattered his nose. He heard and felt the crunching of bone, and both saw and felt the stream of bright red that flowed from it, running into his mouth and down his throat. He could taste the metallic tang.

It was as if he was hovering behind himself, watching the events unfold, only he felt every bit of the pain that his body was experiencing and was powerless to react, and could do nothing to prevent this. In his head, he grabbed Saddler's arm and told him to run,

461

pulling them both in a frantic dash for the stairs, but in reality nothing happened, he just stood there as he took a third, then a fourth punch from his adversary.

What's going on, how is this possible? Let me go, damn it, let
me go!

As he mentally screamed at the obelisk, his body seemed to explode of its own free will, reacting to Saddler at a time when he wasn't even in DJ's immediate thoughts. It moved forward, flailing at Saddler, the punches swinging wildly. Some connected, but the wasted energy and directionless aim made them ineffectual, barely rocking Saddler on his feet. DJ was like a remote control robot being manipulated by an uncoordinated and inexperienced toddler.

Saddler had blocked most of the punches and managed to ease himself out of the corner. He was slowly backing away. "Come on, man; that's enough now. We both got some good hits in; we're both bleeding. Let's drop it and get the hell out of here."

Suddenly, DJ was moving like the trained soldier he was, a man excelling at hand-to-hand combat, knowing how and willing to use lethal force.

No! Don't do this; he doesn't deserve this. Carla needs him;
the baby needs a father, even a shitty one. Let him go; this
isn't his fight.

No one listened to DJ's frantic inner pleas that he was unable to voice. Fear flashed then settled on Saddler's face. He swallowed hard then mimicked DJ's stance, left foot forward and right hand bent up to protect his chin, the left providing the two point cover. They bounced

462

their weight from foot to foot, both ready to move in any direction in a flash.

DJ double fronted, delivering two lead punches from home base, both of them hitting their mark of Saddler's nose before he doubled backed out of his reach. He held his weight on the ball of his right foot, heel raised, ready to move; his understanding of body mechanics as deep as his knowledge of any other kind.

He swiveled as Saddler – seeing he had no choice but to fight until DJ was willing to listen to reason– went on the attack. DJ used his footwork to keep him balanced as he turned; Saddler's lead and front cross punch combination glancing off the side of his head instead of hitting him face on. Saddler tried to follow them up with a left hook that would have more impact, trying to make every hit count, but DJ was too fast, ducking below the hit and darting forward to grab Saddler around the legs in one fluid motion. Crouching low, he lifted and flung Saddler back; jumping to his feet and taking up his stance as Saddler hit the ground face first, eating sand. Seeing that Saddler would take a moment to recover, DJ moved in, delivering a vicious two-handed blow to the base of his spine.

Saddler screamed, the intense pain forcing the air from his lungs. He began to cry, trying to crawl away from DJ before the next blow came, his legs barely responding.

> *Get up, Saddler. Get up and knock me out, stop me, please.*
> *Oh God, please don't let him be paralyzed. Get up for fuck's*
> *sake, get up and fight! Beat me. Beat it!*

In spite of the serious pain DJ's hit had inflicted, Saddler managed to flip himself over. Tears streaked the sand that clung to his face, his chest moved up and down rapidly in hitching breaths.

"I'm sorry, man," he managed to say through his sobs. "I'm sorry for everything. I was a dick, but I was so fucking jealous of what you'd had. I'm sorry about Clara, I truly am, but I love her, man, I really fucking love her and I'll do everything I can to make her happy. I'll take good care of her and the baby, I swear, I promise they'll want for nothing."

I know DJ wanted to say; *I think I knew that all along, and I know that you make her happy in a way that I was failing to do in the end. That's what kept me sane.* He longed to step forward and hold out a hand to Saddler, to help him to his feet and limp out of the bunker together, broken and hurt, but better men than they'd been before and with a deeper understanding of the situation between them. He tried, he tried with everything he had, but it wouldn't let him. He refused to stop fighting his inner battle even as he advanced on Saddler, his face twisted into an evil grin.

Saddler scrambled backwards, finding that his spinal cord hadn't suffered any lasting damage from DJ's hit and his legs were working fine. Using the element of surprise, he raised and bent them under his chin then his knees shot forward, his heavy boots hitting DJ firmly in the groin.

DJ's body crumpled to the ground. He tried to scream, but his mouth wouldn't open. Tears filled his eyes but never fell. The pain was excruciating, and nausea overcame him. Saddler seized his moment, still sobbing as he made a run for the stairs. Against his will, DJ's body reacted.

No, I'm not ready! The pain is killing me! Stay down! Please
let me stay down; please let Saddler go.

The cries and sobs inside his head were pointless. In a flash, he launched himself at Saddler, who'd made it to the fifth step. He grabbed him around the legs and yanked them back towards him, causing Saddler to crash down heavily onto the steps. DJ dragged him; bumping Saddler's chin and face against each step on the way down. He continued to drag, pulling him through the sand back to the rear of the cave beneath the bunker, back to the obelisk. By the back of his jacket, he yanked him one-handed to his feet.

Saddler must have seen the intent in DJ's eyes. DJ watched his expression change as Saddler realized he was fighting for his life. There was no reasoning with him, and the only way out was to win. Inside, DJ wished him luck. Anything was better than being controlled this way.

Saddler made his move, flinging an arm around DJ's neck, trying to maneuver him into a headlock. DJ dug his feet into the sand and refused to budge, retaliating with a rapid-fire series of low body jabs to Saddler's sides, intent on making him relax his hold. Saddler clung on, still trying to twist DJ around by his neck. Changing tactics, DJ launched his weight forward, and they hit the deck together, DJ on top. He straddled Saddler and began hitting and punching him over and over again, turning what was left of his face into a bloody, mashed pulp.

Saddler should have been out cold, but terror and agony gave him an adrenaline rush beyond what he'd ever experienced before. DJ suddenly found himself flung off Saddler, trying to stay on him akin to riding a bucking bronco. He landed heavily on his backside, his back slamming into the obelisk. He hadn't noticed before but the obelisk was glowing, the green light bright and pulsating. He heard that terrible mocking laugh, low and guttural as if it were a spectator enjoying every second of the fight. His back began to burn, and he scrambled to the side, narrowly missing the latest onslaught from Saddler, whose fist crashed into the obelisk. DJ heard the sickening sound of snapping bones.

He seized the moment, rushing Saddler headfirst, slamming into his side and knocking him back to the ground. He was on his feet and kicking hard, aiming for the kidneys. He knew if either of them survived this night they'd both be spitting and pissing blood for months. Saddler rolled and grabbed DJ's ankles, yanking them out from beneath him, causing him to fall. Saddler scrambled to his knees and grabbed DJ's head, slamming it repeatedly against the ground. DJ felt his brain rattle inside his skull, felt the blood pour down the back of his neck from the head wound.

Onward the battle raged, one hour, two, three, more? DJ didn't know. He found himself straddling Saddler once more, right beside the obelisk. He pounded and pounded, blow after blow, left, right, left, right. His knuckles were in pieces, shattering more each time they hit Saddler's skull. Still he couldn't stop. Not until Saddler's panic-filled and pleading eyes turned glazed and lifeless, not until his chest stopped rising and falling beneath him.

DJ gave a deep gasp, and he found himself whole again, staring wide-eyed down at the motionless body beneath him. He reached for Saddler's neck with two fingers, checking for a pulse. Nothing. The smashed skull, open mouth, and staring eyes had already told him that Saddler was dead, but his last sliver of hope was dashed as he failed to locate even the tiniest flicker of life. His leaped to his feet, backing away, unable to move his eyes away from the blood oozing from Saddler's head into the sand beneath him, the pulsating green light of the obelisk growing brighter as the crimson tide was sucked in towards it.

"Oh God, I'm sorry. I'm so fucking sorry. I hated you, but I never wanted this."

Pain wracked DJ's body, and he collapsed, every inch of his body screaming in agony. The punishment it had taken probably wasn't survivable, but somehow he was still here. He'd thought he'd felt every hit, every blow, every kick, but he realized now he'd only felt a fraction, a muted version, enough to hurt and punish to the extreme, but not enough for him to lose consciousness and find relief in the darkness. Unbidden tears flowed down his cheeks, his body in too much pain to actually cry or sob. The bunker swam, and he was certain he'd lose it soon, would pass out, and possibly never wake up.

"Okay, you bastard, I get it. This was a punishment, torture. You've had your fun, and I have to live with my guilt for the rest of my life, however, long or short that may be. Are you fucking happy now?"

As he asked the question, he found himself on his knees, crawling his way clumsily and brokenly towards the obelisk. His limbs were once again moving without his bidding, without his permission. He tried to stop, tried to fling his body in the other direction, but it refused to obey. His terror grew in proportion to his distance, the obelisk looming large in his vision, the light so bright that it hurt his eyes. It seemed to be streaming out of the carved inscription, flooding the bunker with an unbearable brilliance. Laughter screeched and echoed around him as he dragged Saddler's body out of his path. He was on a collision course with the obelisk, and there was nothing he could do to prevent it, nothing was to be allowed to prevent his forward motion.

Reaching the obelisk, he turned around and sat with his back resting heavily against it, panting for breath. Instead of burning, the stone pillar now felt cool, almost soothing. He shivered, the only reaction his body was permitted to do from the several desperate urgings of his fevered mind. Its touch felt disgusting, vile. He wished he could get up, wished he could run, get away from the feel of pure evil, away from the horrific reminder of the man who'd died by his hand, away from this dark place; but it had him now, and it wasn't letting go.

Haven't you tortured all of us enough? You made me fucking kill a man tonight, a fellow soldier, a battle. What the fuck more do you want from me?

Once again, he couldn't form the words with his mouth but nevertheless, the evil within the obelisk heard and answered. DJ didn't

468

know how, but suddenly his M16 assault rifle was in his hands, and his head was bent, watching his fingers checking that it was free of sand and grit, fully loaded, and ready to fire.

> *No! No, no, no, no! This can't be how it ends; I won't let it be how it ends. I'll fight you every step of the way, you bastard! It's you that's going to die, you that's going to be sent down to the pits of hell, not me.*

DJ's head snapped up, and he stared straight ahead. As if in slow motion, he raised the rifle, pausing to stare down into it before jamming the barrel into his mouth. His lips closed firmly around it. He tilted it slightly, aiming it upwards to ensure that it was pointing towards the medulla oblongata, the continuation of the spinal cord into the skull where it formed the lowest part of the brainstem, the control center for the heart and lungs. Every good soldier knew that it was the instant kill spot. He appeared to be the picture of resigned determination, but internally, DJ raged.

> *Alright, if this is the way you want it, fine; do your fucking worst. My battles are coming for you; you'll never win against them all. You're a coward, trying to pick us off one by one. Is that all you can handle, you fucking pussy? If it is then you're screwed, totally screwed, because they'll never stop, they'll fight until they win, that's what we do. You picked the wrong ones to mess with this time.*

DJ pulled the trigger.

The rapport was deafening then died instantly in the dead air inside the bunker; no sound ever echoed here except the laughter. DJ's body jerked once, blood and brains splattering the obelisk and the wall behind, slowly beginning to slide downwards. The rifle given to him to protect himself and his battles fell from his hands. For a second, he was motionless, staring straight ahead, the front of his face untouched while his skull was a gaping, ragged hole behind, then his body slipped sideways, falling with a soft plop into the sand.

The obelisk pulsed and glowed as DJ's spilled lifeblood was sucked in towards it, the guttural laughter the only sound in the now still bunker.

Epilogue

Under the cover of darkness, the restricted area of the base was highly active. Joey had been unable to sleep, bothered by the short, simple service that had been held for DJ while Saddler had received a full military funeral with honors. Suicide wasn't considered an honorable death in the military and therefore, his battle had been denied what should have been rightfully his. Instead, his body was being shipped home and only a small gathering of those who truly knew the man had attended the uncomfortable service.

Joey had been the one who'd found DJ, the one who'd known exactly where to look when the Armament Dogs had discovered that he was missing. While they searched the showers, the chow hall, the phone center, computer lab, and everywhere else they could think of, Joey had slipped away, walking on his own to the bunker. He didn't know quite what he would find, but he knew he didn't want the others subjected to whatever it was. When he discovered the shattered and broken bodies, he'd dropped to his knees and cried.

They all knew that DJ hadn't taken his life by his own hand; that the obelisk had orchestrated it in order to punish him for rallying them into action or to halt their attack upon it. Convincing the U.S. Army of that would be impossible, so all they could do was stand aside as his death was declared a suicide and he was stripped of everything he was; a good, loyal soldier deserving of the highest praise and the deepest mourning. As DJ had known, the Dogs had all vowed to take vengeance upon the obelisk; the plan DJ had put in place still their intention, merely delayed until the heat around the bunker had died down. Joey had stepped outside that night simply to get away from the empty bunk below him and to get some fresh air. Now he was glad that he had.

Early that morning, army personal buzzed around the bunker, but once photographs were taken and the bodies removed, the bunker had been sealed off, and the area had gone quiet. The sudden renewed activity at this early hour made Joey curious. He began to walk, determined to find out what was going on.

He was surprised to find the outer gate of the restricted area wide open. He slipped through, using the other bunkers as cover as he made his way as close as possible to the third, where three LMTVs were parked outside. There, he listened.

No voices reached him, but he thought he heard the sporadic bursts of machinery or equipment of some kind. He ducked back as three men appeared, using hand signals to communicate, obviously checking to ensure that whatever they were about to do wasn't observed. He pressed himself against the wall and held his breath as they made a quick check, too easily satisfying themselves that they were alone.

One disappeared back inside, returning soon providing point to eight other men that were carrying something heavy between them. Joey could hardly believe his eyes when he saw the green glow beneath the loose tarp that covered it.

Damn it; they're taking the fucking obelisk.

It pulsated brightly and rapidly. If Joey was to attribute human-like qualities to it – and he knew he should – he would say it looked either furious or excited. He had no way to tell. He also had no way of finding out just where the hell they planned to take it as they loaded it into one of the LMTVs.

***

In the Whitehouse, Colonel Frank Cooper was feeling uneasy. His request to send Bill King to Iraq had been denied, but it certainly hadn't been ignored. A certain group that had been watching King's research with great interest had been extremely excited about this latest development. Frank had found it increasingly difficult over the years to keep it quiet from his old friend just exactly who'd been funding and guiding his research for the past decade. He knew that if Bill had the slightest inkling as to why they were interested, he would shut down his research and disappear.

Now the powers that be were delighted that they had an opportunity to get their hands on what they believed was the greatest weapon they'd ever come across. Not only that, but it was a blameless weapon, one they could deploy without arousing any suspicion and subsequent retaliation. They couldn't wait to get it into a secure bunker on U.S. soil, to be studied further and to figure out the best way to use it against their enemies. Colonel Frank Cooper felt that perhaps it was time to take a vacation, a long one, as far away from the United States as possible.